# THE RIDER'S QUEST

SPARKS TRILOGY BOOK II

KERRY LAW

Copyright © 2022 Kerry Law

All rights reserved

ISBN-13: 979-8-3615-8023-1

For Colin
Thank you for believing

To LORSOKE
GRIYDAK SEA
NORWEN PEAK
LAKE TOIG
TUNNEL
SHINE
ANTEILL
WEST BARTER
QUORELLE SQUARE
EAST BARTER
HARBOUR
THE PALACE
CITY OF KIERELL
JASTAK PEAK
GRIYDAK SEA
K.Lew

CHAPTER 1

## KICKED OUT

Aimee and Nathine landed in the middle of Quorelle Square, their dragons' talons clacking on the flagstones. Aimee jumped down from her saddle.

'Hurry up, we'll be late.' She waved for Nathine to get a move on. They'd been invited to an important council meeting and Aimee didn't want to put a single foot wrong.

'Who put you in charge?' Nathine complained, dismounting slowly and wincing as she put weight on her injured leg. The burn on Aimee's arm seemed to pulse in sympathy. She knew the agony of an Empty Warrior's hand burning through flesh.

'Sorry, are you alright?' Aimee asked, concern pushing aside her nerves.

'We'll be late if you keep chit-chatting,' Nathine replied, ignoring Aimee's sympathy as she nodded for Malgerus to fly up to the library roof. In a whoosh of bright orange wings he was gone, alighting a moment later on the flat spine that ran along the library's long roof.

'Go on, Jess,' Aimee encouraged her to follow. She wasn't great yet at giving her dragon commands without also speaking them.

By the time Jess was on the roof beside Malgerus, Nathine was halfway up the steps into the council chamber. Aimee hurried to catch up. Inside she followed Nathine up the sweeping staircase to the first floor. There was no time today to admire the painted panels that told Kierell's history or to appreciate the beautiful domed ceiling inlaid with glowing dragon's breath orbs.

A few moments later Aimee and Nathine stepped into the high gallery and found it stuffed full of people. Extra chairs had been brought in, squeezed around the large table, and their occupants were all bumping elbows. There were people standing too, blocking the view out of the full-length arched windows. Even the tabletop was busy—the entire carved surface covered with maps and charts, and handwritten lists.

Aimee took a deep breath to steady the nerves that were jangling inside. All eleven members of the Uneven Council were present, along with Captain Tenth of the city guard. There was also a group of men and women wearing long sky-blue and yellow robes over their clothes. She'd been invited to speak at this meeting and that was a lot of people who were going to be looking right at her. There would be no hiding her unusual face. But she was the girl who'd saved a whole caravan, she could manage this meeting.

'Who are the robed people?' Aimee whispered to

Nathine, as they found a place near the door.

'You've never seen scholars from the university?' Nathine rolled her eyes.

Aimee noticed Jara was sitting at the top of the table beside her twin brother, Councillor Myconn. Aimee planned on staying at the opposite end of the room from her. But just then, Jara looked up and spotted Aimee. Anger flared on her face like a firework.

'What the blazing sparks are you doing here?' Jara demanded, springing from her chair.

'I'm meant to be here,' Aimee replied, having to force her words out. Most in the room had turned to look at her. Thankfully, Councillor Beljarn spoke up in her defence.

'Yes, I invited her, and your other Rider here, to tell the council everything about the army that they saw,' he said, pushing his gold-rimmed glasses up his nose.

'You're loving this, aren't you?' Jara hissed at Beljarn. 'A chance to scuttle back inside the mountains and cower here forever.'

Aimee held her breath as anger darkened Beljarn's face too. The two ex-lovers stared at each other across the room, waves of hate flowing between them.

'I've no idea who specky man is but I'll put one hundred presses on Jara to win any fight against him,' Nathine whispered, and Aimee had to swallow a laugh.

Councillor Cyella stood, her chair making no sound on the plush carpet. She was still wearing her mud-splattered travelling dress. Aimee looked around and realised they were all still in the dirty, sweat-stained clothes they'd been wearing on the tundra. They must have rushed to this room the moment they got back to the city, but that was hours ago. Aimee wondered if they'd been sitting arguing and worrying for all that time.

'Jara, no one is giving up on the plan for peace with the Helvethi but an army of Empty Warriors changes everything. Sparks! We thought they were extinct,' Cyella said. 'So please sit down, and let's hear the girl's account.'

Aimee straightened and smiled to herself. She'd been called a girl, not a freak. Everyone in the room turned to look at her. She stepped forward, mainly because she was worried that if she didn't, Nathine would shove her forward. It was too hard to look at anyone's face so she stared over a scholar's yellow-robed shoulder and out the arched windows.

She told them how she'd been attacked by Empty Warriors. The people who hadn't heard her story before swore as she described monsters which were supposed to have been destroyed three hundred years ago. She was pleased to be able to tell them that she and Jess had killed several. Though she kept to herself the fact that she'd been out alone searching for her dragon because she'd lost control and Jess had flown off.

She described how she and Nathine had captured the Empty Warrior to bring back to the caravan as proof that they still existed, because who would have believed them otherwise? Empty Warriors were half-forgotten monsters from their past. Kyelli and Marhorn had destroyed them all. The burned handprint on her arm was a constant dull ache, as if reminding her what it had cost to capture that single Empty Warrior. When it came time to describe the army, she faltered. From the corners of her eyes she could see worried and frightened faces.

'It's alright, on you go,' said an older councillor with dye-stained hands. Aimee remembered her as the one who'd been sick when she saw the wound on her arm.

Strangely it was Jara who persuaded her to continue. The expression on her face was as dark as the inside of a crack in the mountains, and just as sharp-looking. Aimee felt she had to prove that she'd not wrecked Jara's dreams for no reason.

As she talked she could picture again the hundreds and hundreds of longboats cutting silently through the waves. She described how eerie it was that none of the Empty Warriors yelled orders or spoke at all. She told them that each Empty Warrior had been dressed in dark clothing, with a black breastplate and sword on his hip. She couldn't help a shudder as she described their eyes that had no whites, no irises, and no pupils, just swirling flames.

The only thing she didn't tell the councillors was that the Empty Warriors all had exactly the same face. The two she and Jess had killed, the one they captured, and the ones in the boats had all been identical. Nathine had mocked her when she'd said that before and now, in this room of important people, she was doubting herself.

Nathine added a few observations of her own but

mostly it was only Aimee's voice wobbling out into the room. She felt the familiar prickle in her cheeks and knew she'd gone bright red. It wasn't very Rider-like, but she couldn't help it. When she finished she stepped back beside Nathine, grateful not to be the centre of attention anymore. Nathine leaned over and whispered to her.

'I would have made more of the part where we were incredibly heroic, but you did alright.'

'Thanks,' Aimee replied, smiling wryly.

She was still watching the room keenly and felt a surge of pride when she was called back into the discussion.

'The girl actually spotted the words first,' Councillor Callant was saying. His large shovel beard brushed his chest as he spoke. He had one band tattooed around his left wrist meaning this was his first term on the Uneven Council.

As one, the scholars looked at Aimee. The woman at the front of the group was tiny, with a bun of steel grey hair on the crown of her head. A hundred lines around her mouth and eyes said she'd done a lot of laughing, but today her face was very serious.

'Tell me about the Empty Warrior's breastplate,' the elderly scholar said.

'I brought it back to Kierell, Layanne,' Jara jumped in before Aimee could speak. 'I'll bring it to the university and you can study it. You don't need her description.'

Jara didn't even look at Aimee as she dismissed her

and Aimee felt a pang of disappointment. It was nerve-wracking speaking in front of so many people but she loved that she was here, that she was helping like a Rider should.

'Thank you, Jara,' Layanne said, nodding to her then turning back to Aimee, 'but your Rider not only realised what the creatures attacking her were, she also spotted a carefully concealed message. I would like to hear her description of it first-hand.'

Layanne spoke with authority and a confidence that Aimee recognised. Her aunt Naura had been the same in the kitchen when she was teaching her to bake. It was the authority of a woman who knew her own skills.

'His breastplate was black metal and engraved with a silver tree,' she began to explain. 'It was weird because it was beautiful, really detailed and delicate.'

'Why did that strike you as weird?' Layanne interrupted.

'Because he was a monster and I didn't expect monsters to wear beautiful things,' Aimee explained.

'None of the accounts we have of the Empty Warriors mention them wearing an engraved breastplate. There's nothing in Nollanni's *Founding of Kierell*,' Callant mused.

'What else?' Layanne asked.

'There were words engraved on his breastplate, made to look like part of the tree so you couldn't see them at first,' Aimee continued. 'Along the lower edge it said Ternallo Island and–'

'Marhorn's sparks, where's that?' someone asked,

but Layanne held up a hand for silence and nodded for Aimee to go on.

'There were four lines of writing in the branches of the tree,' Aimee said. Even under the pressure of all the eyes on her she knew she'd be able to repeat them perfectly. She'd thought about them non-stop on the rushed flight back to Kierell, trying to puzzle out what they meant. She really hoped Layanne would understand them and know a way to stop the army.

'The lines said, "We are created through sparks and fire" and "All that we are is hatred" and "We are fuelled by our purpose". The last one was "We will not cease until Kyelli's city is in ashes".'

It felt wrong to be speaking such a threat inside the city's council chamber. By now everyone in the room had already heard rumours of what the breastplate threatened, and the councillors had seen it themselves, but Aimee's words still struck a nerve. She could see it in their wide eyes and bitten lips. She wanted to protect them and looked hopefully at Layanne.

The elderly scholar shook her head. '"We're fuelled by our purpose",' she quoted, 'but what is their purpose? To destroy us? But why?'

Aimee's shoulders slumped. The other scholars were shaking their heads too and her hope that they would have an answer was drifting away like dragon's smoke on the wind.

'How can something be created through a spark and fire?' another of the scholars mused.

'Does it matter?' Cyella shouted, cutting across the

scholars. 'Who cares where they came from or how they were made. There's an army of monsters that are supposed to be extinct, and they're coming to destroy us!'

'We're safe inside the Ring Mountains,' Beljarn said.

'Really?' Cyella glared at him as if it were his fault, but Aimee could see the way her hands trembled. She was afraid. 'The reason we're here inside these mountains is because Empty Warriors forced our ancestors from our old home. They destroyed an entire island and the four kingdoms on it!'

Her words left the room in silence.

'Kyelli and Marhorn were supposed to have ensured we'd be safe,' said a councillor in a small voice. She was one Aimee didn't know, and she looked around the table, her eyes pleading.

'We will be safe if we stay inside our mountains,' Beljarn repeated.

'So we just close the tunnel and sit in Kierell forever?' Myconn asked, his voice as sharp as dragon's teeth.

Beljarn nodded. 'It's what Marhorn wanted us to do.'

'You don't know that,' said a scholar with untidy red hair.

'And what happens when our economy starts to shrivel?' Jara asked, her face as unforgiving as her brother's. 'What about the little shops selling wines from Nallein? Or the merchants who trade in fabrics from Taumerg? Are you willing to never buy another of those padded silk jackets?' She pointed at Beljarn and raised a blonde eyebrow.

'And it's not just the city states we need to keep trading with,' Myconn added. 'Marhorn's sparks, half the things we have in this city come from beyond the mountains. Reindeer meat and skins, the timber from the Ardnanlich forest.'

'Don't forget medicinal herbs from plants that only grow on the tundra,' another councillor added and Myconn nodded at him.

A moment later everyone in the room was naming all the things in their lives that came from beyond the Ring Mountains. Kierell was remote and isolated, and people like Jara wanted to change that. Aimee did too, but she'd never realised how much already came into Kierell from outside the mountains. If they hid away they'd wither, like a limb starved of blood.

Aimee pressed herself against the wall, the arguments swirling around her. The throbbing in her arm had become more insistent and she was grateful for a moment to step back. Nathine elbowed her in the ribs.

'You didn't tell them about the name on the breastplate.'

'Do you think I should?'

Aimee thought it was significant, though she wasn't sure why. There was something about the way the name looked like a signature, similar to when her uncle Gyron had carved his maker's mark into each piece of furniture he made. It suggested there was perhaps someone, somewhere, who had taken ownership of the Empty Warriors. But no one else had mentioned this idea and so Aimee was reluctant to suggest it in case she was wrong.

'You went on and on about the name on the flight back, wondering what it meant,' Nathine said. 'Maybe one of them knows, so tell them.'

Aimee nodded and turned to face the room. 'I think there's someone in charge,' she said, trying to make her words carry over the myriad voices. But she wasn't good at being loud and no one heard her.

'Hang on,' Nathine said, then she bellowed, 'Aimee hasn't finished, she has more to tell you!'

A shocked silence followed Nathine's shout and everyone looked taken aback.

Nathine nudged Aimee and smiled. 'There you go.'

Aimee wanted to punch her. Now, not only was everyone staring at her, but they looked angry that they'd been yelled at in their own council chamber. Still, she needed their attention and now she had it.

'There was a name on the Empty Warrior's breastplate,' she said. 'It was like the signature a craftsman would add when he signs his work. I've seen lots of marks like that because my uncle made furniture.' She felt it was important to explain so they took her seriously. 'I think maybe the person on the breastplate is the one who made the Empty Warriors with sparks and fire, and he's in charge of them.'

'What was the name?' Layanne asked, her shrewd eyes fixed on Aimee again.

'The Master of Sparks,' Aimee said at the same time as Councillor Callant did. He continued speaking.

'I've never come across the name before. Nollanni doesn't mention it. In fact there's nothing in her book at all about the Empty Warriors being created by a person. I—' He broke off to cough. 'Excuse me. I always assumed they were creatures that just existed, like prowlers or dragons. I've read *Founding of Kierell* a dozen times at least and when the Empty Warriors attacked Kierellatta, our old home, she makes no mention of anyone controlling them.'

'And Nollanni is the only source we have and she was writing eighty years after Kierell was founded,' Layanne said, sounding frustrated.

'I wish Marhorn had written a memoir before he died,' said another of the scholars, 'or that Kyelli had left us notes about Kierellatta.'

The mention of Kyelli gave Aimee a sudden idea. 'Why don't we try and find Kyelli?' she suggested, directing the question at Layanne. 'I know no one's seen her in the city for ages but she's almost immortal, isn't she? So she must be out there somewhere.'

Callant shook his head, brushing his chest with his beard. 'I've been trying for years to find any record of where Kyelli went but there's nothing. She just disappeared.'

'Callant's correct. No one even knows if she's still alive,' Layanne added.

'Why are we even discussing this?' Jara asked, bursting into the conversation.

Aimee risked a glance at her. Jara had stood up, hands on the table and she glared around the room.

There were two pink spots of colour on her high cheekbones.

'We have a hundred practical things to sort out, and you're discussing one dull-sparked girl's idea of trying to find someone who's almost a myth,' Jara continued. Her words hit Aimee like a blast of wind making her shrink back against the wall. 'I need to arrange for scouts to fly out and find everything they can about the army of Empty Warriors.

'You,' she pointed at the scholars, 'need to study that breastplate for any clues as to how we can destroy the Empty Warriors.

'We,' her long finger turned to Captain Tenth, 'need to discuss the city's defences. And Myconn and the rest of the council need to work out how we can ask the Kahollin, Ovogil and Takhie tribes for help, if we need it. Which won't be easy since we left them kicking their heels at Lorsoke.'

'Jara's right,' Myconn joined in. His cheeks weren't flushed like his sister's but he had the same steely look in his green eyes. He pointed to a young councillor with short red hair. 'Willow, take notes and start an agenda so this meeting stays on track. We've taken enough detours.'

As people began talking Jara left her chair and slipped through the crowded room. Aimee noticed she took the long way round to avoid passing Beljarn. Then her stomach flip-flopped as she realised Jara was heading for her. She instinctively hunched her shoulders the way she used to when trying to make herself smaller so her bullies wouldn't notice her. For the first time since she'd cut it, she wished for her long hair so she could pull it over her face.

'Get out of here,' Jara ordered. 'Nobody needs your help anymore or your flimsy ideas about getting some lost immortal to fight our battles for us.'

Disappointment thumped down on Aimee. She really wanted to stay, to be a part of this. She was the girl who'd saved a caravan. But Jara was her leader and Aimee had to obey. She wasn't sure if a leader was allowed to kick someone out of the Riders once she had her dragon, but she was worried Jara might try. So she swallowed the lump in her throat, and turned to go. She glanced at Nathine and Jara caught the look.

'Nathine can stay,' Jara said.

That hurt more than being made to leave. There was no reason for Nathine to stay. Jara was just being spiteful. Aimee really wanted Nathine to make a point by leaving with her, but they'd only been friends for two days. She hadn't earned that level of loyalty yet.

So she slipped quietly from the room alone and managed to hold in her tears until she reached the main entrance hall.

CHAPTER 2

## WALK AWAY

AIMEE HEAVED OPEN one of the large wooden doors and left the council chamber. Outside, she stayed in the shade of the portico and tried to push the hurt out of her brain. There were four pillars, carved like dragons, that held up the roof of the portico and Aimee stood with her hand on the cool stone of the nearest one. She wiped her eyes with the cuff of her coat sleeve and looked up at the library roof. Jess was perched on the flattened apex beside Malgerus, her emerald scales gleaming as she sunned herself. She had her wings stretched out, soaking up the heat; she appeared relaxed, except her head was cocked towards Aimee.

'I know, girl, just give me a minute,' she whispered and sent a command along their connection, telling Jess to stay.

It was only two nights ago that Jess had flown away and Aimee had nearly lost her, so she was making an effort not to share negative emotions through their connection. It was hard, though, because right then all she wanted was to slump down and cry.

'I want to be involved, Jess,' she said quietly.

She was scared of what was coming, of the Empty Warriors with their terrifying eyes of swirling flames. The thought of them breaking through into Kierell and burning people with just their hands made her feel sick. When she'd been reunited with Jess, out on the tundra, she'd had the chance to run away but she'd chosen not to. Kierell was her home, and as a Rider it was her duty to protect it. But what could one lone girl and her dragon do?

Dyrenna and Pelathina would be flying back from Lorsoke today. Maybe Jara would assign Dyrenna another task, and Aimee wondered if Dyrenna would let her help with it. They'd probably be flying back pretty quick so might even be home already. Aimee decided to go back to Anteill and see if she could find Dyrenna. There was no point hanging around outside the council chamber just for Jara to ignore her when they all came out.

She hurried down the steps into the square. Up on the library roof Jess sensed her intentions and flapped her wings to take off. Then Aimee spotted Lyrria and she stopped. She still had one foot on the bottom step and stood awkwardly wondering what to do. Could she sneak away before Lyrria saw her? She looked for Midnight and spotted her lying down at the far end of the library's long roof, her barbed tail hanging over the grey tiles.

A few days ago, the sight of Lyrria would have created all sorts of exciting tingles. If Aimee was honest, she still felt them, and that's why she needed to avoid Lyrria. She didn't want to let herself be seduced again. Staring at her from across the square, Aimee felt a tug in her chest. Lyrria's long auburn braid gleamed softly in the sunlight. She wasn't wearing her coat and Aimee's eyes were drawn to the open top few buttons of her shirt. She was leaning against the statue of Kyelli and Marhorn, and the stance made the curve of her hips look so touchable.

Lyrria hadn't seen Aimee yet and stood tossing an apple from one hand to the other. It made Aimee think of the way her tongue often tasted of apple juice. Then she remembered Lyrria in the camp two nights ago, telling stories of stealing apples with her brother, then pretending she wasn't with Aimee. The memory of Lyrria's rejection killed all the tingles. Lyrria wanted to keep their relationship a secret and that proved she didn't really care about Aimee.

Ducking her head, Aimee hurried across the square, willing Lyrria not to see her. Then Jess landed with a whoosh of wings and Aimee groaned. There was no way Lyrria wouldn't spot a bright green dragon. Maybe she could mount up and fly away really quickly.

'Aimee!'

Her heart contracted. She grabbed her saddle but Lyrria popped out from the other side of Jess.

'Hey, what's going on? Has the meeting finished already? I thought they'd be talking till everyone's sparks ran out.' Lyrria smiled, showing her crooked front teeth, the flaw that Aimee loved. 'What did the council decide to do?'

Aimee gaped at her. 'How can you just ask me normal questions like that? Are you pretending that nothing's happened?'

'What do you mean?' Lyrria asked and reached out to touch Aimee's waist.

'No,' Aimee said, though her voice caught a little in her throat.

'What's draining your spark?' Lyrria asked, and she genuinely looked confused.

Aimee felt a rush of anger and was grateful for the boost it gave her. Did Lyrria not even know how much she'd hurt her?

'Hey.' Lyrria smiled. 'I forgot to say, what with the monsters and all, but I like the new hair. It suits you.'

Again she reached out to touch her and again Aimee pulled back.

'Kyelli's sparks, what's up with you?' Lyrria looked annoyed now.

'You said to your brother that I was no one, that we weren't together. You were too ashamed to tell anyone that I've been your lover,' Aimee reminded Lyrria. Her heart was hammering against her ribs like a frantic dragon trying to escape.

'Oh come on, I told you, my brother doesn't need to know who I sleep with.'

'Why not?'

Lyrria threw up her arms in exasperation. 'Just, because.'

'Because I'm a freak and you don't want to admit to anyone that you like me.'

Lyrria opened her mouth to speak but nothing came out. Lyrria, who loved talking, and always had something to say. Aimee felt an urge to hug her but she quickly squashed it. Beside her Jess was shifting uncomfortably, her long talons anxiously tapping the flagstones. Aimee knew that, with her weird face, there might never be anyone else who liked her, but she made herself turn away. She climbed into her saddle.

'Aimee, wait, what is this?' Lyrria's beautiful face looked up at her. 'Don't you want to be together anymore?'

'I don't think we ever were together, not properly,' Aimee replied.

Then, with her chest so tight she could barely breath, she and Jess took off. They soared above the steep grey rooftops as the city spread out beneath them. She didn't turn to see the green copper dome of the council chamber. If she looked back, then she might fly back to tell Lyrria she was sorry so she could see her smile again. Ahead the sharp cliffs rose like an impenetrable wall, their peaks stabbing the blue sky. Aimee pulled gently on Jess's horns and squeezed with her knees, guiding her dragon up and left.

The wind blew Aimee's short curls back from her face and for a moment she closed her eyes. She tried to imagine the wind blowing through her brain, carrying away all the memories of nights she'd spent with Lyrria. It didn't work. Even when she opened her eyes she could still see Lyrria smiling down at her. She saw Lyrria's long hair, free of its braid, and she could feel it gently brushing the bare skin of her chest. In her mind Lyrria's bare, freckled skin glowed in the light from a dragon's breath orb.

'Ugh!' Annoyed at herself she tried to shove the memories away and focus on what she could feel.

Jess's spiralled horns were hard beneath her hands. Her fingers were already cold because she'd forgotten to put on her gloves. She'd forgotten her goggles too, so her eyes were watering. Beneath her she could feel the subtle shifts in Jess's body as she rode the sky and she tried to enjoy sharing Jess's feelings of strength. Inside her chest, though, her heart hurt like someone had grabbed it roughly and was wringing out all the love.

'I did the right thing, didn't I?' she asked Jess as they soared up into the peaks.

Jess sent a pulse of love along their connection and Aimee smiled. Feeling Jess's love was like when she put her cold toes into a bath of warm water. She guided Jess over the training ground then up into the cluster of peaks on top of the Heart.

'Okay, girl, let's go home,' Aimee said. Without her gloves and hat, her fingers and ears were prickling with cold now, and she was looking forward to a cup of tea. 'You know the way, Jess.'

Aimee squeezed her eyes tight shut as Jess dived down one of the vents that led into the Heart. Maybe one day she'd be brave enough to keep them open. For now she'd simply trust Jess.

The huge cavern was empty of Riders as Aimee unsaddled Jess, though there were plenty of dragons on the ledges around the walls. She watched Jess fly up to rest on a ledge halfway up and as she did so, she noticed something about the other dragons. None of them were lying down, they were all crouched or standing, wingtips fluttering or talons clicking on the rock. They were uneasy which meant their Riders were too.

Aimee looked for Black but couldn't see him. Disappointment settled on her. She'd really wanted to talk to Dyrenna. Leaving the Heart she trudged through the tunnels of Anteill, wondering what she was going to do. There were monsters to fight but she felt useless.

She stopped outside the dining cavern and peeked in. It was busy, as if every Rider had gathered in there, waiting for news, for orders, for Jara to come back and give them a plan. Aimee had promised herself she was going to get to know more of the Riders, maybe even make friends with some of the other women. But she couldn't face doing it now. If she went into the dining cavern everyone would want to know what had happened in the council meeting and she didn't want to admit that Jara had kicked her out.

Her fingers were still cold, so she continued along the tunnel to where it narrowed and there were spreading branches of purple quartz in the wall. Here there was a small side door into the kitchen cavern. She slipped inside.

Dragon's breath orbs, hanging on chains from the ceiling, gave the room a comforting glow. A large fireplace had been carved into the far wall, making use of a natural vent for a chimney. All the walls were covered in ledges, some of them natural, others carved. Pots filled the bigger shelves lower down. Above them were stoneware jars and wooden bowls. Running between them all were veins of quartz in the rock, sparkling pink, rich purple and milky white. A huge wooden table filled the middle of the circular room and at one end someone had placed a small yellow jug filled with yolansie flowers, each of which seemed to have a hundred orange petals.

Aranati turned from the table as Aimee slunk in. The beautiful Rider wore her customary frown. In the glowing light her skin shone like polished copper and her long dark hair sucked in the shadows. Aimee stiffened, waiting for questions about the council meeting. Instead Aranati asked something else.

'How's your burn?'

'Oh. It aches, a lot, but it's not hot anymore,' Aimee replied.

When they got back to Kierell last night, Aranati had cleaned and bandaged both Aimee's arm and Nathine's leg. She'd applied a salve of dragon's saliva mixed with oatmeal. It smelled like smoky porridge but had felt really cooling. Aranati had explained that dragon's saliva contained properties which helped a wound heal more quickly.

'Your burn's deep and it'll take a while to heal so be careful with it. Nathine shouldn't be walking around with the one she's got on her leg,' Aranati said, her frown deepening.

Aimee didn't want to disagree so she changed the subject. 'Do you know if Dyrenna's back yet?'

Aranati shook her head. She was measuring tea leaves into a pot and Aimee noticed she was clenching the spoon. Then she remembered, Pelathina was with Dyrenna, and she was Aranati's little sister.

'I'm sure they'll be fine,' Aimee said quickly.

The Empty Warriors couldn't attack Riders in the sky, could they? And if the Helvethi centaurs were upset that the councillors had reneged on their meeting, they wouldn't take it out on Dyrenna and Pelathina, would they? Aimee felt bad that she might have put them in danger and wanted to comfort Aranati. The older Rider was so unapproachable though, with her constant frown and her perfectly beautiful face.

'Do you want some tea?' Aranati asked.

Aimee nodded then waited in silence while Aranati fetched a mug and poured.

'Shall I pour one for Lyrria too? And she likes honey in hers, doesn't she?' Aranati asked. The question threw Aimee off balance.

'Lyrria's down in the city, waiting for Jara, I think,' Aimee managed to stutter.

'Oh sorry, I assumed she'd be with you.'

'Why?'

Aranati looked at her and the deep groove between her dark eyebrows softened a little.

'I've seen the way she looks at you,' Aranati said softly. 'I thought perhaps you two were together.'

The ache returned to Aimee's chest with a vengeance. It wasn't fair. Lyrria was too ashamed of having a relationship with a freak to tell anyone, but it seemed half the Riders knew anyway. Aimee shook her head, trying to knock loose some words, but they were all stuck fast. She took the mug of tea from Aranati and left the kitchen without saying anything. She was being rude but she couldn't face explaining about Lyrria.

She hurried along the tunnel in case Aranati followed or called after her. Rounding a bend, she found herself at the entrance to Dyrenna's workshop. It was dark inside, the rows of old saddles hanging on the wall like roosting bats. She wondered if she sat in there, smelling the leather and oil, would she feel better? She took a step inside then stopped. Without Dyrenna to talk to the room felt sad and empty.

She continued on, carrying her tea, wandering the tunnels aimlessly. During her training she had learned to walk carefully, being light and quiet, but today it felt like the world was pushing down on her and her boots scuffed the stone floor.

She'd worked so hard to become a Rider, learned so many new skills, but now, when warriors were needed, she felt useless. The Riders' strength was their community. They would fight for their city but they'd also fight for each other. Aimee longed to be a part of that, and when she'd saved the caravan she had been. But now she and Jess were alone again. She wasn't strong or skilled enough to save the city by herself.

Without meaning to she walked to the armoury. She

stopped when she realised where she was and pushed open the door. This was where she'd first held a real scimitar. The memory of how good that had felt pulled her into the dark room.

CHAPTER 3

## SHADOWS AND SECRETS

The armoury door swung shut behind Aimee and the shadows closed in around her. Yellow light glowed under a wooden rack of training swords. She put down her tea and fished out a small dragon's breath orb. It must have been kicked under there and left behind. As she held it up the shadows retreated. She clasped it in one hand, her tea in the other, and walked slowly around the armoury.

The room smelled of leather and the cold tang of metal. It made her think of all the hours she'd spent training. Learning to fight, to wield twin scimitars in a deadly dance, and how strong her body had become. All of it was a waste if she couldn't help save Kierell.

She did a circuit of the room and stopped by a rack of scimitars. Their bare blades glinted as the light passed over them. The rack was on wheels and it slid aside, revealing a stalagmite almost as tall as she was. It sparkled with rose quartz. Aimee sat down on the cold stone floor and rested her head against it.

She finished her tea, then put down the mug and orb and pulled her legs up, hugging her knees. She sat in a little bubble of yellow light. Beyond it the room was so full of shadows she couldn't see the door any more. It felt like the shadows were staring at her, admonishing her for hiding like the old Aimee had.

'But what can I do?' she asked them. 'I'm not a hero. I'm not even someone important.'

Annoyed she let go of her knees and allowed her legs to flop back to the floor. Her right heel accidentally kicked her tea mug and sent it skittering away into the shadows.

'Kyelli's sparks,' Aimee swore quietly, worrying that she'd broken another mug.

She grabbed the orb, rose to her feet and walked over into the shadows. The orb's light pushed them away and revealed the back wall of the armoury. There was a large niche in the wall, just above Aimee's head and on it rested a wooden box. It was too small to have weapons inside. The need for something to distract her made Aimee reach up and pull down the box. It was heavy, and even using both hands, she nearly dropped it. She put it on the floor and sat cross-legged beside it.

It was skilfully made and she knew her uncle Gyron would have liked it. A dragon had been carved onto the lid, its wings wide in flight, its mouth open as if roaring. She ran her fingers over it, feeling each wooden scale and the curves of the dragon's body. Stars, clouds and swirls of wind had been carved around the sides of the box, the details inlaid with orallion. The blue-tinged metal glinted in the flickering light from her small orb. At the bottom of the box were four feet, each with curved talons.

She tried the small metal clasp. It wasn't locked. Curiosity made her flick it open. Inside was a book she recognised. It was the ledger Jara had given her to sign after she'd made the climb. The council had an official record of all the Riders, and Aimee had signed that ledger too, but this one belonged to the Riders. Aimee hadn't had a chance to examine it before, she'd been too intimidated by Jara to ask if she could look through it. Taking the ledger out she balanced it reverently on her lap. It was bound in dragonhide that had gone stiff and black with age. The cover creaked as she opened it and a musty, old paper smell filled her nose.

Aimee gasped when she read the lines on the first page. They were signed, by Kyelli. She hovered her fingers over the words, not daring to touch them. Kyelli herself had written them. Her handwriting was spiky but neat and she'd drawn a little picture of a lillybel flower beside her name. Aimee softly read the words aloud.

'Let this be a record of my Sky Riders. Every woman in this book has braved the climb and proved her dedication to Kierell. Your sparks shine brighter than the stars.'

Aimee read it four times. She pictured Kyelli, with her long hair and regal face, sitting somewhere in Kierell, perhaps under a cherry blossom tree, writing these words. Had she looked at the empty pages and wondered who were the girls that would one day fill them? Aimee had always loved the statues of Kyelli down in the city but this was better. This was something Kyelli had actually touched.

She flicked slowly through the pages. There were no other notes from Kyelli but it was impressive to see three hundred years of names. Women who'd all become Sky Riders. She flicked back and looked at the first name. Efysta SaWern. She had a little star beside her name. Aimee wondered what that meant. Eventually she reached pages with names she recognised and she noticed Jara had a star too. It must mark the women who'd become leaders. Then she found her own name, last on the list. She had a sudden horrible thought that if Kierell was destroyed then hers would always be the last name on the list.

'I don't know how, but I won't let that happen, Kyelli,' she promised, closing the ledger.

It was when she lifted the ledger to replace it in the box that she noticed something odd. Not with the ledger but with the box. Aimee had watched her uncle make boxes. Gyron had been meticulous in his work, always using perfect dovetail joints. Aimee had been rubbish at woodwork but she knew enough to know when something was well made. This box had neat dovetail joints on the front two corners but the ones at the back were clunky. The wood looked too thick. She turned the box around, imagining Gyron shaking his head.

She ran her fingers over the wood and felt a tiny

catch at the bottom of the back panel, so carefully hidden she'd nearly missed it. She ran her fingers further along, finding a second catch. Using her thumbs, she pressed both catches and the back panel of the box slid out. She jerked and caught it before it clattered to the floor.

Then she scrambled to catch the thing that fell out of the secret compartment.

It was a piece of thick paper, folded in half twice and yellowed with age. It was coated in a layer of dust and decorated with three crusty dead spiders. Aimee shook them off and then, very carefully, she opened out the paper. It took her a moment to realise she was looking at a detailed and beautifully drawn map of Kierell. There was writing at the edges in Kyelli's spiky handwriting. This was something else she'd made.

An idea hovered at the edge of Aimee's mind, too big and tempting for her to let it come all the way in yet. She glanced at it sideways though. What if there was something on this map that told her where Kyelli had gone?

Another part of her brain told her to put the map back. Maybe it was something very secret that only Sky Rider leaders were meant to see. If it was, and Jara found her with it, she would be in even more trouble. And the last thing she needed was to give Jara another reason to have a go at her.

She folded it back up, then hesitated. She didn't want to put it back. That big, tempting idea pushed a little further into her mind. If this map did contain a clue to where Kyelli was, how could she put it back in its box with the dead spiders? Kyelli had saved them once before. She could do it again. This could be Aimee's way to be involved, to help save the city. What if no one else knew about this map? What if she doomed the city by not using it to find Kyelli?

So she popped the folded piece of paper in her pocket, put the box back together, then heaved it back up into the niche on the wall.

She hurried straight to her room, completely forgetting about her mug and leaving it in the shadows of the armoury. Once inside she took a dragon's breath orb from the cabinet beside her bed and sat it on top. The flickering light filled her little cave room. Her hands were shaking with nerves as she pulled out the map. Unfolding it carefully, she laid it down on the patchwork blanket that covered her bed.

Just then her door swung open and banged against the wall. Aimee jumped and threw her pillow over the map.

'Here you are,' Nathine said, limping in and nudging the door closed. She stood and looked around. 'Your room's smaller than mine but I like the purple crystals above your bed. My room's only got one small line of pink quartz in the wall by the door.'

'Nathine, why are you in my room?' Aimee demanded, eyes nervously darting to the pillow.

'I used to visit Hayetta in her room all the time,' Nathine replied.

Then there was an uncomfortable silence as both

girls thought about their friend who'd died on her first flight.

'Nathine, I need—'

'I thought you'd want—'

Both girls spoke at once and then both dropped into silence again. It was Nathine who broke it.

'I'm not particularly busy right now, so I thought I'd fill you in on what you missed in the rest of the council meeting.'

Nathine spoke with a feigned nonchalance but it was thoughtful of her, and not at all what Aimee had been expecting.

'Okay, but can you knock next time please before you come barging in,' Aimee said.

Nathine shrugged and waved away Aimee's concerns. 'It's alright, I saw Lyrria in the dining cavern with Jara and Sal, so I knew you two weren't in here naked.'

Nathine's words tore open the wound in Aimee's heart. She tried to hide it, but Nathine must have seen.

'Hey.' She took a hesitant step forward then stopped. Her round face looked confused and unsure.

Aimee clamped down on the swelling pain in her chest and tried to sniff some traitorous tears back inside.

'Dragon's dung,' Nathine said. Then apparently decided something because her hesitancy vanished and she plonked herself down on Aimee's bed.

Aimee was shocked. 'But—'

'I know,' Nathine interrupted. 'You'll probably infect me, I'll turn white and all the energy will drain out of my spark, then I'll die.' She shrugged. 'But you might have given me a hug when Hayetta died so I don't want you thinking I owe you.'

She wrapped an arm around Aimee's shoulders and Aimee didn't realise how much she'd been needing a hug until she got one. She leaned into Nathine's broad shoulder and let her tears come.

'Did Lyrria break up with you?' Nathine asked.

'I think I broke up with her,' Aimee gasped between sobs.

'I'm impressed, good for you.' Aimee felt Nathine nod.

'Why is it good?' Aimee asked. 'It feels like a mountain's crashed onto my chest and I can't breathe. It's like she stole a piece of me and ran off, and now I'll never get that piece back. I feel rubbish.'

Nathine gave her a squeeze, catching the edge of Aimee's bandaged arm. Aimee gasped.

'Sorry,' Nathine said.

Aimee couldn't be angry because she knew Nathine was trying to help.

'If you're so super in love, why did you break up with her?'

Aimee struggled for a moment to get her breath and wiped snot from her top lip. 'Because she wouldn't admit to anyone that we were together. She was happy to have fun when she felt like it but she didn't want people to know she was sleeping with a freak.'

'Then you were right to fly away from her. If a relationship has to be kept secret then it's not a good one.'

There was an edge to Nathine's voice and Aimee

knew she was thinking about her father, the way he abused her. He'd threatened to hurt her little brother if she ever told anyone.

'You'll find another girl,' Nathine said, her voice softening a little. 'I mean that mushroom haircut you gave yourself might put some girls off, but I'm sure there will be someone who likes it.'

Aimee choked on a small laugh. Nathine unwrapped her arm from Aimee's shoulders and sat back against the wall. She winced as she stretched out her wounded leg. 'So, do you want to hear about the council meeting?'

Aimee wiped her eyes and nose on her sleeve then nodded.

'Very Rider-like,' Nathine said with a smile, pointing at Aimee's slimy sleeve.

Aimee laughed. Surprisingly Nathine had actually made her feel better. 'Alright, what did they decide after Jara kicked me out? Is there a plan?'

Nathine snorted. 'The Uneven Council is completely out of its depth.'

'They're just scared. I am too.'

'Yeah well, they talked forever, arguing over everything from sending Riders out to destroy the army, to—'

'But we can't, there were thousands of Empty Warriors,' Aimee said.

'I know, don't worry. Jara shot that one down. She might be annoyed at you but she'll protect her Riders. Even forty-five dragons are no match for thousands of those monsters.'

She shuddered and Aimee too felt the sick tug of

fear as she imagined trying to fight hundreds of Empty Warriors. Attacking only three had gotten both her and Nathine injured.

'That councillor with the beard—'

'Callant,' Aimee interrupted.

'Yeah him, he wants to try and find the Master of Sparks, though no one knows where to start. Those scholars are going to bury themselves in books looking for any reference to him. The councillors all agreed with that plan. They think if they can find the person controlling the Empty Warriors then maybe we could negotiate with him.'

'The breastplate said the Empty Warriors' purpose was to destroy Kyelli's city but I don't understand why anyone would want to do that?' Aimee said. 'I wondered if perhaps it's a mistake. Do the councillors think that if they could talk to the Master of Sparks maybe we could stop him?'

'Yes, though the one with the glasses, that Jara kept glaring at—'

'Beljarn.'

'If you say so, well he was arguing for completely blocking the tunnel so no one could ever go outside the mountains again, but also no army could get in. He said it was the only way we'd be safe. Nobody agreed with him but the council has voted to temporarily suspend all caravans. I wish I could see my father's face when he hears that news.'

'Jara won't be happy with that,' Aimee said.

'She wasn't, but the council voted eight to three in

favour. Why does she hate Beljarn so much?'

'Years ago both her parents and Beljarn's parents were killed by Helvethi while out on the tundra trying to make peace,' Aimee explained what she'd learned from Dyrenna. 'Jara wants to fulfil her parents' dream, but I think it made Beljarn afraid of the outside world. Also, he broke her heart.'

'See, it happens to everyone,' Nathine said flippantly.

Her words cut Aimee, just as they always had, but this time Nathine seemed to regret them. 'I didn't mean—' she began, then hesitated.

'It's okay, I know,' Aimee said. 'So the plan is to somehow find the Master of Sparks. What about us—I mean, the Riders?'

'Well, Jara's going to send scouts out to track the army. She wants to know how many there are and if they're actually going to head our way.'

Aimee thought they would. No one would engrave a promise onto thousands of metal breastplates if they didn't intend to fulfil it.

'And then the Helvethi are coming,' Nathine continued.

'Here?'

Nathine tucked her hair behind her ears and nodded. 'Yeah, Pelathina's back and she said the leaders from two of the tribes still want to meet with us so they're coming here. Dyrenna's travelling with them. They'll have to run all the way from Lorsoke if they're going to make it here before the Empty Warriors.'

Aimee thought of Dyrenna in the sky alone, trying to outrun an army of monsters. Fear for her friend pricked at her heart.

'Is it only the tribe leaders who're coming?' she asked, hoping maybe Dyrenna would have two whole tribes with her for support.

Nathine nodded. 'Yeah, the two leaders from each tribe.'

Aimee tried to picture a small group of centaurs walking through the streets of Kierell, their hooves clopping on the cobbles. They'd look so out of place. Aimee had only ever seen the two dead Helvethi on the tundra, killed by Empty Warriors and she was interested to see living ones. That's if Jara let her see them.

'Did Jara assign you a task?' Aimee asked.

Nathine scowled. 'No, she just told me to come back here and wait. I don't understand. She's the one who pushed us to be Riders and now that we are, it's like she doesn't want us.'

Aimee felt bad for her. She'd involved Nathine in her hunt for the Empty Warrior, and it was because of her that Jara was angry at Nathine too. Aimee knew that Nathine had dreamt of being a Rider but now she was being excluded. She wondered about showing her the map. Jara had dismissed her idea of finding Kyelli but Aimee couldn't let it go. Something about it seemed right and she was eager to see if the map could help her.

'I don't think Jara's going to let me help but I want to be involved,' Aimee said. 'I found something which we can use and I thought you'd like to help me.'

Nathine looked suspicious. 'Are you just pitying me because I'm injured and Jara doesn't like me now? Which is your fault by the way.'

Aimee took a deep breath. Building a friendship with Nathine was like taking one step forward and three steps back.

'I'm trying to be nice and I thought we made a good team. I couldn't have saved the caravan or found that army without your help.'

'You've already had one hug today, flattering me isn't going to get you another,' Nathine said.

'I don't want any more hugs from you. I'd have to hold my breath again because your armpits stink,' Aimee retorted without thinking.

Even though Nathine rolled her eyes, Aimee realised that, if she was going to go ahead with the plan that was brewing in her head, she wanted Nathine with her.

'This is what I found,' Aimee said. She pulled out the piece of paper from under her pillow then scooted over and laid it across both her and Nathine's legs.

'Where did you get this?' Nathine asked, and Aimee explained where she'd found it.

'It's a map, see? Of Kierell,' Aimee said, tracing her finger over the drawing. 'It's a picture of what the city looks like when we fly above it. Look, there's the council chamber in the middle, and there's Marhorn Street in Barter. You can see the way it bends slightly at the end when it reaches Tormanlyk Square.'

'It's so detailed and looks exactly like the city does from the air,' Nathine said and Aimee could tell from the way her voice had gone up that she was interested in the discovery too. She was glad she'd shared it.

'I think a Rider made this map because only a Rider sees the city like this,' Aimee said. 'Look at how wiggly the streets of the Palace are. I lived there for seventeen years but there's no way I could have drawn a map of it until I saw it from the air.'

'Look, what are these?'

Aimee followed Nathine's finger as she pointed to symbols on the map. Each one was a little drawing of a tree but they were in places where there weren't any trees, like Quorelle Square. They were also in blue ink whereas the rest of the map had been drawn in black.

'There's another one,' Aimee said, pointing.

'And here.'

'I can see five, no six, of them.'

'Yeah, me too.'

'What do you think they mean?'

Nathine shrugged.

Aimee turned her attention to the writing down the right-hand side of the map, beyond the Ring Mountains and sitting in the Griydak Sea. She explained to Nathine that it was Kyelli's handwriting then she began to read aloud.

'"I created this map with the help of my good friend, Efysta, and her dragon, Dream"'

'Who do you think Efysta is?' Nathine interrupted.

'She was the first leader of the Sky Riders,' Aimee replied.

'You know the name of someone from three hundred years ago but you don't know the names of most of the women you eat breakfast with?'

Aimee felt her face flush. Nathine was right, and she had promised herself she'd change that. But she hadn't done anything about it yet so she kept reading, ignoring her failure.

'"I didn't want to leave any trace but Efysta persuaded me. I don't want to leave Kierell. I've come to love the city and I'm proud of what our survivors have built here but it isn't safe for the people if I stay."'

Aimee stopped reading. 'Why wouldn't it be safe for people if Kyelli stayed? She's the one who saved us from the Empty Warriors in our old home.'

Nathine shrugged so Aimee kept reading.

'"I've left clues in Kierell that point to where I've gone in case my Riders ever need to find me. I hope that you don't. I hope that by taking myself away, what I fear will never come to pass. I beg you, do not come to find me unless you have no other choice. This map is the first clue, though I hope you never need it."'

Aimee looked up at Nathine. She'd been right; the map was a way to find Kyelli.

CHAPTER 4

# FORBIDDEN

Nathine looked at Aimee, her blue eyes wide. 'It's a message from Kyelli. She wrote this.'

The awe on her face mirrored what Aimee was feeling. Nathine obviously admired Kyelli too but instead of feeling jealous, Aimee was glad. It gave her and Nathine something they shared and that was surely a good thing for their burgeoning friendship.

'We could use this map to find her,' Aimee said. 'She'd know how to destroy the Empty Warriors.'

'In the council meeting you proposed trying to find Kyelli and Jara shot you down,' Nathine reminded her.

'I know Jara thinks it's a waste of time but I think we'd be idiots not to try and find Kyelli. We can't save the city ourselves but Kyelli could do it.'

'Have you considered that maybe Jara knows about this map already? You said it was in a box that probably only the leaders of the Sky Riders ever open. What if Jara doesn't want to use the map? Kyelli's written on it that it's only for emergencies.'

'And thousands of spark-less monsters, with nothing inside them but fire, coming to kill everyone, that's not an emergency?' Aimee said, the words tumbling out quickly.

She'd really hoped that by sharing the map with Nathine, she'd instantly think her idea was brilliant and they could fly off on another mission. She could do it alone of course but she didn't want to. She'd struggled through the climb, the training and learning to fly by herself but that wasn't what Riders were supposed to do. They were a community and they worked together. Jara might be excluding her, but Aimee and Jess could make their own little team with Nathine and Malgerus.

'Maybe we should just put the map back and pretend we didn't see it,' Nathine suggested.

'No,' Aimee said and slapped her palms down on her bed. 'Kyelli saved our ancestors from the Empty Warriors so she can save us too. We just need to find her. If she knows there's an army coming to destroy her city, she'll understand why we used the map.'

The map was still on the bed between them and she looked down at it. Now that she knew what it really was, every time she looked at it she felt all the swirling possibilities. If she took up the map and followed its clues she'd be able to actually meet Kyelli. This wouldn't just be a beautiful statue but really her, alive and amazing. She had to do it.

'I'm going to put the map back,' Nathine said. 'You shouldn't have taken it in the first place.'

Alarmed, Aimee reached for it but Nathine snatched

it up first. She bounced off the bed and shoved the map in her trouser pocket. She was out the door half a second later. Aimee jumped off her bed and ran down the corridor. Nathine was limping on her wounded leg and Aimee caught her easily. She grabbed Nathine's arm, dragging her to a halt.

'Can I have the map back?' she asked.

Nathine shook her head. 'No, because you'll use it on this self-appointed mission which Jara thinks is pointless and when she finds out she'll be really pissed. Even more pissed than she is now. And if she thinks I was involved then I'll never get a proper mission.'

Nathine had her angry face on, the one Aimee had hoped she wouldn't see again. She didn't cower away from it, though. Instead she stepped into Nathine's space and glared up at her, head tilted back because she wasn't as tall.

'This *is* a proper mission and if you're going to wimp out then Jess and I will go ourselves,' Aimee said. 'And if you don't give me back the map, I'll break your nose again.'

Nathine's eyes opened wide at the threat. There was still a slight kink in her nose from when Aimee broke it at the nesting site. The air suddenly felt tense, as if it was contracting around them, and Aimee pictured Jess and Malgerus facing off.

'Please come with me and help,' Aimee said. 'You're injured and Jara isn't going to give you any important tasks, which I know is my fault. But I think if we can find Kyelli then Jara will be relieved because she'll have help.'

Nathine stepped back and leaned against the tunnel wall. On a ledge by her head a dragon's breath orb flickered yellow light over her face. If Nathine said no again, Aimee wondered if she could get the map off her without hurting her.

'You know, you look like a constipated dragon when you make that serious face of yours,' Nathine said as she pulled out the folded map and passed it to Aimee. Surprised and relieved, Aimee took the map and gripped it tightly.

'Thank you,' she said. 'A constipated dragon?'

'Yeah, well, now that I can't call you a freak any more I need to be more creative in my insults,' Nathine said, smiling.

'You could try not insulting me at all.'

'But then I might end up liking you.'

Aimee shook her head but felt her lips twitching into a smile.

'So, do you want to help me? I think we should examine the map again and try to work out what the first clue is,' Aimee suggested.

Nathine shook her head. 'I'll help, but we can't just keep inventing missions for ourselves. You need to take the map to Jara and ask permission to follow it.'

Aimee's elation at having won back the map vanished. The thought of going to Jara for permission pulled her down, like a bog sucking at her boots.

'You have to ask her, Aimee, even if she takes it off you and says we have to patrol the cabbage fields instead,' Nathine said.

Aimee knew she was right but it felt like snakes were squirming in her belly. It was like the times when she had to admit to her aunt Naura that she hadn't got something from the market because she'd been too afraid to go out.

'Okay, let's go and ask her,' Aimee said with a lot more confidence than she felt.

Nathine put a hand on her shoulder. 'I don't think it would be a good idea to threaten to break her nose, though. Besides, she's really tall, you'd never reach.'

Aimee figured that was Nathine's attempt at being supportive so she didn't tell her how unhelpful it was. She'd always wanted a friend and never thought she'd have one, so she couldn't complain if Nathine wasn't exactly what she'd dreamed about.

'I made the council listen to me. I can do this too,' she said.

Nathine didn't mock her, instead she nodded and even looked a little impressed at her resolve. Aimee took a deep breath. She hadn't expected to have to stand up to Jara again quite so soon. Clutching the map tightly she started off down the tunnel. Nathine limped beside her and elbowed her in the ribs.

'Aimee?'

'Yes?'

'I want to help,' Nathine said, her voice surprisingly small. 'When I used to watch the Riders with my father's caravan, I wanted to be as strong as them. Mainly because I dreamed of killing my father but also,

I wanted to be able to protect other girls. Being able to save people from Empty Warriors would be good, like being a proper Rider.'

Aimee smiled and mentally pictured adding a few more bricks to the bridge of friendship she was building. She gave the other girl's hand a quick squeeze, letting go before Nathine could make a sarcastic comment.

They tried the dining cavern first but it was empty now, tea mugs abandoned on the tabletops, so they headed for the Heart. As soon as they turned into the tunnel that sloped down towards it, Aimee could hear the overlapping echoes of many voices. She was gripping the map so tightly that she was crumpling it. She stopped at the entrance and took a deep breath.

'I can do this,' she whispered, then stepped into the Heart.

She hadn't seen so many Riders in the cavern since the day of her first flight. They were gathered in groups all across the cavern, and all busy with something. Up round the walls their dragons, sensing their Rider's emotions, were perched on the edge of the ledges. Their wings were fluttering, jaws snapping, heads sweeping side to side as they watched their Riders keenly. Aimee's eyes flew up to Jess. She was near the top of the cavern wall and crouched on a ledge. Her wings were furled but she'd stretched out her long neck and was watching everyone. Her eyes locked on Aimee's and Aimee felt her in her mind, a steadying presence.

Aimee scanned the groups, looking for a blonde head. Everyone had something to do, no one was loitering uselessly. No one except her and Nathine. Aimee's determination to be involved grew even stronger. She spotted Jara striding across the cavern and hurried after her. It was late now and the eternal twilight of the short summer nights floated down from the vents. Jara walked through one of the shafts of grey-blue light and Aimee saw the strain on her face, tightening her features.

As Jara neared the circle of dragon's breath orbs hanging from shepherd's crook poles, Aimee caught up with her.

'Jara, can I speak to you please?'

Jara glanced back over her shoulder, fine blonde hair cutting the twilight. Her green eyes were as hard as Jess's scales.

'Not now, Aimee, I don't have time.'

She turned and continued walking. Aimee trailed after her but Jara ignored her and joined a group of eight Riders. Aimee only knew one name, Sal, the petite redhead at the front of the group. All the Riders had their coats and gloves on, goggles dangling from their fingers.

'Are you ready?' Jara asked. Sal nodded once. 'Alright, I want a full report of the army. Everything. Numbers, as close as you can estimate, any command structure you can see, an idea of how fast they're moving and any siege weapons. I especially want to know if it looks like there's someone in charge. If this army belongs to the Master of Sparks, surely he'll be with it. I want six of you to stay with the army but fly high in case they have archers. Sal, you and another will bring the report back. Does everyone understand?'

The women all nodded then moved away to call down their dragons. Jara gave Sal a quick hug then moved on. Her long legs made it hard for Aimee to keep up.

'Jara?' Aimee tried again. This time Jara ignored her completely.

Another group of Riders were pulling on coats and scimitars. Jara joined them, with Aimee and Nathine trailing after like hatchlings who'd lost their clutch. Aranati spoke as she slipped her scimitars onto her back.

'Captain Tenth is stationing a troop of guards at the caravan compound.'

'Good,' Jara nodded. 'Sparks. I hate that we're stopping caravans from heading out onto the tundra but it's only temporary. The council are announcing the ban on travel tonight so Tenth knows his guards need to be ready before then.'

'Do you think there will be trouble?' asked a Rider with long dark hair.

'I hope not but a lot of people's livelihoods lie beyond the mountains so I can understand if they're angry.' Jara gathered up her hair as she spoke, then let it fall. 'The guards at the compound are more of a precaution.'

'And us?' Aranati asked, the crease between her eyes deepening.

'You can help explain to people. You've seen the Empty Warriors.' Jara put a hand on Aranati's shoulder.

'But I want you to also survey the area around the tunnel, both inside and outside the mountains. If we can't stop the army before it gets here, that's where they'll attack. I want to know what we can do to make sure they do not get through that tunnel.'

'I heard Councillor Beljarn suggested collapsing it,' said the dark-haired Rider.

Aimee saw the anger on Jara's face and recoiled, even though it wasn't directed at her.

'I will not let that happen,' Jara said fiercely. 'When this is over we'll need that tunnel again.' She turned to Aranati. 'Are you good to go?'

Aranati nodded and Jara gave her arm a squeeze before continuing round the cavern. Aimee heard the flap of wings as Aranati and the others called down their dragons. Aimee could tell, from the way Jara kept running her hands through her hair, that she was still angry. It made her even more nervous about speaking to her.

'You're not being forceful enough,' Nathine whispered in her ear.

Aimee shrugged her off. She hurried to catch up with Jara, then stopped dead. Nathine bumped into her and swore. Aimee's eyes were fixed on the purple dragon beside Jara. Midnight. Lyrria's dragon. Then Jara moved to the side and Aimee saw Lyrria. Her heart jumped into her throat and it felt like she might choke on it. The tips of her fingers tingled with unwanted adrenaline.

'I can't,' Aimee whispered.

Lyrria was standing in one of the shafts of twilight

and the soft light caressed the side of her face. Her silver earrings sparkled and Aimee had a sudden vivid memory of kissing her ears. The longing welled up in her and she desperately tried to shove it back down, like trying to close a box that was too full.

She dragged her eyes away and looked up at Jess. Her dragon was crouched now, on the edge of her ledge as if ready to take off. Aimee opened the door in her mind and let all Jess's love flow into her. Her dragon's uncomplicated emotions washed though her brain, pushing Lyrria away.

Jara and Lyrria were close enough that Aimee could hear them talking but she kept her eyes on Jess.

'Aimee!' Nathine hissed but Aimee ignored her.

She heard Jara telling Lyrria to take three others and patrol the ring of mountains. They were to keep a close eye, especially on the Griydak Sea. Jara was worried the army might not all have landed on the beach. Kierell had a small harbour in the eastern curve of the mountains. It made them vulnerable but it was only approachable by boat. Aimee hadn't even considered the possibility of an attack from the sea.

'And make sure you're visible,' Jara said. 'The city's going to be unsettled after the council's announcement tonight. I want people to be able to look up and see they're protected.'

'Alright, I'll make sure I wave periodically,' Lyrria said and even without looking Aimee knew she was smiling her crooked smile.

'Lyrria, I'm serious,' Jara said.

'I know, don't worry. I'll take Lwena, Faye and Orylla.'

Disappointment needled Aimee and she realised she'd been hoping Lyrria would say her name. She stayed staring at Jess until she heard flapping. From the corner of her eye she saw Midnight dive up one of the vents.

'The Empty Warriors will have arrived and killed us all before you scrape together enough courage to talk to Jara,' Nathine said, crossing her arms. She had muscly shoulders and the pose made her look even broader.

Aimee gathered up her determination and marched over to Jara, who hopped over one of the channels that funnelled rainwater and strode towards the back of the cavern.

'Jara, wait, please,' Aimee called as she caught up.

This time Jara spun around. Her eyes flitted from Aimee, to Nathine, and then back to Aimee.

'Aimee, I don't—' she began but Aimee interrupted.

'No, you have to listen to me!'

In her desperation her plea had come out as a shout. It echoed round the cavern and the Riders still there all turned to look at her. Aimee felt her face flush and involuntarily hunched her shoulders. But she couldn't run and hide now. She held out the folded piece of paper but kept a tight grip on it.

'I've found a map that Kyelli drew,' she began, 'it's got a note on it that says we can use the clues in it to find her. I want to try following them. Kyelli says on the map to only do this if it's an emergency but I think the

Empty Warrior army counts as one.'

Aimee was surprised to see a flash of panic in Jara's sharp green eyes. She couldn't be that worried about Aimee being involved, could she? Jara did the thing where she gathered up her hair and then let it fall.

'No one's seen Kyelli in the city for over one hundred years,' Jara finally said. 'She probably isn't even alive anymore.'

'But she's immortal,' Aimee cut in, 'or nearly immortal. She's one of the Quorelle and has thousands of sparks.'

'I don't care if she does, I'm not wasting time trying to find a woman who left us generations ago. Kyelli dumped us inside these mountains then disappeared. She doesn't care what happens to Kierell and doesn't give a dull spark about our future. We can't rely on someone else coming to save us. The Riders are here to protect this city and that's what I'm busy trying to do.'

'You don't need to try and find her,' Aimee said, feeling her voice take on a pleading tone. 'I'll do it. It's…' she faltered then mentally touched her bond with Jess, taking some of her dragon's strength. 'It's not like you were going to give me a mission anyway.'

Jara narrowed her eyes but didn't deny it. Aimee stood her ground, though she was shaking like she was cold. She was very aware of how much it would hurt if Jara said no. The map was her way to try and help save the city. Finding Kyelli was all she could do. She couldn't put it back in the box and forget she'd seen it. It was also her chance to actually meet Kyelli.

Jara shook her head and Aimee felt her heart sink down into her toes.

'It's a waste of time and I forbid you to do it,' Jara ordered. 'Sparks! You're barely a Rider and you think you can fly off on any mission you fancy? I should never have let you steal your dragon this year, I should have made you wait till next year. And it was a mistake to take you with the caravan. I need you to just keep out the way, Aimee. Go and hide in your room till this is over.'

'But Kyelli can save the city. We just need to find her,' Aimee tried again.

'I said no, Aimee!' Jara shouted, her voice sharp as dragon's claws. 'And since you just don't seem to listen, I forbid you to leave Anteill. If I, or any other Rider, sees you in the sky, I'll take Jess and kick you out of the Riders.'

CHAPTER 5

## ARMIES AND PLANS

JARA TURNED AND strode off, her boot heels clicking loudly on the cavern floor. Aimee felt a rush of anger and shame, making her face go bright red. Around the cavern other Riders were staring at her. Everyone had heard what Jara said and Aimee didn't like seeing the pity on their faces. It reminded her of the piteous looks old women used to give her on the streets. She clutched the map tightly and watched Jara speaking to another cluster of Riders.

'Well, there goes that plan,' Nathine said unhelpfully.

Aimee stood in the middle of the cavern feeling lost and had no idea what to say. She felt Jess tugging at her connection and looked up. Her dragon was on the verge of flying down to comfort her. Aimee really wanted to feel Jess's cool scales against her cheek and wrap her arms around her, but she told Jess to stay.

'Sorry I'm upsetting you, girl,' she whispered.

She looked down at the map in her hand. Should

she put it back in the box? If she did, she'd always feel guilty that she'd turned away from something she believed could save her city. If she defied Jara though, would she be kicked out? She'd struggled so hard to make the Riders' community her home, what would she do if she lost that? And what if they killed Jess? A dragon without a Rider couldn't be allowed to live. She could still see Jara and Dyrenna killing Ellana after Hayetta died. The thought of losing Jess was terrifying. Worse than losing the parents she'd never known, and worse even than watching her aunt and uncle cough themselves to death.

Wingbeats echoed round the cavern as another group of Riders headed out into the night. Watching the last dragon's tail disappear up the vent, Aimee realised she was fed up watching other people do things while she hid away. For years she'd looked out at life from her window seat in the loft above her uncle's workshop. She didn't want to just watch any more, she wanted to be involved. When she'd saved the caravan and then gone to the council meeting she'd felt part of the Riders, but Jara had pushed her back to the outside of it all. She turned to Nathine.

'Do you believe Kyelli could help us?'

Nathine stood very still and Aimee wondered what she was thinking. Finally, she shook her head slowly. 'It doesn't matter, we can't go.'

Aimee checked Jara was still with the other Riders and that no one else was near them, then grabbed Nathine's arm.

'I'm going to go anyway,' Aimee whispered, 'and I want you to come with me.'

'Did you chop away parts of your brain when you cut off your hair? Jara just forbid you from leaving Antiell,' Nathine whispered and looked around furtively, checking no one could hear them.

Aimee squeezed Nathine's arm tighter. Her determination had gotten her up the climb, it had pushed her to get Jess and because of it she'd uncovered the greatest threat Kierell had faced in over three hundred years. She wasn't going to ignore it now.

'We're just two girls, we can't save the city ourselves. I'm not even sure all the Riders can save us. But Kyelli can, so we *have* to find her.'

'Jara doesn't want us to,' Nathine said slowly. 'She's got a plan and everyone else is following her orders.'

'This map shows a whole different Kierell.' Aimee tried a different tack. 'It's Kierell as Kyelli saw it. There's a hidden side of the city that no one's seen since Kyelli and Efysta drew this map. Don't you want to explore it?'

Nathine opened her mouth but then didn't say anything. Aimee knew Nathine wanted to explore the map as much as she did. She'd seen the excitement on her face when they'd been looking at it.

'I do, but Jara said no. We can follow the map later, explore the hidden city after this is all over,' Nathine said.

'If the Empty Warriors reach the city, and we can't find a way to keep them out or destroy them all, then there won't be any of Kierell left for us to explore.' Aimee grabbed Nathine's other arm and squeezed it too. 'Kyelli is the only one who can save the city. She's fought the Empty Warriors before. Come on, Nathine.' Aimee gave her a shake.

Nathine's eyes flicked up to Malgerus then back to Aimee.

'You're really willing to risk Jess on this? Because if Jara catches you disobeying her, you'll be separated forever. That's a huge gamble, mushroom head.'

Aimee touched her connection with Jess and felt the warm pulse of her dragon's love. Was she really willing to risk that? After having so nearly lost her, would she chance being separated from Jess again? The more she probed the thought, the more she realised that she didn't see it as a risk. Her flame of determination had been stoked and she knew that if she could just follow the clues on the map, then she'd find the immortal. She'd finally have Kyelli to protect her, just as she'd always dreamed.

'I'm not risking Jess,' Aimee said. 'If we solve the clues on the map then we'll prove that we are Kyelli's Riders. And then, with Kyelli on my side, there's no way Jara will dare to kick me out. I'm pretty sure Kyelli will outrank Jara.'

Nathine looked at her for a long moment. 'Alright, I'll help if it makes you shut up and stop squeezing my arms.'

Aimee smiled at her. 'Thank you. I think we'll need—'

The rest of her words were lost in the blast of cool air that was pushed down the nearest vent as a dragon burst from the ceiling. Large pine-green wings snapped open as Whisper glided to the floor. Aimee was surprised to see Sal back. She'd only just left to scout the army.

'Jara!' Sal yelled but their leader was already running across the cavern towards her.

'What's happened?' Jara called as she reached them.

'You can see the army,' Sal said.

'Already?' Jara's shock swept across her face and she ran her fingers through her hair.

Aimee was taken aback too. When she'd left the army yesterday morning they were still disembarking on the beach. It had taken her and Jess hours to fly back to the caravan from there. Then the caravan had sped home, pushing the horses till they were slick with sweat.

'How can they be in sight so soon?' Jara demanded. 'They can't run faster than a dragon can fly, can they?'

No one for over three hundred years could have answered that.

'Where have they reached?'

Jara was pacing in front of Whisper and his dark green head was following her back and forth.

'They aren't at the isthmus yet,' Sal replied. 'I couldn't see them clearly, they're just a dark blob on the tundra. But it's a really big blob.'

Aimee pictured the narrow strip of land that connected Kierell to the tundra and imagined the Empty Warriors pouring along it, their eyes flickering like thousands of tiny torches.

'How long have we got until they cross it?' Jara asked.

'I—' Sal faltered.

'How long?' Jara repeated. She'd stopped pacing and stood staring up at the red-haired Rider.

'Jara, I can track people, and nearly any animal out there, but that's because my grandpa taught me. But no one even knew the Empty Warriors still existed. I don't know how they'll act, or move, or how fast they can march.'

Jara clenched her fists in front of her face, bringing them to her lips. Aimee suspected she might be biting her knuckles. Her veneer of confidence was cracking.

'That's another reason we need to find Kyelli,' Aimee whispered to Nathine. 'She'll know stuff about the Empty Warriors.'

'I know you're right, but enough with the hero-worshiping, okay?' Nathine whispered back.

Aimee felt the familiar flush in her face and hoped Nathine had just gone in for an easy joke. She'd hate it if Nathine knew how desperately she wanted to meet the woman she'd always admired. To admit to that would make her feel childish, and she was trying to be a grown-up Rider now.

'Give me your best guess please, Sal. I need some information to work with,' Jara was saying.

Sal shrugged her narrow shoulders and chewed her bottom lip for a moment. 'Going by how freakishly quick they've marched already, I'd say they'll cross during the night and be here tomorrow morning.'

'Kyelli's sparks,' Jara swore. Then she was all business again. 'Okay, your mission still stands. I need you to find out everything you can. Numbers, command structure, weapons, everything.'

She shot her glance up at Faradair. He was ready, with his talons curled around the edge of his ledge, wings unfurled. He stepped into the air and glided down to Jara.

'Go!' Jara yelled at Sal, as she pulled on her own gloves and goggles.

Whisper began to flap his long wings, stirring up the air in the cavern.

'I'll tell Lyrria, then Aranati,' Jara called over the whooshing of air. 'We need to make sure that tunnel is secure tonight. It's the weak spot in our defences.' She leapt up onto Faradair's back. 'But my spark will go out before I let Beljarn collapse it.'

Aimee watched as Whisper and Faradair disappeared up the vents.

'Aimee?'

The use of her actual name made Aimee turn to Nathine in concern. She only called her Aimee when something was wrong. Nathine's eyes were wide in her round face and she was hugging her arms close to her chest.

'Aimee, those monsters are going to be here tomorrow. I mean actually here. And we can't stop them from coming.' Nathine looked down at her bandaged leg, perhaps feeling again the agony of that handprint burn.

'My little brother, Lukas, is in the city. He's only eight, he can't fight.'

'Hey,' Aimee said softly and took her hand. Nathine didn't pull away and that told Aimee how scared she was. 'Lukas doesn't need to fight. His big sister is a Rider and she'll protect him.'

Nathine shook her head. 'I saw the army landing on the beach, and you went on and on about the message on the breastplate, but I hoped it was all wrong and that they wouldn't really be coming to destroy us. Why would anyone want to destroy a little boy?'

'I don't know why.'

'Didn't you, at any point, think maybe you were wrong and we were all panicking for no reason?'

Aimee shook her head. 'When I was little and I went out in the city with my aunt, I used to hope each time that it would be different, that people wouldn't curl their lips in disgust or cross the street to avoid me. But then I grew to expect the bad things because they always came.'

'Well, that's depressing.' Nathine still had one arm wrapped tightly around her own ribs.

Aimee smiled at her. 'No, it meant I found ways to be ready for them.'

'Like places to hide?'

'Yeah I know it's not the same, but this time we can get ready by finding Kyelli because she'll know how to stop the monsters.' Aimee squeezed Nathine's hand. 'I'm scared of fighting them again too.'

Nathine pulled her hand free and gave herself a

shake. 'Fighting them doesn't frighten me, sludge brain. But maybe a bit of guidance from an immortal would help.'

'Sludge brain?'

'Yeah, I thought I'd try it out, what do you think?'

Aimee sighed in exasperation. Why did her first friend in the whole world have to be so annoying?

'I think you can do better,' she replied then continued before Nathine could try. 'So, where do you think we start with the map?'

'Well, first it would be good to work out how we're going to get out without any other Riders seeing us. Someone might report us to Jara.' Nathine looked pointedly at the scattering of Riders still in the Heart.

'We could sneak back here in a few hours. It'll be properly dark by then so I doubt anyone will be around,' Aimee suggested.

The twilight that had been coming in the vents was gone. When Aimee looked up she could see a tiny circle of darkening sky at the top of the nearest one. They wouldn't need to wait long for it to be as dark as it got in summer.

'If it's dark when we're flying over the city we won't be able to read the map.'

'We can't read it anyway,' Aimee pointed out. 'We don't know what those tree symbol things mean and I think they're the clues.'

'Okay, so since this is your genius mission, how are we supposed to work out what random trees plonked onto Kierell mean?'

Aimee wished Dyrenna was back. She remembered sitting on the mountaintops, listening to Dyrenna tell the story of Kyelli and Marhorn. She would understand the map better—she knew loads of stories, like a scholar. Then it struck her.

'Councillor Callant.'

'Beardy man?'

'Yes, beardy man. He was really interested in the breastplate when I spotted the wording on it, and he kept mentioning a book about the founding of Kierell.'

'So we take the map to him?'

Aimee nodded.

'Alright, it's your plan,' Nathine said again.

'And if it all goes wrong you'll say you had nothing to do with it?'

'Correct.'

'And if we find Kyelli and she saves the city, then you'll—'

'I'll say it was my idea all along.' Nathine grinned at her. 'I'm glad you've grasped how this works.'

They agreed to meet in the tunnel just outside the Heart in three hours time. Aimee sent a silent goodbye to Jess and left the cavern with Nathine.

Back in her room Aimee felt restless and jittery. She just wanted to get going and kept imagining the Empty Warriors marching closer and closer. Finally she thought maybe she should try to get a little rest and got into bed, but sleep didn't follow her. Lying on her back she stared up at the cluster of purple crystals above her head. Unwanted memories of Lyrria in her bed beside her kept nudging their way into her brain. Finally, exasperated and upset, Aimee got up and took out the map again. In the light of her dragon's breath orb she studied it. She read and re-read the words Kyelli had written, but still couldn't work out what the clues were, never mind how to use them. She finally fell into a doze, propped up in her bed, with the map on her lap.

CHAPTER 6

DARING TO DISOBEY

A IMEE CREPT ALONG the dark tunnel towards the Heart. She kept close to the walls and away from the light of any dragon's breath orbs. It felt odd to be sneaking in her own home. Nathine was already waiting for her in the shadows by the Heart's entrance. She had her coat on, buttoned up to her chin and her wavy hair pulled up into a high ponytail. Her saddle was at her feet, shoved up against the wall. Aimee stepped quietly into the shadows and dropped her saddle on top of Nathine's.

'You still want to do this?' Nathine said in way of a greeting.

'Definitely.'

They were both whispering even though the tunnel was empty.

'Did you go to the kitchen on your way here?' Nathine asked.

'No,' Aimee replied. She'd been too afraid of meeting someone, and sneaking into the store to grab her saddle had been nerve-wracking enough.

'I knew you'd hide in your room and not have any dinner. Here.'

Nathine handed her a piece of spiced fruitcake wrapped in cloth. Aimee was delighted that Nathine had bothered to think about her and bring food. She mentally added another few bricks to their friendship bridge.

'Thank you,' Aimee said.

'Well, you're still really scrawny, like a deflated Empty Warrior.'

Aimee ignored the insult, and shoved aside the image of the horrible way the Empty Warriors had shrivelled when they died, leaving only blackened bones wrapped in skin. She took a few bites of the cake then stuffed it into her coat pocket. Then she peered around Nathine and into the Heart.

'Sparks,' she swore and ducked back.

'Is someone in there?' Nathine whispered. Aimee nodded.

A few shafts of moonlight were coming from the vents in the roof but mostly the large cavern was filled with night. The dragon's breath orbs illuminated a circle around the cavern's centre, like the yellow iris of a dragon's eye. A Rider had walked out into the middle. Aimee pressed herself further into the wall. Through her coat she could feel a knobbly vein of quartz digging into her spine. She didn't dare move.

'It's Fineya,' Nathine whispered, the words sounding squished, as if she hadn't moved her lips.

Aimee didn't know who that was and cursed herself. Was Fineya close friends with Jara? Had she been in the Heart earlier when Jara had forbidden Aimee to leave Anteill? She hoped Fineya was going to fly off somewhere and not come walking out of the cavern. If she did, she'd pass Aimee and Nathine, and they'd struggle to explain why they were huddled in the tunnel looking shifty.

Thankfully, Fineya pulled on her gloves against the nighttime chill and whistled to her dragon. He glided down from the shadows, landing beside his Rider. Light from the dragon's breath orbs danced over his scales making him shine like polished copper. He was bulky looking, his limbs and neck shorter than Jess's and his wingspan wasn't as wide as most of the other dragons. When he moved, though, his scales rippled with a beautiful iridescence.

'Do you know his name?' Aimee whispered.

Nathine looked at her and her face was all screwed up, except her eyebrows which were raised. The expression said she couldn't believe Aimee cared about that right now.

'It's Burnish,' Nathine answered after a moment.

Aimee watched as Fineya and Burnish disappeared up one of the vents. She waited a moment, just to make sure no one else was in the Heart, then hurried into the cavern, Nathine right behind her.

Nathine whistled and Malgerus launched himself into the air. He seemed to have grown every time Aimee looked at him and his bright orange wings looked almost as large as Faradair's now. Aimee looked up at Jess and called to her along their connection. Jess stepped to the edge of her ledge, her talons curling over the lip and stopped. Aimee waited but she didn't move. Instead she just stared intently at Aimee and fluttered her wingtips.

'Come on, girl,' Aimee pleaded in a whisper. All she got was a pulse of unease along their bond. Jess was sensing Aimee's own feelings about doing something forbidden and it was making her unsure about flying down.

'What are you doing?' Nathine hissed. 'This isn't the time to be staring lovingly into each other's eyes. Get her down here so we can go before anyone sees us.'

She wanted to yell at Jess to fly down but she'd learnt that getting angry, and shouting at her dragon, would only scare her off. Instead she took a deep breath and focused on her emotions. Her worries about being caught felt like jagged barbs in her brain. She mentally plucked them out and threw them away. Then she stoked her flame of determination and focused on how great it would be to find Kyelli. She sent that image to Jess.

Jess unfurled her wings with a whoosh and glided down to the cavern floor. She head-butted Aimee gently.

'Good girl,' Aimee smiled as her nose filled with Jess's familiar smoky scent.

'Finally,' Nathine said as she finished buckling Malgerus's saddle.

Aimee hurried to get hers on Jess. She was rushing, so put half the straps in the wrong buckles and had to redo them.

'Hurry up,' Nathine chided her.

'That's not helping,' Aimee said as she tightened the last one.

She grabbed the high pommel and cantle of her saddle and boosted herself up. Just as her bum hit the saddle she heard echoing footsteps.

'Sparks, someone's coming!' Panic made her shout and her voice bounced around the cavern.

'Shut up!' Nathine hissed.

Aimee held her breath and waited. The footsteps grew louder, then a shadow stretched along the floor and into the cavern.

'Go!' Nathine yelled. Malgerus began to flap frantically, his huge wings swirling the air.

The shadow's owner stepped into the cavern. It was Pelathina. Surprise bloomed on her face as she saw Aimee and Nathine. Aimee knew Pelathina was given important missions, like taking communications to the Helvethi. Jara trusted her.

Malgerus was circling the cavern now, his wingbeats making the dragon's breath orbs rock on their poles. Yellow light flashed erratically across the cavern and Pelathina ran through it towards them. She was coming to grab them. To drag them to Jara who'd take their dragons.

'Nathine, fly!' Aimee yelled.

'Aimee, wait! Jara said—' Pelathina began but her

words were drowned under Jess's flapping wings.

Jess swooped around the cavern building speed while Pelathina shouted up at her. Jess dived up a vent and Aimee squeezed her eyes shut. Once in the sky she felt a wave of relief and beneath her Jess gave a small roar.

'Shh,' Aimee told her.

But how long did they have before Pelathina told Jara?

'Do you think she'll follow us?' Aimee asked as Nathine guided Malgerus passed a wisp of cloud and over to her.

'I don't know, but it's too late to go back and say we were only stretching our dragon's wings,' Nathine replied, 'so I guess we're committed now.'

She and Nathine flew over the grey mountaintops and down into the city. They soared above the rooftops of Barter's shops and inns, the normally busy streets quiet in the night. The sky was a deep, dark blue and not quite black—it never got properly dark in summer. The Ring Mountains cast their jagged shadows across Kierell, coating the city streets in darkness. Occasionally Aimee spotted a lantern flickering at a window but they saw no one. She felt a pang of sympathy for all the people cosy in their beds with no idea that when they woke tomorrow, their council would tell them there were monsters at the gate, trapping them in their city.

'Where do you think we'll find Councillor Callant in the middle of the night?' Nathine called across. 'I'm not peering in bedroom windows till we see him.'

'I don't think any of the councillors will have gone to bed. My guess is that they'll still be at the council chamber so I think we should try there first.'

'You know, sometimes you're quite good at this.'

'At what?' Aimee could tell Nathine was looking at her but the darkness hid whatever expression she was wearing.

'At making plans and giving orders.'

'I…' Aimee didn't know what to say to that. People who made plans and gave orders were leaders. They spoke up in front of others without their face going red, without stumbling over words or wishing they could run away and hide. That wasn't her.

The dome of the council chamber was easy to spot. The dragon's breath orbs set into its roof flickered and shone like captured stars. The knot of worry in Aimee's stomach was too tight for her to enjoy the beauty of it. She was scanning the library rooftop and Quorelle Square below, hoping not to see Faradair. Jara had said she was going to see Aranati and help arrange the defences at the tunnel, but surely she'd also report to the council. Had she already done that and left?

'There's no sign of her,' Aimee said. Nathine didn't need to ask who she meant.

The girls landed beside the statue of Kyelli and Marhorn. The sound of Jess and Malgerus's talons on the flagstones echoed around the square and Aimee winced at how loud it was.

She dismounted and Jess turned her head to look up at the library, opening her wings again.

'No, not tonight,' Aimee said, quickly grabbing her saddle to keep Jess from flying up. Sitting on the roof she'd announce Aimee's presence to any passing Riders.

As Aimee had guessed, the council chamber still looked busy, even now, in the middle of the night. Two city guards were standing on either side of the huge wooden doors at the top of the steps. One door was open and a rectangle of yellow light painted the flagstones under the portico.

Now they were here, a sliver of doubt wormed its way into Aimee's mind. What if Callant couldn't help them? No, she told herself not to think like that. He *would* be able to decipher the map. Nathine probably already had an insult lined up for when Callant couldn't help them, so she'd just have to make sure she was made to swallow it.

'Sparks!' Nathine swore.

At the same moment Aimee heard wingbeats above them. She tilted her head back.

'Oh no,' she whispered.

Moonlight gleamed on the unmistakable red of Faradair's scales as he soared over the council chamber, coming from the north. Panic clawed Aimee's belly.

'Get behind the statue, come on!' Aimee called to Nathine.

It was too late to take off, Jara would see them the moment they entered the sky. So Aimee and Nathine ran to the other side of the large statue of Kyelli and Marhorn. Jess and Malgerus followed them, confused but spurred on by their Riders' panic.

'Do you think she saw us?' Aimee whispered.

'I don't know but if she looks round she'll see them.' Nathine pointed her chin at Jess and Malgerus.

The two dragons were standing at the base of the statue watching the girls with their yellow eyes. Their slim bodies might be hidden by the stone pedestal but there was no way their wings would be.

'Tuck your wings in, Jess,' Aimee said and mimed tucking her arms in close to her body. Jess cocked her head and looked up at her. Malgerus snorted a small cloud of smoke. He didn't understand either.

'I wish I could send Jara commands like I do with Mal. Go into the council chamber, Jara, and don't look behind you,' Nathine said.

Aimee held her breath. She heard the leathery snap as Faradair took off and the clack of his talons as he landed on the library roof. She waited with her eyes half closed, dreading to see Jara appear around the statue, her face furious. In her mind she clung tight to her bond with Jess, hoping she wasn't about to lose her.

Long moments passed and nothing happened. Aimee twisted around and moved very slowly, trying to peer around Kyelli to see the rest of the square. Nathine yanked her back.

'I'll look,' she said. 'Your face is too recognisable.'

Aimee wanted to argue but Nathine was right. Nathine darted her head around Marhorn's legs then pulled it back. She smiled.

'Jara's gone inside.'

Relief flooded through Aimee, spilling over into Jess.

Her dragon fluttered her wings and nudged Aimee's chin with her snout. Aimee grinned. Then Malgerus was there too. He head-butted Jess's neck then snapped at her. It wasn't aggressive, it was playful. Jess snapped back. Watching the two dragons Aimee was suddenly reminded that they were clutchmates and that they were still so young. Had they played together before she and Nathine had stolen them? It made her sad to think that maybe Jess and Malgerus had been friends before she and Nathine infected them with their animosity. It was another reason to continue working on their friendship.

'Thanks for looking round the statue for me,' Aimee said, turning to look at Nathine.

Nathine tightened her ponytail, pulling it higher up on her head. 'It's past midnight so maybe your hug quota has reset itself, but if you're only getting one hug a day from me, do you really want to use it now? There's a whole day to get through.'

'You're really annoying.'

Then Aimee laughed. Nathine's sass had a way of cutting through her worries and she wondered if Nathine knew that and did it deliberately.

'Are you up for sneaking into the council chamber?' Nathine asked. 'Because we can't risk marching through the front door now. We might walk right into Jara.'

Aimee stepped out from behind the statue, now the coast was clear, and studied the council chamber. The building was two storeys and circular, capped by the huge copper dome. A band of roof tiles ran around the dome, like a skirt of slate. Below the tiles were the windows of the first floor and some of them were tall, leading out to little stone balconies. Aimee pointed up at them.

'If we can find a room that's empty, then Jess and Malgerus can perch on the balcony and we can sneak inside. Hopefully then even if Jara comes back out of the council chamber she won't see our dragons. They always perch on the library roof so maybe Jara won't think to look anywhere else.'

'There's a lot of ifs and maybes in this plan,' Nathine pointed out, but she still boosted herself into her saddle.

Aimee mounted up too. Jess and Malgerus rose into the air and Aimee steered her dragon towards the left side of the council chamber. She avoided looking at Faradair as they passed the library, but she heard his wings rustle.

'Slow down, Jess.' Aimee pulled gently on her spiralled horns. Aimee was keen to find Callant and Jess could feel that. Her response was speed. 'Slow,' Aimee told her again, pulling a little harder on her horns. Jess's wingbeats became almost lazy and Aimee smiled. She was getting better at controlling Jess in the air.

They were level with the first floor and Aimee pulled gently on Jess's right horn, steering her around the building. She glanced behind to check Nathine was following. Aimee was looking for a window that was dark, meaning the room behind it was empty. All the rooms so far either had lights on or nowhere for the dragons to land.

They flew past another lit-up window and Aimee jolted in surprise. She yanked on Jess's horns to stop her and her dragon growled at the abruptness of it, her feathers flaring. She awkwardly tried to hover but hadn't mastered it yet so swooped away from the building.

'Are you chickening out?' Nathine called.

'No, I'm...' It was too hard to talk and try to control Jess. She was attempting to fly in a circle, skimming the edge of Quorelle Square and back to the council chamber. 'I just...Jess...' She gave up explaining to Nathine. 'Look.'

Malgerus had flown past the excitement-induing window but Nathine easily guided him back. It was annoying how much more skilled she was at flying. With a nudge and command sent along their connection, Jess landed on the balustrade of the small stone balcony. Malgerus flapped in beside her and the two dragons jostled for space on the narrow perch.

'Look,' Aimee said again.

'Beardy man.' The light from inside the room lit up Nathine's triumphant smile.

Through the windows Councillor Callant was hunched over a desk, completely oblivious to the dragons staring in at him. He was alone in the study. Aimee pushed Jess's head forward and her dragon snorted, steaming up the glass, then she began licking it.

'What are you doing?' Nathine asked, half a laugh in her voice.

'I meant for her to tap on the glass with her snout,' Aimee explained, feeling a flush of embarrassment. Jess continued to lick the window.

'Do you think it tastes nice?'

Aimee gave a bemused shrug.

Nathine shook her head and rolled her eyes. 'Councillor Callant!' she yelled.

Aimee winced as, inside, the big man was startled and dropped his pencil. He looked to the door first but Nathine called again.

'This way.'

Callant sat frozen in his chair for a moment as he looked out at the two dragons perched on his balcony, one of them licking his window.

CHAPTER 7

ONLY A RIDER

'IT WOULD BE nice if you opened the window,' Nathine said, pointing at the latch.

Callant's shock released him and he leapt to his feet as if worried about being rude. He lifted the latch and the two large windows swung inwards. Aimee slipped her left foot from its stirrup, swung her leg over so she was sitting sidesaddle and then leapt down onto the tiny balcony. Nathine landed beside her. Callant was staring at them and chewing his bottom lip, which made his big spade-shaped beard waggle.

'I'm sorry we gave you a fright,' Aimee apologised, 'but can we come in and talk to you?'

'You're the girl who found the Empty Warriors,' Callant said. Aimee liked that he didn't say she was the girl with the weird face. 'Sorry, I didn't catch your name at any point.'

'I'm Aimee and this is Nathine.' Nathine gave a little wave. 'Are we okay to come in?'

'Of course.' Callant backed into the study, making

room for them to follow. 'Though normally when people visit me they tend to use the door.'

'We're sort of—' Aimee began but Nathine stomped on her toes.

'Flying in through upper storey windows is part of our Rider mystique,' Nathine said.

'Fair play. If I had a dragon, I probably wouldn't bother with the stairs either,' Callant said, and his beard opened, revealing his grin.

Aimee had been about to tell him a vague version of the truth about hiding from Jara but she realised that Nathine's tactic had better put Callant at ease. He was a big man, tall and broad but he gave the impression of someone who always tried to make himself appear smaller. He looked like he should be the hero of some epic battle, wielding an axe and yelling. Instead he was softly spoken and his study was filled with books and scrolls, not a weapon in sight. The books filled every space on the shelves and teetered in towers on his desk. The wall opposite them, by the door, was covered with pinned up pieces of paper showing neatly made lists and complex family trees.

Aimee liked his study. The walls were lined with beechwood panels and light from three lanterns reflected off the pale wood, giving the room a golden glow. The floor was wooden too but covered with a mishmash of patterned rugs, their edges all overlapping and none of them lying straight. This wasn't a workshop like her uncle's, or the cave where Dyrenna repaired saddles, and there were no tools or finished products, but it was still a room where a skilled person worked at something he was passionate about.

Aimee looked at the open book on his desk. 'Is that the book about when Kierell started?' She'd forgotten the title of it.

Callant looked confused for a moment then his beard split to show a smile again. 'You mean Nollanni's *Founding of Kierell*? Yes. This isn't the original, that's in the library and Lokendan, he's the master librarian, would chop my hands off if I tried to take it home. Though, this,' his fingers hovered reverently over the open pages, 'is one of only three copies so it's still very special.'

Aimee looked at the illustrated first letter and the perfectly neat handwriting. Her mind boggled at the thought of how long it must take to copy out a book. The sound of Callant coughing pulled her away from her thoughts. It was a deep cough that sounded painful.

'I've read Nollanni dozens of times but I've been going through it again,' Callant said once he had breath to speak again. 'Now that we know the Empty Warriors still exist, and given the message on the breastplate, I wondered if that knowledge would knock my brain into a new furrow of thought. Then perhaps something I'd previously not understood in the book would make new sense.'

'And has it?' Nathine asked.

Callant shook his head. 'Not so far. Nollanni was writing eighty years after Kierell was founded so all her accounts are second- or third-hand. There's nothing about how the Empty Warriors were created, or where they came from, or how Kyelli and Marhorn destroyed them.'

'What about the name on the breastplate?' Aimee asked. 'Is there any mention of him, the Master of Sparks?'

'Nope.' Surprisingly, Callant laughed. 'But then that's the fun of academia. There's always something new to discover and study.'

Aimee saw Nathine's angry face appear and she grabbed the other girl's arm, but it wasn't enough to stop the outburst.

'This isn't fun! Having a fiery hand burn through your leg isn't fun! These monsters will be here tomorrow, so there isn't time for you to wallow in old scrolls, pondering great philosophical ideas.'

From behind them Malgerus's growl rumbled into the room. The big man was taken aback and slumped into his chair. Nathine glared at him, their heads almost on a level now he was sitting down. He chewed his bottom lip again, beard waggling.

'I'm sorry, we—' Aimee began.

'Tomorrow?' Callant interrupted.

Both girls nodded.

'I thought I'd have more time to study,' Callant said, looking up at all his books and scrolls. 'I'm sure the answer lies in the past. All we have are fragments of our history, but if I could just put them together the right way…'

'Aimee, show him the map,' Nathine ordered.

Callant perked up at this. 'What map? Something else from the Empty Warriors?'

Aimee shook her head and pulled the folded map from her pocket. Callant leaned back in his chair as she stepped forward and opened it out on his desk. She could see he was instantly absorbed by it and she was glad she'd brought it to him.

'This is incredible. I've never seen such a detailed map of Kierell. And this writing here,' he ran his thick fingers over the writing down the right-hand side. His lips moved as he read it, then he began whispering and finally he was reading the last part out loud. '"I've left clues in Kierell that point to where I've gone in case my Riders ever need to find me. I hope that you don't. I hope that by taking myself away, what I fear will never come to pass. I beg you, do not come to find me unless you have no other choice. This map is the first clue, though I hope you never need it."'

Callant looked up at her, his eyes shining with excitement. 'You found something that Kyelli actually wrote. This is…it's…' but his words trailed off as another coughing fit racked his chest.

'Are you okay?' Aimee asked tentatively.

He wheezed for a moment but waved away her concern. 'My lungs have never been great. It's usually only bad in the winter.' He lifted up the map. 'I can't believe Kyelli drew this. Where did you find it?'

Aimee hesitated. She didn't want to lie to Callant but nor did she want to reveal things that maybe only Riders should know. She looked to Nathine for help.

'It was in an old box,' Nathine said vaguely.

It didn't matter, Callant wasn't listening. 'This is a way to find Kyelli, she left a breadcrumb trail,' he said.

Aimee's heart flipped over in her chest. 'So can you decipher it? You know what the clues mean?'

'Is that why you're here?' Callant asked turning to look at Aimee. 'You want my help to unravel the clues in the map, and then you're going to fly off and find her?'

'Well, we're not here for the nice cup of tea you haven't offered us,' Nathine cut in.

The windows were still open and Nathine shivered in the cool night air. Aimee was cold too, despite her coat, but she was too excited to care. Callant hadn't seemed to notice the cold but he suddenly looked flustered and glanced around searching for something to offer Nathine.

'Ignore her,' Aimee told him. 'Will you help us? I think if we can find Kyelli then she can save us. She and her father defeated the Empty Warriors once before. She might know who the Master of Sparks is and how we find him. Marhorn's dead so she's the only one left who can help us.'

'Of course I'll help you,' Callant rushed to say. 'This is the most incredible document. We have nothing from the early days of Kierell and to have something that Kyelli actually wrote, well, it's momentous.'

He was staring at the map lovingly as he spoke. His beard was split to show his big grin and his thick fingers moved above the map as if they too were sucking information from it. Aimee knew she had to give him time to take it in, to work it out, but she was practically bouncing on her feet with excitement. Random words floated into the air as Callant talked to himself.

'…ah, that does lead there…'

'…didn't realise it was that shape…'

'…is, that? Oh, it is, now…'

'Sorry to interrupt when you're having so much fun, but there's an army of monsters marching towards us as you mumble to yourself,' Nathine said.

Aimee flushed red, even though Nathine was the one being rude. Callant reminded her of her uncle Gyron, and of Dyrenna, and because of that she wanted him to think well of her.

'You're right, sorry.' Callant looked up at them. 'Is this how you see the city? When you're flying, I mean.'

Both girls nodded.

'That's what I thought. This is a view of the city that only someone above it would see, which means only a Rider ever sees Kierell like this. Kyelli says she created the map with Efysta and her dragon. Other maps we have of Kierell are drawn from the ground so they look different. This one's probably more accurate.'

'And? What does that mean?' Aimee asked.

'It means this was meant for you specifically,' Callant replied.

'Me?'

Callant nodded. 'Kyelli drew the map from a Rider's perspective which means she meant for only a Rider to follow it. I think all the clues on it will be things only a

Rider would know.'

Aimee's heart fell into her stomach like it had tumbled from a dragon. She didn't understand the map or even know what the clues were. Had she failed again? Was Kyelli telling her she wasn't a proper Rider?

'What things?' Nathine demanded.

'Well, I don't know yet, but look, the only thing which stands out on the map are the tree symbols in blue ink. They must be the clues,' Callant said.

Aimee stepped closer and dared to put one hand on his desk. He didn't recoil in disgust, in fact he didn't seem to have noticed, so she added the other hand and leaned in to see better.

'There's six of them, all across the city,' Callant mused.

Aimee was staring at the map, willing the answer to jump out at her. She wanted to understand what Kyelli was telling her. But it was just a map and six random blue trees.

She glanced back at Nathine and was surprised to see she hadn't moved from the window. When they'd been looking at the map in Aimee's room she had been full of excitement but now she was hanging back. Then Aimee glanced at Callant. Was Nathine nervous of him? Had her father made her wary of all older men? The thought made Aimee sad.

'Why draw trees?' Callant was still studying the map. 'And why put them in places where there are no trees. Look, this one's right in the middle of Quorelle Square where it's all paved.'

'So why mark it? What's in Quorelle Square?' Nathine asked.

Aimee leaned round to look at the other girl. For her, there had only ever been one thing of interest in the square—the statue of Kyelli.

'It's something for us, Nathine, think,' Aimee said.

'I am thinking, mushroom head,' Nathine scowled.

'Wait.' Callant's finger was flying over the map, dotting back and forth. Then he reached up to the shelves above his desk and pulled down a small book. It had been propping up some others and they slammed to the shelf. He didn't seem to notice. Aimee caught sight of the title as he flipped it open, *Art of Kierell*.

'What do paintings have to do with our map?' Aimee asked as Callant flipped through pages of writing and sketches.

'Not paintings, statues. Yes, look.'

Aimee leaned over again and followed Callant's finger.

'This inked tree marks the statue in Quorelle Square, and then here,' his finger moved north in the city, 'this is the university. There's a mosaic of Kyelli in the courtyard there.'

A memory floated to the surface of Aimee's mind, of sitting in the mountaintops and asking Dyrenna if she had a favourite image of Kyelli. She'd liked the painted carving of Kyelli and Marhorn in the wooden beams outside the White Griffin Inn.

'Where's Lilletorn Street?' Aimee asked, scanning the map at the edge of the Palace.

'Here,' Callant pointed, right where there was another blue tree. 'That must be…' He was flicking through his book.

'It's a carving above the inn there,' Aimee said.

She felt movement and Nathine appeared beside her, on the other side from Callant, drawn over by the excitement of discovery.

'There's the one at the foot of the cliffs,' Nathine pointed.

At the eastern edge of Barter, right where Kyelli had drawn the peaks of the Ring Mountains, was another blue tree. Aimee thought of the statue of Kyelli there, the one that pointed the way up the cliffs.

'Are you sure?' Callant asked, flicking through the book, eyes darting between it and the map.

'Definitely,' Nathine said firmly. 'Whenever I could sneak away from my father I used to go visit that one and look up at the cliffs. I kept waiting for the day that I was strong enough to make the climb.'

'See,' Callant said, grinning up at them, 'things only Riders would spot.'

Despite his size, and huge beard, Callant looked like a little boy, caught up in the excitement of a game.

'So Kyelli put symbols on the map to show where there are statues or pictures of her,' Aimee said.

'But how does that help us? And there are more than six statues of Kyelli in the city,' Nathine pointed out.

'Ah, but you're forgetting this map was drawn nearly three hundred years ago,' Callant replied. 'Look, half of our city is missing.'

Aimee looked and realised he was right. She hadn't noticed it before, but both the east and west curves of Barter were shown as a lot smaller than they were. Now the brick warehouses nearly reached the base of the cliffs. And Shine, in the north, was only a small strip on the map, whereas when Aimee had flown over it, there were streets and streets of big houses and pretty tree-filled squares.

'So, perhaps there were only six statues of Kyelli when she drew this map,' Callant continued. 'The city's littered with them now, but I think we're looking at the originals. This is an incredible window into how our city used to look.'

'Yeah, maybe, but monsters, remember?' Nathine said.

'Sorry. I'm grateful that I was elected as a councillor but it doesn't leave as much time for studying as I used to have and I sometimes…,' he let his words trail off and looked up at the girls. 'Sorry, I'm doing it again. Monsters, I know, so let's head out to Quorelle Square.'

'And do what?' Nathine asked.

'Find whatever Kyelli left for us on her statue,' Aimee said, excitement bubbling inside her.

'Indeed,' Callant agreed. 'There's a hidden layer to this city that Kyelli created but no one's ever noticed it before. We've just got to try and see it.'

Aimee folded up the map and put it back in her coat pocket, then Callant moved to the door as Aimee moved to the open window. He looked back for a moment, confused that they hadn't followed.

'Oh right, dragons. Well, I'll meet you down there.'

He was through the door a moment later. Aimee hurried onto the balcony, her limbs feeling bouncy with anticipation and climbed up on Jess's back. She grinned at Nathine.

'I knew he'd be able to help. This is it, we're going to find Kyelli.'

Nathine mounted up. 'All we've got are the locations of some statues.'

'Yeah but Kyelli hid something on them and I'm sure we'll find it.' With a push of her back legs, Jess launched them into the sky. 'Come on.'

CHAPTER 8

ON THE TRAIL

Faradair was still on the library roof and Aimee could feel him watching them as she and Nathine landed in the square. They'd have to find the clue quickly before Jara reappeared. Callant came jogging down the steps and across the square. Just as he reached them he was engulfed in another coughing fit. Aimee winced at the way his coughs echoed around the empty square. He put his hands on his knees for a moment, gasping. Concerned, Aimee took a few steps towards him but he straightened and waved her away.

So Aimee turned to the statue, eager to see what it was hiding. Both she and Nathine pulled small dragon's breath orbs from their pockets, just little ones that fit in the palm of their hands, but their flames were bright enough to light up the statue.

'I'd love to know how they're made,' Callant said wistfully, looking at the orbs.

Aimee walked slowly around the statue with Jess following her. Nathine and Malgerus circled around the other way. Giving the dragons a wide berth, Callant followed too. They all met on the far side of the stone pedestal.

'So yeah, it looks like a statue. What are we're looking for?' Nathine asked, an edge of frustration in her voice.

Aimee screwed up her forehead and looked at Kyelli's stone face. She was as beautiful as ever. Her face was long and narrow, her eyes almond-shaped. Her long stone hair fell straight to her waist. Aimee had always imagined it as pale blonde, the opposite of her dark brown curls. She had her hands in front of her, holding a book. Her father stood to her right. Aimee had never focused much on Marhorn. He had the same shape of face, though the bottom half of his was covered in a neat beard, the texture chiselled into the stone. They both wore long, flowing clothes, Kyelli a dress and Marhorn a tunic, that looked old fashioned.

Aimee stared up at Kyelli, willing her to reveal something. The longer they stayed the more chance they'd get caught. Jara could walk out of the council chamber at any moment.

'I don't know,' Aimee said, starting to feel desperate. 'Callant?'

He'd twisted his lips to the side as he thought and it made his beard stick out at an odd angle. 'The map was made for a Rider to follow, so there must be something about this statue that only a Rider would notice.'

Nathine stood with her hands on her hips, head tilted to the side, staring up. She was scowling at Kyelli as if annoyed she hadn't left simpler instructions. Then her face changed, scowl slipping away to reveal the younger girl beneath.

'Rider's jewellery!' Nathine exclaimed.

Before Aimee could ask what she meant, Nathine jumped up onto the pedestal.

'Oh, I don't think you're allowed to be up there,' Callant said. 'That statue is an important monument, a piece of architectural history, and if someone sees us we could be in serious trouble.'

Aimee felt bad for making him worry but she climbed up too. 'I promise we won't damage anything.'

'Speak for yourself, scrawny one, I'm going to break open this statue if we need to.'

Aimee tried to give Callant a reassuring smile, to say that Nathine was joking, but Jess was fluttering her wings anxiously. Hopefully Callant couldn't read dragon behaviour.

'Oh come on, there's no one here and even if there were, we're Riders,' Nathine continued. 'We outrank some busybody clerk or librarian. And besides, they wouldn't know we're not on an official mission.'

At Nathine's last words Aimee cast a furtive glance down at Callant. Her chest tightened as she realised he'd heard.

'What do you mean not an official mission?'

'It's a little complicated but you won't get in any trouble,' Aimee said quickly and hoped she was right. 'Nathine, what did you see?' she asked to distract Callant. He stepped between Jess and Malgerus, and placed his elbows on the pedestal, looking up.

Nathine pointed at Kyelli's hands, holding the book. 'Look, Kyelli's wearing a bracelet.' Nathine looked at her. 'You know about Rider's jewellery, right?'

Aimee nodded. She knew of the tradition though it was no thanks to Nathine who, back in her bullying days, had taunted her for not knowing.

'Lyrria told me,' Aimee said, trying not to think about how they'd been together at the time.

'I don't know about the jewellery,' Callant said, raising his eyebrows.

Aimee hesitated for a moment before deciding to tell him. She needed his help and she was already breaking the rules by disobeying Jara.

'Each Rider only wears one piece of jewellery, something special and meaningful, because Kyelli only wore one,' she explained. 'Lyrria, she's another Rider,' and she managed to keep her voice tight as she said her ex-lover's name, 'she said she thought Kyelli's piece of jewellery was a bracelet.'

'It was,' Nathine said, still pointing to the statue.

Aimee had never noticed it before but Nathine was right, Kyelli had a bracelet carved around her right wrist. Aimee doubted she'd ever have spotted it. She didn't know the stories and traditions like Nathine, who'd idolized the Riders her whole life. The bracelet was a cuff as wide as Aimee's forefinger and carved to look like it was engraved. Time, and the freezing Kierell winters, had worn away whatever the pattern had been.

'There's got to be something,' Nathine said as she

peered at Kyelli's arm.

Aimee leaned in too so their heads were almost touching and they both spotted it at the same time.

'There!'

'Told you!'

'What can you see?' Callant looked like he was about to climb up on the pedestal with them now, important historical monument or not.

'It's a letter! No, there are two,' Aimee replied.

Carved onto the side of Kyelli's bracelet, where her left arm protected it from the worst of the wind and rain, were the letters N and P. They had been carved inside a circle, just like the tree symbols on the map. She described to Callant what they could see.

'I told you, something only a Rider would spot.' He grinned at them, obviously delighted to be included in the discovery. 'But what could they mean?'

'They're not her initials so do you think there's—' Nathine began but in her excitement Aimee cut her off.

'Letters on each of the Kyellis marked on the map?' She was grinning too.

'Kyelli disappeared from the city one hundred and three years ago,' Callant said, his voice soft and thoughtful. 'And on the map she said she'd left clues that point to where she's gone, so maybe—'

Her excitement was bubbling over and Aimee cut him off too.

'What if the letters spell out where Kyelli went?'

For a moment all three simply grinned at each other, feeling smug and caught up in the joy of discovering something that no one else had ever spotted.

'We need to check the other five locations marked on the map,' Callant said, moving back from the statue as Aimee and Nathine jumped down.

Jess was standing behind the councillor, her wings half unfurled, tips fluttering. Aimee smiled at her. She was delighted to be sharing another mission with Jess, especially now they knew what they had to do.

'Which one do you want to check first?' Callant asked.

Aimee pulled her eyes from Jess, opened her mouth, then hesitated. She'd been picturing swooping over the city on her dragon, gathering up the clues. Callant couldn't do that. A pair of dragons could fly back and forth across the city much faster than a man could run through the streets. And with the way Callant kept coughing, Aimee doubted he was much of a runner. Blue was already seeping into the sky and they only had a day until the Empty Warriors arrived. Callant had been helpful though, so how did she tell him that he'd slow them down without being mean? Nathine had less tact.

'We'll be much quicker if you don't come with us.' She was already mounted up and Malgerus was snapping at the air.

Callant's disappointment was obvious. For such a big man he managed to slump into someone a lot smaller. Aimee didn't want him to feel left out. She knew that feeling and it was horrible. Besides, he'd been helpful so far and what if they needed his knowledge again. She pulled out the map, studying and calculating.

'Callant, why don't you head for the statue at the bottom of the cliffs. In the meantime, Nathine and I will go to the one at the White Griffin Inn, get the letters, then meet you at the cliffs,' Aimee suggested.

Callant seemed delighted with this. He was so tall and broad, and his beard seemed to take up so much of his face, that Aimee had thought he was much older. Seeing his excited eyes, shining in the glow from her dragon's breath orb, she realised he was only in his mid-twenties, just old enough to be a councillor.

'I'll see you soon,' Callant said, then hurried away across the square. Aimee had mounted up before he disappeared down the alley beside the library.

'Look at you giving orders to councillors,' Nathine said.

'I wasn't ordering him,' Aimee protested.

Nathine didn't need to say *oh really*, her look said it for her. Then both girls were in the sky and Aimee was focusing on the next clue. The short summer darkness was almost over and the city was becoming clearer as they flew above it. Aimee looked at the paved streets and rows of red-brick buildings, the market squares and the wooden stalls that would soon be filled with traders. For her, growing up, the city had been a place of fear, something to hide from. Today for the first time, it was somewhere she wanted to explore.

As they flew over the eastern curve of Barter, Aimee's stomach rumbled. Daring to take a hand off Jess's horns, and only because they weren't very high up, she pulled out the cake Nathine had given her and took another few bites. Crumbs tumbled down into the streets below. The air was still and their dragons' wingbeats were loud. Aimee turned Jess south and they glided to the edge of the Palace.

They landed at the end of Brewers Lane. The street behind her was straight as an arrow but the buildings along it were a higgledy-piggledy cluster of big barns with small round turrets attached to their sides and roofs. A fast-flowing river ran behind the buildings. The water came all the way from Lake Toig, nestled up in the mountains between the peaks, and down Toig waterfall before running through the eastern edge of the city. In the still morning air Aimee could hear the creak and splash of the waterwheels. Brewers Lane was home to the city's grain mills and breweries. Jess's nostrils flared and Aimee felt her disgust at the yeasty stench in the air.

She looked around for the White Griffin Inn. It was at the corner of two streets and its wooden shutters were closed over all the windows. Aimee walked over, Jess clicking on the cobbles behind her, pulled out a dragon's breath orb and studied the inn. Nathine stood beside her and the swirling flames lit up the two girls with their green and orange dragons. The rest of the street was still dark.

The inn had two storeys, capped with a steep roof of grey slate. A covered porch stuck out from the closed front door and the carving was above this. Two wooden figures, about half the size of Aimee, were nestled in an alcove in the wall above the porch. Kyelli stood on the right, her father on the left. It was a nice carving but Aimee still didn't like it as much as her statue in Quorelle Square.

'I can't see a bracelet from here,' Nathine said. 'Can you?'

Aimee shook her head and doubt seeped into her belly, like water coming in under a door. What if they were wrong? What if the N and P on Kyelli's bracelet didn't mean anything? They'd be back to the start and Aimee had no idea what they'd do then.

She looked up and down the street. It was empty. She could hear night workers in the grain mills and breweries, but no one was outside to see them. She tucked away the dragon's breath orb, then quickly she sprang at the porch, grabbing the lip of its roof. Pain shot through her arm as the muscles under her burn stretched, and Aimee gritted her teeth against it. She braced her leg against the wooden beam which supported the porch roof and pushed up. She got her chest and elbows up onto the roof, then hooked her heel on the lip. Pushing off the wooden beam she scrambled onto the roof, landing on her hands and feet like a cat.

She looked down to tell Nathine to climb up too when suddenly Malgerus was in her face. He snorted a cloud of smoke which washed over her with the deep musky smell of woodsmoke. His huge wings were doing backbeats as he hovered beside the inn, blowing Aimee's hair off her face. Nathine sat on his back grinning.

'Oh,' Aimee said, 'I didn't think of that.'

Nathine laughed then she pointed to the carving. 'Look, she's wearing a bracelet.'

Aimee stepped carefully across the steep roof, holding onto the apex with one hand. Up close the carving was blocky. Kyelli's dress was all blunt edges instead of flowing folds of cloth. But she did have a wide cuff carved around her right wrist. At the edge of her bracelet, tucked in where her wooden arm rested against her wooden hip, was a circle.

'Tell me there are letters,' Nathine called.

'Yes! This time it's an L and A,' Aimee replied as she worked her way carefully back to the edge of the porch roof.

Once at the lip she swung her legs over and lowered herself down. She landed in a crouch just as the door to the inn opened. Aimee straightened up slowly and found herself facing a young man wearing a flour-dusted apron. Light poured out of the room behind him.

'Hey, what are you doing? Were you up on my roof?'

He stormed out of the porch and Aimee skipped backwards, banging into the pillar supporting the porch. All her old instincts were screaming at her to hide. She was trembling, but she clenched her fists. And she readied herself to tell him to go stick his head in a slimy bucket because she didn't care what he thought of her face.

Then she felt a weight on her shoulder and felt Jess's cool scales against her cheek. The man looked at the dragon's head on her shoulder and clapped his hands together. Flour puffed into the air.

'Oh, you're a Sky Rider, sorry for shouting at you. Can I help you with something?' he asked, sounding oddly eager.

Aimee gaped at him. He didn't say anything about her weird face.

'No, we need to be heading off. Your inn looks nice though, maybe we'll fly by sometime for a drink,' Nathine said, and Aimee was envious of the easy way she spoke to a complete stranger.

'Oh, hello,' the man said, stepping out of his porch to smile at Nathine. 'I didn't see you. Wow, your dragon's huge. It's…they're both…sparks! Sorry, I've never seen a dragon up close before. My brother works for the ManJarlane family and he's been beyond the mountains twice now. On his first trip, the Riders with the caravan killed a prowler that had been stalking them all the way up the side of Lake Ceil. Were either of you on that trip?'

Aimee and Nathine both shook their heads. Aimee glanced at Nathine and saw she was biting her bottom lip as if to stop herself from laughing.

'Sorry,' he apologised again. He ran a hand through his sandy-coloured hair, leaving a dusting of flour on his high forehead. 'You must think I'm a dull-sparked fool. But I can't wait to tell my brother I've met two dragons. Anyway, you need to go, don't you? I'm sure you've got important things to do. More important than making rye bread I'm sure.' He laughed and held up his hands.

To Aimee he seemed really sweet, and she realised

that last year she'd never have found that out about him. To her, everyone in the city was the same because all she ever saw of them was their disgust and fear at her freakish appearance. Meeting this young man had made her realise there were all sorts of people in the city and maybe she could get to know some of them.

She gave the man a wave once she'd got back into her saddle. He waved back with both hands then a thought flitted across his face.

'Hey, do you know what's going on with the caravans? My brother popped in for a pint last night. He was supposed to be going to Lorsoke next week but isn't now because the city guards are closing the tunnel. Is it something to do with the Helvethi? I thought we were supposed to be making peace with them? I voted for Myconn SaSturn, as did loads of people round here. He's been promising a new future where the Helvethi aren't our enemies and I believed him.'

'It's only temporary,' Nathine told him as Malgerus began to flap.

Malgerus took off and the man shielded his face with his hands as displaced air blasted over him.

'Temporary?' he called up to Nathine when he could see again. Then he looked at Aimee. 'If there's trouble with the Helvethi, you'll be out there, protecting us, won't you?'

'Yes,' Aimee replied.

She couldn't stand to tell him there was something much worse than centaurs heading for the city and that they'd be here in a few hours. How would someone like him, with his floury hands, ever survive an Empty Warrior attack? She wanted to fix things so he could bake bread and drink with his brother, and never have to even see an Empty Warrior. To do that, though, she needed Kyelli's help.

She caught up with Nathine and they skimmed the rooftops of the Palace, heading west across the city.

'You're good at talking to people,' Aimee said.

'It's not hard,' Nathine shrugged it off, then she caught Aimee's eye. 'When I travelled with my father's caravan I always made a really big pot of tea in the evening and took it round offering cups to everyone. I got chatting to a lot of different folk—merchants and reindeer hunters, their families that they brought with them.' She turned away from Aimee and looked up at the Ring Mountains. 'It was a way of avoiding my father.'

'I—' Aimee began but Nathine cut her off as she always did when Aimee tried to offer her sympathy.

'Besides, I brew a really good cup of tea.'

They flew in silence for a few minutes. When Aimee had lived in the Palace she hadn't appreciated what a jumble it was. Skinny red-brick buildings were all crammed together and nearly every one had some sort of wooden extension bolted on. The wooden panels had all turned silver with age and they seemed to merge into the steep grey rooftops. The Palace didn't have groves of birch or hazel trees like Shine and Barter, but it did have colourful doors. They flew over the three inter-twisting streets that made up Twisted Rope Alley and Aimee saw doors painted mustard yellow, berry red, sky blue and even one that was striped green and purple.

Then they reached the scrublands between the Palace and the base of the Ring Mountains, and they swung north. Aimee pushed Jess's horns gently and she swooped into a dive, levelling off just above the grass. Aimee slowed her down with a squeeze of her knees and Jess landed beside the small statue.

Callant was already there and Aimee could tell by the look on his face that something was wrong.

CHAPTER 9

COGS AND STEAM

AIMEE AND NATHINE dismounted and raced each other to the statue. Aimee won, because Nathine was limping. She crouched beside the statue and winced. Malgerus snorted a small cloud of smoke that Aimee had to wave away.

'Are you alright?' Callant asked. He stepped towards Nathine, hand reaching out. The gesture was all concern but Nathine still hobbled backwards away from his touch. Aimee threw Callant a *it's not your fault* look and turned to Nathine.

'Is it your leg?' Aimee asked, concerned for Nathine.

'No, it's listening to your stupid questions that causes me pain,' Nathine snapped, then added, 'Every now and then I get a shoot of pain like that monster's put his hand on me again.' She winced as she straightened.

'I do too,' Aimee said. 'When the Empty Warrior grabbed me it felt like my whole arm was on fire. If you need to go back because your dressing—'

'I'm fine,' Nathine interrupted, 'and you need me to

help solve this thing.'

Callant was chewing his bottom lip again, beard waggling as he listened to them. 'When you and Jara killed that Empty Warrior, the one you brought back to the caravan, lava poured out of it. Are you saying that can burn through your skin?'

Aimee nodded. 'Their palms are all black, and cracked, so you can see the fire flowing inside them. If they touch you it burns through everything.'

'Marhorn's sparks,' Callant swore. 'There's nothing in Nollanni's book about the Empty Warriors themselves being weapons.'

'That's why we need Kyelli. We need to know more. We've got all these stories about our past, but no real facts,' Aimee said.

She looked down at the statue. This one was carved stone and Kyelli's head came up level with Aimee's shoulder. Long grass and wild thyme grew around her feet. Her left arm stuck out, pointing at the cliffs and the route to the Sky Riders' home. Aimee remembered standing in tears and looking at this statue four months ago. Back then Kyelli's pointing arm had told her what she should do and Kyelli had been right. Aimee was counting on her to help again.

'So what's wrong with this one?' Nathine asked. So she too had seen Callant's worried face when they landed.

'There are no letters,' Callant replied.

'You probably didn't look properly.'

'Of course I did,' Callant insisted, folding his thick

arms, 'and there aren't any letters.'

Aimee refused to believe that. She was so sure they'd worked it out, that there were going to be letters on each Kyelli marked on the map. And once they had all the letters it would give them the name of wherever it was that Kyelli had gone. Aimee crouched down to inspect the statue.

'Were there letters at the White Griffin Inn?' Callant asked.

'Yes, L and A,' Aimee replied.

'Maybe we were wrong about them.' Callant looked down at her. 'When you were describing the breastplate you mentioned craftsmen signing their work. Perhaps that's all the letters are, initials of whoever made the statues. We might have to go back to Quorelle Square and start again. Can I see the map?' Callant held out his hand but Aimee ignored him.

'No, this is how we find Kyelli.' She ran her hand over the stone, down Kyelli's arm. 'There's no time to start again. We won't…'

Her words trailed off as her fingertips brushed Kyelli's stone ones. The cuff of her long sleeve came as far down as the back of her hand. Her wrist was hidden. In desperation Aimee leapt up and grabbed Kyelli's left arm but it was the same. Callant was right, there was no bracelet and no hidden letters.

'Maybe the letter is carved somewhere else,' Aimee said.

She began running her hands over every inch of the statue, examining each notch and groove in the stone.

The sky was lightening to a pale blue and there was enough light to see now without dragon's breath orbs. Nathine joined her and when they found nothing, Nathine kicked the statue.

'Kyelli's sparks!' she swore. 'What do we do now, Aimee? We're back to the beginning. If we go back to Quorelle Square now we'll probably run into Jara who'll banish us both to the Ardnanlich Forest or a tiny rock in the middle of the Griydak Sea. Then she'll take our dragons so we have to live there forever like hermits. I'll end up killing and eating you.'

'This is often what studying history is like,' Callant said. 'You get a thread and you follow it, back through the scrolls and books, but sometimes it breaks off and you have to retrace your steps. If we examine the map again perhaps we'll see what we've missed.'

'There isn't time!' Nathine yelled, turning her anger on him. 'We have a few hours before we're trapped in the city with an army trying to break in. This isn't history. Those monsters exist, here, now. So stuff your threads, and your theories, into your stupid beard!'

Behind them Malgerus growled, his ruff of feathers flared.

'Nathine, would you shut up for a minute,' Aimee said straightening up.

'Why? Am I disturbing the scholarly atmosphere? I doubt silence will make any difference to Beardy's thinking.'

'No, Nathine, it's you who needs to think,' Aimee said, as patiently as she could.

'Why me?' Nathine snapped.

'You figured out that the clues were hidden on Kyelli's bracelet because you know more about the Riders than I do. And Callant is right, that was something only a Rider would spot. So think, what else do you know about Rider lore?'

Aimee was pleased to see the anger fade from Nathine's face as she looked back at the statue, considering it. She walked around it slowly, inspecting the statue like a merchant examining an object before deciding how much to pay. Aimee wondered if she'd picked up that mannerism from her father, though there was no way she'd ever mention that.

The grass rustled as Callant moved beside her.

'Is she always this angry?' he asked, very quietly.

'Yes,' Aimee smiled ruefully. 'Don't take it personally.'

She silently willed Nathine on. Beside them Jess and Malgerus both stood stock still, their heads titled to one side as they watched their pensive Riders.

'Yes!' Nathine called, startling Aimee and making their dragons flutter their wings.

'What did you find?' Callant called as he and Aimee rushed around the statue to where Nathine was bent from the waist, staring at Kyelli's hip.

'Look,' Nathine pointed and grinned.

'Are you seeing anything?' Callant asked Aimee 'Because I'm not.'

Annoyingly, Aimee couldn't see anything either. 'What am I supposed to see?'

Nathine sighed deeply. 'Come on, it's your skin that's not right, there's nothing wrong with your eyes. Look.'

'It's just a round lump of stone, part of her dress.'

'No it's not. The stone's been worn down by rain but look at how perfectly round that lump is and see the line underneath it? That's the edge of a pocket and the circle's poking out of it.'

Aimee stared harder, trying to build up the worn stone in her mind's eye. Then she spotted it. 'It's the top of a pair of goggles.'

'Finally. I thought my spark was going to run out before you realised that.'

'Goggles?' Callant asked.

Without planning it Aimee and Nathine both pulled their flying goggles from their pockets and waved them at Callant. Realising they'd done the same thing, they laughed.

'Did you know Kyelli invented the Rider's goggles and made the first pair herself?' Aimee shook her head and Nathine continued. 'They're really tricky to make and she only told one glassmaker, Telthon Sand, how to make them and he passed on the method to only his most skilled apprentice. And that's how it went, each passing it on to the best so that there's only one glassmaker in the city now that can make our goggles.'

'This is fascinating,' Callant said and Aimee could hear the genuine interest in his voice.

She too liked learning these pieces of Rider history, even if Nathine wasn't as good at telling the stories as her uncle had been, or as Dyrenna was.

'So, what do the goggles on the statue mean?' Callant asked.

'I think...' Nathine began as she pulled a short dagger from her belt.

Aimee and Callant watched as she slipped the point of her dagger into a tiny crack at the edge of the stone goggles. She ran it around the circle and along the pocket. Crumbles of dried mortar pattered down on their boots. Nathine dug her dagger in further and prised the stone apart. It pinged off and hit Aimee on the chest.

'I actually didn't do that on purpose,' Nathine said with a grin.

Aimee didn't mind if she had because Nathine had discovered something. The goggles were a cap over a hole in the statue and now they could see inside it. In his excitement Callant took a step forward, then seemed to decide that this was their discovery, and gestured for the girls to look first.

'The statue's hollow inside,' Aimee said.

'From the outside you'd never be able to tell,' Nathine said, rocking back on her feet to look again at the whole statue.

'There's something in here,' Aimee said excitedly as she peered inside.

'What?' Callant asked and Aimee could feel the eagerness coming off him in waves.

Nathine leant forward again beside Aimee. The hole in the statue was the size of Aimee's splayed hand and they had to be right up close to see inside. Aimee felt the pressure of Nathine's head pressed against the side of her own, touching her, and smiled to herself.

Inside the statue there was a jumble of cogs and gears, all connected by metal bars. It looked like a more complicated version of the pulleys on the outside of the warehouses in Barter. They were for lifting heavy goods up to the lofts, though. It made no sense to have a pulley inside a statue.

'Do you know what all the cogs and chains are for?' Aimee asked, really hoping that Nathine would because her family owned several warehouses.

'No, why would I know?' Nathine replied and Aimee's excitement at the discovery ebbed back out like the receding tide.

She turned to look up at Callant. 'Do you know about cogs and stuff?'

'Let me see.'

Aimee and Nathine moved aside to let Callant peer into the statue. 'Fascinating.'

'If he starts on about wading through books again, following cake crumbs, I'm going to let Malgerus bite him,' Nathine said.

'Shh,' Aimee replied, shaking her head. 'Callant, do you know what they're for?'

He pulled his head back, opened his mouth to speak, and coughed instead. It was a frustrating few moments before he'd recovered enough to speak again. Aimee could feel Nathine's impatience.

'There was a boy I studied with at the university,

Rejok, and his father had been all the way to Taumerg once,' Callant finally said, 'and he told his son, that in Taumerg they'd been building all sorts of machines that work and move using cogs and steam.'

Aimee didn't understand how steam could move a machine.

'But we don't have anything like that in Kierell,' she pointed out. 'So how did a machine get inside this statue?'

'That is a conundrum,' Callant agreed, 'especially when you consider that we're assuming the statues on the map are the oldest ones, made when Kierell was built. Marhorn organised the building of Kierell as soon as he brought his surviving people here, which was three hundred and three years ago. Because they were busy building a new home I don't think anyone went outside the Ring Mountains for years. Also, Nollanni hints that Marhorn forbade it.'

'So how could they get this machine from the city states and pop it in a statue?' Nathine asked.

'I don't think they could have. It was about fifteen years ago that Rejok's father was in Taumerg, and he said the machines were a new thing. There was a lot of excitement around them. So if the city states didn't have these steam machines three hundred years ago, and Kierell didn't either, then they shouldn't have existed.'

'Just like Empty Warriors shouldn't exist any more,' Aimee said quietly.

'Indeed, so what is this machine inside the statue and why is it here?' Callant mused.

Exasperation edged with panic had crept back into Aimee's mind. Why had Kyelli made the clues so damn hard? She wondered if any other Rider had ever tried to follow them and given up.

'This is so annoying!' Nathine exclaimed.

Disgruntled she sat down on the grass and glared up at the statue as if it had offended her. She picked up the circle of stone she'd prised off and twirled it over and over in her hand. Aimee was thinking furiously, rummaging through her thoughts, hoping that if she could get them in the right order then she'd know what to do next. Callant was staring at the stone in Nathine's hands, and sucking in his bottom lip as if he was trying to inhale his beard. With a grunt of annoyance Nathine drew back her arm to chuck away the circle of stone.

'Wait!' Callant called, but Nathine threw the stone.

Aimee dived forward and snatched it from the air. Nathine's glare switched itself to her.

'I was trying to hit that rock over there,' Nathine said.

Aimee ignored her and handed the stone to Callant. 'Have you thought of something?'

'Seen something, look. And good reactions, by the way.'

The circle was much smaller in his hand than it had been in Nathine's. He flipped it over, and on the side that had been hidden inside the statue, there was a carving. Because it had been protected from the weather, the lines of the image were still clear. It was a dragon, breathing fire.

'Look.' Aimee passed the stone back to Nathine, who studied the fire-breathing dragon for a moment then gave Aimee a *so what* look. Aimee peered back through the hole in the statue then looked at Callant.

'I don't understand,' she said, face all scrunched up.

'This is another clue meant for a Rider,' Callant replied.

'Kyelli might have understood that machine thing inside the statue, and maybe her Riders did hundreds of years ago, but we don't know anything about cogs and stuff.'

The panicky feeling was rising in Aimee's chest again. Was this a test Kyelli had set? Was she about to fail?

'I know a little about it from listening to Rejok, though it's mostly theory, but let's look, come on.'

Callant knelt by the statue and motioned for Aimee to join him. She did so hesitantly but he didn't seem bothered about having her weird skin near him. She peered into the statue. It was dark inside and she had to wait for her eyes to adjust. Just inside the hole there was a small tank with a lid and a long tube coming out the top of it. At the top the tube connected to a bunch of small cogs. None of it made any sense to her.

'Do you have a flask of water?' Callant asked.

'Yes, but—'

'And your dragon, we'll need him too.'

'Her,' Aimee corrected, 'she's called Jess. Have you figured it out?'

'Maybe.' Callant chewed his lip.

Aimee ran over to Jess, rummaged in her saddlebag and pulled out her water flask. Jess head-butted her on the shoulder and growled softly.

'Come on, girl, we need you too,' Aimee told her and Jess followed her back to the statue.

Nathine was looking up at Callant sceptically. Aimee looked down at Nathine, still sitting on the grass, and noticed she had her hands under her wounded leg, lifting it slightly off the ground.

'Here.' She held out a hand and gently pulled Nathine to her feet. She didn't protest and Aimee knew her hunch had been right. Nathine's leg was hurting again but she didn't want to admit it. That was the real reason she'd sat down, not because she was annoyed.

'Rejok said cog machines worked with steam,' Callant said, head swinging round to look at the girls.

'But we don't understand that,' Nathine said.

'I don't think we need to understand it, that's what so clever about this carving.' Callant held up the stone. 'It's telling you that all you need is dragon's breath. Imagine you had a kettle of water for tea and—'

'I'm going to need a cup of tea if you keep babbling on,' Nathine said.

Aimee ignored Nathine's sarcasm because she suddenly understood what Callant was thinking. 'He's right, Nathine, imagine you got Malgerus to blast the kettle with flames, the water would boil really quickly and make a burst of steam. It would also probably ruin the kettle so it's not a good way to make tea, but I think it'll work for this.' She turned to Callant. 'That's what you're thinking, isn't it?'

Callant's beard opened and his grin appeared. 'Precisely. I think if we make a burst of steam it'll make the piston move and then the cogs will turn.'

'Alright but then what?' Nathine asked.

'I don't know, but let's find out.'

Aimee held out her water flask. Callant looked at it, then down at his thick-fingered hands and back to Aimee. 'I think you might need to do it. My hand's never going to fit through that small hole.'

Aimee nodded, nervous but keen to help. 'What do I do?'

'First we need water in that small tank, so you'll need to fill it,' Callant explained.

Aimee reached through the hole and into the statue, feeling around until she touched the cold metal of the small tank. There was a lid with a catch and it took her a moment but she managed to flip it open. She withdrew her arm then squashed her water flask, squeezing it through the hole. Balancing her flask on top of the tank she carefully pulled out the stopper. It was really awkward to do with one hand.

'You're making the constipated dragon face again,' Nathine told her.

Aimee closed her eyes so she could more easily focus on only what she could feel with her fingertips.

'Maybe I should get my flask ready in case you spill the water from yours into Kyelli's feet,' Nathine offered.

'No, I can do this,' Aimee said, still with her eyes closed.

She lined up her flask mouth with the hole, then quickly tipped it up. She heard the water pour into the tank.

'See, told you I could do it.' She beamed at Nathine then turned to Callant. 'What's next?'

'This is where we need your dragon. Can you give her instructions? Does it work like that?' Callant asked.

Aimee felt her face flush. 'She sometimes does what I tell her,' she admitted.

Callant turned to Nathine. 'Alright, how about your—'

But Aimee cut him off. 'Jess can do it.'

Callant didn't understand that he was being insulting, he just wanted to unravel the next piece of the puzzle, but Aimee still felt a twinge of hurt.

'What does she need to do?' Aimee asked again.

'Well, we need that water in the tank to boil and make a burst of steam,' Callant said.

Aimee nodded. Jess was watching her with her unreadable yellow eyes but Aimee could feel her dragon's eagerness. She sensed Aimee was keen to do something even if she didn't know what it was.

'Jess, you have to blow fire into the hole and aim at the tank of water,' Aimee explained. She took hold of Jess's head and gently pulled her towards the statue. Jess growled, unsure. 'It's okay, girl,' Aimee reassured her.

She pictured Jess doing what she'd asked and once she had the image clear in her mind she pushed it along their connection. Thankfully, Jess seemed to understand because she moved closer to the statue.

'You know she won't be able to give a full blast of flames because she's not fully grown yet,' Nathine said behind them.

'I know, but she only needs to boil some water not heat up a bath big enough to fit your smelly body in.'

Callant laughed and Nathine glared at him. Jess eyed the hole then nudged it with her snout. Aimee watched, her entire body tense like a bow string, as Jess's black tongue flicked out and she licked the stone. Then apparently satisfied she closed her lips around the hole and blew flames inside.

There was a moment where Aimee thought nothing was going to happen, then she heard the hiss of steam. Jess jerked her head back in fright and snapped at the statue. Aimee laughed.

From inside the stone she heard a thump and the creak of cogs. Both she and Callant pressed their eyes up to the hole to see what was going on. Nathine protested because she wanted to see too. The metal piston moved, the cogs turned and then from their left came the sound of grinding stone. They all looked at each other then ran around to the front of the statue.

Amazed they watched as a crack appeared in the stone of Kyelli's sleeve. Then in a puff of dust her sleeve moved, the cuff of it pulling back up her arm, revealing her stone wrist.

'She's wearing a bracelet!' Nathine shouted.

'You did it, Jess.' Aimee hugged her and Jess nuzzled the back of her neck.

Her heart was beating a tattoo against her ribs with

the excitement of solving the puzzle and she was sure her spark must have gotten brighter. With a grinding sound the cogs halted and Kyelli's stone sleeve stopped moving. It had gone far enough up, though, for Aimee to see all of her bracelet. This one was also a wide band and carved right at the edge were the letters S and E.

CHAPTER 10

FACING UP

'BRILLIANT, RIGHT, WHICH one's next?' Nathine asked.

Aimee looked at her and couldn't help but laugh. Nathine's blue eyes were wide with excitement and her round cheeks were flushed pink. Fear of the Empty Warriors was a constant in Aimee's mind, like a stone in her boot she couldn't tip out, but she was enjoying solving Kyelli's clues. She liked working as part of a team, and being accepted in that team.

'Hang on, we should be writing these letters down,' Callant said. He rummaged in his pockets for a moment then looked at them sheepishly. 'Do either of you have a pencil?'

Callant had come running out of the council chamber without anything, not even his coat. Aimee did have her coat, and her hat, gloves and goggles, and a half-eaten piece of cake in one pocket that was now mostly crumbs. But she didn't have a pencil.

'I've said it before, it's a good thing you bring me on

these missions of yours,' Nathine said as she stuck her hand into Malgerus's saddlebag.

She pulled out a small blue, leather-bound book held closed with string. At the end of the piece of string she'd tied a pencil. As Nathine slipped it free, Aimee wondered what the book was, but didn't dare ask. Their friendship was certainly growing but angry-Nathine still lived quite close to the surface. She passed Aimee the pencil.

'Don't lose it because I'll want it back.'

Aimee took out the map.

'Wait!' Callant exclaimed. 'You can't write on that. It's a valuable artefact, a piece of Kierell's history. We need to preserve it for posterity.'

Aimee looked up at him. 'Kierell won't have a future if we don't find Kyelli. And I'm sure she wouldn't mind me writing on her map. I'll do it on the back so you can't even see it.'

Aimee turned the map over and wrote P, N, L, A, S and E.

'Where's Pnlase?' Nathine said, looking over Aimee's shoulder. 'It doesn't sound like a real place. Maybe Kyelli couldn't spell.'

Aimee spluttered. 'She's immortal, and saved our ancestors, and taught us how to bond with dragons. And she wrote on the map with a load of perfectly spelled words.'

'Sparks, Aimee, it was a joke. I didn't mean to offend your super, amazing hero.'

'She *is* a hero, she…' but Aimee let her words trail

off when she saw the smirk on Nathine's face. 'You're so annoying. And Malgerus is stupid.'

Callant was repeating the letters quietly to himself and completely ignoring the girls' silly argument.

'Well,' he finally mused, 'there's nothing on the map to say what order you should visit the statues in.'

It took Aimee a moment to get her head away from being exasperated with Nathine and back to their quest.

'So the letters are all jumbled up and we'll need to re-arrange them?' she asked.

'Yes, it's an anagram.'

'If she's such a hero of the people, why did Kyelli make the clues so difficult to follow?' Nathine complained.

Callant looked like he was about to say something but then the hole in his beard closed again. Aimee envied him his ability to not always rise to Nathine's bait. She made a point of making Nathine watch as she tucked the pencil securely into one of her inner coat pockets. Then she held out the map so they could all see it. There were three more tree symbols marking statues they hadn't yet been to.

The sky was a pale blue, tinged with pink but Aimee thought they still had a couple of hours before the city woke up. And then only a few more hours until the Empty Warriors arrived. She desperately wished they had more time.

'Callant, do you need to go back and do councillor-ish things?' Aimee asked.

'Councillor-ish?' he laughed and Aimee felt her face

go red. She hoped he didn't think she was stupid and that, like Nathine sometimes said, her brain was patchy like her face.

Callant shook his head. 'When I left the council meeting last night, everyone was…busy. Myconn and his sister have been directing preparations with Captain Tenth. They're anticipating a siege, and I can't believe I'm saying that. Layanne and her scholars have the breastplate to try and wrangle any more clues from it about who the Master of Sparks is. Then the council want to try and find him, to negotiate with him. And it seemed like there was so much going on but…' Callant's words trailed off and he shrugged.

Aimee understood. 'You wanted to help but you didn't know what you could do.'

'You're very observant,' Callant said.

He'd said it like a compliment but Aimee wasn't sure what to make of it. She didn't think she was observant, only that she knew how he felt because Jara had made her feel the same way.

'I've only been a councillor for a few weeks,' Callant continued, 'so it's all still new to me. I always wanted to be a scholar, and you should have seen how proud my father was when I was accepted at the university. I thought his spark would shine right out of his chest.' Callant looked at the two girls and smiled. 'I imagine your parents were the same when you became Riders.'

Aimee's old grief at losing her family resurfaced, like mud stirred up from the bottom of a pond. She knew Gyron and Naura would have been so proud of her, but they'd never know what she'd accomplished. She couldn't meet Callant's eye in case she started crying. She glanced at Nathine who was scowling and looked like she might punch Callant.

'I've said something wrong, haven't I?' Callant looked so timid sometimes. It was surprising in such a big man.

'Did you not like being a scholar?' Aimee asked. She didn't want him to feel bad but she needed to change the subject. He didn't know she'd climbed because she was all alone and that Nathine climbed to escape her abusive father. Thankfully Callant took the hint and continued his story.

'I loved being a scholar actually, but studying made me realise how little we know. All our knowledge is what we've written ourselves during three hundred years inside these mountains. It's so insular and limited. There are other cities out there with different books, full of new ideas. I want us to be able to access those, to share them. It's why I stood for election. I wanted to support a peace with the Helvethi so we could be free to travel safely across the tundra.'

'But now the Empty Warriors have gone and marched all over those dreams,' Nathine said and Aimee was surprised to hear sympathy in her voice.

'Yeah, but I want to find a way to fight them and when you said you were going to find Kyelli,' he nodded at Aimee, 'I thought this was a way I could help. So I guess for me, this *is* the councillor-ish stuff I need to be doing.'

Aimee was glad. She felt better having Callant along with them. Kyelli might have created the clues for Riders but without Callant they'd still be staring, frustrated, at the map with no idea where to begin. Aimee believed she could find Kyelli but it was nice to know that if she got stuck she could turn to Callant for help.

'So, which one next?' Nathine asked as she mounted up. Malgerus shifted beneath her, keen to be back in the sky.

'I think we should split up again,' Callant suggested. 'We only have a few hours and I can't cross the city as quickly as you can.'

Aimee opened out the map. 'Why don't you head here,' she pointed to the north,' and we'll fly to the university?'

Callant shook his head. 'It makes more sense if I go to the university. I know where the Kyelli is there and it's also closer. It'll take me ages to walk up to the north of the city. You should check that one and then meet me at the university.'

Aimee hesitated. What Callant proposed made sense but she didn't want to go north. She couldn't say that without admitting why, though. So reluctantly, she agreed.

'Great, then there's only one more after that,' Callant said. Then with a quick wave he turned and began jogging across the grass towards the warehouses of Barter. Aimee noticed him clutching his chest as he turned in between two buildings and heard his coughs echoing back from the brick walls.

She looked down at the map in her hands. The streets and buildings of Shine stopped at the northern edge of the city and there was a blank strip, then four rectangular buildings were marked. The tree symbol was on the western-most building. It was an area of the city Aimee had never been too.

'Right, off up to where the fielders live,' Nathine said. 'They have their own little community up there.'

The field workers' community was where Lyrria had belonged to before she made the climb. Of course she wouldn't be there now, but her past was. It was where little Lyrria had run around with her brothers and sister. If Aimee went there she wouldn't be able to stop thinking about her. She wondered if Lyrria still knew any of the people there. Were her parents still there? Parents Aimee would never be taken to meet, because Lyrria was too ashamed to bring home a freak for a girlfriend.

'Hey, Aimee, those Empty Warriors are still coming.'

Nathine's shout jolted her from her thoughts and she realised she'd been staring blankly across the city.

'What's wrong?' she called.

'Nothing,' Aimee lied quickly.

'Oh really?' Nathine pointed at Jess.

Aimee's dragon had hunched down, pressed her belly into the long grass and furled her wings. Aimee could pretend she wasn't upset but Jess had no guile in her and she was sharing Aimee's heartache.

'Lyrria's surname is Field,' Aimee said by way of explaining.

'Ah, and that's why you wanted Callant to go get those letters instead of us. But Lyrria's not going to be there, she's patrolling the mountains,' Nathine pointed out.

'I know but...' Aimee's words were pulled back down by the heaviness of her heart. She wasn't sure how to describe to Nathine what she was feeling. Surprisingly though, Nathine seemed to understand, in her usual unsympathetic way.

'You don't want to go see and where she's from because you were hoping one day to wander through the crop fields hand in hand, and sit on her old bed, gazing lovingly into each other's eyes and be mightily impressed when she told you daring stories from her childhood. And now you can't do that because you won't let her hands back under your shirt.'

As grateful as Aimee was that Nathine understood, her cheeks still flushed, and she decided she didn't want to discuss Lyrria with her any more. Instead she coaxed Jess up from the grass.

'I could go and get the next letters myself,' Nathine offered as Aimee climbed into her saddle.

'No,' she said firmly.

Kyelli had set these clues, and to be worthy of finding her, a Rider had to solve them all. She wasn't going to finally stand in front of Kyelli having only managed some of them. What if Kyelli knew she'd wimped out of one of them?

'You know, this is your mission, so you could have ordered Callant to go to the fielders' community,' Nathine said.

That idea horrified Aimee. She couldn't dish out orders, that was something Jara did. People obeyed Jara because she looked and acted like a leader. No one was going to jump to do what Aimee asked, especially not a councillor.

'I can't order people around,' Aimee said as she climbed into her saddle.

'Why not?'

'Because.'

'If you keep shooting down all my ideas I'll start thinking you don't like me,' Nathine said as Malgerus began to flap.

Aimee starred over at her in disbelief. Nathine had hated her for four months and made it clear that the last thing she ever wanted was Aimee's friendship. Now Nathine was saying she would be upset if Aimee didn't like her. Her lips were downturned and she looked hurt. Aimee felt bad and started to apologise just as Nathine flipped her expression and grinned mischievously. Aimee couldn't decide if she was more relieved or annoyed.

'I've never had a friend before,' she told Nathine, 'and I'm wondering if they're all as annoying as you?'

Nathine didn't answer but her grin widened as Malgerus took off. Aimee watched them soar upwards, Malergus's bright orange scales contrasting beautifully with the pale sky. Aimee took a deep breath and touched Jess's mind with her own. It was calming. Jess didn't worry about what people thought or who was supposed to be in charge, she just followed Aimee and trusted in her.

'You're right, Jess, we can do this.'

Her stomach lurched and wind blasted her face as Jess shot into the sky. They caught up with Malgerus and the two dragons skimmed around the outer edge of the city, following the curve of the mountains. They flew fast, the wind whipping Aimee's short curls back from her face. She looked north and nerves jangled inside her. She wasn't going to stop, though.

CHAPTER 11

# DIDN'T TELL

Aimee and Nathine flew past the last street in Shine and over a wide band of trees. Birch, rowan and hazel all grew together in a dense tangle and Aimee wondered if that was deliberate. Were the trees there so the privileged old families in Shine didn't need to look at the poorer people who grew their food? Growing up in the Palace Aimee knew her uncle, and the tradespeople filling the streets around them, weren't well off, but at least their skills were respected. Aimee couldn't understand why the people who dug up their potatoes weren't also valued. She was glad the distinctions in the city didn't apply to the Riders' community.

Beyond the trees were the rectangular buildings marked on the map, only there were seven of them now, not four. It was like Callant had said, the city on the map was smaller, showing only what had been built at the time.

Stretching from the buildings all the way to the northern curve of the Ring Mountains were the fields and orchards that fed the city. They were every shade of vibrant, from the bright greens of new leaves, to the rosy reds of apples and the blush pinks of blossoms on the waeberry bushes. There hadn't been many growing things or open spaces in Aimee's life in the Palace. She thought she might have liked to grow up here instead. Then she realised she'd actually have hated it here because there was nowhere to hide in open fields. Not like the twisting streets of the Palace where she'd grown adept at finding the concealed alleys and shadowy doorways.

'Do you think the new buildings were added to the east or west end?' Nathine called over, interrupting her thoughts.

They'd slowed Malgerus and Jess, and now the two dragons hovered over the edge of the trees. Aimee realised Nathine had a point. The map showed the clue was on the western-most building but was it still the western-most one?

'We'll need to start at that end and check them till we find the right one,' Aimee said.

It would take longer and that was frustrating. They'd spent ages at the last statue and the morning was slipping away. She'd hoped this would be an easy one. She pulled Jess's left horn and pressed her ribs with her right knee, turning her so they flew towards the end of the long, wooden buildings. They landed behind the last one and Aimee felt Jess's pleasure at landing on plush grass rather than the rock of the mountains or the slate of a roof.

In Kierell all the buildings were red brick with grey slate roofs but the field workers' communal houses were wooden, silver with age, and many had moss on their wooden roof shingles. They were all raised off the ground on short, thick stilts and the gap under the buildings was large enough that Aimee could have crouched and walked under them.

'Have you seen the faces?' Nathine said.

Aimee felt a jolt of panic as she thought Nathine had spotted people watching them. Then she realised Nathine had dismounted and was looking closely at the wooden stilts. Aimee joined her and saw that each thick post was carved with snarling, menacing faces. She looked closer and felt a cold horror slip down her spine.

'They're Empty Warriors,' she gasped.

Nathine peered closer. 'Kyelli's sparks,' she swore.

The faces on the wooden posts all had flames carved in their eyes. They were also identical. Every single face Aimee could see looked exactly the same. It was just like the Empty Warriors she'd seen in the boats.

'Oh sparks, no,' Nathine said.

Aimee thought she'd seen something terrible in the carved faces but when she looked round Nathine's head was tilted back. A golden dragon was soaring towards them. Aimee recognised it. Harmony. She pictured Aranati's perpetually stern face and winced. Maybe Pelathina hadn't told Jara that she'd seen Aimee and Nathine leaving against orders, but had told her sister instead. Apart from Jara, Aimee couldn't think of a Rider she'd least like to explain herself to. Aranati was always so serious and looked like the sort of person who'd never broken a rule.

'What do we do?' Nathine asked. In her panic she forgot Aimee's wound and grabbed her arm. The pain was like fire licking her bone and Aimee stifled a scream.

'Hide,' she panted through gritted teeth.

She dropped and scurried under the wooden building, then waved frantically for Nathine to follow. She motioned for Jess to sink down and sent the command along their connection. Jess crouched low in the grass and tucked in her wings.

'Well it's alright for you,' Nathine whispered as she lay down beside Aimee, 'your dragon's green.'

Aimee's arm was still throbbing and she tried to breath out the pain. She peeked from under the edge of the building. Harmony skimmed the copse of trees then glided towards the buildings.

'She's gone to the other end,' Aimee told Nathine in a whisper.

She stared intently along the row of buildings. She could see under them, all the way to the end. Then she noticed something about the wooden stilts on the next building along.

'Stay,' she told Jess, holding out a palm towards her like Dyrenna did with Black. Then she began to crawl under the building and towards the next one.

'What are we doing?' Nathine whispered, following her. 'If we get caught Jara won't get a chance to punish you because I'm going to let Malgerus eat you, freaky skin and all.'

'I just need to check something,' Aimee replied.

She reached the edge of the building, sprinted across the gap between them and ducked under the next one. The thick posts supporting this one were carved with faces too. Like the others, these faces were all the same as each other.

'These faces are all a different person,' Aimee said, half to herself.

'What do you mean?' Nathine asked. She'd followed and crouched beside Aimee.

'The faces on the other building were all the same face, like copies of one person. The ones on this building are all the same too, but it's like they're all copies of a different person.' Aimee ran her hand over the carvings. They were in the shade and the wood was cold beneath her fingertips. 'This person has a taller forehead and a wider nose.'

'How did you even notice that?'

Aimee hesitated, just for a moment, before explaining.

'When I was little and my aunt took me out, I used to study faces. I kept looking for someone with one like mine,' she said, then hurried on before Nathine could say anything. 'But there's also something else different about these faces. Their eyes don't have flames carved in them.'

Nathine peered closer. 'They've got triangles.'

'I think they're supposed to be mountains.'

'Really? Well they're rubbish-looking mountains. I could have done better than that. So, what do they mean?'

Aimee shook her head. She had no idea. Did this mean there were Empty Warriors out there with something else inside them, something other than fire? Was this something Layanne and the scholars should know about too? She needed to check the other buildings. Moving in a crouch she scurried along and under the next building. Nathine followed and didn't complain. The stilts of this one were all carved with a woman's face, the same woman, over and over. In her eyes the grain of the wood had been chiselled deeper so she seemed to have woodgrain eyes. The next building had a man again with a squarish jaw and cogs carved in his eyes, like the ones inside the Kyelli statue.

Aimee and Nathine reached the fifth building but its stilts weren't carved at all. Aimee ran a hand over the smooth wood in confusion. She looked along at the next two which were also devoid of carvings. Four buildings had creepy Empty Warrior faces and three didn't.

'The buildings with the carvings are the original ones, the four marked on the map,' Aimee said as she realised what it meant. 'The people who built Kierell carved Empty Warriors on them but later, when the other buildings were added, they didn't carve any. Maybe because by then they'd forgotten about the Empty Warriors.'

'Okay, but what does that mean?' Nathine asked. She was plucking out blades of grass in frustration. 'Why would anyone want to carve scary monsters that killed everyone onto their homes?'

'I don't know but maybe we're supposed to understand something from them.' Aimee thought about the council chamber and the painted panels on the wall curving up by the staircase. They showed Kierell's history but was there more to them too? She wished Callant was with them. 'It's like Kyelli wrote our history in the city's buildings, like she wanted to tell us something but also keep it hidden. Does that make sense?'

'No, not really.'

Aimee thought about the way as a little girl she'd gone out into the street with big ideas about making friends, then when the other children appeared, all she'd done was hide.

'Maybe Kyelli was scared,' she suggested.

'Of what?'

Aimee shrugged.

'Couldn't she have just written a book like a normal person and left it in the library with a sign saying, "Read me if the Empty Warriors come back". Why did she hide the story in cryptic clues on maps, and statues, and creepy carved faces?' Nathine threw a bunch of grass stalks at the Empty Warrior faces.

'Kyelli must have a reason for doing it this way,' Aimee said. She began to run back along underneath the buildings.

Nathine followed. 'I know she founded the Riders but I'm really starting to dislike Kyelli.'

'I'll tell her you said that when we meet her.'

As they reached the last building Aimee heard voices. She and Nathine froze. Two sets of boots appeared at the edge of the building. Aimee slowly lowered herself to the cold grass, grateful that their black clothes would meld into the shadows. One pair of boots was scuffed and muddy, the other were black Rider's boots. Both pairs stopped at the corner of the building.

'All of it? We can't give anything to the Guilds?' asked a man's voice.

'Yes, Sorjern, every crop that's picked is to go to the council warehouses on Halkell Street,' Aranati's voice replied.

'The Guilds won't let us give everything over to the council. I can easily send the normal supplies, but there will be an uproar if I take what's been planted for others.'

'You're head of the Growers Guild.'

'I am, but the other Guilds have all placed orders with us worth thousands of presses to them. The ManAllakan family has paid for nearly a full field of cloudberries. Their cloudberry liqueur sold well with traders from Soramerg last year and they've plans to make twice as much this year.'

'They might not be selling any to Soramerg,' Aranati said and though Aimee couldn't see her she could picture her frown.

'Look, I've heard these rumours about monsters with no sparks coming back to life. It's nonsense. Probably spread by the Helvethi to keep us off the tundra. I'm surprised you Riders are taking it seriously,' Sorjern said.

'The Empty Warriors are back,' Aranati advised. 'Now, I'll repeat your orders, the council will be taking all the food and you've to bring it to the warehouses on Halkell street.'

Aimee heard the rustle of paper and assumed she'd handed Sorjern the council's orders.

'You can't be serious?' Sorjern asked.

'The warehouses on—'

'Yeah, I got it but I don't know if this'll be enough.' Aimee heard paper flapping. 'The Growers Guild doesn't have the same authority as the others. It never has.'

'It does now,' Aranati told him. 'The council voted on it last night.'

'Well, that's something new.' Sorjern sounded pleased. 'The council's never bothered much with the Growers before. I guess things are changing, finally. Once we've got this peace with the Helvethi settled, I'll have the authority now to travel out to the city states. Folks have been bringing back rumours for years that they've got farming methods that can double a yield and even pick the crops for us!'

Aranati didn't reply and Aimee wondered if she was feeling the same guilt that she was. This man, like the baker they'd met earlier, was looking forward to the better future that ties with the north would bring. If they couldn't stop the Empty Warriors, though, that future would be lost. Aimee had managed to change her own life and she thought everyone should have that chance. She wanted to crawl out from under the building and promise Sorjern that she'd help him.

Without meaning to, she shared with Jess her desperate desire to do something. She heard the snap of her wings and looked around. Jess had risen, stretched out her wings and was cocking her head from side to side as she stared right at Aimee.

'Stupid dragon, what's she doing?' Nathine hissed.

Aimee waved at her to lie down, but she didn't understand the sudden panic she was feeling from her Rider. She growled. Aimee's heart flipped over in her chest.

'Stay here,' Aranati's voice ordered, and Aimee watched with dread as her boots passed the building and rounded the end. Roused by Jess, Malgerus had stood up too. Nathine was hissing frantically for him to move but both dragons heard Aranati coming. Aimee felt like freezing water from the Griydak Sea was pouring into her chest.

Aranati walked round the end of the building and Aimee watched as her shiny boots stopped. Jess and Malgerus were peering round too. Aranati must have been looking right at them.

The hunt was over.

Aranati was going to find them and tell Jara they'd disobeyed her. They'd be kicked out of the Riders and lose their dragons. The map would never get solved and they'd have to face the Empty Warriors alone.

Then Aranati crouched down and her face appeared right in front of Aimee's. She had a childish urge to squeeze her eyes shut. Aranati's customary frown deepened as she took in the two girls lying under the building. Aimee held her breath and grabbed hold of her connection with Jess. Could she and Jess get away before Jara separated them? But Aimee didn't want to leave the home she'd found. Or the city she wanted to save.

'Please,' Aimee whispered. It was all she could manage.

'Have you found a way to reach Kyelli?' Aranati asked. Her head was tilted to one side, her long dark hair brushing the grass.

Aimee shook her head. 'Not yet, but we're close.'

Aranati stared at them for a moment longer and then to Aimee's disbelief she straightened up and walked back to Sorjern.

'Sorry, it's nothing,' she said to him. 'Do you understand your instructions?'

He must have nodded because Aimee heard Aranati whistle and saw Harmony's golden-scaled legs appear as she landed on the grass. A moment later Aranati and Harmony were gone. Aimee dared to breathe out.

'Why did she let us go?' Nathine asked and the confusion in her round face mirrored Aimee's own.

Aimee shrugged. She had no idea why Aranati had covered for them.

'Okay, well that was more nerve-wracking than doing the climb,' Nathine said with a sigh of relief. 'Come on, let's get this clue.'

Nathine crawled out and, favouring her injured leg, carefully got to her feet in the gap between the first two buildings. Aimee followed and as she stood up, she saw

Kyelli. The end wall of the building facing them was covered with a mural. It must once have been beautiful but the paint had faded and peeled like flaky skin. Flecks of orange, yellow and purple still clung to the flowers but mostly they were brown and sad. The sky was peeling blue and the once bright dragons looked like ghosts flying through it. Right in the centre were Kyelli and Marhorn.

It was hard to tell but Aimee thought that Kyelli's hair had been painted a coppery brown and she was wearing a flowing dress that was still mostly yellow. Aimee didn't like seeing Kyelli looking so neglected.

'Right, get out the map and note down the letters. I'll read them out,' Nathine said as she stepped closer to Kyelli. 'If I can, that is.'

The paint on Kyelli's arms was peeling so badly Nathine had to press it back on with her fingertips.

'Can you still read them?' Aimee asked, pulling the map and pencil from her pocket.

'There's an R.' She peered closer and Aimee crowded in too. 'And a C.'

'It's not a C, it's a G.'

'No it's not.'

'It is, look there's the small line that makes it a G.'

'That's a line in the wood.'

'It's not. That one's definitely a G,' Aimee insisted and wrote the two letters on the reverse of the map.

'Well, if you're wrong…' Nathine left her sentence hanging.

'What?'

'Your mission, your fault.'

'I'm not wrong.'

'Alright, mushroom head, what are the letters we've got now?'

'P, N, L, A, S, E, R, G,' Aimee read out.

'I really hope after we've been to the last two Kyellis that this makes sense.'

'Me too.'

She was counting on Callant figuring it out once they had all the clues.

CHAPTER 12

## ARRIVAL

THE CITY WAS waking up as Aimee and Nathine flew over Shine towards the university. The red brick buildings were the colour of rust in the early morning sunshine and between them groves of birch trees rustled their leaves. It looked so calm, so ordinary, but Aimee saw the city differently now. She wondered if she was seeing it as Kyelli had, not as a place of buildings and lives, but as a story mapped out and told in statues, murals and carvings.

What did the faces on the support posts mean? What else was hidden in plain sight that no one had ever spotted? Aimee thought of the little carved Kyelli she'd been able to see from her bedroom window in the loft. There were hundreds like that across the city. Were any of those hiding something important? And what about the council chamber? It had painted panels on the walls by the staircase, Aimee remembered admiring them, and the table in the high gallery was all carved. Had Kyelli made those too and hidden truths about their past in them?

The enormity of it was overwhelming, like flying into a huge cloud and not knowing which way was out. Jess slowed beneath her and Malgerus pulled ahead. Noticing, Nathine twisted round in her saddle.

'What's wrong now?' she called.

'What if we can't find her in time?' Aimee said.

'Hey, I thought you were being all confident now?'

'I am, but all we've got are a bunch of letters and it feels like there's more of our past, of the Empty Warriors story, hidden across the city. What if we're meant to understand it all? We don't know what any of it means yet.'

Jess's feathers were half raised, green tips pointing out from her scales and she'd slowed her wingbeats so much Aimee began to worry they might fall out of the sky. Nathine had to steer Malgerus in a wide circle to come back and meet them. Her high ponytail streamed out behind her as she skilfully flew her dragon in beside Aimee and matched Jess's pace.

'Do you see that long building with the twin peaked roof and all the skylights?' Nathine pointed.

They were flying over the edge of Shine, above a copse of hazel trees, that separated the rich people's houses from the eastern curve of Barter.

'Yes.'

'That's my father's main warehouse. It'll be stacked with reindeer hides, fresh from the tanners and all rolled up ready to sell. In the back there's a kitchen where they cook the reindeer meat into smoked sausages. Finished ones will be hanging in clusters from the rafters. The ones with fennel were always my favourite. And somewhere, running through it all, probably getting in the way, will be my little brother.'

Nathine turned to look at her and Aimee saw a shadow of the scared girl she'd glimpsed before.

'You told me that if we found Kyelli, then she could get rid of the Empty Warriors,' Nathine continued. 'You convinced me, with that determined frown of yours, that the map was the key to doing it. And that we could follow it, find her and save the city. Lukas has a bright spark and there's no way I'm letting a monster burn that from his chest. So, mighty quest leader, don't you go cracking on me now.'

'Or Malgerus will eat me?' Aimee said.

'Oh not just Malgerus. I'm starving, so I'll eat at least one of your arms.'

It wasn't the soft, comforting words Aimee always imagined a friend gifting her, but there was something about Nathine's brusque manner that always seemed to cut straight through the mess in her head. She smiled, then remembered the cake in her pocket. She fished it out, though what was left was mostly squashed and crumbly.

'I've still got some cake if you're hungry.' She offered it to Nathine.

'Ugh, I don't want mushed cake from the bottom of your crummy pocket.'

'It's still good,' Aimee insisted.

Nathine shook her head. 'Come on, Beardy's probably at the university already.'

Aimee shoved the cake in her mouth and chewed quickly as she pushed Jess for more speed. Then movement in the sky to the west caught her eye. She could see at least five colourful dragons in the air above where the tunnel was. As she watched, they soared up and over the mountains, the jagged outline of Norwen Peak to their left. Then they hovered in the sky. Two more dragons were flying towards them from the city.

'Jess, they're here,' Aimee whispered, as if the Empty Warriors might hear her.

She had to see, hoping she was wrong but knowing she wasn't. She felt Jess's muscles work harder beneath her as they climbed into the sky.

'What are you doing *now*?' Nathine called, but followed them up. Malgerus's bigger wings meant he quickly caught Jess.

The city grew smaller, and the sky grew bigger, as they rose above the level of the mountaintops. Aimee saw the sea first, surrounding the mountains, then she made herself look towards the strip of land that connected Kierell to the tundra.

The Empty Warriors' army had arrived. The people of Kierell were trapped.

'Kyelli's sparks,' Nathine swore.

Aimee just stared. She could barely see the grass on the isthmus, it was so covered by Empty Warriors. They were too far away for her to make out any details but somehow that made it worse. They were a swarm, and how could you fight a swarm? Against that backdrop the few dragons in the sky looked so small. If they dived down onto the army they'd be lost like flower petals, tumbling and sinking into a raging black river.

Aimee and Nathine were out of time.

'Aimee!' Nathine called.

'I know! Let's go.'

She pushed Jess into a dive. The rooftops of the city zoomed up towards her, blurry through her streaming eyes. With a snap of her wings Jess levelled out above the twin peaked roof of Nathine's family warehouse. Aimee turned her dragon north-east and they sped towards the university. Its red brick walls rose to a collection of peaked roofs, each one steeper than the last. They made the whole roof look like a miniature mountain range.

'There's Callant,' Nathine called.

A tree-lined path led from Hylwen Street to a brick archway, it too capped with a steep grey roof. It was the entrance to the university and Callant was sitting on a bench just outside. As their dragons spiralled down, Aimee could see the top of Callant's head. Amongst his thick brown hair there was a thinning patch at the crown, despite him only being in his mid-twenties.

Jess's wingtips brushed the trees as they landed and Aimee felt her amusement as if the leaves had tickled her. She wished then that she and Jess could be exploring the city for fun, getting to know each other better. Aimee loved knowing that Jess would protect her and fight for her, but she also wanted to know what Jess liked. She wanted to learn what smells she enjoyed or her favourite weather to fly in.

Maybe they'd get that chance once they'd found Kyelli and Aimee could hand saving the city over to her.

Callant had been hunched over but he looked up as they landed. Malgerus was tapping his talons on the flagstone path, revealing that Nathine was anxious.

'What are you doing just sitting here?' Nathine demanded.

Callant had one hand pressed to his chest, his face was as red as the brick building and his eyes were shiny with tears.

'Are you alright?' Aimee asked, swinging down from her saddle.

He gripped the arm of the bench and sucked a breath into his wide chest. 'I'm fine. I ran nearly all the way here and my lungs did not like that.' His voice was hoarse.

'Maybe if you trimmed your beard you'd be able to breathe properly,' Nathine said. 'In the meantime, why don't you lounge here while we go and get the letters.' Nathine looked through the archway. 'Where's the Kyelli here?'

Aimee knew by now that it was fear which made the mean version of Nathine come to the fore, but she felt bad because Callant wouldn't know that. She didn't want him to feel bullied.

'Nathine, give me your waterskin,' Aimee said, holding out her hand.

'Drink your own.'

'I poured mine into the statue.'

Nathine sighed, in an overly dramatic way, and fished out her waterskin. Aimee passed it to Callant. He took a few big gulps and smiled gratefully.

'When I was little, and I had a winter cough, my aunt used to brew me thyme tea,' Aimee said.

Callant shook his head. 'I've drank so much thyme tea that I swear, if I have any more I'll drown my spark. It's never made any difference to my cough though.'

Aimee didn't know what to say. That was the only helpful suggestion she had.

'Here.' Callant held out the waterskin.

'Nah,' Nathine shook her head, 'you can keep it.'

She'd dismounted and walked towards the archway leading into the university. 'Come on, let's get these letters.'

'I've—' Callant broke off to cough, wheezed for a moment then continued. 'I've got them.'

'Great, what are—' Aimee began but Nathine spoke over her.

'Are you sure what you've got is right?' Nathine stood, hands on hips. Malgerus was still tapping a talon on the flagstones.

'It's my lungs that don't work properly, not my eyes,' Callant replied.

Aimee couldn't help herself and she laughed. Callant and Nathine both turned to her, looking puzzled and annoyed respectively.

'Sorry, it's just that when Nathine thinks I'm being stupid she tells me that my brain's patchy as well as my skin,' Aimee said.

'Well right now it's being very patchy because we need to make sure we've got all these clues right and you'd be an idiot if we just trusted beardy here.' Nathine jabbed a finger in Callant's direction.

Callant stood up, towering over both girls. 'And why am I not trustworthy? If I hadn't helped, you'd still be turning that map all around and upside down trying to work out where to start.'

'Aimee would have figured it out. And besides, you're too slow.'

'I don't have the advantage of a dragon.'

'You don't have a chest that works either.'

The two were standing toe to toe, faces flushed as they glared at each other. Malgerus's ruff of feathers was sticking straight out and he'd half crouched so his head was level with Nathine's.

'You look like you're big and strong but you're useless. How will you fight the Empty Warriors?' Nathine snarled, her top lip curled.

'This is my way of fighting!' Callant boomed.

'Kyelli's sparks, stop it!' Aimee yelled, thrusting herself between them. 'Nathine, do you have to be mean to everyone who's not your friend?'

'I wasn't being mean, I was only pointing out that—'

'Shut up.'

Amazingly she did. After knowing how Nathine's father had abused her, Aimee understood her anger. She got why Nathine carried it around, why it infused her personality, and why, when she was scared, she lashed out at others. But they didn't have time for it right now.

She took Nathine's hand and pulled her away from Callant. Nathine didn't resist, though Malgerus continued to watch Callant, orange head cocked to one side.

'We need him, Nathine, because we can't solve this on our own,' Aimee said. 'I know you're scared and when you're scared it reminds you of being afraid of your father and that's—'

'He can't touch me any more.'

'I know, and would you shut up and let me give you some sympathy for once.'

To Aimee's astonishment, Nathine smiled ruefully. 'There you go, giving people orders again.'

'Not people, just you. Can we get back to finding Kyelli now?'

The smile slipped from Nathine's face and without it, or her anger, she looked so much younger than eighteen.

'My father had a beard like his,' she said quietly.

Aimee grabbed her and pulled her into a hug. Nathine was taller so Aimee's words were muffled by her shoulder.

'Callant isn't him.'

'I know.'

'You could get Malgerus to rip off Callant's beard with his talons,' Aimee joked.

'Now there's an idea.'

Nathine grinned as she stepped out of the hug and tightened her hair in its high ponytail. Aimee turned back to Callant.

'I'm sorry we—'

'No, I should be apologising. I shouldn't have lost my temper like that. It wasn't very councillor-like.' He looked to Nathine. 'Are we okay?'

'Yeah, Beardy, you can buy me a cake when this is all over to apologise. I like those meringue ones with the layers of raspberries and cream. So, what were the letters?'

'The ones on the mosaic were I and R,' Callant said.

'Mosaic?' Aimee asked.

'Yes, on the south wall of the courtyard there's a mosaic of painted wooden tiles. Kyelli has a wide bracelet on her left wrist. I can't believe I never noticed it before, but then that's what this map is showing, isn't it? Another layer to the city.'

Aimee longed to step through the archway and see this Kyelli but there was no time. She quickly wrote the two newest letters on the back of the map, waved the pencil at Nathine to prove she still had it, then stowed it back in her coat pocket.

'So, only one more then we'll have all the letters of the anagram,' Callant said. He seemed to have recovered from his coughing fit and he clapped his big hands together. 'Let's see the map.'

Aimee flipped it over and they all gathered round to look. The last tree symbol was at the north-west edge of Barter, right on the mountains.

'I know that one, it's above the tunnel,' Nathine said. 'There's a face carved into the rock.'

'Interesting. I never noticed that when we went

through,' Callant said.

'It's quite high up and it's only a face.'

'That can't be right then,' Aimee said. 'A face won't have a wrist and bracelet.'

'There are no other statues in the caravan compound. I know, I've been enough times,' Nathine said.

Aimee decided to trust her. She nodded and folded the map away.

'Will I meet you there?' Callant asked.

Aimee felt all awkward, but she didn't want Nathine to get in first and say something Callant might take as offensive, so she made herself speak.

'It's right on the other side of the city. It'll take you an hour to get there, even if you run, but I don't want you to hurt your chest again. And also, it might not be safe.'

'What do you mean?'

Aimee took a deep breath. She hadn't wanted to tell Callant that the army was here because she didn't want to see the fear on his face. Not when she couldn't do anything to take it away. But he'd find out soon. The whole city would.

'The Empty Warriors are here,' Aimee said quietly.

'Marhorn's sparks! Already? I should maybe...' his words trailed off and he looked towards the council chamber. Its green copper dome was visible above the vista of peaked roofs.

Aimee knew what he was thinking. 'You became a councillor because you wanted to help people?' Callant nodded. 'Well, we need your help to solve this anagram.

Myconn and the others can handle the council stuff.'

Callant chewed his bottom lip for a moment, making his beard waggle above his chest. Then, to Aimee's relief, he decided to keep helping them.

'I'll meet you somewhere halfway then. How about at the library?' Callant suggested. 'There's a side door off Dorwentden Street.'

'Sounds like a plan,' Aimee agreed.

She and Nathine mounted up and Callant stepped quickly back as their dragons began to flap.

'Hey!' he called up. 'Be careful.'

As they soared up into the sky Aimee took those two little words with her. Callant was a scholar and councillor, a proper city person, and he was concerned for her safety. Despite her weird face he didn't wish her ill. Aimee grinned and the wind hit her teeth, making them cold but she didn't care.

Then she focused on where they were going.

The handprint burn on her arm throbbed and she felt sick at the thought of all those Empty Warrior hands waiting outside the city. They wouldn't break though the tunnel, would they? They couldn't, not before she'd found Kyelli.

They passed over the council chamber and Aimee pulled on Jess's right horn, steering her towards the caravan compound. Beneath her own fears she could feel Jess's uncomplicated joy at being in the sky. She wished she could share it.

'Aimee!' Nathine called over the rushing air. 'Jara's probably at the tunnel.'

Aimee's heart sank into her stomach. She thought of how angry and fierce Jara had looked when she had forbidden her from leaving Anteill. She couldn't let Jara stop them now, not when they only had one clue left. But how could they get it without Jara seeing them?

'How high above the tunnel entrance is the carved face?' Aimee called over.

'Pretty high,' Nathine replied.

Aimee thought for a moment, picturing the peaks above the tunnel. The huge bulk of Norwen Peak was to the left of the tunnel and its lower flanks broke up into a series of smaller summits. Then the cliffs were sheer down to the caravan compound. They couldn't just fly up to the face, everyone in the compound would see them. They'd have to approach from above, but without their dragons being seen.

'Nathine, we'll need to land above the tunnel and climb down to the carving.' Aimee explained her plan.

'Jara will still see us if we fly over the caravan compound and into the peaks.'

'I know, so we'll need to fly into them from outside the Ring Mountains.'

Both Jess and Malgerus had slowed and now Nathine turned.

'You mean fly over the mountains somewhere else on the curve, fly along the outside and…no, Aimee.'

'Yes, we have to.'

'I'm not flying over that army.'

It was the only way to get above the tunnel without being seen. They'd have to fly above the Empty

Warriors and back into the Ring Mountains. The thought of thousands of those monsters right beneath her scared Aimee too. But the Empty Warriors weren't going to take Jess from her, Jara was.

'It's the only way to get the last clue, Nathine. Unless you'd rather go and wait with Callant.'

'That was low,' Nathine protested.

'You must be rubbing off on me.'

Aimee turned Jess to the north and they flew over Shine and out across the fields. Malgerus pulled ahead and Aimee could feel Jess bristling but she kept her flying steady. The two dragons skimmed over neat rows of pear trees, their wingbeats rustling the leaves. Aimee expected to see workers in the orchards and fields but there was no one. She wondered if that was odd?

The fields went on and on, stretching all the way to the bottom of the Ring Mountains. She supposed Kierell could easily feed itself, even with an army blocking the gate to the tundra. There was the small harbour in the eastern curve of the mountains which meant the fish market would always be stocked. They wouldn't get any reindeer meat from the tundra, but it was a luxury anyway.

So Kierell would be fed but trapped. What would happen to the city if no one could leave ever again? Aimee thought it would be like her, hiding in her aunt and uncle's loft, never going out and letting the world slip by, unexplored and unexperienced.

And that's only if the Empty Warriors didn't break through and kill everyone.

Passing over potato fields they reached the sheer grey cliffs of the Ring Mountains. Here the rock was streaked with smoky-white quartz that ran down it like trickles of ice. Over to the east Toig waterfall spilled down the cliffs, pouring from Lake Toig which was hidden between the peaks. Malgerus was racing ahead and Aimee urged Jess for more speed. Malgerus pumped his wings, a few huge beats, before Nathine pushed his horns and he shot into an upward dive. His bright orange scales flashed against the grey rock.

Refusing to be outdone, even though Nathine was proving to be a better flyer, Aimee copied. After a burst of speed Jess tucked her wings and dived upwards. Aimee felt like she'd left her stomach below and it was replaced with a ball of adrenaline. The cliffs shot past. The green fields fell away. Up above the sky rushed towards her. It was awesome and intoxicating. For a few moments everything else disappeared. It was just her, Jess and the sky.

They didn't make it as far up as Malgerus and Nathine before Jess's speed ran out and she had to start flapping again. Aimee didn't care. Her mind was full of Jess's joy and she sent back her own, sharing their love of the sky. As they reached the summits Aimee followed Nathine across a wide plateau of scree. Ahead was a narrow ravine. Malgerus was heading straight for it.

'Nathine! We won't fit.'

'We will!'

Aimee winced in anticipation as Malgerus sped into the dark between the walls of rock. Jess was going too fast for Aimee to change course without hurting her or crashing. They flew into the ravine behind Malgerus. Aimee shrieked and Nathine whooped. They fitted, but only just. Jess had a little room but Malgerus's wingtips brushed the rock.

Then they burst out over the sea. Grey-blue waves rolled into the cliffs, while spray danced in the wind, and Aimee smelled the salty tang. They swooped down towards the waves and Jess followed Malgerus along the outside curve of the mountains. Out here there was nothing to show that a city lay on the other side. The tundra was a green smudge on the horizon and the Griydak Sea stretched out to Aimee's right, seemingly going on forever. The Empty Warriors had Ternallo Island written on the bottom of their breastplates. Was it out there somewhere?

They followed the outside curve of Beargleall Ridge and Norwen Peak grew larger as they approached, its summit capped in snow even now, in the middle of summer. Then the isthmus appeared, and along with it, the army of Empty Warriors.

CHAPTER 13

## BOLTS AND WINGS

AIMEE FELT LIKE someone had sucked out all her breath. There were thousands of them. The Empty Warriors covered the isthmus that connected Kierell to the tundra. She couldn't see any green grass, only the black and grey of the army. Malgerus roared.

'Shh,' Aimee hushed him, feeling a bit panicky now they were getting close.

'They're going to see us anyway,' Nathine said. 'Mal and Jess are the only bright things out here.'

'Why are they all just standing there?' Aimee asked.

'I don't know, but it's creepy.'

The Empty Warriors were standing in rows, facing the Ring Mountains, all perfectly still. None had made campfires, or were sharpening weapons, or were gathered around chatting. They simply stood, waiting, like statues. Nathine was right, it was creepy.

Both girls had unconsciously slowed their dragons.

'We fought three of them and we were both injured. Sparks! The city doesn't stand a chance,' Nathine said.

'It will once we have Kyelli to help us,' Aimee replied.

'Do you think the Master of Sparks is down there?'

Aimee shuddered. 'I hope not, but where else would he be? This is his army.'

The shadowy figure of the Master of Sparks had been looming in her mind and now, looking down at his army, Aimee's spine prickled at the thought of him watching them. They needed Kyelli before they could face him.

Even flying slowly they were running out of sea and soon they'd be above the army. A few heads turned to look at them. She knew to expect it, but still their fiery eyes made Aimee shiver. Jess growled as she felt her Rider's unease. There were no shouts and no one pointed up at them. There was no noise at all from the rows and rows of warriors. It was so eerie.

'They all look the same!' Nathine exclaimed.

'I said that!' Aimee pointed out.

'Maybe you did, but look, they're like twins but thousands and thousands of them.'

Every Empty Warrior had the same symmetrical face, wide mouth and black hair. Their expressions were all utterly blank, though. And their eyes flickered with fire—no irises, no pupils, no whites, just orange flames. How could something that looked like a man, but didn't have a spark, be alive?

They all wore the same black boots, dark grey trousers and shirt too, and that's what made the army look so dark. Their breastplates were black as well and each one was engraved with the same silver tree. Aimee wasn't close enough, and no way did she want to be, to see the writing on their armour. She knew it was there though. Their purpose to destroy Kyelli's city was engraved on their chests.

Aimee didn't see any archers but still they kept above bow range as they flew over the eerily silent ranks of the army. In front of the gates that led into the tunnel there was a clear space in the rows of warriors. Here dozens of Empty Warriors were busy with several gigantic tree trunks. They were stripping the branches and fastening the trunks together. All around, the other Empty Warriors stood perfectly still, not even watching.

'Sparks! They've got half of the Ardnanlich Forest with them,' Nathine exclaimed.

'They're making a battering ram,' Aimee said, as her brain put together what she was seeing.

'They'll bash through the mountains with that, never mind the gate.'

Aimee looked at the gate, solid metal a foot thick and barred from the inside. It had been built in the days of Marhorn.

'It'll hold,' she told Nathine.

'Oh, you're an expert on siege warfare now? Do you think they dragged those trees all the way from the forest?'

'They must have,' Aimee replied.

It would have been a near impossible task, pulling those gigantic trees for miles across the bogs and tussocky grass of the tundra. The army didn't have any horses so the Empty Warriors must have dragged the trees themselves. And they had still made it to Kierell in two days. Aimee didn't think a human army could have travelled that quickly. Jess and Malgerus flew high above the half-constructed ram and towards the cliffs above the gate.

There was no warning yell, no shouted order, just silence from the army below. Then came the bolt that tore through Malgerus's wing.

He roared in agony, the sound bouncing off the cliffs. Nathine screamed too, sharing her dragon's pain. The bolt was barbed and lodged in the membrane of Malgerus's wing. They had been flying well out of bowshot range. No human would have had the strength to shoot a bolt that high.

'Nathine!' Aimee yelled.

Malgerus was flapping frantically but there was a rope attached to the end of the bolt and the Empty Warriors below were reeling him in. He twisted frantically, trying to grab the bolt in his teeth and pull it free but he couldn't reach it without tucking in his wing, and if he did that he'd fall from the sky.

'Mal, stop it!' Nathine cried as she struggled to stay in her saddle.

The Empty Warriors yanked the rope and Malgerus was pulled downwards. He was roaring and puffing small spurts of flame. Aimee didn't have a plan, she just acted. Reaching across her shoulder she slid free one scimitar and with her other hand she pushed Jess's horn. Jess dived. Aimee gripped the single spiralled horn so hard that it hurt. She squeezed Jess tight with her knees, every muscle in her legs clenched. Terror blasted through her like wind hitting her face. Malgerus was an orange blur at the edge of her vision.

A few feet above the Empty Warriors she pulled on Jess's horn. She felt her bum slip in the saddle and screamed as Jess levelled off. Another bolt flew up. Jess whipped her head to the side and it flew past her snout. The movement made them veer to the left and they almost missed the rope. Aimee had to stretch her right arm out as far as it would go, feeling the strain of muscles in her armpit. She used Jess's momentum for strength and her scimitar sliced clean through the rope that was pulling Malgerus down.

He flapped frantically upwards, his wing trailing the length of severed rope. His flying was erratic, his injured wing dripping blood down onto the army. Nathine was having trouble controlling him and Aimee could hear her swearing.

'Nathine, get into the peaks!' Aimee called.

She pulled Jess up from the army and steered her towards the safety of the mountains above the tunnel. She hoped Malgerus's instinct would be to follow.

This time she heard the clank. She yanked on Jess's left horn and her dragon banked that way, her wings becoming vertical. The bolt cut through the air right where they'd been, hovered for a moment as if it was looking for them, then began to tumble back down. Jess levelled off without Aimee telling her to and headed for the mountains again. Aimee glanced around and was relieved to see Malgerus following, right on Jess's tail.

The entire time the Empty Warriors hadn't made a single sound.

A few moments later the dark peaks enveloped them and they were safe. Nathine landed on a wide ledge facing the grey and white bulk of Norwen Peak. Malgerus skittered on the rock, his injured wing trailing. Aimee and Jess had barely landed before Nathine started yelling.

'You idiot! That was the worst of your stupid half-baked plans. Oh yeah, let's just fly over an army of monsters. I've always wanted to be target practice. Now my dragon's crippled!'

'Nathine, I—'

'No, don't. Keep your hugs to yourself.'

She jumped down from Malgerus and without her on his back he sank to the rock, belly on the ground. His orange scales were so vibrant against the grey rock. He was snorting rapidly, small puffs of smoke drifting away on the breeze. Aimee could feel Jess's sympathy and knew her dragon wanted to help.

Nathine stroked Malgerus's feathers then stepped towards his injured wing. The barbed bolt was still stuck through it. Dragons had few blood vessels in the membrane of their wings but there were still spots of red around the wound and on the rock.

'Shh, be still Mal,' Nathine said softly, reaching towards the bolt. But Malgerus was in her mind and he knew what she was going to do. Before Nathine's fingers reached the bolt he scrambled backwards, trailing his wing and growling.

'Blazing sparks, Mal!' Nathine yelled. 'I need to pull it out.'

Malgerus growled again, his orange lips curling back to show his long curved teeth. They'd only been bonded for a month but already Aimee could see Malgerus was like Nathine—he reacted to fear and pain with anger.

Nathine took a slow step towards him and Malgerus shuffled back.

'Damn it! I'm trying to help, Mal.'

Aimee knew she was but Nathine would be feeling Malgerus's hurt like it was her own and that was the problem. Nathine was a swirling mix of anger and pain, and added to his own pain, Malgerus wouldn't know how to deal with that.

Aimee jumped down from Jess. She wasn't sure yet how she could help and before she could do anything, Jess rushed forwards. Malgerus had backed himself up against the lichen-spotted crags at the back of the ledge. Jess tucked in her wings, making herself smaller, and crouched in front of him. Malgerus growled at her, but Jess gently nudged his snout with hers. He stopped growling. Jess rubbed her head against his and Aimee heard the rasp of their scales. Malgerus sank a little lower to the ground. Then Jess stretched out her long neck and took the bolt in her teeth.

'What's she doing?' Nathine cried, panicked.

Aimee grabbed her to stop her from getting in Jess's way.

'Let her help,' Aimee said softly.

Nathine was as rigid as a spear shaft, her round cheeks flushed red, but she stayed back. They watched as, with her teeth, Jess pulled the bolt up and through Malgerus's wing. A small spurt of blood came with it. Jess spat away the bolt and trailing length of rope. Then Jess licked the wound. Malgerus held still during her ministrations. When Jess was done the two dragons head-butted gently and Jess clicked back over to Aimee.

Released from Aimee's grip, Nathine ran at her dragon and flung her arms around his neck, pressing her face into his orange feathers. Jess stepped close to Aimee and gently nudged her. Aimee smiled and stroked the slippery scales of Jess's long neck.

'Good girl,' Aimee told her.

Jess and Malgerus had always been so wary of each other because of their Riders' shared animosity, that Aimee often forgot they'd been clutchmates before the girls had bonded them.

'Will he be alright?' Aimee asked her dragon.

The hole in Malgerus's wing membrane was as wide as her spread fingers. It wasn't bleeding much but he was still crouched with his belly pressed to the rock. Would he still be able to fly? They didn't have time to wait for it to heal. Aimee knew that if it had been Jess injured, then she'd want to do anything to keep her away from danger. But they had to keep going.

'Nathine, I'm sorry that Malgerus is hurt but we have to get the last clue,' Aimee said softly.

She saw Nathine's shoulders hunch and when she span around Nathine was wearing her angry face. A strand of long hair was stuck to her lips and she snatched it away.

'I'm not going.'

'But Nathine—'

'No, you little piece of dragon's dung, I'm done with this stupid mission of yours. I'm not risking Malgerus anymore. He was nearly shot from the sky!'

'But we're going back inside the city now. There are no Empty Warriors there.'

'No, just our leader who we've disobeyed and if she sees us, she'll kick us out of the Riders and kill our dragons!'

Malgerus raised his head to Nathine's shoulder and growled. His yellow eyes were fixed on Aimee. She heard Jess stretch out her wings behind her.

'We're so close though, Nathine. Only one more clue and we'll have solved the puzzle of where Kyelli's gone. We can bring her back. She'll be able to protect us against the Empty Warriors, and Jara.'

'I don't care!'

Malgerus's head inched forward and Aimee saw green from the side of her eye as Jess's head appeared beside her.

'You just want to run and hide behind Kyelli,' Nathine accused.

'No, that's not it. Nathine, she can help us, she can stop all this.'

'Is she just another older woman for you to fantasise about since you can't have Lyrria?'

The insult thumped Aimee in the chest, knocking

away any retort. It was all the worse because she'd lowered her guard—she wasn't prepared for insults from Nathine anymore. They were supposed to be friends now. She felt tears gathering. Tears because Nathine had been mean again, tears because she'd broken up with Lyrria, and tears because she was scared of the army outside. Talons clicked on the rock as Jess stalked forward. Behind Nathine, Malgerus rose up to his full height.

Aimee's skin felt tight with the tension in the air. A few minutes ago Jess and Malgerus had been clutchmates but now they were being ruled by their Riders' emotions and would snap at each other if Aimee and Nathine became any more hostile. She had to take Jess away before she got hurt. Even injured, Malgerus was so much bigger and stronger than Jess.

'Will you wait here while I go and get the last clue?' Aimee asked tentatively.

'No chance.' Nathine was stroking Malgerus's scales. 'Mal and I are going back to Anteill and we're going to stay there like we should have done. And if Jara comes back looking for you, I'll tell her exactly where you are.'

Aimee couldn't think of a retort for Nathine so she simply turned away.

'Come on, Jess.'

Jess kept head-butting her as she climbed into her saddle. She could sense her Rider's need for some comfort. Aimee ran a hand along her snout and pressed her forehead to the cool scales on Jess's neck. Her ruff of feathers flattened in pleasure.

'I know, I love you too, girl. It's just you and me again, but we can do this.'

She glanced back at Nathine but the other girl wasn't watching her. She had her face pressed against Malgerus and he'd wrapped his long neck around her. Strands of Nathine's wavy hair were caught on his spiralled horns. Aimee left them.

CHAPTER 14

CAUGHT

AIMEE AND JESS flew from the ledge and between the peaks. The mountains were deep here and it was a few minutes before Aimee saw Kierell again. The sun shone on its red brick buildings with their steep slate roofs, tall birch trees poking up between them. At the centre, the dome of the council chamber was easy to pick out. From the sky it all looked so peaceful. It was such a contrast to the terrifying army just on the other side of the mountains—two different worlds separated only by the peaks.

Jess landed on a small ledge high above the caravan compound. The ledge was narrow but ran back into the mountains and was overlooked on both sides by steep-sided cliffs. Aimee dismounted and led Jess back into the shadows where she wouldn't be seen by anyone below. There was a scree slope and beyond that a buttress of rock. Aimee led Jess behind the buttress, into the cold shadows.

'You have to stay here,' Aimee told her firmly, 'but

I'll be back really soon, I promise.'

Jess cocked her head and regarded Aimee with her unreadable yellow eyes. Inside her head Aimee felt a tug on their connection, like someone pulling her sleeve.

'I know, but we can't risk Jara, or another Rider, seeing you.'

Jess took a step forward.

'No,' Aimee told her, making her voice loud and strong. The command echoed back from the cliffs above them. Jess cowered and Aimee felt the rebuke in her mind. She ignored it because she really needed Jess to stay.

'I'll be very angry if you try to follow me,' Aimee said, keeping her voice stern. She sounded like her aunt had when she'd scolded Aimee for hiding and refusing to go out.

'Stay, stay, stay.'

She began walking backwards, repeating that one word in her mind and pushing it along her connection to Jess. Her dragon sank to the ground and furled her wings. Aimee turned away. A few feet from the cliff edge she dropped to her hands and knees and crawled to look over the lip. Even without Jess, someone might spot her.

Before the caravan of councillors had left, the compound had been chaos, but of the organised kind. Today it was just chaos. The city guards had built a semi-circular barricade across the area in front of the gate. Aimee could see they'd used merchant's boxes and crates, wagons and spare wheels. It was haphazard but jammed together tight. Guards stood along the city side of it, their multicoloured patchwork cloaks making them easy to spot.

Beyond the barricade the compound was full of shouting people. Aimee couldn't make out their words but she could see their confused faces. The council's decision to close the tunnel had become public knowledge and people weren't happy about it. Aimee wanted to go down and explain to them what she'd just seen on the other side of the mountains. She wanted to tell them the barricade wasn't to keep them in, it was to keep the monsters out.

The crowd surged like the sea but instead of waves rebuffed by the cliffs, they were people pushed back by the guards. Aimee could see Harmony perched on top of a wagon in the barricade, her golden scales beautiful in the sun. Aranati must be down in the crowd somewhere. Aimee scanned the rooftops and spotted Faradair on top of the blacksmith's forge.

Jara was here.

There were two other dragons, one pale lavender and the other deep teal, perched around the compound. The Riders were sensibly keeping their dragons away from the crowd. Aimee wasn't sure she'd be able to keep Jess under control if she was down there, being pressed on all sides by angry people and trying to calm them, all while keeping a lid on her own fear. She was having to keep a tight hold on Jess just to keep her behind the rock buttress.

Suddenly a man got passed the guards and scrambled up the barricade. The swell of voices from below grew louder. Aimee watched as he reached the top and began picking up boxes and flinging them off the barricade. Wooden crates smashed on the flagstones. Wine poured from one like blood. Reindeer leather gloves tumbled from another and were trampled underfoot. Three guards climbed up the barricade and dragged the man back down.

'…can't keep us in here!'

Aimee caught his words as he yelled at the guards. She was shocked. Last week the city had been full of hope and optimism for the future. The Guilds were preparing for a new life of opportunities across the tundra. The world had been opening up. Now everyone was trapped. Aimee could imagine the shouting man's anger spreading through the city, as infectious as fear.

She had to help them. So she pulled off her scimitars, leaving them lying on the rock, then lay on her belly and swivelled around so her feet were at the edge of the cliff. Then she slowly pushed herself backwards along the ground, her legs inching out over the edge. She reached the point where her waist was at the cliff edge and she folded herself in half, her feet coming down to touch the cliff face. The toes of her boots scrambled on the smooth rock. For a sickening moment Aimee thought she wouldn't find purchase.

Then her feet found a crack and she wedged them in. Slowly she lowered her upper body down till she was facing the cliff, her cheek pressed against the sun-warmed rock and her arms above her head, fingertips gripping the ledge. Pain flared in her wounded arm but she gritted her teeth against it.

All the fear of doing the climb came rushing back, only this time she was climbing down and that felt a hundred times harder. She wouldn't be able to see where she was putting her feet. For a long moment she stayed there, frozen, her arms too shaky to move. Fear pounded in her head like a heartbeat.

'Come on, I can do this. Just climb down, check the letters then climb back up. Easy.'

She began to edge down the cliff face. She'd feel her way slowly with each foot before moving. It grew a little easier after the first part as the rock became less sheer. Her fear was still palpable and talking to herself was a good distraction.

'Well, Callant was right, this one is definitely a clue only a Rider would get. Though Kyelli probably expected one of her girls to simply fly up, collect the letters and soar away again.'

She risked a glance down between her feet and the sight made her dizzy. The caravan compound was closer now but still far enough away that the fall would kill her. If she splatted on the flagstones, Jara would certainly see her. Though at least she'd be too dead to be in trouble.

The sounds of chaos were louder now and Aimee could hear some of what was being shouted.

'You're not listening, you dull-sparked idiot! My brother's out there working with the trappers. He needs to get back in but you've locked the bloody gate!'

Guilt and horror filled Aimee's mind. She hadn't

thought of the people who went out into the nearby tundra to work. The hunters and trappers, the woodsmen on the edge of the Ardnanlich Forest. Had the Empty Warrior army found them? Had those people tried to run home and been caught by those fiery hands?

Jess tugged at their connection and Aimee tried to squash her fear and guilt.

'Stay, girl.' She sent the command firmly.

She continued to climb down. It was slow going and she felt like she was making no progress. Her left foot found a really good hold and she lowered her body down. Her hands touched smoother rock, stone that had been worked. She'd reached the carving of Kyelli.

Kyelli's face was larger than Aimee was tall. She looked down and realised the really good hold her left foot had found was Kyelli's bottom lip. Aimee hoped she wouldn't mind. It was hard to get an idea of what the face looked like since she was pressed up against it. Aimee twisted her head around to look at Kyelli's left side. All she could see were outlines of carved rock. She shuffled further along Kyelli's lip.

Hair had been chiseled in the rock and just along from it were long lumps that looked like fingers. That was a relief. If she had a hand then surely she had a wrist and a bracelet. It was too hard to make out shapes so close to the rock so Aimee would have to feel for the letters. Making sure she had a good hold with her left hand she let go with her right.

She gasped in pain as the handprint burn on her arm stretched with her muscles. Breathing rapidly to try and control the waves of pain she ran her fingers along the rock. She felt Kyelli's hand, the smooth rock of her wrist and then an edge. Up over the edge Aimee felt around desperately. Her left arm was quivering.

Then Aimee's fingers found the letters. She traced them slowly, twice to make sure she got it right. An A and a G. She was about to pull her hand back when her fingers brushed the edge of an indent. Puzzled she stretched further, her shoulder muscles screaming. There was another letter, a T. She'd almost missed it. Her stomach did a horrible plunge at the thought that she'd nearly messed up this clue. She stretched even further but the rock after the T was smooth. No more letters.

She pulled her right hand back and grabbed the rock at the top of Kyelli's head. She gave her left arm a quick shake. The pain was lessening but she still wished she had time to slather on more of Aranati's salve. It had felt so cooling, but that would need to wait till later. Then she began to climb back up. At least it was easier this way, and she could see how far she had to go.

The shouting down in the compound grew louder, more panicked, but Aimee ignored it and focused on climbing. She had all the letters now. She just needed Callant to rearrange them and then she'd know where Kyelli had gone. The tails of Aimee's coat flapped out behind her as she reached and stretched for the best holds. The shouting below grew more frantic.

Aimee could see the lip of the ledge, she was nearly up. There was a crash below and more yelling. Aimee kept climbing.

'Keep back! You, no!'

The shout was loud enough that Aimee heard it. Something was going on down there. A dragon's roar split the air. Aimee stopped climbing. Her toes were wedged into a narrow crack and her arms were above her head, fingers wrapped around a jutting spur of rock. She twisted her neck and looked down.

The crowd had grown angry and swarmed the barricade, trying to dismantle it. Guards were attempting to shove them back. Faradair had landed on top of a wagon and he roared again. Aimee searched for figures in black, looking for the Riders. One guard had climbed on top of a tower of boxes and was pushing people back down with the butt of his spear. Aimee watched horrified as a man reached up and grabbed the guard's ankles. The guard yelled and dropped his spear. Then he snatched up a crossbow.

'No, don't,' Aimee whispered, helpless and horrified.

The climbing man yanked on the guard's ankles and he fell, toppling backwards off the barricade. The thud of his landing was lost in the noise but something flew up from his hands. A crossbow bolt.

Aimee only saw the flicker of movement as the arrow shot directly at her. She screamed and twisted to the side. The arrow bounced off the rock, just where her left hip had been. But she'd twisted too frantically and her hands slipped. She scrabbled at the rock with her fingernails, tearing them. The weight of her flapping coat pulled her away from the cliff.

'Please,' she whispered, then screamed. 'No!'

She fell, tumbling off the cliff like a detached shadow. Her mind went blank. Then a hundred thoughts raced through her brain at once. The lead one was Jess. But she'd so firmly told Jess to stay. She closed her eyes as the compound rushed towards her.

Then she was snatched from the sky.

'Jess!'

She felt talons around her thighs but when she looked up, the dragon holding her was sapphire blue. It took him only a few wingbeats to carry her up and over the lip of the ledge. He laid her gently on the rock and Aimee gasped with relief. Her heart was thundering in her ears and for a long moment she just lay there, letting the what-ifs race through her mind. Then she pushed herself up to sitting, wanting to see who'd saved her.

Pelathina stood with one hand on her dragon's neck. Aimee felt like her stomach had fallen back down the cliff. Pelathina had tracked her down. She was here to take her back to Jara. Aimee took a deep breath.

'I'm not going. You'll have to tie me up, and even then I'll get Jess to bite through the rope.'

Pelathina frowned, and it made her look like her big sister, Aranati. 'Sparkly sparks, why am I kidnapping you?'

'Because you saw me and Nathine leave the Heart. You know Jara has forbidden me from trying to find Kyelli. So Jara sent you to track us down and you're going to take us back for punishment.' Aimee looked at Pelathina's now bemused face. 'Aren't you?'

'So it's true?' Pelathina asked, her face lighting up. 'You've got a way to find Kyelli.'

'No. Maybe.' Aimee was confused by the direction this conversation had taken. 'Didn't Jara send you?'

Pelathina shook her head. 'Frennia heard you in the Heart, when you told Jara about the map. All the Riders are whispering about how we'll get to meet Kyelli if you find her.'

Aimee didn't know who Frennia was and she didn't like the thought of other Riders whispering about her. But Pelathina was smiling at her. She had the same graceful face as her older sister, with the same high cheekbones and pointed chin. Their expressions were opposites though. Aranati was always frowning but Pelathina seemed to smile, a lot. And when she did, cute dimples appeared in her light brown skin.

'Are you okay? Where's your dragon?' Pelathina asked.

Aimee jumped to her feet.

'Jess!'

A second later she appeared, half running, half flying. She barrelled into Aimee almost knocking her back on her bum. Her growl was rumbly, more like a purr. Aimee pressed her face into Jess's fluttering feathers and savoured the wave of love in her brain.

'I'm sorry, girl, I shouldn't have demanded that you stay. We'll do everything together from now on, I promise.'

Jess licked her face and Aimee winced as her rough tongue left a trail of saliva down her cheek.

'Thank you, I think.'

Pelathina laughed and smiled at her, her teeth small and white in her bronze face.

'So why you were climbing up a cliff? After we did the climb I told Aranati I was never going to climb another cliff, ever. It was terrifying! Why would you want to do that again?'

Aimee wanted suddenly to sit down with Pelathina and hear her story. But now was not the time.

'How did you see me?' she asked instead.

'I was heading down to the caravan compound from Anteill. I was looking for Jara, and Lwena said she'd be there.'

Mention of the compound made Aimee suddenly remember the fight. She rushed over to the edge and looked down, expecting to see a full-out battle now. Thankfully things had calmed down, sort of. The Riders and guards had control of the barricade again. Now all four dragons were perched on it. Aimee couldn't see their Riders but she imagined them in the crowd, trying to explain, trying to spread some calm. Aimee didn't envy them.

Shouts still drifted up but Aimee couldn't hear the words now. The crowd had swelled and she wondered how long before it turned ugly again. If the Empty Warriors broke through and all those people were still there, they'd be slaughtered by glowing swords and hands that burned.

'They don't understand,' Aimee said.

She'd been talking to Jess but Pelathina answered.

'How could they? Inside these mountains they've always been protected. They don't understand how lucky they are.' Aimee detected a note of sadness in Pelathina's voice. 'No one down there has ever seen a war, nor their parents or grandparents. For them, battles belong in history books.'

Aimee looked down at the scared people.

'We're running out of time. I have to find her.'

Pelathina ran a hand through her cropped black hair, making it all stick up. It ruined her graceful look but she didn't seem to care.

'So you really are on a quest to get Kyelli to come to our rescue?' Pelathina asked.

Aimee nodded but offered no more details, still not quite sure how much she could trust Pelathina.

'You keep your cards close to your chest, don't you?' Pelathina smiled at her, cute dimples appearing again. 'My da would have called that *gurt-sekrit*.'

Aimee was about to ask what that meant but didn't get a chance because Jess and Skydance's heads whipped around, staring back along the ledge between the peaks. Pelathina reached back for a blade and Aimee grabbed hers from the ground.

Malgerus emerged from the shadows, his orange scales making him look like a torch coming out of the darkness. Nathine was walking beside him.

'Alright, mushroom head, I haven't forgiven you, and your mission is stupid, but maybe you're right. I was—'

Nathine's words died when she spotted Pelathina.

She glared at the Rider and her round cheeks flushed. The three girls stared at each other in silence, until Pelathina broke it with a laugh.

'If you were a dragon, your ruff of feathers would be sticking straight out right now,' Pelathina said to Nathine.

Aimee didn't mean to but she laughed too. Nathine turned her glare on Aimee. Beside her Malgerus shuffled from foot to foot. Aimee suspected that she'd been about to get an apology from Nathine but guessed there was no way Nathine would go through with it in front of someone else. Aimee didn't mind. What mattered was that Nathine had come after her.

'I've got the last letters,' she told Nathine. 'There were three, A, G and T'

Nathine flashed a look at Pelathina.

'It's okay,' Aimee said. 'She won't tell Jara.'

'No, in fact I'd help you if I could but I'm due to report to Jara, then the council. Amazingly, only Myconn bothered to learn Helvetherin. The rest of the council can't speak a word of it so another translator will be handy.'

'You can speak Helvetherin?' Aimee asked.

'The Helvethi are in the city?' Nathine asked at the same time.

Pelathina laughed. 'You're like excitable little hatchlings.'

Nathine bristled at the endearment and looked ready to point out that Pelathina was only about two years older than them. Pelathina continued, though.

'Yes, we managed to get back here with four of the Helvethi leaders before those monsters blocked our way. They're at the council chamber. And yes, *bi yaryhk tain Helvetherin.*'

Her dark eyes seemed to sparkle and Aimee couldn't help feeling a tingle in her belly. And she couldn't stop herself from watching Pelathina's pretty face.

'We need to go too,' Aimee said, and was annoyed when her voice came out a bit squeaky.

'Good luck,' Pelathina said, then swung herself up onto Skydance. The bronze of her skin contrasted beautifully with the sapphire blue of Skydance's scales. Pelathina gave a mock salute then Skydance swept off the cliff. His body was narrower but longer than Jess's and he was very graceful in the air. Aimee turned to Nathine.

'Can Malgerus fly?' she asked tentatively, in case she provoked Nathine's anger.

Nathine mounted up. 'Even with a hole in his wing he'll still be faster than Jess.'

There was a whistling sound when Malgerus took off, as the air passed through his wound, but he still made it into the sky. Aimee and Jess followed. They stuck close to the mountains but on the city side this time. Aimee trusted the upheaval down in the caravan compound would hold Jara's attention as they made for the library.

CHAPTER 15

## PUZZLING IT OUT

Jess and Malgerus landed on Little Allgar Street just as a troop of city guards ran past. Their colourful patchwork cloaks flapped behind them and their chainmail jangled. Aimee heard shouting from the direction they were running. More trouble? More angry people? She didn't have time to think about it because Callant came running at them.

'Did you get it?' he asked excitedly, then doubled over, coughing.

Aimee and Nathine dismounted.

'Yes we got it. There were three letters this time,' Aimee told him. She didn't mention that it was only she who'd followed the last clue and that Nathine had nearly given up. Callant wouldn't have understood the pain Nathine had been sharing with Malgerus.

'Three?' Callant wheezed, straightening up.

Aimee nodded. 'A, G and T.'

'What does that give us now? Do you have the map there?' Callant stretched out his thick-fingered hand.

Aimee unfolded the map and passed it to him. She pulled out Nathine's pencil, waved it at her again to prove she hadn't lost it, then gave it to Callant. She watched him hesitate, pencil hovering over the back of the map where Aimee had scribbled the other letters.

'I'm sure Kyelli won't mind if you write on it,' Aimee said.

'I know a dozen scholars who'd disagree.' He lowered the pencil, lifted it, then lowered again.

'My spark's going to run out before he does anything. Give it here.' Nathine snatched both map and pencil. She spread out the paper on the wall of the library and added the last letters.

Callant looked horrified and Aimee laughed at his expression. It was as if Nathine had graffitied on the council chamber.

'Right, brainy, you're up. What do these mean?' Nathine stabbed the letters with the end of her pencil.

Callant took the map from her before she poked a hole in it, and stared at the letters. He chewed his bottom lip, beard waggling. He kept touching the letters in random orders, trying to make a word of them. Aimee silently willed him on.

As they waited Aimee heard a commotion in the western curve of Barter. She looked along the quiet street. One of the reasons she'd always hated going out in the city was because it was so busy. Kierell had grown in the three hundred years since Marhorn and Kyelli had founded it, and now its streets were crowded with people and businesses. No one ever moved away from

Kierell, and because of the encircling Ring Mountains, there wasn't a lot of space for the city to expand into. So it was crowded. However, the street Aimee was looking at was empty.

The carved wooden fronts of the shops were open but no one was queuing outside. Further along, an inn had tables outside under a spreading alder tree, but no one was sitting at them eating sausages or pastries for breakfast.

'Where is everyone?' Nathine asked, as if she'd been in Aimee's mind.

Aimee shrugged. 'I hope they haven't all gone to the caravan compound too.'

'There might be a riot.'

Aimee really hoped not but the mood at the compound had been ugly. People were confused and angry. The council had promised them a new future and now they were locking it away. But people couldn't see what waited for them outside the mountains. To them, the Empty Warriors were gone, destroyed by Marhorn and Kyelli, nothing but history and legend.

'Hurry up, Callant,' Nathine ordered. 'Do you have a brain in your skull or stale porridge.'

Callant shook his head. 'I can't make a place name from these letters.'

'But the map says to use it to find Kyelli. So the clues must point to where she's gone,' Aimee insisted.

'I can make two phrases,' Callant said. He was still tracing the letters over and over, and hadn't looked up from them.

'What are they?' Aimee asked eagerly. Behind her Jess fluttered her wings.

'Well, the first one is *palest grain*,' Callant said.

'Grain? Like the crop?' Nathine asked in disbelief. Malgerus snorted a small cloud of smoke which drifted up under the eaves of the building opposite. 'I doubt Kyelli's been hiding in a field of grain for one hundred years.'

'True. I'm sure our ploughs would have unearthed her by now.' Callant tried a joke but Nathine just glared at him.

'It can't be that, so what's the other phrase?' Aimee asked.

Callant looked at her. 'The only other thing I can make the letters spell is *Pagrin's Tale*.'

'Who's Pagrin?' Aimee asked.

'Well, that's the problem. I've never heard of him and if this is another clue then surely he'd be someone Kyelli expected us to know,' Callant said and Aimee heard the frustration in his voice. 'Do you recognise the name? Is it something to do with the Riders?'

Aimee shook her head 'I've never heard it, and isn't Pagrin a boy's name?'

'Great, so we've hit a dead end,' Nathine said, rolling her eyes.

'Unless there are more letters,' Callant suggested.

'There were only six trees inked on the map,' Aimee pointed out.

Callant went back to staring at the map. Nathine folded her arms and glared at everyone. Aimee wasn't going to give up. It had to mean something. She stared at the brick wall of the library and let her eyes become unfocused. In her mind she tried to travel back through the stories her uncle had told her. Had he ever mentioned a Pagrin? Aimee had loved her uncle's stories and she always paid attention, but she couldn't remember him ever telling her about someone called Pagrin.

Then her eyes snapped back into focus as she realised what she was looking at. The library.

'Could it be a book?' she asked.

'Could what be a book?' Nathine said, looking sceptical.

'Pagrin's Tale. It might be a story and if it is, it could be in a book,' Aimee explained.

'Yeah, but Kyelli's not in a book,' Nathine said, still doing her best to be unhelpful.

'Unlikely, we'd—'

'Don't you dare say "because she'd have fallen out from between the pages already" or some other terrible joke,' Nathine warned Callant.

'I was going to say it's unlikely to be a book because I've worked my way through every volume on Kierell's history that the library has,' Callant replied, with a hint of smugness.

'Well, maybe it's not a history book. It could be a steamy romance. I bet you haven't read all of those,' Nathine teased.

Callant's mouth fell open, making his beard crumple into his chest. 'The library of Kierell doesn't have those sorts of books.'

'Oh I bet it does, illustrated ones and everything. The scribes probably fight each other for the jobs copying out those,' Nathine continued.

Callant's face had gone as red as the brick wall and he spluttered as Nathine laughed. Aimee however was annoyed at them both. At Callant for being so easily wound up and at Nathine for being, well, Nathine. She stamped her foot and behind her Jess growled.

'There are monsters outside banging their way in!' she yelled. 'I don't care what kind of book it is, we have to find it, so can you two shut up. Please.'

Nathine gave her a knowing look. 'You're giving people orders again.'

Aimee ignored her. She turned to the blue door in the wall beside them. Like all doors in the city it was carved wood, and this one was decorated with a repeating pattern of letters and quills. Aimee took the handle, then stopped. She looked at Callant.

'Does…eh…is this the way into the library? I've never been before.'

Callant's grin appeared in his beard. 'Oh, you're going to like this. The library is beautiful and I love showing it to someone for the first time.'

'We're not looking for a tour. Monsters, remember?' Nathine said.

'Nathine, shut up,' Aimee said without turning around.

'What about Mal and Jess?'

Then Aimee did turn. Jess cocked her head and took a small step forward. Aimee couldn't leave her down in the street. If someone came around the corner and got a fright at seeing a dragon they might scream, then Jess would get angry or scared, and that wouldn't be good. Jess would have to go on the roof and Aimee would hope that Jara stayed at the tunnel.

'Up you go, girl,' Aimee said softly.

Jess flew up and disappeared over the eaves of the library roof. Aimee heard her talons click down on the flat top. Nathine looked at her intently for a moment then signalled for Malgerus to follow.

'Okay,' Aimee nodded to Callant and grinned. 'Let's go get this book.'

CHAPTER 16

HIDDEN

CALLANT LED THEM into the library, a building Aimee had never really thought much about before. To her, the only good thing about the library had been the small alley down the side that was a shortcut to Baker's Row. It had been a good escape route from her bullies.

They followed Callant along a short corridor then out into the library proper. Aimee gaped. Growing up she was used to the cramped space of her uncle's workshop and the loft above. She'd never been in a building so bright and open. The library was one large, cavernous space, open all the way to the rafters. Carved wooden pillars stood proudly along the walls, holding up the huge curved roof beams. Looking up at the ceiling was like being inside an upturned boat.

Aimee's feet were following Callant, but her eyes were roaming the room. Rows of shelves, twice as tall as she was, stretched from wall to wall. Everything was wooden—the herringbone floor, the walls, the rows of pillars, the rafters and the tall bookshelves. And all that wood was carved. Little goblins peered down at them from the edges of shelves, dragons flew up and around the pillars, and the wall panels had been carved with scenes from a city of towers that overlooked a sea of wooden waves.

It must have taken years and hundreds of skilled people to build the library. She wished her uncle could have seen it. He'd have loved it. He always said he could feel his spark shining brighter when he saw good craftsmanship. In the library he'd have been glowing.

High up, where the pillars met the rafters, there were long windows that let the summer light stream in. Because the light floated down from above, it seemed to fill the whole cavernous space. It didn't shine directly on the books, though, so they wouldn't fade in the sun. Aimee was impressed by how many books and scrolls were stacked neatly on the shelves. Her aunt and uncle had never been able to afford any books. All Gyron's stories were in his head.

Nathine ran one hand along the edges of the shelves. 'My father has seven books, and he displays them in his office like they make him a great man. I was never allowed to read them.'

Seven was impressive for one man to own but there must have been hundreds and hundreds on the shelves around them. And every one of them painstakingly copied out by scribes and decorated by the illustrators. These shelves were home to thousands of hours of skilled work. Callant was right, Aimee loved the library.

He led them straight down the middle, their boots clicking on the floorboards. As they neared the other end there were no more shelves on the right-hand side. Instead there were rows of big solid desks. Each one held a complete book in a stand and sheets of paper to make a new one. Scribes hunched over the desks, quills scratching. A few looked up as Callant, Aimee and Nathine passed, perhaps grateful for a quick break from their writing. The wall behind the scribes had a huge window and sunlight streamed in over their desks, bathing everyone in yellow.

There was a big desk sitting by itself at the far end, its wooden legs carved to look like piles of books. An older man with neat cropped grey hair and a trimmed beard looked up from his work as they approached. Aimee guessed he was Lokendan, the master librarian Callant had mentioned earlier.

'Ah, Councillor Callant. Have you come to return your overdue books perhaps?' the man asked. He carefully put down his quill beside a huge ledger.

'Not right now, but I will,' Callant replied.

'The late fines will still apply, even if you are a councillor,' the librarian said.

'Of course.' Callant waved away the talk of fines and changed topic. 'We're looking for a book.'

Lokendan finally noticed Aimee and Nathine, and his thin eyebrows shot up as he took in their black clothes and scimitars. Then his narrow eyes slid over Aimee's face and his lip curled, just a little, but enough for Aimee to know he didn't like her half-colourless face.

'Could you direct us to a book called Pagrin's Tale?' Callant continued.

Lokendan's eyes slid back to the big councillor and he shook his head. 'We have no books with that title.'

Aimee stared at him. He couldn't know the names of all these books, could he?

'It might be a very old one, from just after Kierell was founded, or maybe even from Kierellatta,' Callant pressed on.

The thin librarian drew himself up. 'I have been master librarian for thirteen years. I know every scroll, ledger, book and scrap of parchment that the city owns. There are no books from Kierellatta, as well you know, Callant. Marhorn and his daughter brought us here with nothing. Kierell was built from scratch, and everything in here has been written in the last three hundred years.'

Nathine leaned close and whispered in Aimee's ear. 'I bet his spark's as dull as an old coin dropped in a muddy puddle.'

Aimee wanted to laugh but there was a sinking feeling in her stomach. If Pagrin's Tale wasn't a book, then what was it? She wondered again why Kyelli had made the clues so hard. Callant and the librarian continued to disagree. Nathine took a step forward but Aimee grabbed her arm, pulling her back.

'I don't think you yelling at him is going to help,' she said.

'What about threatening him? I could get Malgerus to bite off his toes, one by one.'

'That's not…' Aimee's words abandoned her. Her chest squeezed shut, making her suddenly thumping heart feel like it was trying to break out.

Nyanna Page stood staring at her, mouth open. She was wearing a pale blue dress and her blonde hair was in a low ponytail that cascaded over one shoulder. Aimee's palms tingled and her traitorous eyes swept over Nyanna, trying to take in all of her beautifulness at once. She had forgotten how lovely she was. It was like the past four months hadn't happened and Aimee was back to being a shy girl standing in front of her first love.

'Freak, you're still alive?' Nyanna said.

Despite everything Aimee had learned on her journey to become a Rider, the insult tore through her, just as it always had. She noticed Nyanna was holding three books, clutching them to her chest like a shield protecting her from Aimee's freakishness.

'We all thought you'd died, same as old Gyron and Naura,' Nyanna said.

The casual way Nyanna spoke of the loss of her family reminded Aimee that she'd always been cruel. But she was also beautiful, with her perfect hair and slender fingers that Aimee had always fantasised about, imagining them entwined with her own.

'You just disappeared, but no one's missed you,' Nyanna continued. 'I'm amazed your stunted spark is still burning. You aren't coming back, are you? Because I've really enjoyed being able to walk through the streets without being blindsided by your patchy cow face.'

All the years of loving Nyanna and being bullied by her had slammed back down around Aimee like a cage. She was trapped by her emotions. Nothing had changed. She was still the freak with no home and no friends. A pretty girl would never fall in love with her. She felt tears in her eyes.

'Hey, what's going on?' Nathine nudged her.

'What?' Aimee blinked at Nathine.

'If I'd spoken to you like that, you'd be stamping your feet and yelling back at me. I thought you didn't let anyone call you a freak anymore.'

'But she is a freak, look at her,' Nyanna said, pretty pink lip curled in disgust.

Aimee looked back at her. Her beautiful blue eyes, the same shade as her dress, were narrowed as she watched them, a bit unsure now. She noticed Nathine's hand on Aimee's arm and visibly shuddered. Aimee found herself wanting to explain, again, that she wasn't infectious, just different.

'Sparks, Aimee.' Nathine punched her lightly on the arm.

Aimee couldn't pull her eyes away from Nyanna though. There was a piece of gold leaf, possibly from an illustration she'd been working on, stuck to the curve of her collar bone. Aimee wanted to reach out and gently brush it off. She felt Nathine's eyes on her.

'Oh, I get it,' Nathine said. 'She was the girl you liked before Lyrria, but I'm guessing she turned you down.'

Aimee felt her face flush. Nathine could be oddly

perceptive at times, usually the wrong time.

'Do you think I'd let someone like her touch me?' Nyanna looked affronted that Nathine would suggest any sort of link between her and Aimee.

Aimee still couldn't find any words, just like she never could in front of Nyanna. Nathine stepped forward and looked Nyanna up and down. Nyanna clutched her books tighter.

'What are you doing?' she asked, wary.

Nathine ignored her. 'You can do much better than her, Aimee. Put her in a fight and she'd crack like an empty dragon's egg.'

Aimee laughed, she couldn't help it. Once again Nathine's scathing remarks had cut through her messy emotions.

'What happened to you, freak?' Nyanna asked, looking angry now the girls were laughing at her. 'And I don't like your friend.'

'The feeling's mutual, bookworm,' Nathine said.

Aimee smiled at Nathine. Their bridge of friendship just got a handrail, with some twirly embellishments. She turned back to Nyanna.

'I became a Sky Rider, that's what happened to me,' Aimee said. 'I'm not dead in a gutter, my spark's brighter than ever and if you try to kick me down, I promise it'll be you who ends up on the ground this time.'

Aimee shifted her shoulders making the hilts of her scimitars waggle behind her head. Nyanna's eyes opened wide as she finally took in more of Aimee's appearance than just her face. She made no retort. It seemed she'd finally run out of insults.

'Nice one,' Nathine said.

'Thanks.' Aimee grinned. 'We'd better go, we've got the world to save.'

'Yeah, no time for colouring in pictures.'

Aimee laughed as she and Nathine turned away. Maybe it was Nathine rubbing off on her, but she couldn't help turning back to throw in one last word. Nyanna was still staring at them, her pretty face open with confusion.

'Do you still see Pairen?' Aimee asked. Nyanna nodded, unsure. 'Tell him from me that my dragon says hello.'

'Kyelli's sparks, you're on form with the retorts today,' Nathine said.

Aimee smiled, in her heart as well as on her face. For years she'd dreamed of standing up to her bullies, and today she'd done it. And it felt even better than she had imagined it would. It was like there were bubbles fizzing in her veins.

Then she saw Callant's face and the bubbles all popped. He'd turned away from the librarian's desk and was walking towards them, shaking his head.

'There's no record of a book called Pagrin's Tale,' he said.

'There has to be,' Aimee insisted. It had to be a book because otherwise she was all out of ideas.

'It didn't seem like the right answer to the clues,' Nathine said and her tone was actually gentle. 'I mean why would the map point to a book?'

Aimee didn't have an answer for Nathine. Frustration roiled inside her. From the corner of her eye she could see Nyanna still watching them. After acting all big and important she couldn't let Nyanna see her floundering so she walked away down one of the isles alongside the wooden shelves. The outer wall of the library was to her right, shelves of books and scrolls to her left. She wanted to pull the books down off their shelves and throw them to the floor. She wanted to tear through each one because she didn't believe the librarian, he had to be wrong.

Angry with herself, and Kyelli, she leaned back against one of the wooden pillars that supported the vaulted ceiling. Was there some Rider thing that she was missing because she wasn't good enough? She tilted her head back and stared up at the ceiling. Gyron would have liked it. The pillars supported graceful arches of timber and the bracing beams between them made a pattern of triangles. It was neat and perfect. Except, there was something tugging at Aimee's brain.

She stared hard at the beam above her, then back and forth along the length of the ceiling, checking. She pulled away from the pillar she'd been leaning against and compared it to the ones on either side. It was a different wood. Every other pillar and beam looked like they were made from oak, but this one was birch. It was a lighter colour.

'Palest grain,' Aimee whispered.

She sprinted back down the aisle, boots skidding on

the polished floor. Nathine and Callant were arguing again so she barged in the middle and grabbed Callant's shoulder. She shook him, though she could barely make the big man move.

'You said the letters also spelled out the words palest grain, right?'

'Yes, but—'

'I've found the palest grain. That's the clue,' Aimee interrupted him.

Callant chewed his bottom lip and Nathine looked at her sceptically. It was as if neither one wanted to have to tell her again that she was wrong.

'You can bring your scepticism with you, but I'll prove you wrong. Just come, please,' Aimee begged.

'We'd better go because she's got that determined look on her face,' Nathine told Callant. 'She won't give up till we follow her.'

Aimee ran back down the aisle. 'Here.' She slapped one hand on the pale pillar and pointed up at the beam with the other. 'It's a lighter colour of wood than all the others.'

'Maybe they ran out of the other wood when they were building,' Nathine suggested.

'I'll bet you my Rider's jewellery that I'm right,' Aimee said.

'What?' If possible, Nathine looked even more sceptical now.

'If I'm right about this being the clue, then you have to buy me mine. But if I'm wrong, I'll buy you yours.'

'Deal,' Nathine agreed. 'And I hope you've got a

secret stack of presses because I want jewels as sparkly as the councillors wear.'

Callant patted the wood beside Aimee's hand. 'What are you talking about? How is this pillar the clue?'

'It's the palest woodgrain in here so there's got to be something on it,' Aimee explained.

'I'm sorry, but I just can't picture Kyelli with a little knife, carving into a beam the place she'll go. She was a timeless immortal, not a rebellious teenager,' Callant said.

'There's something here, I know it,' Aimee replied, looking at the beam, not Callant.

'Really sparkly jewels,' Nathine said.

'But you're not going to check the whole beam, are you?' Callant asked, looking up at the rafters. Aimee nodded and grinned.

'How?'

'Easy, I'll climb it,' Aimee replied.

'You'll what?' Callant exclaimed.

'Oh, the bookish people are going to love us for this.' Nathine grinned mischievously.

It was just like climbing in the rafters of the loft above her uncle's workshop. Aimee shimmed up the pillar, hooked her heel on a skinny supporting beam and pulled herself up. A moment later Nathine swung up beside her. Below them Callant was chewing his lip and looking around anxiously. Aimee looked along the curving span of the pale beam. It rose in a graceful arc then met the ceiling in the centre of the cavernous library. From up here the triangles of supporting beams made the roof look like a spider's web.

'Oy! Get down from there, you'll damage something. Vandals!'

Aimee glanced down to see Lokendan rushing through the stacks towards them. His yells didn't bother her though. People had been yelling at her all her life. She spotted Nyanna's golden head below and had a sudden urge to show off, to run along the beam, high above the bookcases, just to prove that she could. They had to take their time though, examining the beam as they went.

'I'll go first,' Aimee said. Nathine looked like she might argue but then, thankfully, didn't.

Aimee began to crawl along the beam, eyes sweeping the wood as she went. Below her Lokendan continued to shout but Aimee ignored him. The beam was just wide enough for both her knees but she barely noticed the growing drop. The height of the library ceiling seemed nothing when compared to soaring above the city on Jess.

'In my father's warehouse there were high shelves built against two walls,' Nathine began speaking behind her. 'It was where all the rolled-up reindeer skins were stored, after they'd been dried and tanned. I used to climb up to the highest shelves and hide amongst the skins. It was really warm up there and my father could never find me.'

Aimee was surprised that Nathine was sharing this memory with her, and annoyed that she'd done it at a time when she couldn't give her a sympathetic hug.

'So that's why you're good at climbing,' Aimee said.

'That's why I'm better at it than you.'

The beam curved towards the ceiling and Aimee could see that soon her head would be bumping against it.

'Have you seen anything?' she asked Nathine.

'Nope. No secret messages or weird symbols.'

Aimee felt the panic rise up in her like she was going to be sick. If she was wrong what could she do? Give up? Hide back in the shadows of the armoury and wait for the Empty Warriors to destroy everything?

Then she spotted it. Right at the top, where the beam met both the ceiling and the curving beam coming from the opposite wall of the library. There was a trapdoor, hidden in the ceiling.

CHAPTER 17

# LOST AND FORGOTTEN

THE TRAPDOOR WAS cleverly concealed. It had been painted the same pale cream as the plasterwork ceiling, so its edges hardly showed. There wasn't a handle or a bolt, just a round indent the size of a fist that from the floor probably just looked like a shadow. Aimee looked down and it seemed that everyone in the library had gathered to look up at her.

'Did you know there's a door up here?' she called down, aiming her question at Lokendan.

'A door?' he called back.

'I'd take that as a no,' Nathine said behind her. She'd crawled right up next to Aimee and was peering over her shoulder at the ceiling. 'So are you going to open it, or do I get to push you off and do it myself?'

'I'm doing it,' Aimee said quickly. 'This was my discovery.' She reached up, then stopped. 'What if Kyelli's in here?'

'Don't be an idiot.' Nathine snorted a laugh. 'The most powerful woman who's ever lived isn't hiding in a secret attic. Even with thousands of sparks in her blood, she'd have starved to death by now.'

'Maybe immortals don't need to eat,' Aimee countered.

'Just open it, mushroom head.'

Aimee bunched her fist into the shallow indentation and pushed. Something clicked then the door gave. She pushed it upwards and a shower of dust cascaded down. She blinked and coughed, Nathine doing the same beside her. It was pitch black beyond the trapdoor.

'Well, come on, don't just sit there waiting for your spark to run out,' Nathine urged, practically climbing over Aimee in her excitement.

'So you admit I was right?' Aimee asked as she tentatively poked her head up through the hole.

'Yes, you were right.'

'That means you owe me some jewellery,' Aimee said.

'No need to be so smug. How big a diamond would you like? Size of your eyeball? Size of your head? I've got about fourteen presses so I'm only several thousand short.'

Aimee blocked out Nathine's nonsense and peered into the blackness around her. There was a hidden room up here but the light from the library was only making the shadows deeper.

'Hello?' she said softly, half-hoping, half-fearing for an answer. Nothing came.

She braced on the edge of the trapdoor and pushed herself fully into the room. Sitting on the edge with her legs dangling down she must have looked funny from below, just some legs sticking out from the ceiling.

'Sparks, it's dark in here,' Nathine said as she poked her head up.

Aimee moved away from the hole to give Nathine space to climb through. Her feet scuffed in the dust, sending tiny grey waterfalls down into the library.

'Do you have a—' Nathine began to ask but Aimee cut her off by pulling a dragon's breath orb from her coat pocket.

'Wow,' Nathine breathed as the orb lit up the room.

They were in an attic that stretched the entire length of the library. Even Aimee's dragon's breath orb couldn't illuminate it all and the ends remained in shadow. Hundreds and hundreds of books filled the attic in stacks and teetering piles, overflowing from crates and boxes. Aimee stood up and held the orb high. The flat roof was only a few hands' breadths above her head. She realised it was flat because it was where the dragons perched. Jess was just above her.

'Why would someone hide all these books?' Nathine asked, walking towards the nearest crate. Its wooden top was open and books spilled haphazardly from it. She ran a finger across the top of one, drawing a crescent moon in the thick dust.

'I don't think anyone's been up here for years, maybe since the library was built,' Aimee said.

'Really? What gives you that idea?' Nathine replied as she pulled a sticky clump of cobwebs from her ponytail.

'Why has Kyelli led us up here?' Aimee asked. She was learning that Nathine's sarcasm was a force of habit and as such didn't really need acknowledging.

'Kyelli didn't lead us up here, you did,' Nathine pointed out.

Aimee carefully stepped around a waist-high pile of books and headed further into the attic. She had to weave around the stacks and step over crates on the floor.

'Hey, come back with that light,' Nathine called and Aimee heard her following.

As the dragon's breath orb revealed more and more books, Aimee's shoulders slumped. Were they going to have to check every book up here looking for more clues? That would take weeks. The Empty Warriors might have broken into the tunnel already. Time felt like the dust on the floor, swirling away as Aimee walked through it.

She set the orb on top of a pile and picked up a book at random. It had a blue cover and gold lettering. She flipped it open. Something was weird. It didn't look right.

'Nathine, this book isn't made up of writing.'

'What are you on about, dusty brain? All books are written. That's what your scribbly girl and her friends down there do all day.'

Aimee stared at the pages in her hands. It definitely wasn't writing. Every word and letter was neat, precise and angular. They ran in tiny rows, hundreds of words per page and all uniform. It wasn't handwriting.

Something else had made these words. She shoved the book at Nathine and picked up another. It was the same. Neat letters, made of ink but not handwritten.

'Aimee, look.' Nathine dumped her open book on top of the one Aimee was holding. 'These drawings are of things like the cogs and pulleys inside the statue at the cliff.'

Aimee stared, amazed and confused by what she was looking at. She flipped a few pages and there were more drawings of machines, big and complicated ones, all with gears and levers.

'If we have books about the machines they have in the city states, why are they hidden up here?' Aimee asked, looking at Nathine.

The other girl just shrugged. 'No idea, but what's more strange, is who hid them up here.'

'You think Kyelli hid them?'

Nathine shrugged again. 'Who else?'

Aimee didn't like that implication. These were books that could help the city, and Kyelli wouldn't have kept knowledge from her people, would she? Kyelli had saved them. She and her father had helped the survivors build Kierell. Wouldn't they have wanted their new city to have every advantage? She stared at the hundreds of books around them. So many stories, tales, ideas and learnings, all forgotten. Why?

'Things shouldn't be hidden away, they should be out in the world,' Aimee said softly, thinking of the years she'd spent in self-imposed isolation.

She walked around a stack of books that touched the

ceiling, like a stalagmite grown too tall in a cave. There was a small wooden lectern behind the stack, and lying on it was a leather-bound notebook. It didn't look like the hidden books, it looked more like the ones down in the library. Aimee picked it up. The corners were dog-eared and some of the stitching had split, trailing threads. It was tied closed with a yellow ribbon.

Intrigued Aimee carried the notebook into the circle of dragon's breath light. There was something embossed on the cover. She brushed off the dust, accidentally wafting the cloud of it at Nathine.

'Hey, do you mind?' Nathine said, between coughs.

Aimee didn't mind, in fact she barely heard Nathine. There was a tree on the cover of the book and it was the same as the little trees on the map, the ones that marked the statues. The ones that Kyelli had drawn. Aimee's heart beat a tattoo against her ribs and she was sure she heard Jess moving on the roof above them. She plonked down on the floor, sitting cross-legged and not caring about the dust or spiders.

'Found a good book, have you?' Nathine asked, dripping sarcasm. 'Gotten bored of your quest and thought you'd like to curl up here and read stories instead. Would you like me to fetch you some tea and cake?'

Aimee untied the ribbon and opened the notebook. 'Yes,' she whispered. This book was a proper one that had been handwritten and the writing was spiky but neat, just like on the map.

This was Kyelli's notebook.

She almost dropped it. Her hands were shaking and she had to sit still for a moment and digest what she was seeing. She was holding a journal that Kyelli had poured her thoughts into. No one had been this close to their people's saviour in over a hundred years. She could read this and actually know Kyelli. She eagerly flicked through it and was delighted to find that every page was filled.

'No, wait, go back a page.'

Nathine's voice startled her. She hadn't even realised the other girl was crouching and looking over her shoulder. She reached around Aimee and flicked the pages back. A drawing of faces filled one whole page.

'Empty Warriors,' Nathine said.

'They're like the ones carved onto the stilts beneath the fielders' houses,' Aimee noticed.

She ran her fingers over their eyes. Some had flames for eyes, others little mountains, all the female faces had woodgrain eyes and a few, not as many, had cogs in their eyes.

She turned the page. The header said *Empty Warriors* and it had been underlined three times. With her heart pounding she scanned the first lines of writing.

*They brought so much death. Even now that they're gone and we're safe, I still have night terrors. I can see Kierellatta crumbling, fires tearing through our beautiful streets, buildings levelled, their stones crushing whole families. All those people we couldn't save. Father tells me the nightmares will fade and I hope he's right, because forever is a long time to live with these images in my head.*

Aimee flicked over the next few pages. The section on Empty Warriors continued.

'Kyelli's written about the Empty Warriors and I bet she's explained how she and her father defeated them,' Aimee said excitedly.

She'd found answers.

'Well, we didn't find Kyelli, but look at you being the hero again,' Nathine said.

'You helped too. That makes us both heroes.' Aimee held up the journal. 'But if this helps us save the city, Kyelli will be the real hero. She'll be our saviour again.'

Nathine looked at her and she had a funny expression on her face, as if she was chewing Aimee's words and didn't find the taste quite right. Still, Aimee jumped up tucked the journal inside her belt to keep it safe.

'Come on, we need to show this to Callant.'

Aimee couldn't wait to see the grin on Callant's face and the relief in his eyes when he realised they'd found information on how to defeat the Empty Warriors. She lowered herself down out of the trapdoor and onto the beam. Everyone in the library was still staring up and when they spotted her questions flew like a flock of starlings. Aimee ignored them all, scanning the crowd for Callant. At least his big beard made him easy to spot.

'Callant!' she yelled, excitement making her not care who saw or heard her. 'We did it!'

'What? Sparks, is Kyelli up there?'

Aimee laughed. 'No but I think we've found answers and I know you love a good book.'

He shoved through the crowd, making his way to the base of the pillar, eagerly waiting for her. Aimee hurried down, her boots slapping on the floorboards as she dropped the last few feet. She opened her mouth to give Callant the great news but Lokendan shoved the councillor aside, and grabbed Aimee's arm. He towered over her, more than a head taller.

'By Marhorn's thousands of sparks what gives a freak like you the right to come into *my* library and go climbing around on the ceiling with your dirty boots. This is a sacred place of knowledge. It's not for the likes of you.'

Buoyant from her discovery, and standing up to Nyanna earlier, Aimee let her words fly at Lokenden before she had a chance to think about them.

'The likes of me? I'm the girl who saved the entire council. I'm the Sky Rider who, with Kyelli's help, is going to save the whole city.'

Nathine dropped down beside Aimee in a crouch then stood up slowly and treated Lokendan to one of her best scathing looks.

'Nice one, Aimee, though if I was you, I'd let one Empty Warrior through and Lokendan can stare into his flaming eyes as he touches the books in here and whoosh!' She waved her hands in front of the librarian face making him flinch. 'The whole library will be incinerated.'

Lokendan looked horrified and he turned spluttering to Callant. 'It's true then? These rumours flying all over the city about the Empty Warriors having returned, or followed us here from Kierellatta?'

Frightened whispers fluttered through the gathered crowd. Callant nodded, confirming the rumours.

'Yes, there's an army of them beyond the tunnel, so leave Aimee alone and let her do her job,' Callant said, turning from the master librarian.

Aimee heard the murmurs in the crowd, some refusing to believe it was true, others panicking.

'So,' Callant asked, 'how are you going to save the city?'

'I'm not going to save it, Kyelli is.' Aimee untucked the journal from her belt and passed it to him.

He began flicking through it and the moment he realised who the author was he too almost dropped it. He stared in awe at Aimee.

'This is...I mean she wrote...'

'I know.' Aimee smiled. 'And I'm sure she'll have written in there how she defeated the Empty Warriors last time. Then we can do the same again and we'll be safe.'

'Alright, we need to study this properly and carefully,' Callant said, his thick fingers trembling. 'Let's go back to my office and as soon as we find something, we'll take it to the council.'

Aimee thought of trying to explain to Councillor Myconn that she'd disobeyed his sister, again, but it was okay because she'd found a way to help them. She doubted she'd get to that second part. Even in her imagination his hard green eyes bored into her.

'Will you come with me to the council?' Aimee asked, looking up at Callant.

He was flicking through the journal. 'What? Oh yeah, of course.' He looked up and his grin split his beard. 'Right, come on. I'll pop the kettle on the stove in my office. I'm going to need some tea to calm my nerves before I can study this properly. Kyelli wrote it!'

'I know.' Aimee laughed. 'And we can leave the tea-making to Nathine. I hear she brews a lovely cup.'

Nathine scowled at her but it wasn't a real scowl, Aimee could tell because her blue eyes sparkled with excitement.

'Still annoyed I made you come on this mission?' Aimee asked as they exited via the library's large double doors.

'You're being smug again. It's not very Rider-like.'

They'd just stepped outside and the doors were swinging closed when Aimee heard Lokendan shouting after them.

'Good riddance. And you still owe twelve presses in late fines, Councillor Callant!'

Aimee turned to joke with the councillor but her eyes were caught by the crowd in Quorelle Square. Then she noticed the angry shouting. It wasn't a crowd, it was a mob.

CHAPTER 18

THWARTED

Aimee, Nathine and Callant stood on the top step of the steps leading down from the library doors to Quorelle Square.

'By Marhorn's thousands of sparks,' Callant cursed.

'Who are they?' Aimee asked.

'There goes that cup of tea,' Nathine said.

All three had spoken at once and no one answered Aimee's question. As they watched, more people trickled in from the side streets around Quorelle Square. They gathered in ever-growing groups and Aimee could feel their confusion solidifying in the air. People looked around as if searching for someone with answers. Friends called to each other, asking if they knew what the deal was. Beneath it all, Aimee could feel the undercurrent of fear.

She ran halfway down the library steps and looked up at the roof. Jess stared back down at her. She was shifting from side to side, her wingtips fluttering, and her ruff of feathers was up framing her long head.

'Stay!' Aimee yelled, and threw the command along their connection. 'Please, please, please,' she added in a whisper. She couldn't have Jess swooping down and landing in a crowd. She'd feel threatened and lash out. Aimee could feel Jess's desire to get away from all the tense emotions, but to her great relief Jess settled back down on the roof. She curled up, long tail hanging down against the tiles, looking miserable.

'Sorry, girl,' Aimee whispered, then she ran back up the steps to Nathine and Callant. Nathine had her eyes closed and Aimee guessed she was telling Malgerus to stay.

Three boys Aimee's age appeared from the alley that led to Baker's Row. One of them ran up the library steps to look across the crowd.

'There's Master Ignorkic, by the scribes' hall,' he called to his companions, then skipped back down the stairs three at a time, and the boys began working their way through the crowd.

'They were wearing the badges of the Carpenters Guild,' Aimee said. Her uncle had kept his in a beautiful beechwood box with roses carved on the lid.

'Yeah, lots of them are but also, that big group at the front, they're from the Stonemasons,' Nathine pointed out.

'What are they all doing here?' Callant asked.

One group of stonemasons had pulled out sheets of paper and were waving them at the council chamber. This rippled through the crowd, and it soon seemed like everyone held paper, the sheets fluttering and rustling as they were held aloft in bunched fists.

Aimee caught snatches of the stonemasons' words.

'…already forked out three hundreds presses…'

'…took on two additional apprentices and now who's going to pay for them…'

'…you promised!'

'…contract isn't worth a damn. I'll let my spark run out before I trust another councillor…'

'Oh, sparks,' Callant breathed beside her. 'The Stonemasons and Carpenters Guilds were given contracts for building a road to Lorsoke. They'll have invested thousands of presses in this project.'

'But now they can't go out to build a road, no one can,' Aimee said.

Callant's beard brushed his chest as he shook his head. 'And now they're worried for their livelihood. That, and feeling betrayed by their council.'

Aimee felt a stab of guilt. She'd convinced the councillors to turn back. She'd stalled the peace talks with the Helvethi. She looked at a group of apprentices, boys and girls a handful of years younger than she was, and they looked so vulnerable. Young faces screwed up fiercely as they followed their masters' protests, but against an Empty Warrior, they'd be helpless. She had to find a way to make the tundra safe for them.

'We need to read Kyelli's journal,' Aimee said. 'If we can't get to your office, Callant, then we'll go somewhere else quiet.'

'Oh I'm sure we can get through this crowd. Nathine's scowl can carve us a path and we'll follow in her wake,' Callant said.

Nathine opened her mouth to retort but Aimee spoke over her. 'Don't start, Nathine.'

Aimee's eye was drawn by movement in the crowd. Three people broke away from the front, two men and a woman. They stomped up the steps to the council chamber, waving their useless contracts. Two guards in their multicoloured cloaks stepped in front of them, barring their way. More guards stood stoically behind them. The council chamber doors were firmly closed. No one was getting in to yell at the councillors.

The guards tried to urge the three people back down to the square but a moment later one of the men lay sprawled on the steps. Aimee hadn't seen what happened. Did he fall or did one of the guards shove him? A hush fell over the crowd, lasting a few heartbeats, then the shouting erupted. Aimee watched, dreading any violence.

'What do we do? How do we help?' she asked, looking at Callant, but the big man was staring at his council chamber and shaking his head.

'We get out of here before this turns ugly, that's what we do,' Nathine said.

'We can't,' Aimee argued. 'These are people of Kierell, we're meant to protect them.'

'Not from getting angry and shouting. We can't protect them from fighting with each other.'

His two companions had helped the fallen man back to his feet. They stood huddled together on the bottom step staring up at their council chamber, confused as to why they were suddenly barred from it. More city guards had appeared and their numbers barricaded the steps.

Down in Quorelle Square people were still appearing from side streets and the cafes around the square had emptied. There had to be more than just the Carpenter and Stonemasons Guilds here now. Aimee wondered, if her uncle had still been alive, would he be here shouting protests. She couldn't picture gentle Gyron amongst these angry faces.

A group of girls had climbed up the statue of Kyelli and Marhorn to see over the crowd, and Aimee wanted to tell them to get down. That was her statue of Kyelli and she selfishly didn't want other girls climbing all over it.

The currents of fear and anger in the crowd were growing stronger. Aimee could feel them tugging at her. A man with the Stonemasons Guild badge embroidered on the back of his long coat elbowed his way to the front of the crowd. People quietened as he began calling for the Uneven Council to get out here and explain what was going on. His words sent angry mutterings of agreement through the crowd.

Aimee grabbed Callant's left arm, the one with his councillor band tattooed around his wrist, visible because he had his sleeves rolled up.

'Callant, you have to go back into the library and stay there. If anyone in this crowd realises you're a councillor they'll be mad at you,' Aimee said.

'What she means is, they'll beat the spark out of

you,' Nathine added.

'It's not gotten that bad,' Aimee cautioned.

'It might, though.'

Callant looked down at them, chewing his bottom lip. 'I don't think—'

'Sparks!'

Aimee span around at Nathine's curse, expecting to see people advancing up the stairs to yell at Callant, and probably them too. It was worse. A blood-red dragon swooped from the sky and landed on the library roof. Jara was here and there was no way she hadn't spotted Aimee—she'd just landed beside Jess and Malgerus. Aimee's palms prickled with panic but this time she couldn't run and hide.

Jara slid carefully down the roof tiles, lowered herself off the gutter and dropped to the top of the steps. Aimee was vaguely aware other Riders had appeared too but Jara completely filled her vision. Her blonde hair was tied back and her ponytail swung angrily as she strode over.

'Aimee Wood, I distinctly remember forbidding you from leaving Anteill, so what the blazing sparks are you doing here?' Jara demanded.

'I found—' Aimee began but Jara continued, cutting her off.

'You are proving that the only thing you're good at is disobeying orders.'

'I didn't mean—'

'The Riders work together, and that means everyone has to do as they're told. I warned you, that if you disobeyed me again I would take Jess and—'

'Jara, if I may interrupt for a moment.'

'No, Callant, you may not,' Jara snapped back, not taking her hard green eyes from Aimee.

In the square below the crowd had begun to yell and Jara had to raise her voice further.

'I've got one mob here, a riot at the tunnel and this unrest will spread. Councillor Bylettie was attacked by a gang of apprentices from the Logger's Guild. They threw stones at her. People are angry at the council, they're furious with my brother and they're pissed off with me too. We promised them a new future, with change and progress but now I'm forced to lock them inside the mountains and threaten anyone who tries to get out. And I've got four Helevthi leaders thinking that I've betrayed them because we didn't bother to show up at Lorsoke.'

'But the Empty Warriors—' Aimee tried again.

'And every time I turn around there's your freaky little face, undoing ten years of work!'

There were pink spots on Jara's sharp cheekbones and she seemed to tower over Aimee, high as a mountain peak. Aimee cowered. She heard a rustle of wings and glanced up at the library roof. Faradair was pinning Jess to the roof with his powerful forelegs, his long snout inches from Jess's neck. Jess lay submissive, trying to show her belly. Aimee could feel her fear washing into her mind.

Tears flooded Aimee's eyes. 'Jara, please don't hurt her.'

Even over the crowd Aimee heard the steely ring as Jara slid one scimitar free. Nathine and Callant instinctively stepped back, but Aimee froze. Jara's eyes were hard as emeralds as she pressed the tip of her blade to Aimee's chest.

Aimee felt like her thudding heart was going to burst right out and impale itself on Jara's scimitar.

'Please, I found…' but Aimee couldn't get the words out past the choking fear squeezing her throat.

Then a hand appeared on Jara's arm as another Rider stepped close and a soft voice said, 'Calm, Jara, she's trying to help.'

It was Dyrenna. There was a moment that went on forever and then finally Jara lowered her blade. Aimee's eyes flicked up to the roof. Faradair released Jess and Aimee felt like she'd drunk a barrelful of relief. She wanted to hug Dyrenna. Taking strength from having the older Rider on her side, Aimee grabbed her chance.

'I know I disobeyed you but I followed the map, the one that Kyelli left us. I persuaded Nathine and Councillor Callant to help me but it was my idea so don't punish them. Kyelli left clues all across the city, hidden in plain sight. And it worked because, well we didn't find Kyelli, but we found a journal she's written.'

Aimee took the journal from Callant and began flicking through it, searching for the pages about Empty Warriors. Before she got to them, Jara snatched it from her hands.

'This! You disobeyed me for some book? I've got a city hovering on the brink of chaos, and an army of monsters trying to break in, and you think an old book's going to save us?' Jara snarled.

'I think Kyelli's left us notes on how to defeat them. There are pages—'

'Kyelli's gone. She left the city, left us and we're on our own,' Jara interrupted again.

'Jara, maybe we should listen to Aimee,' Dyrenna said in the calm way she had. 'There's so much we don't know about our past, and there are truths buried in the old stories. We thought the Empty Warriors were gone but we were wrong. We need to know more.'

It was a long speech for Dyrenna and Aimee was very grateful for it. It did nothing to change Jara's mind, though. In fact, she thought she saw a look of fear sweep over Jara's face, just for a second.

'The past is gone and is of no use to us right now. This is about Kierell's future and at this rate, our city isn't going to have one.'

Jara shoved Kyelli's journal into her inside coat pocket and began to turn away.

'No!' Aimee called, blinking tears of desperation from her eyes. 'We need to read it. Kyelli's the only one who can save us.'

'No, my Sky Riders are going to save us and since you're so desperate to help, you can join Pelathina's mission,' Jara said, pointing with her chin.

Pelathina was hurrying along the top of the library steps. Aimee felt a jolt in her stomach as she saw the bronze-skinned Rider, her short dark hair becoming tousled as she pulled off her hat and goggles.

'Jara, no, you can't send Aimee out there,' Dyrenna said, grabbing Jara's arm and pulling her close. Her words were low but Aimee could still hear them. 'She's in no way prepared for that.'

When Aimee was eight she'd snuck downstairs one night to her aunt's tiny kitchen and eaten a whole jar of Naura's raspberry jam. The neighbourhood children had beaten her earlier and she wanted something sweet to make herself feel better. But it made her sick and she'd thrown the whole lot back up. She felt that same horrible sickly feeling now as Dyrenna and Jara stared defiantly at each other. What was Pelathina's mission and why did it make Dyrenna look so afraid?

'She wants to be the big hero. All I'm doing is giving her the chance,' Jara said. She pulled her arm from Dyrenna's grip and turned back to Aimee. 'I'm ordering you to join the party of Riders heading over the mountains and into the army. While you're out there you could try doing something useful, like killing as many Empty Warriors as you can.'

Aimee rocked back on her heels as if Jara had punched her. Fight the Empty Warriors? The burned handprint on her arm throbbed in time to her racing heartbeat. Fighting three of them had nearly killed her. There were thousands outside the gate. Simply flying over them had nearly cost Nathine her life and her dragon. A handful of Riders against that many was a suicide mission.

Pelathina reached them and Jara instantly announced that Aimee was joining her mission.

'Jara, I can speak four languages and what you just said doesn't make sense in any of them. No offence, Aimee, but we need Riders with experience and dragons that are mature enough to breath fire. Aimee's only been a proper Rider for a few weeks.'

'She's right,' Dyrenna added. 'I'll go instead.'

'No,' Jara replied fiercely, the pink spots on her cheeks glowing. 'I need you here with me.'

Aimee caught a glimpse of the crying woman in Jara's eyes, the one who leaned on Dyrenna for support. Jara would never let Dyrenna take her place.

'Jara, you said volunteers only for this mission, and Aimee's not put her hand up,' Pelathina said.

'Damn it, Pelathina! I've had enough of people not doing what I say today. Aimee is going with you, or she's no longer a Rider, and Faradair will rip out Jess's throat.'

'No!' Aimee cried. 'I'll go!'

'Jara—' Pelathina tried again but Jara rounded on her, face hard with anger, mouth a thin slit, and stared Pelathina down. 'Okay,' Pelathina held up both hands as if trying to calm a dragon, 'but I don't think this is right.'

'Nothing about today is right,' Jara threw back at her.

'What about Nathine?' Aimee asked tentatively, worried her actions were going to put Nathine in danger again. 'She can't fight the Empty Warriors, Malgerus is injured.'

'She can help us get this crowd calmed down and

dispersed.' Jara waved at Quorelle Square. Anger still rippled through the square like waves, rebounding off the council chamber and through them all. More city guards had appeared, their colourful cloaks making them easy to spot.

Callant had been watching the crowd and suddenly he doubled over with one of his coughing fits. Aimee placed a hand on his shoulder, feeling useless because she couldn't help him. Callant sucked in a huge breath, but then began coughing again. Using the noise as cover Aimee turned quickly to Nathine.

'You have to steal the journal from Jara.'

'What?' Nathine looked horrified at the suggestion.

'Please.'

'How?'

Aimee smiled. 'You're always saying my plans are rubbish, so come up with your own this time.'

Nathine tightened her hair in its high ponytail then shoved her hands in her coat pockets. 'Fine.'

'You'll do it?'

'Yes, but then what do I do?'

'I'll come back, and we'll work out the next step together.'

Aimee could see the fear in Nathine's face. 'Aimee how will you come back? That army...' her words trailed off.

'I'll find a way, because Jara's clutching at empty dragon eggs. She doesn't know how to fight the Empty Warriors. No one does. That's why only Kyelli can save us.'

'Aimee, go.' Jara's order cut sharply into her thoughts. 'I'm sick of seeing your face.'

Without looking at her, Aimee gave Nathine's hand a quick squeeze. Then she hurried past Jara, head down like she used to when walking the streets.

CHAPTER 19

## FEAR AND RIBBONS

Aimee caught up with Pelathina at the corner of the library. The other Rider had stopped and was looking out over the crowd, a sad expression on her face.

'I want to tell them to let go of their anger because it won't help,' she said softly.

Aimee was worried about the crowd but she could also sympathise with its people. 'They can't choose not to feel it,' Aimee said. 'They're scared and they don't understand.'

Pelathina smiled like Aimee had said something amusing and Aimee looked back at her, confused.

'What?' Aimee didn't understand how Pelathina could be smiling right now.

'I carried my anger all the way here from Marlidesh like it was the most important thing I had,' Pelathina replied, her eyes going all distant as she looked back at something Aimee couldn't see. 'But if I'd kept it, I wouldn't be a Rider.'

Her reply made so many questions bubble up in

Aimee, about Pelathina, where she was from, why she and her sister had made the climb, but she knew now wasn't the time.

'Will you tell me your story? Once all of this is over,' she asked, a little tentatively because this was only the second time she'd spoken to Pelathina.

'Sure.' Pelathina's smile widened, cute dimples appearing on her cheeks. Then she jumped and grabbed the lip of the library's overhanging roof and pulled herself up.

As Aimee hoisted herself up beside Pelathina she felt the sickening fear of their mission again. 'I don't understand Jara. We can't kill enough Empty Warriors to stop their army.'

'That's not what Jara's ordered us to do.' Pelathina reached the flat top on the roof and her dragon, Skydance, gently head-butted her. She stroked his sapphire-blue ruff of feathers.

Jess practically scrambled down the roof tiles to meet Aimee. With her boots slipping on the slate Aimee hurried up, feeling her dragon's eagerness to get away from the noise, the shouting and the whirlpool of emotions down in the square. Pelathina was already in her saddle, and Aimee quickly mounted up too.

She really didn't want to go. Dread at facing the Empty Warriors was sucking at her, pulling her down. She looked up at the sky, and couldn't make herself fly up into it. Jess sensed her unease and misinterpreted it. She swivelled her long neck around and snapped at Skydance. Shocked, Aimee tensed, waiting for Skydance to react like Malgerus would have done. But he didn't. Pelathina had put a hand on the top of his head and he stayed motionless and calm. Aimee was amazed at the level of control Pelathina had over him.

'How did you stop him from biting Jess?' she asked.

Pelathina smiled that beguiling smile of hers. 'Happiness.'

Aimee didn't understand but there was a calmness and an ease about Pelathina that gently tugged at her. She didn't know what that meant so she went back to asking about the mission.

'So what does Jara want us to do?'

'We're to find the Master of Sparks, and assassinate him.'

Aimee was confused. 'I thought the council want to try negotiating with him.'

'The council do, and as far as they're concerned we're off to find him. But if he is out there with his army, Jara wants us to kill him, rather than bringing him back to the city.'

'We're going against the council's orders?'

'Haven't you spent all morning disobeying Jara's orders?' Pelathina pointed out but not in a mean way, in fact she looked amused.

Aimee wasn't sure what to reply. Somehow Jara going against the council felt different, wrong, though she couldn't put her finger on why. Pelathina was still smiling and her face was open with happiness. In direct contrast to her sister, she seemed to always be smiling. Why was she so cheerful? Pelathina sat with confidence in her saddle, not overbearing confidence like Jara had, more a quiet understanding of who she was and being content with that. She was small, not much taller than Aimee, and her cropped black hair didn't make her look boyish, instead it somehow made her look more feminine. Maybe because Aimee could see the back of her neck, and her eyes followed the soft curve of it down into her coat collar, eyes drifting further down, searching for glimpses of more curves.

What was she doing? Aimee jerked her eyes down to Skydance, horrified at the thought that Pelathina might have seen her ogling. Then she noticed something, and blurted out a question over her embarrassment.

'Why do you have ribbons tied to your saddle?'

Pelathina plucked at a few of the colourful silk strands tied at various points to her saddle, running them through her delicate fingers. The colours looked even brighter against her bronze skin. 'Ha, you should have seen Jara's face when I added these. She was not impressed, but she let me keep them in the end. I know black is the Riders' thing,' and she gestured to her own clothes, then Aimee's, 'but I grew up wearing saris of every colour, and I miss that sometimes.'

The questions about Pelathina rose to the surface again, but before she could ask them, Pelathina frowned, looking so much like her sister.

'Alright, we're heading to Norwen Peak to meet the others. You can follow me and Skydance,' Pelathina said, looking up to the sky.

She was about to take off and Aimee had to follow

her. She had to join this mission, or Jara would kill Jess. But the memory of fighting the Empty Warriors on the tundra was holding her down like chains locking her to the library roof. Talking to Pelathina just now had given her a small tingle in her belly. She didn't want Pelathina to think badly of her, didn't want to admit to her that she was terrified. But even that couldn't make her move.

'Hey,' Pelathina caught her gaze and held it. 'Stick with me and I'll watch out for you, okay?'

First Nathine had stood up for her, and now Pelathina, who she barely knew, was offering to look after her. Was this what having friends felt like? Was this what being part of a community was like? It gave Aimee a glow inside, as if her spark was pulsing. It gave her the courage to follow Pelathina into the sky.

They swooped over the city, Skydance flying so fast Jess could barely keep up. The colourful ribbons on Pelathina's saddle danced in the wind. Aimee heard disembodied shouts from the streets, and as they flew over the caravan compound she noticed the angry crowd was still there, clustered around the barricade. Pelathina flew high up through the mountains. She didn't weave between the jagged peaks like Aimee would have done. Instead she steered Skydance almost to the snowy summit of Norwen Peak, his blue scales glittering brighter than the sky. Aimee felt a blast of cold air as Jess swept after him, their wings stirring up eddies of snow.

Then they were over the mountains and she could see the army. Fear squeezed her heart with an icy hand.

Jess caught her fear and slowed, letting out a low growl. Did she remember what had happened to Malgerus only a few hours ago?

'Shh, girl.' Aimee tried to calm her, but it was hard to do when her own panic was rising like the tide.

Skydance tucked his wings into a dive, and it took a lot of urging for Aimee to get Jess to follow. Halfway down the outside of the Ring Mountains Skydance levelled out and Aimee spotted the other dragons, colourful against the grey rock. They were waiting on a wide ledge overlooking the army. Skydance landed beside them, Jess following.

They dismounted, and for a moment, were hidden from the others by their dragons. Pelathina took Aimee's hand, surprising her so much she almost jerked hers back.

'I'm not insulting your bravery, but you shouldn't be here,' Pelathina said, quickly and quietly. 'Jara rushed your training, sent you to steal your dragon too soon, and now you've been thrust into this battle without any time to learn dragonback fighting skills.'

Aimee looked down at Pelathina's brown fingers entwined with her own. Pelathina's hand was warm, and it made Aimee's feel tingly. She didn't want Pelathina to think she was useless.

'Jess and I can fight. We saved the caravan,' Aimee said, though her voice came out sounding like a little girl's rather than a grown woman's.

Pelathina stepped closer, slightly taller, her nose level with Aimee's eyes. 'You did, and everyone respects you for that, but you've a lot to learn, and getting yourself killed today won't prove anything.' She gave Aimee's hand a squeeze. 'And you'll never get to take me out for cheese.'

'I need to buy you cheese?' Aimee stuttered, no idea how the conversation had turned to that.

'Yeah, it's in the Riders' rulebook, that if you save someone from falling off a cliff, then they have to buy you a thank you. I know a small bakery on Veijarnt Street that does these rolls with salted ewe's milk cheese baked into the middle. They're so good they'll make your spark explode.'

Pelathina was smiling at her again, and Aimee found herself grinning back. Then a flicker of her sister's frown crossed Pelathina's face.

'Fear is like smoke,' she said, 'it blows into your mind, obscuring everything else, all the happy thoughts, the confident ones, the knowledge that things will get better. And no matter how tightly you close your mind you can't stop that smoke seeping in through the cracks. The secret is not to fight it, or get lost in it, but to let it blow on out the other side. Then you can be the amazing person you really want to be.'

Aimee was a little stunned as Pelathina led Skydance over to the others. She couldn't figure her out. Why was she being so nice to her? How did she manage to be so cheerful all the time? And why was she offering to look out for her? Her experience of assistance so far had been both Jara and Lyrria shoving her towards being a Rider, letting her either succeed or fail on her own.

She didn't have time to worry about it as she and Jess followed Pelathina over to the cliff's edge and the other Riders. They were standing beside their dragons, some with their arms around their dragon's necks, and watching the army. The only sound from below was the thud, thud, thud of the battering ram.

Aimee recognised Aranati, her arms crossed and the head of her golden dragon, Harmony, resting on her shoulder. Beside her was Sal, her long red ponytail swishing as she shook her head at something. Beside her Whisper stretched out his long, pine-green wings, before snapping them closed again. The Rider at the end was an older woman Aimee didn't know. She turned as Aimee approached, disbelief clear on her face.

'Dirty, dull sparks, what's the newbie doing here?'

'Jara sent her,' Pelathina replied.

'And what?' the older Rider continued. 'Dyrenna was too busy doing her hair? Feljanna is out shopping for new underwear?'

The Rider's sarcasm was sharp, Aimee felt it cutting at her and her lack of experience, but it seemed to slide off Pelathina like rain sheeting off the cliffs.

'We've got a dream team right here, Lwena, who else do we need?' she gestured round at the five of them.

Beside Lwena her pearly white dragon snorted a large puff of smoke. Lwena stroked her under the chin. 'Glaris says, could you go back to Jara and ask for another three thousand fully-trained Riders, all with adult dragons who can breathe fire.'

'Glaris doesn't talk to you,' Sal said, joining the

conversation. Her words whistled slightly through the gap between her front teeth.

'She does, don't you my girl,' Lwena crooned at her dragon. Glaris rubbed the side of her head gently against Lwena's cheek. Aimee liked that Glaris's pearly white scales were the same colour as Lwena's hair. 'And don't you look at me like that, frowny-face,' Lwena added, looking pointedly at Aranati. 'Just you wait till you've been bonded for thirty-four years, and maybe you'll hear your dragon's voice too.' She took Glaris's head in both hands. 'Do you want to eat Sal, my darling? You could start with her bum, it looks quite juicy.'

Aimee was staring at Lwena. The older Rider was starting to sound a little bit crazy. Pelathina caught her look and leaned in, smiling. 'Normally we keep her and Glaris locked in a tiny cave down at the bottom of Anteill. But don't worry, it's a nice cave, with lots of sparkly crystals for her to stare at. They probably talk to her too.'

Sal hiccupped a laugh, obviously not worried about Glaris eating her bum. Even Aranati's frown lessened a degree. Then Lwena let go of her dragon and stepped in front of Aimee, hands on her hips. Her eyes were the pale blue of an early morning sky, and Aimee felt uneasy as they assessed her. She'd pulled a necklace from her shirt and was tugging on the silver chain. It was her Rider's jewellery and through her fingers Aimee could see the pendant was a little bird.

'So, your dragon looks almost fully grown but I'd bet my jewellery she hasn't given a full blast of flames yet. You've had, what? Four months training, rather than the year a recruit's meant to have. You've never fought multiple foes from dragonback. And I'll bet you can't fly a loopback manoeuvre.'

Aimee felt everyone's eyes on her, Riders and dragons. The familiar hot rush rose up her neck and into her cheeks. Her throat did its usual and closed, trapping her words inside. When she was on a mission with Nathine, she could easily order the other girl around, but that's because they were equals, both new and both learning. But with these women, Aimee was amongst experienced Riders, and they knew better than she did.

'Lwena, this is the team you've got. I think we're all awesome, Aimee included, but if you're not happy, the city's that way,' Pelathina pointed a slim finger over her shoulder. 'We'll complete the mission ourselves.'

Glaris snorted another puff of smoke which Lwena waved away from her face. 'Not a chance. You think I'm letting these bastards destroy my home.'

'Can we get on with the mission now, please,' Aranati said, soundly like a parent scolding her wayward children.

They all stepped back to the edge of the cliff, Aimee joining them with Jess behind her. The thudding of the battering ram had continued the whole time they'd been talking. With every beat it sent another pulse of fear up through Aimee's feet and through her body. But the women beside her didn't look afraid, so Aimee pretended she wasn't either.

'How do we find the Master of Sparks in all of that?'

Lwena asked what Aimee had been wondering too.

The army below them stretched from the cliff walls all the way back across the isthmus. Rows and rows of Empty Warriors stood still and silent, waiting to march through the mountains and slaughter everyone. The way they just stood there was really creepy. Somehow Aimee found it worse than if they'd all been yelling.

'What are they?' Sal breathed the question beside her.

'Not human, that's for sure,' Lwena replied and shuddered.

Aimee remembered the words on the breastplate. 'They were created through sparks and fire,' she said.

'Well, that makes no damn sense.' Lwena shook her head.

'It's another question the university scholars are grappling with,' Aranati said. 'If the Master of Sparks is somehow controlling them, or if he was the one who gave them their purpose, as it says on the breastplate, does he know how they were created?'

Aimee wanted to say that Kyelli knew and the answers were in Jara's coat pocket, but Aranati kept talking and she didn't get a chance.

'Sal and Lwena, you take the western half of the army. Fly from here to the tundra and look for anyone that's wearing a different uniform, or that's giving orders, and looks like they could be the Master of Sparks. Pelathina and I will fly along the eastern half. We'll meet you at the back. Hopefully one of us will have spotted him and we can then plan how to take him out.' Her serious face turned to Aimee.

'Aimee can fly with us,' Pelathina said.

Aranati thought for a moment, then nodded. 'Alright, they don't appear to have any units of archers, so fly low and examine everything you can.'

'They'll fire up bolts,' Aimee blurted out. 'I don't know how but they can shoot up really big bolts that'll cut through a dragon's wing then they'll try to pull you down out of the sky.'

Everyone was looking at her, all a bit incredulous. 'It happened to Nathine and now Malgerus has a hole in his wing.'

'What the blazing sparks was Nathine doing flying over that army?' Lwena demanded.

'It was my plan,' Aimee admitted. 'We were chasing the clues.'

'Glaris says, what are you on about?'

Lwena was a bit mad and kinda scary, but Aimee wanted to tell her about the clues, the map, Kyelli's book, the way to fight the Empty Warriors, but Aranati cut her off, again.

'That's not relevant right now, but thank you for the information, Aimee. Alright, don't go too low and keep a watch out for each other.'

The Riders took Aranati's orders and mounted up. Aimee did too. Jess was nervous underneath her, talons clacking on the rock, wingtips fluttering. Her ruff of feathers was half raised and when Aimee ran her hand over them, each one quivered. She closed her eyes and was about to take a deep breath to calm herself when the air around her boomed with a particularly loud thud. She jumped in her saddle.

'Sparks, that sounded like they cracked the door to the tunnel. It's a foot thick,' Sal said.

'Time to get moving. Remember to watch out for each other.' Aranati and Harmony swept off the cliff and into the sky.

The others followed with Aimee last to take off.

CHAPTER 20

FIRST TO DIE

The five Riders swooped off the cliff and into the sky above the army. Their dragons glittered bright against the dark rows of warriors below—golden and sapphire blue, pearly white and pine green, and Jess's scales gleaming like emeralds. The wind rushed at Aimee as they dived, blowing her short curls off her face. She blinked instinctively but there was no need, her goggles stopped her eyes from streaming. Lwena and Sal peeled off, heading for the western half of the army, and Aimee followed Pelathina.

They levelled off too far down. Aranati had judged a bow shot but so had Aimee when she and Nathine had been here. But Aranati was in charge, so Aimee followed behind and stared fearfully down watching for flying bolts.

Empty Warriors filled the world below them, standing in rows so tightly packed Aimee couldn't see the grass through them. At the narrowest point of the isthmus warriors at the edge of the army were standing with their feet in the cold shallows of the sea. They'd been there for hours, weren't their feet numb with cold? Why didn't they stand somewhere else? Aimee shuddered. Everything the Empty Warriors did seemed more and more inhuman.

And they were utterly silent. A few faces turned to watch the Riders fly over, their fiery eyes like dragon's breath orbs. Every face Aimee saw was exactly the same. She thought of the faces carved in the wooden stilts of the fielders' homes. Why were they all the same? Was that answer now in Jara's pocket too?

'Alright?' Pelathina called from ahead.

Aimee wanted to shout back that she wasn't, but Pelathina appeared so at ease that Aimee didn't want to admit her guts were squirming inside her like worms. So she just gave a small smile.

'Pellie, pay attention,' Aranati ordered from up front, without turning around.

Aimee felt chastised too and turned her eyes back down to the army. Every row they passed over looked the same. Every warrior was identical. Aimee thought of the Riders, with Jara in charge and the more experienced Riders given missions to lead. She thought of the city guards, who had a captain, and sergeants for each district of the city. Even the city itself had the Uneven Council. There was always someone in charge, someone giving the orders. But the Empty Warriors didn't appear to have that.

She thought again of the breastplate and the engraved words that said they were fuelled by their purpose, and the way the name, Master of Sparks, had looked so much like a signature.

'Where are you?' she whispered, eyes opened wide as she tried to scan everything below her.

She heard a clank then a hiss, and reacted without thinking. 'Move!' she yelled.

At the same time she tugged Jess's right horn and they veered that way. Ahead Pelathina did the same, Skydance's long wings carrying her further out. Aranati swooped left, just as a bolt shot into the sky between the three of them. Its barbed head split the air just behind Harmony's tail.

'Thanks!' Pelathina called as the bolt tumbled back down.

'How did they fire something so high?' Aranati called, almost hanging out of her saddle as she peered down at the army. 'It can't have come from a bow, they must—' The clank and hiss came again. 'Another one!' she yelled.

Aimee panicked and pulled on Jess's horn too hard. Jess growled her annoyance and snorted smoke, which blew straight into Pelathina's face just as she too tried to swerve.

'Sparks!' she swore and pulled Skydance into an upward dive. His long barbed tail swished, almost hitting Aimee. She yelped and pushed Jess into a downward dive. She knew instantly she'd made a huge mistake. This time there were three clanks and hisses, loud amongst the silent warriors. She glanced down to see all three heading right for her.

'Up, Jess!'

She switched from pushing on Jess's horns to pulling on them, trying to steer her out of her dive. It was an awkward thing to try and do but amazingly Jess flared her wings, stopping their dive, then flapped furiously for more height. It was as if Jess had understood her command before she'd pulled on her horns.

'Good girl!' Aimee called over the rush of wind. Then yelped as a bolt shot right past them. Jess swerved one way, then instantly swooped back the other as another bolt pierced the air beside them. She didn't see the third one, but by then she was high up and back beside Pelathina and Aranati.

'Everyone alright?' Aranati asked.

'My spark's still burning,' Pelathina answered.

'I'm really sorry,' Aimee apologised to her.

Pelathina flew Skydance around and under Jess, the colourful ribbons streaming from her saddle.

'Don't worry, I crashed right into Arri when I was learning to fly,' she called up.

A brief smile flickered over Aranati's face, making her look more like her sister for a moment. Watching Skydance cut effortlessly through the sky, and the relaxed way Pelathina sat in her saddle, Aimee couldn't imagine her ever flying badly.

'Alright, we need to fly back down,' Aranati announced.

They were about halfway along the army. Aimee watched as Pelathina seemed to think for a long moment then simply nodded.

'But we'll get shot,' Aimee blurted out.

'Follow me, okay?' Pelathina's face was kind. 'Swerve when I do, make for the high sky if I shout at you to, and keep checking for any sign of the Master of Sparks.'

That sounded like an awful lot of instructions, on top of swallowing her fear and keeping Jess under control. She couldn't help picturing Lyrria when she had been training them, simply expecting them to learn because she thought she was the best teacher. Aimee had loved trying to impress her, but suddenly she felt like she hadn't actually learned anything.

'Hey,' Pelathina cut into her thoughts. Aimee looked up and the other girl was smiling at her, not a cocky, knowing smile like Lyrria had, but an understanding one. 'You can do this.'

Aimee nodded. 'I can.'

'Good. And remember, we're going to the bakery for those baked cheese rolls.'

'Pellie, stop flirting and fly,' Aranati yelled.

Pelathina rolled her eyes at her sister, then without waiting pushed Skydance into a dive. Aimee and Jess followed and the army came rushing at them again. Pelathina levelled off, less than a bowshot above the warriors this time. A few heads turned to look up at them as Jess opened her wings with a snap, stopping their dive. Aimee forced herself to meet their fiery eyes and not turn away. Trying to keep one eye on the army and one on Skydance, she followed Pelathina. Row after silent row passed below them—the same face over and over again until Aimee felt dizzy.

This time she saw the machine as she heard the clank. It was a contraption of gears and levers, operated by two warriors.

'Left!' Pelathina yelled. Skydance and Jess banked left almost in perfect synchronicity. Another clank. 'Right!'

Skydance moved so smoothly and Aimee struggled to keep up. She pulled on Jess's right horn, squeezed with her left knee, and Jess did swoop right, but slower than Skydance. The bolt barely missed Jess's wing and Aimee yelped.

'Alright?' Pelathina called.

'Yes,' Aimee lied.

They flew on. Aimee scanned the rows, looking now for both the Master of Sparks and the bolt-firing machines. She also wondered how the Empty Warriors had gear machines like the one inside the Kyelli statue, like the ones the northern cities had.

Abruptly the rows of warriors stopped and there was a space below them, filled with bolt-firing machines. A thicket of bolt tips pointed up at them. A wave of sick fear swept over Aimee, and feeling it, Jess roared.

'Sparks!' Pelathina swore. 'Fly upwards, Aimee!'

Skydance pointed his snout to the sky but didn't go until Jess did. Aimee crouched on Jess's back, tucking her elbows in, making herself narrower, as Jess flapped frantically for the high sky. She felt Jess's ribs between her knees, working like bellows as she panted with effort. Aimee glanced down and saw Pelathina tearing up the sky behind them.

'Go!' she yelled at Aimee, just as the clanks started.

It sounded like a hundred weapons being fired, and the bolts shot into the sky after them. There was no way to dodge that many. Aimee squeezed her eyes shut, trusting Jess to keep going. Skydance roared and Aimee glanced down in time to see the bolt that sliced along his hind leg. Blood droplets spurted into the sky. The barbs didn't catch though, and the bolt tumbled away.

'Keep going, Aimee!' Pelathina yelled.

She heard the clanks of weapons firing again and cried at Jess for more speed. She could feel her dragon's fear pulsing in her mind. They burst through a cloud, momentarily blinded but still heading upwards. Then she caught sight of blue and black from the corner of her eye and looked across to see Pelathina waving for her to slow down.

'You can stop now, Aimee,' she called.

Aimee could feel that Jess wanted to keep going, to fly as far from the army as she could. Aimee had to push hard on their connection before Jess responded to the hands on her horns and Aimee's legs guiding her body. They slowed and Aimee looked down. The army was rows of black dots impossibly far below. Aimee felt her stomach clench. She'd never been this high on Jess before. She sat still in her saddle and waited for Pelathina to fly over to her. Skydance was snorting small puffs of smoke and Pelathina stroked his feathers.

'Is he okay?' Aimee asked.

'I can feel his hurt, and that's always hard, but I

don't think the wound is deep,' Pelathina replied, then she too looked down at the army. 'This isn't working. Let's get back to Aranati.'

A golden spot had reached the end of the army below. Aimee scanned the other side and saw Whisper and Glaris, though they were flying above the sea and curving around to Aranati, avoiding the army. They must have been attacked as well. The hopelessness of trying to fight the Empty Warriors washed through Aimee again.

'You look thoughtful,' Pelathina said.

Aimee wanted to explain to Pelathina about Kyelli's diary and demand that they all fly back into the city and take it from Jara. That they find Kyelli and let her deal with the Master of Sparks. The more Aimee thought about him the more he grew in her mind, becoming a terrifying shadowy figure. But Aimee didn't say anything. These women knew what they were doing, they were skilled, had years of experience and Aimee was a newbie who still struggled to control her dragon.

Also, every time she thought about going back to the city all she could see was the heartrending image of Jess pinned to the library, Faradair's teeth at her neck.

'We should get back down to your sister,' Aimee said.

Pelathina studied her for a moment, Skydance flying slowing around Jess. 'You shouldn't keep thoughts inside. They're born in your brain but really they want to be free and out in the world, otherwise they get all twisted.'

It was the most interesting thing someone had ever said to encourage her to speak, but Aimee still shook her head. Pelathina stared at her for a moment longer, her eyes big through her goggle lens, then pushed Skydance into a dive. Aimee followed a moment later. Thankfully Jess's eagerness to speed after another dragon outweighed her unease at flying back towards the army.

Aimee and Pelathina joined the others beyond the back rows of the waiting army. The five dragons flew slow circles around each other in the air, their Riders calling across to each other.

'This isn't working worth a damn!' Lwena echoed what Pelathina had said to Aimee. 'Newbie was right about the shooting bolts and we can't get close enough to see anything. Though have you noticed they all have exactly the same face? What's that all about?'

Whisper glided under Glaris as Sal spoke. 'Those bolt weapons, they shoot directly upwards. The only target you could hit with one, would be a dragon.'

Harmony hovered, her golden scales glittering like sunshine. 'Meaning that this army knew they'd need weapons to neutralise Sky Riders.'

'So this Master of Sparks creep knows about us, and wants us taken out specifically,' Lwena added.

'That doesn't help us find him,' Pelathina pointed out.

'Argh! Right, I say we grab a warrior, fly back to Viewpoint Ledge with him, and make him tell us where their Master's hiding,' Lwena suggested.

'They don't make any noise,' Pelathina pointed out.

'I don't think they can speak.'

'Well, ribbon-girl, do you have a better idea? Because Glaris says we're wasting our time out here.'

Aimee heard the clank and whipped around, looking back towards the army. But it hadn't come from there. Moving so silently that no one had heard them, four Empty Warriors had sneaked across the heather beneath them.

'Fly!' Sal yelled, but too late.

They'd been flying lower to the ground and the bolt still had all its momentum as it reached them. It burst through Glaris's chest in a spray of blood and crunching of bone. The four other dragons roared, but Glaris couldn't—she was already dead. Her pearly wings folded as she began to tumble from the sky.

'Grab her!' Aranati yelled.

Lwena was screaming, her face splattered with her dragon's blood. Harmony and Skydance swooped after the tumbling Glaris. The Empty Warriors were winding in the bolt, pulling them down. They didn't need to, Glaris was gone and Lwena was plummeting with her. Aimee watched horrified as Skydance swooped in and plucked Lwena from her saddle, cradling her in his taloned back feet. He flapped up into the sky, and as he did, Harmony glided under him and Aranati reached up and wrapped both arms around Lwena, pulling her down into her own saddle. She held the still-screaming Rider in front of her.

Glaris hit the ground beside the Empty Warriors. Aimee could see the end of the bolt sticking right out of her back, it had pierced her clean through. Lwena's screaming intensified as the Empty Warriors began to hack off Glaris's head.

'Aimee, come on!'

Pelathina's shout pulled her eyes from the horrific scene. Harmony and Whisper were already high in the sky, heading back towards the mountains. Jess was flooding her with fear and anguish, but she managed to half close the door in her mind and steer Jess after the others.

CHAPTER 21

A DIFFERENT WAY

THEY REACHED THE shelf of rock that Lwena had called Viewpoint Ledge and landed there. Lwena was still screaming as Pelathina and Aranati lifted her off Harmony and laid her gently on the ground. Aimee dismounted too and stood useless, one arm wrapped tightly around Jess's neck. Jess lay her head on Aimee's shoulder and kept gently nudging her. Seeing a dragon torn from her Rider had upset Jess as much as it had Aimee.

Lwena's white hair was streaked with red, her dragon's blood, and her pale eyes were huge, staring up at the sky as if searching for her dragon. It was awful to watch.

'My Glaris, I can't hear her any more,' she wheezed, her voice raw from screaming.

She tried to push herself up but Aranati gently, but firmly, eased her back down. That was when Aimee saw the spreading pool of blood on the rock. Lwena was splattered with her dragon's blood, but there wasn't enough of that to puddle on the rock. Lwena was injured too.

'Help me hold her,' Aranati ordered.

Sal and Pelathina crouched down, one on either side of the injured Rider and placed their hands on her, pressing her onto the rock. Her screams were warbling cries now.

'Aimee, get over here and help!' Aranati's shout took her by surprise. It wasn't that she hadn't wanted to help, it was just that normally people didn't like her touching them. After a quick reassuring surge on her connection to Jess she ran over.

'What can I do?'

'Hold her feet,' Aranati ordered. Her frown was deeper than ever. 'I don't want her kicking me in the face as I try to help.'

Aimee grabbed Lwena's ankles and pushed them down. Lwena bucked but the three Riders held her firm. Her cries of anguish felt like barbs piercing Aimee's heart. She saw Sal was crying, big fat tears dripping off her nose and landing unnoticed on Lwena. Aranati flipped out a knife and cut Lwena's coat open, buttons pinging off and splatting into the pool of blood. Then she sliced open her shirt too. Her vest underneath had been a pale pink, now it was soaked in bright red. Aimee gagged as the coppery stench of blood hit the back of her throat.

'Glaris!' Lwena cried and tried to pull free.

'Hold her, she's going to tear her wound open wider.' Aranati had pulled a leather pouch from her saddlebag.

There was a spot of deeper red on Lwena's abdomen that was pulsing blood. With dawning horror Aimee realised what had happened. The bolt that had speared Glaris had shot right through her and stabbed her Rider as well. Aranati opened her pouch and rolled it out, bandages, bottles and instruments all in their right place.

'Arri.' Pelathina's voice was soft in the silence now Lwena had stopped screaming.

Aranati looked at her patient. 'No, Lwena come on, don't go after her. Let her go and stay with us.'

Aimee gripped Lwena's boots as she watched the sorrow spreading across her face. Aranati was pulling things out of her pouch. She pulled off her coat and rolled up her sleeves.

Aimee was staring right at Lwena's blood-splattered face as her spark flared. It had been burning through energy, trying to save her, but it had run out. There was a bright flash in her eyes then her spark went out forever.

'Arri, it's too late,' Pelathina said softly, releasing Lwena.

Aranati threw down the dressing she'd been preparing. '*Gari chingreth!*'

Her words were in a different language but Aimee could still recognise swearing and she agreed with whatever Aranati had said. Pelathina reached across Lwena's body and squeezed her sister's shoulder. Sal gently closed Lwena's eyes. Everyone grew blurry as

Aimee's eyes filled with tears. She felt Jess lay a comforting head on her shoulder and she stroked her dragon's feathers. All four remaining dragons had crouched down, bellies close to the rock, and each was pressed up against their Rider.

Aranati was the first to recover. She packed away her medical supplies then pulled her coat back on.

'We can leave Lwena for now and collect her body later. No one will disturb her here,' Aranati said, buttoning up her coat. Then she turned to look back down at the army. The thump, thump, thump of the battering ram had continued this whole time, like a heartbeat of the army. A heartbeat that Lwena no longer had.

'Arri, no, you're not going back down there,' Pelathina said, standing up too.

Aranati didn't turn around. 'We have to find him, Pellie, it's the mission we volunteered for.'

'That was before we knew they had weapons designed specifically to target Riders,' Pelathina argued.

'We'll be more careful.'

'It's not about being careful, we can't fight these monsters, Arri.'

Finally Aranati turned back to them. 'So we just give up? We let them break through the mountains and destroy this city that took us in? We let them murder the people who gave us a home when we had nowhere else?'

Aranati was yelling now. She was always frowning but Aimee had never seen her lose control like this.

Beside her Harmony's wingtips fluttered and her sinuous neck was weaving back and forth like a snake's. Aimee sat cross-legged beside Lwena's body and watched the sisters argue. She didn't know how to interrupt or stop them. She looked across at Sal, but the other woman was huddled around her own knees, Whisper's dark wings wrapped around her.

'I'm not giving up, but I'm not flying down there to die!' Pelathina had grabbed her sister's arm.

'And I'm not abandoning my mission.' Aranati shook her off.

'I won't let you go. *Lalthash il athinsa vard!*'

'*Vard? Omn deshilta!*'

The sisters were nose-to-nose now, yelling in each other's faces. As Aimee watched them, it felt like everything was breaking down. Jara was furious at her, the Guilds were angry with the council, and now two Riders, two sisters, were screaming at each other. No one in the city was equipped to deal with this. The Empty Warriors weren't inside Kierell yet, but they were already breaking it.

'We need help,' Aimee told Jess. Her dragon nudged her cheek. Her scales were cool but her breath was hot as it washed over her. Aimee knew what Nathine would tell her if she was here. The thought actually made her smile and, imagining the *know-it-all* look on Nathine's face, she stood. Jess raised up behind her and looked over the top of her head.

'Hey! Stop arguing!' Aimee yelled.

Pelathina and Aranati shut up and turned to look at

her. Even Sal pulled herself out of her grief and looked up.

'I don't want to go back down there,' Aimee said, pointing at the army, 'and it's not because I'm new and useless, it's 'cause I have a better way to fight them.'

'Kyelli,' Pelathina breathed the name.

Aimee nodded. 'I've almost found her.'

'What?' Sal looked confused.

'Really?' Pelathina looked excited.

Aranati frowned at her. 'Jara forbade you from looking for her.'

'I know, but you saw us, me and Nathine. When we were hiding under the workers' house and you didn't tell Jara.'

'No, because honestly, I didn't think your quest would come to anything. I didn't think you were doing any harm. But you did go against Jara's orders.'

'I did, but Jara only ordered me not to follow the clues because she's scared and she has so much else to think about,' Aimee quickly defended herself.

'I've known Jara for four years and she doesn't do anything without a purpose,' Aranati said. She'd pushed her goggles up onto her head so they held her hair back like a hairband. It drew attention to her crumpled forehead and the deep frown between her eyes. 'What if there was another reason Jara didn't want you to find her?'

'Such as what? That she doesn't want to be outranked by someone?' Pelathina asked.

'That's unfair, Pellie. Jara's always been a great leader, and she puts her Riders above everything.'

Sal unwrapped herself and rose slowly to her feet. Whisper still had one wing draped over her shoulder. 'Except that now she isn't a good leader. Now she sent us out here to die.' She pointed down at Lwena's bloody body. 'Four against ten thousand!'

'We weren't here to fight them,' Aranati argued.

'Then what's the point?' Sal's narrow face had gone as red as her hair. 'Jara's wrong. She shouldn't have taken the councillors out onto the tundra, she shouldn't be trying to keep the tunnel open and she shouldn't have ordered us out here to be killed by monsters! I'm with Aimee.' Sal stabbed a finger in her direction. 'Jara can't lead us through this, we need someone else.'

Aimee's mind reeled as the implication of Sal's words hit her. She hadn't been proposing replacing Jara, just getting Kyelli to help. Sal's words sounded awfully close to mutiny. Aimee wasn't looking to lead a rebellion against Jara, was she?

She thought back to the way Jara had rushed them through their Rider training, and she blamed Jara for Hayetta's death. She was angry at Jara for kicking her out of the council meeting and excluding her. The thought of standing up to Jara made Aimee's belly squirm, but she'd stood up to Nyanna, a girl who'd bullied her for years. Maybe she did want to replace Jara with Kyelli. Surely she'd be a better leader. They were Kyelli's Sky Riders after all.

'What does "almost found" Kyelli mean?' Sal asked her.

Aimee explained about the map, and the clues she, Nathine and Callant had followed. She told them about the hidden room in the library's roof and the diary they'd found up there.

'Her actual diary?' Sal asked. Her fingers were quivering as if they longed to touch it.

Aimee nodded and gave a brief smile. She liked seeing that other women revered Kyelli as much as she did. It made her fascination with the immortal seem less childish.

'Sparkly sparks,' Pelathina smiled at her. 'And she wrote in her diary where she's gone?'

Aimee shook her head. 'I don't know. Jara took it before we could read it. But I did see that there's a whole section where she's written about the Empty Warriors. So if we can read that, I'm sure we'll learn how they're created and how we can destroy them.'

'And if the diary tells you that, do you still want to find Kyelli?' Aranati asked, still serious, still frowning.

Aimee nodded. 'Of course, I...' she struggled for words. How could she explain to Aranati that she needed Kyelli, just like she'd always needed someone to fight her bullies for her.

There was silence for a long moment as the other three Riders considered what Aimee said. She worried she hadn't convinced them. She'd never been very good with words—she'd had too little practice speaking to other people. Things sounded good in her head but somehow always seemed to come out a bit muddled.

Sal was staring down at Lwena's body, her face still

shiny with tears, and one of Whisper's dark green wings still draped across her slim shoulders. The sisters stood at the edge of the ledge, watching the army. Harmony and Skydance stood close together too, their long tails intertwined, sky-blue scales twisting around golden ones. Aimee couldn't help thinking how beautiful the sisters looked. Their bronze faces seemed to glow, as if their sparks were shining through their skin. The wind picked up Aranati's long black hair and pulled it out like ribbons. As Aimee watched, Pelathina ran a hand through her cropped black hair, making it stick up in a way that looked cute rather than fierce.

The wind plucked at Aimee's short hair too and from one eye she could see dark brown curls, and from the other, pure white curls. Pelathina and Aranati looked so much more like Riders than she did, even if they weren't from the city. If they found Kyelli would she be disappointed to see Aimee, a freak, as one of her Riders? Perhaps Aimee should pass the quest over to the sisters, let them go find her.

Jess nudged her, not very gently and Aimee stumbled. She could feel the love in their connection and knew Jess was trying to encourage her, even if she hadn't yet learned how hard she could push her Rider. Aimee put a hand on Jess's cool scales to steady herself. Jess's shove had been enough to knock her away from the melancholic pool she'd been circling.

She stroked Jess's feathers and felt her dragon's pleasure at the contact. Jess was a constant reminder of all she'd achieved, she had to stop forgetting that.

Her boots were almost touching the pool of blood around Lwena and Aimee looked down at the dead Rider. She'd barely known Lwena for half an hour, but her death saddened her. She'd seemed confident, a little crazy perhaps, but strong too. She'd wanted to protect her city and now she was gone and couldn't fight any more. Aimee decided then to borrow a little of Lwena's confidence, and maybe in that way Lwena could keep fighting with them.

She took a deep breath, pulled her goggles down over her eyes and tried to look Rider-ish. 'I'm going back to the city to get the diary and find Kyelli,' she announced.

Her palms were tingling and her heart was thumping faster than the battering ram below. The three women all looked at her, their dragons too.

'You can stay here and watch them break into the tunnel,' she pointed at the silent rows of Empty Warriors, 'or you can come and help me. With Nathine too, because I wouldn't have got all the clues without her, and she's annoying but she's my friend now, and well, I want her to be involved.'

Her voice had trailed off a bit in the last part as she felt the pressure of their eyes. It was easy to start talking confidently, but really hard to keep going. It was as if her confidence was a dam that burst when she spoke, gushing out at the start then trickling by the end.

She turned away from them and boosted herself up into her saddle. For a moment no one else moved and she thought she would be flying back alone. That was alright, she and Jess were used to being alone. But then Aranati nodded at her.

'Sal, can you take Lwena back home?' Aranati asked.

Sal nodded, a few fresh tears adding to the wetness on her cheeks. 'She should be laid to rest with Glaris.'

Aimee looked out at the army and dreaded to think what those monsters had done to Glaris's beautiful body. If that had happened to Jess, she'd want to be dead too.

Sal jumped onto Whisper's back and walked him towards Lwena.

'Wait,' Pelathina called, and knelt beside her body. She had a pink ribbon in her hand, one of the ones from her saddle. Very gently she tied it around Lwena's wrist. 'When I first put these on my saddle Jara was pissed at me, said we were supposed to be inspiring guardians, not children going to a party. Lwena though, she thought it was so funny that she bought me my Rider's jewellery. She told me our individual quirks were what made us Riders.'

Pelathina untucked a long gold chain from the collar of her shirt. The bottom third of the necklace was strung with colourful beads. To Aimee it looked like she was wearing a cluster of rainbows.

Pelathina stood and Whisper gently gathered up Lwena's body in his talons. Aimee tilted her head back as she watched Sal and Whisper rise into the sky, thinking that at least Lwena got to fly one last time. As she looked back down, Pelathina was smiling at her. It was a sad one, but still a smile. How did she do that?

'What's your plan?' Aranati asked from Harmony's back. Her dragon was standing stock still, tense, showing that Aranati was feeling unsure.

Aimee floundered. She didn't really have a plan. She wasn't even sure where she'd find Nathine.

'Don't worry, my sister likes to have everything mapped out before she does anything. She even has all her breakfasts planned for at least the next month,' Pelathina said. In contrast to Harmony, Skydance was weaving side to side, his wings half unfurled and fluttering. It was as if he could never stay still. 'It's pancakes with berries tomorrow.'

'Shut up, Pellie,' Aranati said but with no venom in her voice. 'Jara is our leader, but each Rider is a leader too. You may be asked to lead a caravan, or plan a scouting mission. The people in the city look up to us as their protectors, and you can't hide from that responsibility.'

Aimee wasn't a leader, she knew that she didn't have what it took, but she understood what Aranati was telling her. She couldn't expect people to come along with her unless she had a plan. So she quickly formulated one that she hoped sounded okay.

'First we need to discover if Nathine has the diary, or if it's still with Jara. I can't work out what's next until we have Kyelli's diary. So, we need to find Nathine.'

'How? She could be anywhere in the city and time is not our friend,' Aranati pointed out.

Jess nudged her and she had a sudden flash of inspiration. 'Jess can find Malgerus. They're clutchmates, so she can lead us to him, and Nathine will be where Malgerus is.'

Aranati nodded once, then took off. Aimee looked across at Pelathina. 'Did that sound okay?'

Pelathina smiled that lovely smile of hers. 'It sounded good to me, but remember, it's your plan, so own it, and others will follow you.'

Skydance took off, Jess following a moment later. Pelathina looked more natural in the air than any of the other Riders, and Aimee felt a tingle in her belly as she watched her. Now wasn't the time or place for tingly feelings, but she allowed herself a moment to enjoy it.

CHAPTER 22

## FOUND AGAIN

Aranati and Pelathina flew fast and Aimee could feel Jess struggling to keep up. She was almost fully grown in terms of size, but she didn't yet have the strength of an adult dragon.

'You're doing great, girl,' Aimee said. Her words were lost in the wind but she sent them along their connection too.

They cut between the lesser summits around Norwen Peak and back to the city. Harmony and Skydance dived through the sky, golden and sapphire scales glittering in the sun, and levelled off above the caravan compound. As Jess followed Aimee was dismayed to see the crowd in the compound had grown. The barricade had been reinforced and there were more city guards, easy to spot in their colourful patchwork cloaks. Aimee could feel the anger coming off the crowd like heat rising from a bonfire.

There were dragons perched on the barricade, and Aimee caught sight of a purple one. Midnight. She pushed Jess's horns, urging her for more speed. She didn't want Lyrria to see her. They reached the market streets of Barter, all the stalls with their coloured awnings weirdly quiet today. Harmony and Skydance slowed, letting Jess pull ahead.

Now they were lower, and flying slower, Aimee pushed her goggles up onto her forehead and scanned the streets opening up before them.

'Alright girl, I really hope you can do this. Find Malgerus.'

She thought of a moment when Jess and Malgerus had been close. There weren't many since she and Nathine had fought so often. Finally she settled on the memory of Jess pulling the barb from Malgerus's wing and mentally pushed it along her connection to Jess. At the same time she tried to think of what having a clutchmate would feel like, and ended up picturing Nathine throwing insults at Nyanna for her.

It must have worked because suddenly Jess tipped her wings and banked left. Aimee squeaked in surprise then yelled. 'It's working, Nathine's this way!'

Aimee loosened a few of the ties in her mind which she used to control Jess, and she let Jess choose their direction. Lyrria had told them to never let their dragon fly without being the one in charge, but Aimee was beginning to question a few of the things Lyrria had taught them.

The three dragons skimmed over steep grey roofs, Jess in the lead like the tip of an arrow. It was only a few minutes before Aimee spotted Malgerus. He was perched on the peak of a two-storey building, his orange scales bright against the slate roof tiles. His serpentine head swivelled as Aimee, Pelathina and Aranati approached, and he fluttered his wings, his ruff of feathers quivering. It was almost as if he'd been waiting for them.

Malgerus's building faced a small courtyard and that's where they landed. The flapping of their dragons' wings echoed from the close walls and it sounded like a whole flight of dragons had descended into the square. Aimee didn't need to worry about Jess scaring any people though, there was no one here. She could hear snatches of shouting from further in, near the centre of the city. She dismounted and pressed her face against the cool, slippery scales of Jess's neck.

'Well done, girl,' she said, but also retightened her hold on Jess. Her dragon didn't seem to mind and in fact Aimee could feel Jess's pleasure at the praise, it was like a burst of sunshine in her mind.

'I wasn't sure that would work,' Aranati admitted as she pulled off her goggles, folding the strap neatly before stowing them in a pocket. 'I've never seen a dragon track another dragon before.'

'Well, it just kinda made sense to try,' Aimee said. She felt a blush on her cheeks at Aranati's praise. Pelathina gave her a quick smile as she tugged off her own goggles. She'd made her hair stick up again and Aimee had a sudden urge to run her fingers through it. She shook the thought away.

'Hey, look who came back with her spark still burning, it's my annoying new friend.'

Aimee found herself smiling as she heard Nathine's voice, the characteristic sarcasm making it instantly recognisable. She turned to see Nathine was propping open the blue door to a small cafe. She was holding half a pie and took a bite, wiping a smudge of gravy from the side of her mouth with the back of her hand.

'You're eating?' Aimee's stomach had felt so full of fears and worries for the last few hours that she couldn't imagine putting food in it as well.

Nathine finished the pie, crumbs sprinkling her boots. 'Yeah, it's lunchtime,' she replied with her mouth full.

'Well, it's nice to hear that you were worried about me,' Aimee said.

'Only because you left me with Callant, and sparks, he's boring. He goes on about Kyelli more than you do, and all these other dead folk from history. Why do I care who was on the Uneven Council fifty years ago?'

Nathine stepped out into the courtyard and Callant appeared in the cafe door behind her. He had crumbs in his beard.

'Because it's our history, it matters,' Callant said.

Nathine turned to him, but Aimee reached out and grabbed her hand. She didn't have time to adjudicate another argument between the two.

'Did you get Kyelli's diary?'

Aimee's voice was full of hope, but the way Nathine's face filled with anger told her everything. Up on the rooftop Malgerus growled.

'No, and how was I supposed to manage that anyway?' Nathine snapped, going on the offensive as always. 'Jara was surrounded by city guards. She and Captain Tenth had to gather every guard they could just to calm that crowd in Quorelle Square. But it got worse and all those angry people are still barricaded in there, and it's taking nearly every guard in the city to keep them there. Jara doesn't want a riot spreading.'

'What about the councillors?' Aranati asked, and it was Callant who answered.

'They've shut themselves in the council chamber. The mob outside are calling for them all to resign.'

Aimee saw guilt on Callant's face. 'You're more help to them, and the city, by being here with us,' she told him.

'I hope so,' he replied, before he coughed, blowing all the crumbs out of his beard.

'So, we have to go back to Quorelle Square and find a way to get the diary from Jara,' Aimee said.

'No, mushroom head, Jara's not there anymore,' Nathine said. 'She went off with Dyrenna to a warehouse in Barter. They've got the Helvethi leaders hidden there. Dyrenna was worried what would happen if the crowd saw the centaurs.' Nathine crossed her arms, hunching up her shoulders, and she was wearing her angry face. 'Everyone was ready to be friends with the Helvethi, but not anymore. I heard shouts in the crowd, people from the Stonemasons and Carpenters Guilds saying that because the Empty Warriors appeared out on the tundra that somehow the Helvethi called them.'

'That doesn't make any sense.' Callant shook his head, beard waggling. 'The Empty Warriors are from our past, not the Hevlethi's.'

'I'm sure you tried your best,' Aimee reassured Nathine, but she was disappointed. They still had so much to do, so many clues to unravel and they needed that diary.

'Of course I did,' Nathine immediately retorted, then her face softened and she dropped her arms. She was like a dragon lowering her ruff of feathers. 'But, Aimee, Jara really doesn't want you to have that diary. She was so pissed off when she took it from you. And remember how she nearly had Faradair bite Jess's head off.'

'What?' The crease on Aranati's forehead deepened to a canyon. 'Jara would never threaten another Rider's dragon.'

'She did, Arri, I saw it too,' Pelathina said, taking her sister's hand. Aranati opened her mouth to speak but Pelathina continued. 'I know it doesn't sound like her, but there's something going on with Jara. She's not acting like the Jara who welcomed us after the climb and gave us a home.'

'She's worried for the future of the city,' Callant said. 'All the plans she and Councillor Myconn made have been torn to tatters. She's worked so hard to create a safe passage across the tundra and now all hope of that's been trampled into a bog by that army. It must be hard for her.'

Aimee knew Callant was right but she thought

about what Pelathina had said, and put her words alongside the way Jara had behaved since Aimee found the map. She almost seemed afraid of what Aimee would do with it. Why? Pelathina was right, something was up with Jara.

'I don't know, Pellie, I'm not sure I feel okay with stealing from Jara,' Aranati said.

'Then why did you come down here with us?' Pelathina asked. She was still holding her sister's hand.

'From what Aimee said, I thought Nathine would already have the diary,' Aranati admitted.

'Oh hang on, so you're saying it's okay for me to run all the risks stealing from our leader, but not for you to do it?' Nathine threw the question, then folded her arms again.

'That's not what I meant. It was more...actually I don't know what I meant.' Aranati's dark eyes were pleading as she looked around the courtyard. 'Aimee, what do you want to do?'

Aranati looked at her, everyone did. She thought for a long moment, wanting to make sure she got her words right before they came out. Whatever Jara's reasons, she'd been behaving like one of Aimee's bullies. She'd belittled her, and ostracised her, and made her feel that her ideas and plans were a pile of dragon's dung. But Aimee didn't let the bullies get to her anymore. She wouldn't let them put a cage around her.

'I want to get Kyelli's diary, read it and find a way to destroy the Empty Warriors, and hopefully find Kyelli too,' Aimee announced. 'I think we'll need to do that without Jara's permission, and probably by lying and stealing from her.'

She saw Aranati wince at that. Even Callant looked a little unsure. Finally Aimee decided she'd had enough of everyone's indecision. All they were doing was wasting time. She wasn't a diplomat or a councillor, she wasn't going to persuade people with her eloquent words.

'Damn your sparks!' She stamped her foot and behind her Jess growled. 'I'm going to get the diary. Nathine you're coming with me.' She continued before the other girl could disagree. 'Callant we'll need to move fast, so I'm sorry but you're staying here. But we'll be back, and then we'll need your knowledge again, once we have the diary to read.' She spun on her toes to look at the two sisters. 'I don't really know you both but you're coming too because I think four Riders will be better than two, because well, they just will.'

Silence settled in the little courtyard as she finished. There was a long pause where Aimee began to regret speaking out, but then Callant nodded at her. Nathine tightened the high ponytail on top of her head and grinned. Aranati still looked unsure, but Pelathina was smiling, cute dimples appearing on her bronze cheeks.

'Alright, last one on their dragon has to make me tea for a month,' Aimee called as she grabbed her saddle and swung herself up.

'Hey, not fair!' Nathine complained as she whistled for Malgerus.

He swooped down off the roof and by the time he landed beside Jess the others were already in their saddles. Nathine winced as she swung her wounded leg over, but Aimee knew better than to comment on it.

'So, still giving people orders then?' Nathine asked, one eyebrow cocked.

'They weren't orders,' Aimee protested. 'I just wanted everyone to stop arguing.'

'Uh-huh.' Nathine sounded unconvinced as she and Malgerus took off.

Aimee felt good as Jess rose above the peaked rooftops. Outside, above the army, she'd felt helpless, like a stick being tossed around in a stormy sea. She'd felt like she could do nothing good. Now, as she pulled Jess's left horn, steering her back towards the warehouse district, she had a clearer purpose and she liked that. Seeing three other dragons flying alongside gave her a little buzz too.

The jumble of streets below them untangled, becoming wide enough for wagons. Normally these were busy streets, wagons and workers jostling together, warehouse doors wide open as goods were stored or unloaded. Today there was no one. Aimee flew over an abandoned wagon, tipped on its side. Two boys ran past, one jumping up to set the wagon's wheel spinning.

Where was everyone? Were they hiding? Aimee hoped so, but the faint shouts that came along the wind suggested people were off swelling the mob in Quorelle Square, demanding answers from their councillors.

Aimee glanced over at the Ring Mountains. Could she still hear the thump, thump of the Empty Warrior's battering ram? Or was she imagining it? Was it the pounding of blood in her ears? It felt like her heartbeat was ticking away the minutes until they ran out of time. She pushed Jess for more speed and felt the air swirl around her as Malgerus, Harmony and Skydance sped up too.

Faradair and Black were perched on the long roof of a warehouse that backed onto the scrublands around the base of the cliffs. It was good to see Black. Aimee hadn't had a chance to speak to Dyrenna for a few days and she missed the older Rider, missed her quiet company and the way she seemed to anchor down wayward emotions.

Black sat still on the warehouse roof, wings wrapped around himself, long neck tucked in, but his eyes followed them as Aimee and the others gave the warehouse a once over, checking if anyone was outside. Faradair followed them too, but with his whole body, turning circles as they flew around, his long talons clacking on the tiles. Aimee was sure his yellow eyes were fixed on Jess. His ruff of blood-red feathers stuck straight out, quivering.

'Now would be a good time to share your plan,' Nathine called to her.

Aimee didn't want to land Jess beside Faradair—the memory of his teeth at Jess's neck was still vivid in her mind.

'Let's leave our dragons on this roof,' Aimee said, guiding Jess down onto the warehouse opposite. Her nerves made her forget to communicate clearly to Jess what she wanted and they nearly overshot the roof's peak. Luckily Jess caught it with her talons, realising at the last moment what Aimee wanted her to do. Aimee wobbled in her saddle as she kept moving forward and Jess pulled herself back. With a flash of panic she squeezed her thighs around Jess. Her dragon growled, loud enough for everyone to hear, as she settled onto the roof.

Aimee glanced around, hoping everyone else had been too busy landing to noticed what a mess she's made of it. But of course they'd all seen. Beside her Pelathina laughed, but not the cruel laugh of a bully, more a tinkling laugh of amusement.

'You chose a good hatchling,' Pelathina said, nodding to Jess. 'She understands you well, and I think she has the confidence that you're lacking. You could learn from her.'

Pelathina swung from her saddle, landing neatly, the balls of her feet balanced on the roof's peak. She was so graceful, so sure of everything she did. She didn't have the cocky self-assurance of Lyrria, or the brazen confidence of Jara. Pelathina's looked hard won somehow, and Aimee liked that.

'I don't think I'll ever have that much confidence, but I guess that's okay if maybe Jess has enough for both of us,' Aimee said as she lowered herself carefully from her saddle, holding on to Jess for support.

'Just choose to have it,' Pelathina said.

'What? I can't just choose to be confident.'

'A man with an arrow in his shoulder taught me that you can choose to be anything.'

Pelathina's dark eyes seemed to sparkle, as if her

spark was made of happiness. Again Aimee wanted desperately to ask for her story. She promised herself that if they found Kyelli and passed saving the city over to her, then she'd be brave and take Pelathina for those cheesy rolls. And she'd ask her all the questions now buzzing round her brain like bumblebees.

The Riders wove around their perched dragons and followed Aimee to the end of the roof. There was a wooden walkway around the first floor of the warehouse and they jumped down onto it. Aimee landed in a crouch and as she straightened she noticed the pulley affixed to the building's gable end. Its cog and chain made her think of the machine inside the Kyelli statue, the drawings in the strange books they'd found and the bolt-firing machines the Empty Warriors had. There was something about it that held her attention but she wasn't quite sure why. It was like someone was prodding her, but she was too asleep to really feel it.

'So, what now?' Nathine asked, and Aimee blinked, looking away from the pulley.

'Now we go steal a book,' she replied.

CHAPTER 23

THIEF

AIMEE COULD FEEL Black and Faradair watching them as they moved on silent feet across the street. She tried not to think too deeply about what they were about to do, about what she was about to make everyone do. If she was wrong about the diary being their salvation, her life—and Jess's—would be forfeit. She'd have to flee before Jara caught up with her.

She pushed the thought aside, but it was a bit like trying to shove heavy barrels by herself—they didn't go far.

They reached the shadows cast by the warehouse's brick wall and stopped. Beside them a set of big double doors were firmly shut, but they had a small person-sized door in them and it was open a crack. Aimee could smell leather and oil from inside. Above the door hung a sign, painted with a stylised horse, needle and thread. It was a saddlemaker's workshop. Aimee wondered if Dyrenna had chosen it specifically.

Angry voices drifted out through the sliver of open

door. Aimee picked out Jara's voice. She was speaking haltingly, in a language Aimee didn't understand.

'The Helvethi are saying they can't fight the Empty Warriors,' Pelathina translated. 'There are only two tribes now who would help the city, and between them, they can only muster around a thousand warriors.' She moved closer to the door to listen, tilting her head like a dragon. 'Jara's offering Riders to bolster their number.'

Aranati shook her head. 'That's suicide. She wouldn't send us out there to die. You must have misunderstood, Pellie.'

'My Helvetherin's good, you know that,' Pelathina said softly.

'How does Jara sound?' Aimee asked.

Pelathina gave her a rueful smile. 'Even more pissed off than she was back at Qurorelle Square.'

Ideas flitted through Aimee's mind like startled butterflies, and they all seemed as delicate and as easily crushed. A grating of talons made her look up. Faradair had crouched on the peak of the roof above them, his long neck stretched to its full length as he stared down at them, his yellow eyes narrowed. Then from behind, Aimee heard a collective rustle. Looking over her shoulder to the roof opposite she saw four dragons all with their ruffs of feathers raised and their wings half extended. Malgerus was tapping the tiles with one foot, a rapid staccato that echoed down the street. Skydance was weaving side to side as if he couldn't keep still. Jess had lowered herself, belly resting on the roof and was staring across at Faradair.

No one's dragon was calm, which told Aimee that everyone's emotions were running high. Maybe she could use that and combine it with her ability to slip through a crowd unnoticed. A plan pulled itself together in her mind.

'Pelathina, if things get messy in there, can you explain to the Helvethi what we're doing?' Aimee asked.

'Sure, but are things likely to get messy? What are we going to be doing?'

'I have an idea.'

Pelathina smiled at her quizzically. 'Care to share your idea?'

Aimee shook her head. She didn't want to tell anyone her plan in case they thought it was stupid.

'She's got that determined look on her face again,' Nathine said. 'When she's wearing that, it's easier just to follow her.'

Aimee threw Nathine a smile, grateful for her support. She stepped away from the wall and faced the door. It had been in the sun and its wood was warm as Aimee placed her hand on it, pushing it open all the way. She stepped inside, her plan firm in her mind.

In other circumstances Aimee would have found the rich smell of leather comforting inside the saddler's workshop—it reminded her of Dyrenna's little cave. A huge wooden rack covered the wall to Aimee's left, containing rows of tools, all neat and in their places. Workbenches filled most of the floor, with saddles in various states of completion sitting patiently on top. At the back bridles made a web of leather straps, hanging from the rafters.

The Helvethi were gathered at the end of the workbenches and Aimee felt a thrill when she spotted them. The only Helvethi she'd seen before were the father and son out on the tundra, the ones the Empty Warriors had killed. They looked so different, and powerful, and really tall. There were two males and two females. Tribes always had a pair for leaders, and these were the leaders of the Kahollin and Ovogil tribes. The reddish-brown fur of their backs and legs looked soft in the diffuse light of the workshop.

'Aranati, Pelathina, what happened?' Jara's voice cut through the workshop, her question fired as direct as an arrow. 'Please tell me you found the Master of Sparks.'

Aimee was standing in front, had been first through the door, but Jara ignored her completely, didn't even look at her. Earlier that would have made her upset, made her want to jump up and down, waving her arms. Right now, Jara dismissing her was part of her plan. But she had to check it was going to work so she tried speaking.

'Jara, we're here because—' she only managed a few words before Jara snapped at her.

'Shut up, Aimee. Sparks, you're like a sock with a hole in it that no matter how often I throw away still seems to end up back in my drawer.'

She stepped closer and glared at Aimee, and Aimee backed down. She looked around and realised the Helevthi were all staring at her, their eyes roving over the colourless side of her face. The elder of the males looked disgusted and leaned back, away from her, even though there were three workbenches between them. Aimee kept hold of her plan, waiting.

'Lwena's dead,' Aranati was saying.

'No, Lwena wouldn't die, she's too experienced.' Jara did the thing where she gathered her hair up on her head then let it fall. Her high cheekbones were flushed pink and there was a wild, desperate look in her green eyes. Aimee recognised it from the night she'd watched Jara cry broken-heartedly in Dyrenna's arms. She looked like a woman coming apart at the seams.

'Jara, we can't go back out there, not a single one of us,' Pelathina said, her voice gentle, like she was talking to a child.

'We have to find the Master of Sparks.' Jara's voice was amazingly still firm. 'Once the Master of Sparks is dead, we get the Helvethi to threaten the army's rearguard and position Riders in the air above the army. With the Master of Sparks gone we're in a strong position to end this without losing the city, or the tunnel.'

'Jara, how? There must be ten thousand Empty Warriors out there. What can a few Riders do against so many monsters?' Aranati put her hands gently on Jara's shoulders. 'They can shoot us out of the sky, Jara. That's what happened to Lwena.'

'No.' Jara shoved Aranati's arms away and stepped back. 'The council are holed up in their chamber and Beljarn's in there arguing for the tunnel to be caved in. It'll only be so long before people start to agree with him. Then we'll be trapped inside these mountains forever. Sparks! Give it a few weeks and the city will start turning on itself.'

Aimee heard rattling on the roof and knew Faradair was as agitated as his Rider. That was good, it played into her plan.

'Calm, Jara.' Dyrenna emerged from behind a rack of saddles and put an arm around Jara's shoulders. But Jara shoved her away as well.

'Aranati, you will go back out to the army. Take someone else to replace Lwena and I want—'

'Jara, they pulled Glaris from the sky and hacked off her head!'

Aimee jumped at Pelathina's outburst. Jara looked startled for a moment, then shook her head, flyaway blonde hair swishing. It was as if she refused to believe what was actually happening.

Aimee heard the clop of hooves on floorboards. Two of the centaurs had come closer, the young female and the older male. They had small tails, like a deer, and theirs were flicking in a way that reminded Aimee of Jess fluttering her wingtips when she was unsure. The female had a face full of freckles and her red hair was bound in intricate braids wrapped around her head.

'*Ulus yavj bania er, Jara?*'

Her words rolled like they were tumbling down a hill before emerging from her mouth. She waved at Aimee and the others, then pointed at Jara and seemed to repeat her question. Jara replied, her Helvetherin words halting. Aimee watched the exchange until the female centaur said something while gesturing right at Aimee, and Pelathina sucked in her breath.

'She called me a freak, didn't she?' Aimee asked.

'Near enough,' Pelathina replied, and though the insult hurt, as it always did, Aimee appreciated Pelathina's honesty.

Jara's voice was raised again and she was gesturing at Aimee, who didn't need Pelathina's translation to know that Jara was saying nothing good about her.

Aimee could feel the tight swirl of emotions in the air and decided now was her moment. A childhood of being called a freak had taught her to make herself smaller. Years of fearing insults, or worse, in the streets had taught her to slip through crowds almost unseen. The sound of her bullies' running footsteps had taught her to be fast. She used all of these skills now.

Everyone had huddled together, drawn by Jara's arguing. Aimee had drifted towards the edge, no one noticed her, and that played perfectly into her plan. Jara had ignited everyone's anger and they were all distracted by it, as Aimee had hoped they would be.

Now was her moment.

She tipped her shoulder and slipped sideways between Pelathina and Aranati, round the back of one of the male centaurs, and under one of Jara's waving arms. Without pausing she slipped a hand into Jara's coat pocket where she'd seen a squarish bulge. Her fingers closed on the diary and she pulled. Clutching it to her chest, she span on her heel, dived between two of the centaurs and ran for the door. It was a long moment before anyone realised Aimee had even moved, and by then she had a head start.

She was preparing to send a command to Jess the moment she was outside, when she heard a crash and a drum of hooves. One of the centaurs had leapt over two workbenches in one go and landed right in front of her. She tried to stop but her boots skidded on the wooden floor. From the corner of her eye she caught a sweep of black hair.

'Aranati!' she yelled and flung the diary.

Then she crashed into the flank of the centaur and fell to the floor. She instinctively put her hands out to break her fall and as her palms smacked into the floorboards, pain flashed up her wounded arm. She cried out as the burned handprint began to throb. The centaur towered above her and Aimee realised it was the young female with the red, braided hair. A tattoo of geometric patterns ran down her cheek from below her right eye making her look somehow even more foreign than her deer-like body did.

The centaur yelled something at Jara, then reared up on her hind legs. The hooves of her forelegs crashed back to the floor, landing either side of Aimee's knees. She felt the vibrations through the floorboards under her bum.

Then she lowered down and Aimee shrank away, but not fast enough. The cold edge of a curved dagger pressed to her throat.

'You, not friend of Jara. You, enemy of peace,' the centaur said.

Aimee didn't dare move, she hardly dared to breathe. Her throat pulsed against the dagger. Everyone had been converging on her and now they stopped, like statues. Aimee stared up into the centaur's eyes—large grey eyes the colour of clouds over the tundra.

'Pelathina.' Aimee barely moved her lips as she spoke. 'Can you tell her that I'm not her enemy, please?'

Aimee heard Pelathina's voice come from behind her, fast and breathless. The centaur above Aimee snarled something back. Aimee's heart was pounding in her chest and every beat sent a pulse of pain into her burned arm. The unintelligible words flowed over her head and Aimee really hoped they didn't contain her death.

Then a hand, and the arm of a black coat, appeared in her vision. For a moment Aimee thought it was Pelathina, then she realised the hand was pale, not brown. It rested softly on the centaur's wrist, fingers enclosing the taught tendons that gripped the dagger. Aimee flicked her eyes and was shocked to see Jara on the end of the arm.

'*Sala, ugu, ne ugu.*' Jara's words were a lot slower than Pelathina's had been. 'She is a Rider, Sala.'

Any joy Aimee might have felt at Jara claiming her as one of her own was dampened by the dagger which didn't move. Above her head one of the other centaurs spoke. Sala's grey eyes left Aimee's face, then a never-ending moment later, the blade left her throat.

Aimee was about to thank Jara, hoping that perhaps they could take a tentative step towards being civil again, but Jara got in first.

'I can't have a Helvethi killing a Rider inside Kierell. There are still Riders who don't trust the Helvethi and I'll never get them to support our alliance if they think a centaur murdered one of their own. Even if it was the freak that they killed.'

Jara had spoken without even looking at Aimee, and her words stung liked Aimee had been pricked with gorse. She tried to put a lid on her hurt, as Dyrenna stepped close to Jara.

'Jara, that isn't fair, Aimee—'

There was a splintering crash, like a felled tree toppling, and everyone jumped. Aimee scrambled back on her bum in case Sala's dagger reappeared. The small door to the workshop fell inwards, slamming to the floor. Aimee heard the roar and knew instantly that it was Jess. She tried to get through the gaping doorway but her wings wouldn't fit. She got herself wedged and roared again in frustration. Aimee could feel her tugging at their connection, as if she could use that to pull Aimee closer to her.

'Jess!'

'Blazing sparks!'

'*Sundrak!*'

Everyone shouted at once, but only Aimee moved. Her boot heels beat a rhythm on the floor as she ran for the door. Jess saw her coming and roared again, still trying to wriggle through a door that was way too small for her.

'Get her under control! Dull-sparked fool!'

Jara's command flew through the air after Aimee. She reached Jess and grabbed her dragon's head, pulling it down towards her own. She pressed her forehead against Jess's and imagined sending calming thoughts straight through their touching skulls. With one hand she patted Jess's feathers, trying to coax them to lie flat again.

'It's okay, girl, I'm safe,' she whispered. 'Now you have to ease off, please.'

Jess snorted a puff of smoke that wreathed Aimee's face. It tickled her nose but she didn't pull away. Instead she inhaled deeply, enjoying Jess's warming smell of woodsmoke.

'You shouldn't have done this,' Aimee told her, whispering, 'but thank you.'

It still amazed her that this incredible creature would risk her own life for her.

'Aranati, give it back.'

Aimee turned, but kept a hand on Jess, her scales becoming warm under her palm. The melee of people had split in two. Jara stood, Dyrenna by her shoulder and the Helvethi ranged in a semi-circle behind her. Sala still had her dagger bared, and the flinty look in her grey eyes said she was considering sticking it somewhere. Facing them, Aranati and Pelathina stood side by side, Nathine shifting uncomfortably behind them.

Aranati held the diary in both hands, her fingers almost camouflaged on its brown leather cover. Jara reached out, her long, slender fingers extended towards the diary.

'Aranati, don't you betray me today as well.'

Aimee guessed Jara had meant for the words to come out fierce as claws, but instead they wobbled. Everyone in the room must have heard the tears waiting just behind them. Aimee felt a pang of sympathy for her. But it didn't make her want to give in to Jara's orders, instead she wanted more than ever to find Kyelli. Only their city's saviour could take away the strain before Jara cracked.

Aimee drew strength from Jess, took a deep breath and stepped forward. 'Aranati, give the diary to me.'

Aranati's dark eyes swirled from Jara to Aimee and back to Jara. Her faced was screwed up with anguish and indecision.

'Please,' Aimee and Jara both said at the same time.

CHAPTER 24

## Missing

Aimee caught Pelathina's eye and wrinkled her forehead in a question. Surely if anyone could sway Aranati it was her sister, and Aimee was pretty sure Pelathina was on her side now. But Pelathina shook her head, gave a rueful smile and mouthed the word *stubborn*. Aimee felt a twinge of annoyance. Pelathina could at least try to persuade Aranati.

The tension in the warehouse was like a taught rope, twisting, straining, creaking. Jara snapped it with her outburst.

'Kyelli's sparks, Aranati! I shouldn't have to be begging you to listen to me. Does four years of friendship mean nothing to you?'

Aranati was gripping the diary so tight that Aimee could see the bony ridges of her knuckles. She took a single step forward, and Aimee held her breath.

'Lwena and Glaris were killed, Jara,' Aranati said softly. Her head was titled down, her words falling on the diary in her hands.

Jara sighed deeply. 'I'm sorry, and I feel the pain of that too, don't think I don't.'

'But you'll still send us back out there?'

Jara pulled the strands of her blonde hair up onto her head then let them fall. 'You don't need to go, Aranati. I'll find someone else.'

'I'm not a coward.' Aranati looked up, the frown deep on her face. 'I watched my parents murdered before I was taken as a slave. Surviving that taught me courage I will never lose.'

Pelathina reached out and gently took her sister's hand. Jess growled in Aimee's ear and she realised she'd been gripping her neck. She shoved her hands in her coat pockets and gripped the lining fabric instead, twisting it in her fingers.

'I'm sorry, I didn't mean it like that.'

As Jara stepped forward she glanced around and happened to catch Aimee's eye. Aimee was sure she saw fear flit across Jara's face, like clouds blown across the sky on a windy day. Then her cheeks flushed with anger and she stepped purposely towards the sisters. Aranati pulled back, bumping into Nathine who grabbed her to keep from falling.

'Damn it!' Jara lost patience. The anger that had been roiling inside her since the caravan turned back, spilled over again. 'Give me the diary or I will take Harmony and kick you out of the Riders!'

Aranati looked as if Jara had slapped her. When she spoke her words were soft clouds beside Jara's lightening.

'You would threaten to take another woman's dragon? You may as well threaten to steal the spark from my chest. Every one of us deserves our dragons, and that includes Aimee. Yes, we voted you as our leader, but we are Kyelli's Riders and you have no right to take that from us.'

Aimee saw it again, the fear flit across Jara's face. It came when Aranati said Kyelli's name. What was she afraid of? Losing her position as the Sky Riders' leader if Kyelli came back?

'Never in three hundred years has a woman been expelled from the Riders,' Aranati continued. Her lilting accent made her words even softer. 'We have all risked our lives to become part of our Riders' community, and we protect each other, as well as the city. It seems you have forgotten that.'

Aranati slipped the diary into her coat pocket and turned away from Jara. A wave of relief crashed over Aimee. Aranati began walking towards the door, Pelathina and Nathine right behind her. Aimee expected Jara to dash after her in a burst of fury. But she didn't. Instead she seemed to slump, as if Aranati's choice had sucked the energy from her spark.

'Come on, girl, out of the way.' Aimee gave Jess a gentle shove backward out of the doorway.

The Riders filed out. Aimee was last, and before she left, she looked back into the workshop. The centaurs had watched the whole exchange in confused silence but now they'd huddled together talking animatedly in their own language, stubby tails flicking. Sala caught Aimee's glance and narrowed her eyes.

Jara had buried her face in Dyrenna's shoulder and Aimee wondered if she was crying. It was mean, but Aimee hoped she was. As a girl she'd always wished she could make her bullies cry, rather than the other way round. She also felt elated that Aranati had chosen her. It meant she trusted her more than she trusted Jara right now.

Just as Aimee was about to turn away, Dyrenna gave her a small nod. Aimee really wished the older Rider would come with them, but from the motherly way she held Jara, Aimee knew her place was here. Looking after Jara was Dyrenna's self-appointed task, and Aimee could respect that, even if right then she didn't think Jara deserved a hug.

Outside Skydance, Harmony and Malgerus were landing in the wide street beside Jess. Their dragons were skittish, even Harmony, and their Riders were silent, as if not quite believing what had just happened, what they'd just done. As she jumped into her saddle and took Jess's horns, Aimee glanced up at Faradair. He was crouched low on the workshop roof, his long red tail and neck lying flat against the tiles. His blood-red feathers drooped on either side of his head. Above him Black stood as still as a gargoyle, wings wrapped around himself, but eyes watching everything.

Then they were in the air and soaring back across the city. Now that relief had washed away the fear of defying Jara and facing down a dagger-wielding Helvethi, Aimee felt her excitement bubble up again.

She was back on Kyelli's trail. Now all they had to do was read the diary. Callant and Aranati could learn about the Empty Warriors and how to defeat them, but what Aimee really wanted was to find that one word which would tell her where Kyelli was. Beneath her Jess shared her excitement and sped up, riding the air currents above the city.

Time still felt like it was running away from them, but now that they had the diary they could catch it. They could fix this before the army broke through into the tunnel.

Callant was waiting for them in the little courtyard by the cafe, his bearded face watching the sky. He lumbered to the side as the four dragons swooped in to land. There was barely enough space for them all in the courtyard, even with their wings tucked. Aimee could feel Jess's desire to be back in the sky again. It tugged at her like a friend urging her to leave her chores and come play.

'I can't believe I did that,' Aranati moaned as she dismounted, clutching her head in both hands. Harmony nudged her gently.

Aimee could see Aranati was shaking, the residue of fear and adrenaline still clinging to her. Aimee looked down at her own hands, ignoring the patches of colourless skin dotting her knuckles. She was shaking too.

'We had to Arri,' Pelathina reassured her. '*Shuraksh*, I promise.'

Aranati looked at her sister and slowly shook her

head. Pelathina spoke again, softly, her words unintelligible to Aimee.

'How many languages do you speak?' Aimee asked trying to steer the conversation away from worrying about Jara and any retribution that might be coming their way.

'Four,' Pelathina replied, turning to Aimee. 'Though my Glavic, the language they speak in the city states, is a bit rusty. If we were in a tavern in Taumerg, you wouldn't want to trust me to place your food order.'

'What's your and Aranati's language called?'

Pelathina face lit up with her lovely smile and Aimee felt a completely inappropriate tingle in her belly. 'It's Irankish.'

'I saw a merchant at Lorsoke once who had the same bronze colouring as you,' Nathine said. 'He told me he was from somewhere even further north than the city states where the sun shines all the time. Is that where you're from?'

'Oh, well now, a girl doesn't go dishing out stories of her past as easy as dragon's fire. You'll need to at least buy me cake first.'

Pelathina had been answering Nathine's question, but she was looking at Aimee. That tingle spread upwards making her heart thump faster.

'Did you get it?' Callant suddenly burst out. He'd been watching from the fringes of their conversation, dancing from foot to foot in agitation.

'No, beardy, we thought we'd just get you to write your own version and we'd use that instead.' Nathine's sarcasm was there but it wasn't as sharp as usual. She was rattled by what they'd done too.

Aimee realised then, there was no turning back. By organising other Riders to steal from, and disobey Jara, Aimee had crossed a line she hadn't even realised she was approaching.

Callant was still watching everyone intently, confusion on the part of his face not concealed by beard. Aimee took pity on him. She'd have hated to be left behind too, even if it meant not crossing that line.

'Yes, Callant, we've got the diary and now we'll need your knowledge of history and the city, and stories and stuff.'

He nodded eagerly and held out one thick-fingered hand. Aimee pointed to Aranati, who'd pulled the diary from her pocket, guilt written all over her face. She handed it to Callant as if it was a burning brand that she was keen to be rid of. Callant took it and stroked the leather cover, running his fingers over the embossed tree. Awe shone on his face as if the light of his spark was shining through his cheeks.

'Callant!' Nathine elbowed him.

'Yes, sorry, it's just so amazing to hold this little piece of Kyelli.'

'You're as bad as Aimee.' Nathine shook her head.

Callant sat on a stone bench at the edge of the courtyard and the Riders all crowded round. Their dragons milled around the courtyard, picking up on their Rider's excitement and unable to stay still. Malgerus playfully snapped at Jess.

'I've got tea,' Callant announced, placing the diary on his lap and fishing around under the bench. He pulled up a patterned teapot and a stack of small cups.

'Really, now?' Nathine's lip curled.

'Well, when I'm studying I always find having a cup of tea calms me down and helps me focus.' He looked up at them all, teapot in one hand, cups in the other.

Aimee couldn't help smiling at him. 'That's really kind, Callant, but we don't have time.'

'And tea's horrible,' Pelathina added.

'You don't like tea?' Nathine sounded as if Pelathina had admitted that she didn't have a spark. 'What's wrong with you? I brew the best tea and I'll bet if I made you a cup you'd love every sip.'

'Nathine, shut up,' Aimee interrupted. 'Pelathina…' her words stuttered out. She didn't feel comfortable chastising someone she'd only really met a few hours ago. She looked instead at Callant. 'Please read the diary, and you can drink the whole pot of tea after.'

To Aimee's relief, Callant put down the pot and cups, and opened Kyelli's diary. Aimee leaned over his shoulder, eager to see every single word Kyelli had written, every thought she'd shared. The pages of the diary rustled as Callant leafed through till he came to the section with the heading *Empty Warriors*, underlined three times.

'Go back a page first,' Aimee said.

Callant obediently flicked back, revealing the page covered in drawings of faces. Callant's fingers hovered over the paper, moving across the different types of faces, the ones with flames for eyes, others with little mountains in place of pupils, the female faces that all had woodgrain eyes, and finally the few at the bottom who had cogs in their eyes.

'We saw faces just like these carved into the fielders' homes,' Nathine explained for the others who hadn't been there.

'Sparkly sparks, what are they?' Pelathina asked.

'I think they're different types of Empty Warriors,' Aimee replied.

'There are more of them?' Aranati sounded horrified.

'I don't know. All the ones in the army had fire in their eyes, didn't they? Not other things.' Aimee looked to the sisters for confirmation. They both nodded and Aimee didn't know if she should be relieved. Were there others out there? Did Kyelli and her father destroy the ones with other things in their eyes but not the fire ones?

'Well, hopefully the answers are in here,' Callant said, then began to read aloud.

*They brought so much death. Even now that they're gone and we're safe, I still have night terrors. I can see Kierellatta crumbling, fires tearing through our beautiful streets, buildings levelled, stones crushing whole families. All those people we couldn't save. Father tells me the nightmares will fade and I hope he's right, because forever is a long time to live with these images in my head.*

*Efysta says I should write down my fears to get them out of my head. She tells me that if I confine them in the pages of my diary, they'll have less control over me.*

'Who's Efysta?' Pelathina interrupted.//
'Shh,' Nathine scolded her.//
'She was the first leader of the Sky Riders,' Aimee said, whispering though she wasn't sure why. Then she prodded Callant to continue.

*She knows a lot about control, now that she has her dragon, Dream. And she's so strong. I know the other four will vote for her to be their leader.*

'There were only five Sky Riders back then?'//
This time it was Nathine who interrupted and everyone shushed her. She scowled at them but waved for Callant to continue.

*I've lived for hundreds of years, and I'll live for hundreds more, but right now I don't feel nearly as brave as those women who've taken up my challenge to become Sky Riders. Not one of them has seen more than twenty-five summers, but their courage far eclipses mine. Back in Kierellatta I feared nothing, but that was before control was lost, before the Empty Warriors destroyed everything.*

Callant turned the page and there was a little sketch of a woman with short spiky hair, riding a dragon.

Aimee assumed this was Efysta and she envied her because she'd been friends with Kyelli.

> *I do wish, when everything fell apart, that I could have helped my father more. He won't tell me how many sparks it cost him, but I can see in the lines at the edge of his face that he doesn't have the life inside him that he once did. Father won't let me carry the guilt for not helping. I'm hundreds of years old but he's still trying to look after his little girl.*
>
> *When it got out of control, and the Empty Warriors began to destroy everything, we quickly realised that only an immortal could stop them, only we Quorelle could undo them. Of course, we didn't call them Empty Warriors at first, but that's what they became. It was my brother who gave them that name, and it's a good name for something which is the opposite of us, something with not a single spark.*
>
> *I wasn't going to mention my brother. His death, it still eats at me. The other nine Quorelle died too, but he's the only one I mourn. Now father and I are the last.*

Callant's voice had gone wheezy as he read the last sentence and now he doubled over as a coughing fit engulfed him. Exasperated Nathine made to grab the diary from him, but he pushed her hand away. He straightened up, face red and chest still bucking with suppressed coughs.

'Have you tried—' Aranati began but Callant cut her off.

'Don't say thyme tea.' He shook his head but threw her a smile.

Aimee was happy for the interruption because her mind was reeling from what she'd learned. Kyelli didn't stop the Empty Warriors last time, her father did. But it sounded like she knew how it was done. And she had a brother. Aimee's uncle had never mentioned him in any of his stories. And, worst of all, Kyelli said that only one of the Quorelle could undo the Empty Warriors. Whatever undoing them meant.

Callant finally had enough breath to keep reading.

*I'm getting ahead of myself. I suppose if, like Efysta says, I'm to tell this story, then I should start at the beginning. I should start in Kierellatta. Oh, I loved it there. I'm sure our survivors will create a home and a city here, inside these mountains, but it'll never be quite the same. Each of the three other domains had their capitals—Mornvello, Trivethon and Deltance. I know I'm biased, because Kierellatta was our family's city, but it was the nicest. I still can't believe it's gone.*

Callant turned the page, and the next one was blank. He flicked back in case he'd accidentally turned over two at once, but he hadn't.

'Where's the rest?' Aimee asked, a sudden panic gripping her chest.

'I don't know.' Callant thumbed through the remaining few pages at the back of the diary—they were all blank.

'Perhaps, for some reason, Kyelli didn't get a chance to finish writing,' Aranati suggested, her frown as deep as ever.

'No.' Aimee refused to believe that.

She snatched the diary from Callant, went back to the last page of writing, flipped it over and spotted the stubs. Right in at the spine of the diary there were raggedy stubs of pages. She felt herself sinking, as if a bog of despair was pulling her down. Across the courtyard Jess huddled on the flagstones.

'Someone's torn out the rest of the section about Empty Warriors,' she told the others.

CHAPTER 25

## NOT GOOD ENOUGH

AIMEE SWALLOWED THE lump in her throat and felt tears in her eyes. It wasn't fair. Listening to Callant reading Kyelli's words she'd felt so close to her, but whoever had torn out the pages had snatched away all chance of Aimee finding her. This was it, the end of their quest, and she'd failed. She'd lost all chance they had of saving the city, and their lives.

'Oh sparks, we've betrayed Jara for nothing,' Aranati's voice fluttered with panic.

Aimee looked at her and she stared back, her dark eyes full of accusation. Aimee had led them here. She'd convinced them to cross that line and disobey their leader. It had seemed worth the risk when Aimee was sure they'd find Kyelli. Now, if the others lost their dragons, if Jara kicked them out of the Riders, it would be her fault.

'It wasn't for nothing, Arri, we've learned that—' Pelathina began, trying to pick up the pieces.

'That what, Pellie? That only one of the immortal

Quorelle can destroy the Empty Warriors, and that all the others died, leaving only Kyelli. And we've still got no clue as to where she's gone. *Gari chingreth!*

Harmony had begun flapping, trying to take off, to get out of the small courtyard that suddenly felt very cramped. Aranati pulled away from her sister's reaching hand and ran to comfort her dragon.

'It doesn't make sense,' Nathine said, taking the diary from Aimee. She turned to the front and began angrily flicking through pages. Aimee winced at how roughly she handled the diary. Reams of writing and pages of drawings slipped past under her fingers. 'There's all this other stuff about Kyelli, and the city,' she held up a page with a drawing of Quorelle Square and the council chamber half built, 'so why leave it and only take the last few pages?'

'Because there's a secret on those pages that someone doesn't want us to know,' Pelathina suggested.

'Yeah, but who doesn't want us to know? Aimee and I found this in a hidden room in the library's roof. The dust up there was so thick you could have drowned in it. No one had been up there in hundreds of years.'

'So, you're saying the only person who could have removed the pages was Kyelli herself?' Callant pondered.

'Why would she write about the Empty Warriors then tear out the pages? What kind of idiot leaves a map and a bunch of clues, if they lead to nowhere?' Nathine asked, her voice brimming with anger.

'*Asnjing* sparks!'

They all looked up at Aranati. She was standing in

the middle of the courtyard, one arm around Harmony's neck, her dragon's golden head resting on her shoulder. Her frown was a bottomless crevasse in her forehead.

'We shouldn't have done this.' Aranati shook her head, long dark hair swishing across her back. 'We should have left the diary with Jara and done as we were told.'

'Done what, Arri? Gone back out to the army and got ourselves killed like Lwena?'

'At least we would have been helping, Pellie, doing what a Rider is supposed to do.'

'We are helping!'

'You've got an old diary that tells us nothing. This is a dead end!'

Aranati was right and the bog of desperation finally pulled Aimee in over her head. She slumped down on the bench beside Callant. Her heel caught the teapot, knocking it over. Hot tea puddled round her feet and she barely noticed. Jess's talons clacked on the flagstones as she walked over and laid her head in Aimee's lap. Aimee felt the surge of love through their connection, like warm sunshine in her mind, but instead of comforting her it made her cry. She'd risked Jess for nothing. Would Jara tear them apart?

She looked around the courtyard.

'I'm sorry.'

She'd hoped the words would come out strong, to show she meant them, but they were a wobbly whisper.

'Quiet,' Aranati ordered.

Aimee felt like someone had squeezed her heart. Her apology wasn't good enough. Would Aranati persuade the others to turn on her? Would they hand her over to Jara to save their own dragons?

Then she realised Aranati had turned her face to the sky. They all had. She'd been telling everyone to be quiet, and she looked afraid. Aimee strained to hear whatever Aranati had.

Then she heard it. It was muffled but unmistakable. Thump, thump, thump.

'That sounds like the battering ram, but we shouldn't be able to hear that all the way from the other side of the mountains,' Pelathina said.

'No, unless…' Aimee left her words hanging. She didn't want to voice what she thought. If she said it out loud that might make it real. And she didn't want it to be real.

'Oh great blazing sparks! Finally, some Riders. Aranati! The gate's down! They've broken through into the tunnel!'

The yell came from the sky and Aimee looked up to see Whisper flapping towards them, his long green wings almost brushing the sides of buildings. Aimee's heart dropped into her toes. It was real, the army was inside the tunnel. It'd taken them less than a day to break down a gate that had held for three centuries. Now they were battering the inner gate. Aimee shuddered. A single gate was all that was keeping the monsters from the people in the caravan compound.

And Aimee had failed to find the one person who

could have saved the city. She felt sick.

'Aranati?' Sal shouted from Whisper's back. They hadn't landed, just kept circling the courtyard above, Rider and dragon both too anxious to stop moving.

'I heard you,' she called back, 'now stop telling the whole world. The last thing the city needs is an injection of panic.'

'What do we do?' Sal was still shouting. 'I can't find Jara.'

'She's at the ManYoven workshop on Lolforn Street,' Aranati pointed towards Barter.

'Okay. Then what?' Sal asked as Whisper made another pass.

'Honestly, Sal, I don't know,' Aranati admitted.

Aimee watched Whisper disappear over the buildings, then looked back down at her patchy hands. There were thousands of people in Kierell and she'd been an idiot to think she was the one to save them. Apart from Nathine, every other Rider was more experienced than she was. All the councillors understood the city and its needs better than she did. Those scholars from the university were way more clever than she'd ever be. Perhaps she should have given them the map. With all their learning maybe they would have seen something that she missed, followed it in different ways. But now it was too late.

Jess growled, low in her throat, the sound vibrating on Aimee's thighs. She stroked Jess's feathers. She was just one girl and her dragon. In the excitement of the quest for Kyelli she'd forgotten that. She should have handed over the search to someone better.

Then Aimee realised something was missing—there were no sounds. She expected the others to be arguing and panicking, for the courtyard to be echoing with their voices, but it was eerily silent. She looked up, half expecting to see everyone had disappeared when she wasn't looking. She wouldn't blame them for flying off and leaving her there. Instead, they were all watching her. And their faces were resolute, not panicky.

Nathine tightened her ponytail, pulling it higher up on her head. 'So, what do we do now?'

Aimee waited for someone else to answer, then with a feeling like her insides had shrivelled, realised the question had been directed at her.

'Why are you asking me?' She focused on Nathine, because that was easier than trying to meet everyone's eyes.

'You're the one with all the plans.'

'But you're always telling me my plans are stupid. And look how this one turned out!'

She hadn't meant to shout, nor stand up and glare at them all. Nathine was wearing her *you're an idiot* look. Callant was looking up at her expectantly from the bench. Pelathina and Aranati were standing side by side, one sister frowning, the other wearing a small smile like she knew something no one else did.

'Yeah, your plans are stupid, but better a stupid plan than no plan,' Nathine said.

'But all I've done is waste a day on a pointless quest and get us all into serious trouble. Callant could have been doing important councillor-ish stuff, and you could all have been helping Jara calm that mob, or stop riots, or protect the people at the caravan compound.'

'Ugh! You're so annoying.' Nathine stomped over, shoved Aimee back so her bum landed on the bench again and stood over her, hands on hips. Malgerus was behind her, his body hidden by Nathine's so his orange wings looked like they belonged to her instead.

'All day you've been giving orders to councillors, walking roughshod over stuffy librarians and telling off older Riders. I may have said in the past that your brain is as patchy as your face, but it isn't really. It works just fine, so why can't you realise that you've been happily dishing out authority like you owned it. And I think sometimes that's all authority is, just talking the talk.'

'But—' Aimee began.

'Don't interrupt when I'm being nice to you,' Nathine continued over her. 'We've all followed you today and it's definitely not because I like looking at your bum. I wanted a way to help, to do anything that would protect my little brother. You gave me that. Every little gang needs a leader, and you're ours. With your stupid determination you gave me hope that there's a way to fight those monsters, so don't bloody well take it away now!'

Aimee gaped at her but Nathine just kept on going.

'If you hadn't been so bloody determined, and bossed everyone around, including important councillors and Riders, then we'd probably all be out there fighting the Empty Warriors and getting shot from the sky one by one. You'd definitely be dead by now, though Mal and I might still be alive. So get up, mushroom head!'

When Nathine had finished her little tirade Aimee sat stunned. She'd never thought of herself as a leader, never wanted to be one. She'd just wanted to find Kyelli, and she'd needed help to do that. Callant nudged her in the ribs and she turned to look at him on the bench beside her. He lifted his chin, pointing his beard at Nathine.

'Your friend and I haven't always seen eye to eye today, but she's right. I suppose, being a councillor, technically I should be in charge here, but it's not been me who's led this quest. We only got here because of you.'

'But here's just a dead end,' Aimee said quietly.

Callant nudged her again. 'Do you know what makes a great scholar?' Aimee shook her head. 'Someone who, when their research funnels them into a dead end, resets with a cup of tea, re-examines everything, and finds a way out.'

'We can't do the tea part because I knocked over your teapot.' Aimee splashed her boot in the puddle at her feet, and actually smiled a little.

'The great thing about tea is you can always brew more. I hear Nathine makes the best cup of tea this side of Lorsoke.' Callant's beard opened to show his grin.

'Oh it's better than anything the Helvethi can brew, and probably nicer than any cup in the city states too,' Nathine added, her face looking very serious, but Aimee could see the smile in her eyes.

'Though nothing beats a strong, dark coffee,' Pelathina said, coming to crouch beside Aimee so their eyes were on the level.

'What's coffee?'

'It's the best thing ever, and I miss it so much. But, if we can destroy this army, and get the councillors back out there to make peace with the Helvethi, we can make the tundra safe. Then who knows, maybe some enterprising merchant will trade coffee beans all the way from Marlidesh to here. Sparkly sparks, I can still remember how good it smells.' Pelathina closed her eyes for a moment, savouring her memory. 'Arri, think we could persuade someone to open a little coffee house in Kierell, like the one our parents had?'

Aimee watched as Aranati's frown lessened a little at that suggestion. She must have been happy because Harmony nudged her playfully, her wing tips fluttering. Aimee looked for Skydance and saw he'd hopped up onto another bench and was shifting from foot to foot, talons clicking on the stone, eager to be off. Malgerus was still behind Nathine, his wings making her look amazing. And Jess had uncurled and raised her head from Aimee's lap. She stared at Aimee with her yellow eyes and Aimee could feel the longing in her to be back in the sky.

Looking at everyone's dragons Aimee could tell the three other Riders were all keen to get moving, to continue with their quest, to do something to save the city. They could all fly off on their own and find other ways to help, but they didn't. They stayed, waiting for her.

Pelathina was still crouched beside her, a cheery smile on her pretty face.

'How come you are always so happy?' Aimee asked. 'Even when everything's going wrong, you always smile.'

'Because four years ago on the tundra crossing I made a decision to be happy,' Pelathina told her.

'What, always?'

Pelathina nodded. 'As much as I can be, yes. Before Aranati and I came to Kierell, there was a lot in my life that made me angry, vengeful and sad. But if I can put that aside and choose happiness, then you can put aside your lack of confidence and chose to continue leading this quest.'

'The tea-hater has a point,' Nathine chimed in.

Aimee ignored her and focused on Pelathina. In fact she was finding it hard to look anywhere else. Her brown eyes were intense, but her smile was soft and cute. It was an intriguing combination.

'You're still going to tell me your story sometime, aren't you?' Aimee asked.

It was a simple question, and one she'd asked other Riders, but it somehow felt like she was asking Pelathina more, like there were other words hidden underneath what she'd said. She found herself holding her breath, waiting for an answer.

Pelathina prodded her knee, cheeky and playful. 'Once you've saved the city, I will.'

And Aimee felt like there was more to Pelathina's

simple answer. It set the butterflies going in her stomach and it was an effort to drag her eyes away from the other girl.

'Can I see the diary again?' Aimee held out her hand to Nathine.

'Well, finally, that took long enough,' Nathine complained as she passed it over.

Nathine had closed it and Aimee ran her fingers over the beautiful tree embossed onto the leather cover. Kyelli had touched this, had created it, and surely she meant for her Riders to have it and use it. Aimee opened the diary at the torn-out pages again, childishly hoping that they'd have magically reappeared.

'What's that?' Pelathina leaned over, looking at the diary upside down. She was so close that Aimee could smell her—a sweet, earthy scent that set the butterflies going again. Aimee followed Pelathina's slender bronze fingers, trying to banish the image of those fingers intertwined with her own.

At the bottom edge of one of the torn-off pages there was a little triangle of paper where the page hadn't ripped out neatly. There would be a corner missing from that page, wherever it was.

'There are words on it!' Aimee exclaimed, her voice loud with her excitement.

'Let me see.' Nathine crowded over Aimee's shoulder.

'Watch the teapot!' Callant warned her as Nathine's boot heel stomped down on the spout, breaking it. But then he knocked over the pile of cups as he knelt up on the bench to peer at the diary. Pelathina giggled at the tinkling crash as all the cups toppled over and broke. Aimee laughed too, maybe at the smashed cups, maybe at the joy of discovery, or maybe just at having people huddled so close to her, jostling her, touching her, not one of them caring about her weird skin.

'Well, come on, sludge brain, what does it say?' Nathine elbowed her.

Pelathina gently pressed the little scrap of paper flat. There were two words on it.

'Dragon's Tears,' Aimee read aloud.

CHAPTER 26

## ANGER AND POETRY

'What does that mean?' Nathine demanded. 'If I make Mal cry then Kyelli will magically appear? That kind of nonsense only works in children's stories.'

Aimee barely heard Nathine. She was watching Callant because he was tugging at his beard, the way he did when he'd thought of something.

'You know what Dragon's Tears means, don't you?'

Aimee's heart beat a quick tempo in her throat as she waited for Callant to answer. He pursed his lips, making his beard point sideways.

'I recognise the phrase, I'm just trying to remember where I've seen it.' He closed his eyes, thinking.

'Well, if it's somewhere in the clutter of his office it'll take till next summer to find it,' Nathine said, folding her arms.

'Shut up, Nathine,' Aimee said automatically, all her attention focused on Callant, willing him to remember.

'Yes! It's on the table!'

He jumped to his feet, then immediately doubled over, chest rattling with his coughing. They had to wait till he had his breath back. Aimee was practically vibrating with impatience. Finally, with one hand to his chest and the other wiping his streaming eyes, Callant straightened.

'There's a map carved on the table in the high gallery of the council chamber,' he wheezed. Aimee pictured the big oval table. It had been littered with papers and cups of tea the two times she'd seen it. 'It's not a detailed, accurate map like the one you've got, Aimee, it's more like an artist's drawing of bits of the city. But the table does mirror the Ring Mountains outside, and I normally sit at a chair that's beside the carved north-eastern curve of the mountains. There are a few lines of poetry carved on the map there, and that's where I've seen the phrase Dragon's Tears.'

Callant looked around at them, triumphant. Aimee smiled to see him caught up in the same excitement she was. Then his face fell.

'I can't get into the council chamber. The councillors are inside and they've barricaded the door against the crowd outside.' He chewed his lip, making his beard waggle.

'That's fine, we,' Nathine gestured round at the Riders, 'can fly up to the first floor windows and get in that way.'

Callant nodded, trying not to look dejected. They kept having to leave him behind. Aimee knew that feeling of being excluded, and it was horrible. This clue was Callant's discovery, not hers or Nathine's, he deserved to be there when they unravelled it. Their quest was reignited, but only because of him and Aimee wanted to find a way to include him.

'Is there a secret back door into the council chamber?' she asked.

Callant shook his head but Aranati answered. 'Yes.'

'Really?' Callant's eyebrows shot up into his unruly hair.

Aranati hadn't moved from beside Harmony. She was the only one who hadn't crowded round when Aimee reopened the diary. Her frown deepened and she looked like she regretted speaking.

'Can you tell us where the secret door is?' Aimee asked gently.

Instead of answering, Aranati hunched her shoulders and drew in on herself. Pelathina had said that Aranati liked to have things mapped out before she did anything. Aimee's plans were more the make-it-up-as-you-go-along type. She was about to try convincing Aranati when she realised she wasn't the best person for that. Aimee had seen that Aranati trusted one person more than anyone else in the world.

'Pelathina, can you talk to her?' Aimee whispered.

Pelathina nodded, unfolded herself from her crouch and went to her sister. She spoke quietly, in their own language. Aimee waited. Nathine opened her mouth, probably to make some unhelpful comment and Aimee threw her a look. Nathine scowled but kept her sarcasm to herself. After a few minutes the sisters turned to face them.

'It's in the alley just off Vik Street. It leads into a short tunnel that brings you out in an office at the back of the council chamber,' Aranati told them. 'Jara told me about it. Apparently it was built by a member of the Uneven Council back in Kierell's first century so he could sneak out to his favourite pie shop. Rumour is Marhorn used the tunnel too, for the same reason.'

'Why couldn't you have told me about him when you were droning on about old councillors?' Nathine threw the question at Callant. 'Pie-man sounds way more interesting than the woman who designed sewers.'

The hole in Callant's beard opened but Aimee got in first. 'Ignore her. Aranati, can you show Callant where the secret door is? And the rest of us will fly straight to the council chamber. You can meet us there, and Callant we'll meet you inside, in the high gallery.'

'That sounds like a plan to me.' Pelathina smiled.

'I have seen more detailed plans before,' Aranati said.

'Don't worry, it's all Aimee's idea, so just do what I do,' Nathine told her as she mounted up. 'If the plan works, steal the credit and if it all goes horribly wrong, then blame Aimee because she led us all astray.'

'I'm not sure you're helping, Nathine,' Aimee said.

'I'm always a great help. You'd never have got this far without me.' Nathine grinned at her as she pulled on her goggles and tightened the ponytail on the crown of her head.

'Well I for one am in. I'm choosing Team Aimee,'

Pelathina declared.

Skydance barely stood still for a second and Aimee was amazed that Pelathina didn't miss her saddle as she mounted up. And once she was seated on his back, he was still weaving side to side, as if he couldn't wait to be off. Aimee mounted up too, feeling Jess's strength beneath her. Pelathina's description of them as Team Aimee had made her spark feel like it was glowing bright as a full moon in her chest. She'd unintentionally brought this little group together but now it felt important to keep them together. She thought of Pairen and Nyanna, and their gang of bullies. Now Aimee had her own gang.

Beneath Aimee, Jess gave a rumbly satisfied growl.

'I know, girl.' Aimee smiled.

A few moments later they were in the sky. Aimee could feel Jess's urge to soar up into the freedom of the clouds and tightened the connection in her mind, like winding in a rope. With Malgerus pushing ahead, Jess and Skydance followed him towards the council chamber. Harmony split off towards the eastern curve of Barter, Callant jogging in the streets below. Aimee let Malgerus and Skydance pull ahead as she slowed Jess, and watched Harmony. She skimmed a red-brick clocktower then hovered above an alley, her wings making backbeats that swirled the smoke from a nearby chimney. Happy that Aranati was doing as she'd said, Aimee pushed Jess to catch up with the others.

They approached the council chamber from the north, so the building blocked their view of Quorelle

Square, but Aimee could hear the crowd. It sounded twice as loud and three times as angry as it had a few hours ago. She found herself hunching in her saddle—her ingrained reaction to loud voices. Jess wasn't cowering though, so Aimee took strength from her and made herself sit tall.

The arched windows curving around the council chamber's high gallery reflected the city and the curve of mountains behind them. Aimee smiled as she saw her own reflection riding through the sky, with two other dragons alongside.

'We can land on the balcony,' Pelathina called as she pushed on Skydance's horns and he shot past.

His reflection filled three windows as he landed with a whoosh, sapphire wings extended to full width. Aimee carefully guided Jess in beside him and was really pleased when her talons clicked down on the stone balustrade neatly. She snorted a small puff of smoke.

'Yeah, I know, girl, you land better when I don't overthink it. Stop being so smug,' Aimee told her dragon with a wry smile.

There was a stone balcony following the curve of the arched windows, large enough for a person, but not a dragon. Pelathina jumped down first, Aimee and Nathine just behind her. Their dragons stayed perched above them on the balustrade. One of the windows must have also been a door, because it swung open, startling Aimee.

'Sparks! What are you lot doing here?'

A Rider stepped through the door. Lyrria. Aimee's

heart dropped down into her knees. Lyrria's shirt was undone one more button than was strictly proper. Her intricately braided hair curled beautifully over one shoulder. She leaned against the doorframe, the pose emphasising the curve of her hips. Then she caught sight of Aimee.

'Hey.'

It was all she said. For once, she seemed to have no more words. Aimee watched the emotions slide from her face like masks—surprise, confusion, then delight that quickly gave way to worry, and was the last one guilt?

Then before anyone could speak Harmony landed beside Malgerus.

'Callant's on his way,' Aranati announced.

Movement through the windows caught Aimee's attention and she turned. Her traitorous eyes wanted to linger on Lyrria, still in the doorway, but she pulled them away. She could see gesturing arms and hear angry voices.

'What's happening inside?' Aimee asked Lyrria, and was pleased when her voice didn't wobble.

'The councillors are all arguing about if they should collapse the tunnel. Did you hear? The Empty Warriors have broken down the outer gate,' Lyrria said.

Aimee and the others nodded.

'They can't collapse the tunnel. I know they're frightened but surely the council wouldn't trap us inside the mountains.' Aranati looked around at them all as if seeking support.

'It'll kill a whole bunch of those Empty Warriors,

any that are inside the tunnel will be crushed, and it'll stop the rest of them from getting near us,' Lyrria said, stepping fully out onto the balcony.

'Yeah, but we'll be trapped,' Pelathina added. There was an edge to her voice that Aimee hadn't heard before.

'Well, not us, we can still fly out,' Lyrria replied with a smile. 'Though, with Helevethi *and* Empty Warriors on the tundra now, I can't see why we'd want to.'

'Oh, those poor Helevthi,' Pelathina said, rubbing the back of her head and making her hair stick up. 'Those four leaders who're with Jara, if we collapse the tunnel they'll be trapped here forever. They won't be able to get back to their tribes.'

'Well, they shouldn't have come to Kierell in the first place,' Lyrria said with a dismissive wave of her hand.

Aranati rocked back on her heels as if Lyrria's words had shoved her. 'They came to offer their help. They're here because they believe in the peace Jara's been trying to build.'

'I lost a brother and a sister to Helvethi arrows, so forgive me if I don't weep because a few of them might get separated from their families.'

Anger flashed across Lyrria's freckled face, but it was tinged with sorrow. Aimee had to swallow a sudden urge to reach out and hug her. She disagreed with what Lyrria was saying. But being this close to Lyrria again had opened the box of memories that she'd pushed to the back of her mind. Right then, Lyrria could say whatever she liked, if only she'd kiss her neck again and send tingles through her body.

And that was the thing, Lyrria would do exactly that, if Aimee let her. If Aimee accepted that Lyrria would never fully love her, and would always be ashamed of her. If Aimee asked, knowing Lyrria, she'd probably whisk them off somewhere private right now, even with enemies battering at the city's gates. She'd be up for a bit of fun before any real fighting started.

Behind her, Jess fluttered anxiously, causing Skydance to shuffle away from her, talons clicking on the stone. Aimee took a deep breath and firmly closed the door on her longing.

'If that tunnel hadn't been there, Arri and I would never have been able to get into Kierell. We'd have been eaten by prowlers or drowned in a bog somewhere out on the tundra. We wouldn't have found this safe home,' Pelathina was saying, that edge in her voice getting sharper.

'Well, that didn't happen and you're both safe.' Lyrria shrugged. 'And besides, it's not like there's a stream of people from the city states, or your country, knocking on our door every day.'

'That's because the tundra crossing isn't safe!' Pelathina threw up her arms in frustration. 'But if it were, people would come. Different people with new ideas, and stories, and lots of exciting things we could learn.'

'Do we need that?' Lyrria shrugged again, even more nonchalant this time, though Aimee had a feeling she was acting more casual than she felt.

'And that's your problem right there, Lyrria,' Aranati said, crossing her arms.

'My problem?' Lyrria demanded.

'You've never quite accepted us, have you? You don't like that we're from somewhere else. We're not descendants of the people Kyelli and Marhorn saved, and you think that makes us lesser,' Aranati accused.

On the balcony railing, both Skydance and Harmony had cocked their heads forwards, ruffs of feathers puffed up and quivering. Aimee anxiously looked around for Midnight, but couldn't see her.

'Hey.' Lyrria held up both hands, as if showing she was unarmed. 'I've never said that.'

'No, never in so many words.' Pelathina's eyes narrowed, her face almost as frowny as her sister's.

There was a horribly tense silence. No one was looking at Aimee, but she was staring at them all, and inside her chest it felt like someone was siphoning the energy from her spark. Everything was breaking down, even the Riders, though she understood it was because they were scared. Aimee used to argue with her aunt in the same way. Naura was always trying to persuade Aimee to go out, to stop hiding her odd face, but Aimee had been bullied enough to be scared of everything beyond the safety of her front door. So they argued. Aimee still loved Naura but she'd yell at her sometimes till they both cried.

Aimee glanced through the arched windows into the high gallery. Councillors stood around the table, gesticulating, the same argument raging in there as well. Before, Myconn had most of the councillors on his side, but now that monsters from legend were banging to get in, would they decamp to Beljarn's side? Would they vote to seal the tunnel?

Aimee felt a hand grip her wrist and was startled to see Nathine beside her. Aimee looked up at the taller girl. Worry always made Nathine's round face look younger. It stripped her of her constant anger, and she became not a bully, but a scared girl.

'This,' she gestured to the argument swirling around them, 'isn't why we're here.'

'But—'

'Don't tell me you've forgotten the plan already? This whole thing was your idea, and we're all following your orders, remember, mushroom head?'

Aimee's intended protest came out as a half laugh instead. 'You're right.'

'I know. Now tell them to shut up and let's get on with solving this last clue.' Nathine let go of her wrist and elbowed her in the ribs, causing her to take a stumbling step forward.

Lyrria and Pelathina were practically yelling at each other now, with Aranati trying to calm them both. Aimee didn't know how to intervene in that, how to assert her voice, or her will, over their fierce argument. She also didn't want to draw Lyrria's attention. So she took Nathine's hand, and pulling the other girl along, slipped past them and into the high gallery.

'Aimee, what—' she heard Lyrria begin but then she

was inside and the clamour of councillors' voices drowned out her ex-lover.

She slipped through the window-door at the same moment that Callant barged in the other door. He was wheezing, hand clutching at his barrel-like chest. Sweat trickled down the sides of his face, soaked up by his beard. His eyes were bright and excited, though, and they flicked around the room till they found Aimee. He grinned and gave her a thumbs up.

'Callant, how did you get in here?' Myconn demanded.

'Has the crowd dispersed?' Cyella asked, hopeful, jewels sparkling as she fluttered her fingers.

'No time, sorry.'

Callant shoved his way through the councillors, and around the table to Aimee. He gave her arm a brief squeeze as he passed her, and thankfully it was her uninjured arm, because he gripped like he was trying to crush her bones. He reached the end of the table, close to the windows. It was littered with papers, and with one sweep of his big arm, he sent the whole lot fluttering to the floor.

'What the blazing sparks, Callant?' a young councillor beside Myconn demanded.

Callant ignored him, and beckoned Aimee closer. She tried to pretend everyone in the room wasn't looking at her and hurried over to Callant, pulling Nathine along with her. The layout of the carved map on the table matched the geography of the city outside, with the edge of the table carved like the Ring Mountains. They were standing by the north-eastern curve. Closest to these cliffs was the part of the city that Aimee's uncle had always called the smelly streets. It was the brewers, the tanners and, further north closest to the fields, the abattoirs. Between the buildings and the mountains was a stretch of fields, carved on the table with little flowers and cows. A stream wiggled across the fields, filled from the Toig waterfall. Beside the waterfall, carved into the wood, were four lines of poetry.

> *Placed safe and hidden away*
> *Though I may yet rue the day*
> *The essence of me, always here*
> *Behind the Fall of Dragon's Tears*

CHAPTER 27

# HERE

'IT'S THE WATERFALL,' Callant said. 'It must have originally been called the Fall of Dragon's Tears and we've forgotten that name.'

Excitement filled Aimee to the point where she felt like she could fly without Jess. She stood straight and looked out across the city. Lake Toig was hidden between the peaks, but its waterfall poured down, gleaming silver in the summer sunshine.

'She's just there,' Aimee whispered.

'Who?' Nathine nudged her in the ribs.

'Kyelli.' Aimee laughed and pointed at the poem. 'Always here? She never left us, Nathine. Kyelli's been in the city this whole time, keeping a watch over us.'

'From behind a waterfall?' Nathine looked sceptical but that only made Aimee laugh more.

'Maybe she has a palace inside the mountains, carved out like Anteill, with chandeliers of dragon's breath orbs.'

Aimee shook Nathine as she tried to make the other

girl see what she could see, to feel the anticipation that was reaching boiling point inside her. They were a short flight away from meeting Kyelli. She turned to look at Callant and saw the same light of discovery shining in his eyes, yet he gave her a sad smile.

'You're on your own for this one,' he said. 'It'll take me forever to run out to the waterfall, and besides, I think I'm needed here.' He gestured around the room.

The councillors were still arguing, and the noise was like a nest of angry bees. Beljarn and Myconn were practically nose to nose, yelling in each other's faces. One woman had slumped in a chair and held her head in her hands, crying. Another was shouting to anyone who'd listen that her husband was still out in the Ardnanlich Forest. Aranati was moving between them, trying to restore some calm, and failing badly. Lyrria stood by the window-door, hands on hips, shaking her head at everyone.

If Aimee could bring Kyelli back here, then the councillors wouldn't need to make this decision. The diary pages were missing, so they couldn't learn how to destroy the Empty Warriors themselves, but Kyelli knew. In fact, only she could do it. What they had read in her diary said that only one of the Quorelle could undo the Empty Warriors.

'Callant, can you stall them for an hour?' Aimee asked, tilting her head to look up into his face. 'Keep them arguing, and don't let them collapse the tunnel until I get back here with Kyelli?'

The gap in Callant's beard opened to show a wry

smile. 'I don't think keeping this argument going will be an issue.'

'Thank you, and I'm sorry you can't come with us.'

Callant shrugged his big shoulders. 'Say hi to Kyelli for me.'

Aimee felt she wanted to acknowledge Callant's help somehow, so she stuck out her hand for him to shake, aware that he might not want to touch it. He looked down at her white-speckled fingers and shook his head. Then grinned and pulled her into a hug. He smelled sweaty, but Aimee didn't give a damn. She was sure her spark just got brighter.

'Well, you're not getting a hug from me,' Nathine told him as they pulled apart. 'I've used mine all up on Aimee.'

'Maybe don't let Nathine be the first person to speak to Kyelli, just in case she pisses her off and Kyelli decides to stay in hiding,' Callant said to Aimee, in a conspiratorial whisper loud enough for Nathine to hear.

She threw him a glare and tightened the ponytail on top of her head. 'Let's go, Aimee.'

Aimee nodded and turned to gather up the others. She found Pelathina right behind her, smiling as she pulled on her goggles. Aimee looked around for Aranati but she'd disappeared into a knot of four arguing councillors.

'She's staying here,' Pelathina said. 'I don't think Lyrria has the temperament to stop this lot from killing each other.'

Aimee thought about the way Lyrria had always

goaded the recruits when she'd been training them and had to agree with Pelathina's assessment. She threw one last look at Callant, but he'd already waded into the discussions, then she led the way to the door. Just as she was about to step through, Lyrria grabbed her hand. Aimee felt an unwanted tingle as Lyrria's soft skin met her own. A rush of memories invaded her brain.

But then Lyrria dropped her hand, and Aimee wondered, if they'd been alone would she have held it? If there had been no one around to see her touching the freak?

'Does Jara know what you're doing?' Lyrria asked, and Aimee had to stop herself from staring at her lips.

'Yes.' It wasn't a lie, Jara did know, she just didn't want them to do it.

'When you're back, and we can hand this mess over to Kyelli, can we talk?' Lyrria asked softly.

Aimee wanted to immediately say yes, and her lips almost formed the word before she stopped herself. Sunlight from the open door coated one half of Lyrria's face, making the freckles on her other cheek stand out more. The copper strands in her hair gleamed and her silver earrings, the flowers with the lapis lazuli in the centre, swung gently as she cocked her head. Her brown-green eyes had gone all soft, they way they had when they'd been together.

Sparks, she was beautiful.

'Aimee?' Lyrria prompted.

'Maybe,' Aimee replied, then stepped through the door before she did something stupid, like kiss her.

Outside Jess, picking up on Aimee's excitement, tried to rush over to greet her by hopping off the balustrade and down onto the balcony. Except that the balcony was too narrow and her wings were too wide. She got half-wedged and growled at everyone for a moment before she managed to scramble back up onto the balustrade, talons leaving scratches in the stone.

'Uh-huh,' Nathine said and shook her head as if Aimee was some hopeless student she'd tried and failed to teach.

Pelathina laughed, light and musical. 'I think Jess is an example of what would happen if a child were bonded with a young dragon.'

Aimee felt slightly offended at that, just when she'd been starting to really like Pelathina. 'I'm not a child.' She drew herself up, trying to look taller and more Rider-ish.

'No, but you're sweet, and you haven't yet learned to tuck away your emotions like older Riders do. It's endearing.' Pelathina swung herself onto Skydance's back and looked more at home there than she did on the ground.

'I told you there'd be someone who liked you despite your mushroom hair,' Nathine leaned in to whisper before climbing the railing and into her saddle.

Aimee shook her head. She wasn't going to take romantic advice from Nathine, and besides she was wrong, Pelathina was friendly with everyone, that's just the way she was. And also, now was not the time for these thoughts, because they were off to finally meet

Kyelli.

Aimee didn't need to tell Jess to fly fast, she knew, and they sped through the sky, streets whizzing past beneath them. Malgerus and Skydance, both larger than Jess, should have pulled ahead, but Aimee was practically vibrating with excitement and Jess kept pace with them, snout nosing out in front. Aimee squeezed Jess's spiralled horns, knobbly knuckle bones sticking out because she gripped so tight. She was like a kettle coming to the boil and she wanted to scream into the wind to release some of the swirling mix of anticipation, excitement and delight that was filling her up. Jess did it for her, roaring as they tore through a cloud, ripping it to whispery shreds.

The smelly streets ended, giving way to fields, the River Toig meandering through them. Aimee's eyes followed the river ahead to the waterfall, sparkling like falling beads of silver in the summer sunshine. She'd never thought about it before, but it was a beautiful spot, and perfect. Kyelli should live somewhere beautiful. Aimee pictured the little drawings scattered throughout Kyelli's diary and imagined her sitting on a ledge beside the tumbling waterfall, mountain flowers growing beside her, perhaps with a cup of steaming tea as she sketched in her diary.

Would she be grateful to Aimee for bringing back her diary? Had she missed it all these years? Knowing she had to leave it behind as a clue, but wishing she still had it so she could fill those waiting blank pages at the back. Then Aimee remembered the torn stumps, and the missing pages. The thought niggled at her, but she shoved it away. So what if the Empty Warrior pages were missing, they were about to have Kyelli herself join Team Aimee.

At the bottom of the falls the river tumbled over rocks. Aimee steered Jess down so they skimmed above the frothy water. The spray hit Jess's belly, beading on her emerald scales, and Aimee could feel her delight at experiencing something new. Then they reached the shimmering fall of water and Aimee pulled Jess's horns to make her stop. Jess was getting better at hovering and the back beats of her wings stirred up silvery spray from the waterfall.

Nathine and Pelathina stopped their dragons too, Malgerus and Skydance hovering to the left of Aimee. Looking across at the other girls in their long black Riders' coats, crossed scimitars on their backs, and their dragons gleaming bright orange and sapphire blue beneath them, Aimee thought they looked amazing. She felt a buzz of excitement from Jess in her mind and realised that she probably looked amazing too. She grinned across at the other girls. Pelathina smiled back. Nathine rolled her eyes and shook her head.

'So, how do we get in?' Nathine asked.

'You're kidding, right?' Pelathina said, her smile getting even wider, her dimples deeper.

Without waiting for anyone to answer, she pushed on Skydance's horns. He gave a few big wingbeats, speeding towards the waterfall, then tucked his wings just as he and Pelathina disappeared through the silvery spay. Aimee laughed as his swishing blue tail disappeared.

'Well, I don't hear roaring, so they must not have smashed into a rock face,' Nathine said. 'Looks like you were right and there's something behind the waterfall.'

'There is.' Aimee's cheeks were aching, her grin was so big. 'Kyelli's in there. Race you through.'

She pushed on Jess's horns.

'Hey!' Nathine yelled as Aimee and Jess disappeared.

CHAPTER 28

## GUARDED

Aimee instinctively closed her eyes as they passed through the waterfall. Cool water splashed her face but they were through so quickly that it wasn't enough to soak her. She blinked droplets from her eyelashes and they fell down to bead on Jess's scales. Malgerus burst through right beside them, his large wings spraying her with water.

'Hey!' It was Aimee's turn to yell.

Nathine cocked her head and gave her a smug grin. Aimee laughed. Then she looked around. They were inside a huge cavern that stretched the height of the waterfall. It was larger even than the Heart, its roof reaching deep into shadows. Diffuse light came through the waterfall, gently coating a maze of stalagmites. The rock of these myriad cones was patterned with quartz, just like in Anteill, sparkling in purple, pink and milky white.

The roar of the waterfall seemed muffled inside the cavern, and Aimee jumped when Pelathina spoke, her voice echoing.

'There's a path down there, look.'

The three Riders were slowly flying deeper into the cavern and Pelathina guided Skydance down, pointing between the stalagmites. Aimee steered Jess with her knees, following Skydance and saw it too. A shiny path wiggled along the cavern floor, the rock worn smooth as if by years of footfall. But who would be walking that way so often that they made a path? Kyelli?

Aimee felt like her heart skipped a beat, then sped up to make up for it. Her eyes scanned ahead, following the path, searching for Kyelli. The leathery snaps of their dragons' wingbeats echoed back from the shadowy cave walls. The light from the waterfall slipped away behind them and they flew for a moment through darkness. Then Aimee spotted two balls of orange flame. Dragon's breath orbs. Of course Kyelli would have dragon's breath orbs.

The orbs were each bigger than Aimee's head and they hung from shepherd's crook poles, just like the ones in the Heart. Aimee liked that they had the same decoration in their home that Kyelli had in hers. The sparkling stalagmites grew smaller, then disappeared entirely as they reached an area of flat cave floor. The empty space towered above them, and Aimee wondered if the dragon's breath orbs marked the entrance to a tunnel. Surely Kyelli had tunnels and rooms, just like the Riders did, somewhere cosy to live without shadows hanging over her head.

Skydance was the first to land, Jess and Malgerus

touching down either side of him. Jess flicked out her tongue, tasting the air.

'Stop! What are you doing here?' a voice called out, young and a bit quavery. A boy's voice. Definitely not the voice of an immortal woman.

Confused, Aimee dismounted, but kept a hand on the cool scales of Jess's neck. The dragon's breath orbs hung above her head now, and there was something in the shadows beyond them. It wasn't a tunnel entrance, but looked more like a large stone box. Then someone stepped into the light of the orbs.

Aimee's heart seemed to swell and then deflate all within a few seconds. It wasn't Kyelli. He wore the chainmail and colourful patchwork cloak of a city guard. Orange light coated his face and Aimee saw he was only a year or two older than her. He levelled a spear at them, but its tip wavered, and his eyes flicked nervously up at their dragons. Aimee was impressed. Not many people would stand their ground against three dragons.

'Halfen?'

It was Nathine who spoke. She stepped closer to the boy and her face screwed up, but her eyes were wide, disbelieving. Behind her Malgerus dropped to the floor, making himself smaller, his feathers half-raised and quivering. It was odd behaviour and made Aimee wary.

'Nathine?' The boy lowered his spear, resting the butt on the ground. He turned his head side on to them, angling one ear towards the girls. He looked delighted to see Nathine, a huge grin on his face. 'Wow, you're a Sky Rider now?'

Aimee waited for the sarcastic reply from Nathine, maybe something about thinking a dragon made a nice fashion accessory, but oddly it didn't come. Instead there was a look on Nathine's face that Aimee hadn't seen before. She was ashamed. Aimee was intrigued. Clearly Nathine and Halfden knew each other from before Nathine made the climb, and Aimee wondered what their story was.

'Halfen, I…you're a guard?' Nathine stuttered which was very unlike her.

'Yeah.' He waggled his shoulders, making his cloak swish. 'Well, you know I always wanted to be a Rider, but they don't let boys make the climb. In fact the guards almost didn't let me join because…' His words trailed off and he gestured at the side of his head. 'But eventually they did, though I think that might have been because your father paid someone.'

Aimee watched Nathine's face harden at the mention of her father. Halfen must have seen it too because he carried on quickly.

'Anyway, the training was tough, and I think the instructors worked me twice as hard as everyone else, but I did it. And now I'm a guard.'

He straightened his head and smiled at Nathine. He seemed to be waiting for something. Aimee watched but Nathine didn't return the smile, and slowly Halfen's drooped too.

'To be honest, being a guard isn't as good as I thought it would be. My sergeant always assigns me the worst duties, like this one.' He swirled a finger at the cavern around them. 'I'm not sure they trust me with anything else.'

Aimee watched as Nathine bit her bottom lip, clearly struggling to find something to say. It wasn't like her. Aimee would need to wait to find out their story though, because right then Pelathina pulled them back to their mission.

'I'm genuinely sorry to interrupt this reunion, but I have a lot of questions,' Pelathina said.

'Huh, it's normally Aimee who has all the questions,' Nathine replied, and she looked relieved to have an excuse to turn her attention away from Halfen.

Halfen gave Pelathina a deferential nod, then his eyes flicked to Skydance behind her and he couldn't help a smile. He had a round, open face, and smiling suited him.

'I'm sorry,' he said, 'I didn't mean any insult when I said this was one of the worst guard duties. Obviously it's very important, but it's also pretty boring. Though the secrecy adds some excitement.'

'Secrecy?' Pelathina asked.

Halfen nodded. 'Yeah, because you know no one knows about this place except the city guards, and the Sky Riders. I can't even tell my da when I'm on guard duty out here.'

Pelathina looked at Aimee and Nathine in turn, her eyebrows up and slanted, asking a question. Both girls shook their heads—they had no idea what he was talking about either.

'What *are* you guarding?' Pelathina asked.

Different questions raced through Aimee's mind. Why did Kyelli need a guard? And why a city guard and not a Rider? And where was she? Was this some sort of test they had to pass?

Halfen had angled his left ear towards them again, as if struggling to hear, though the roar of the waterfall was far behind them. His round face was wrinkled in confusion.

'We guard Marhorn's tomb, as per Kyelli's instructions,' he explained. 'Before she left the city she told Captain Elt, he was in charge back then, that she wanted her father's tomb always guarded. We've done it ever since. So, like I said, it's important, but honestly, it's a job they give to the youngest recruits, or as a punishment.'

He waved grandly behind him at the stone box. Aimee had never thought about it before, she was usually only interested in Kyelli, but Marhorn would have a tomb somewhere. Though she still didn't understand how Kyelli's immortal father could have died.

Nathine was first to step forward, and as she did, Halfen put a hand on her arm. Nathine flinched from his touch and he hurriedly withdrew the hand. Nathine wasn't looking at him, but Aimee was, and she saw the crushed look on his face. It was a look she recognised, a look she'd worn. Aimee began to suspect that Halfen liked Nathine, in a more-than-friends sort of way.

'It's just a tomb,' Nathine said, shrugging.

She was standing at the foot of it and the huge block of stone came halfway up her chest. She leaned forward, propping her elbows on it. Halfen looked appalled for a second then laughed. The sound echoed back at them from the cave walls.

'You never did have much respect for any authority.' He gestured at Nathine's casual stance.

'Would you, if you'd had my father?'

Aimee had expected Nathine's response to be cutting, but she'd said it softly, and she finally looked at Halfen again.

'No,' he replied so quietly Aimee barely heard him. He looked like he wanted to touch Nathine again, but he didn't move.

Pelathina was inspecting the tomb, running her hands along all the edges, and crouching down to inspect the stone slabs of its sides. It had been crafted from the rock of the Ring Mountains and it glittered with wiggling lines of white and pink quartz.

'It's a pretty tomb,' Pelathina said, her slim fingers tracing a line of sparkling pink quartz, 'but there's nothing on it.'

'What do you mean?' Nathine asked, still leaning casually at the other end.

'No engravings, no secret messages, no clues as to what we do next.'

'Huh.' Nathine straightened up. 'Aimee?'

Everyone looked at her, even Halfen, but she had no idea what to do next. She couldn't help fearing that Kyelli was somewhere nearby, watching them, waiting to see if they unraveled this last clue and were worthy enough to finally meet her. If they failed, the city was doomed. She stepped between the orbs and put a hand on the cold stone of Marhorn's tomb. Pelathina was right, it was blank, not even his name was carved on top.

'Have you ever seen anyone else in here? Like maybe someone living here,' she asked Halfen.

He was standing beside her but as she spoke he switched to her other side. She looked at him quizzically.

'Sorry, you were on my bad side.' He gestured to his right ear and suddenly his titling head, and comments about the guards almost not admitting him, made sense. He was deaf in one ear. 'Living here? You think someone lives in this cave? What would give you that idea?'

'You're sure? You haven't maybe seen Kyelli?' Aimee asked, all her hope pouring into those two little questions.

'Kyelli? Like, *the* Kyelli?' Halfen's round face was half grinning, half wary, as if sure he was being made fun of but didn't get the joke.

Suddenly Aimee felt foolish too, and the urge to cry welled up inside her. But she shoved it back down, and stoked her flame of determination instead. She was not going to fail now.

'I've been on duty here at lot. I'm sure I get assigned this one more than anyone else, though no doubt my sergeant would deny that,' Halfen continued. 'And the only other person I've ever seen in here is your leader, Jara.'

'What?' Aimee, Nathine and Pelathina all exclaimed at once.

CHAPTER 29

## MORE SECRETS

'DID YOU SAY Jara's been here?' Pelathina asked.
'She knows about Kyelli's home?' Aimee added her own question before Halfen had a chance to answer Pelathina's.

Aimee felt like someone had stolen half the energy from her spark, like they'd punched her in the chest and sucked it out. She'd shown Jara the map, asked to follow it, and Jara had forbidden it. But all this time she knew where the clues led? Jara knew Kyelli was here. She knew where to come to ask for help, and she hadn't. They'd wasted hours unravelling all the clues when Jara could have just come and fetched Kyelli this morning, or last night, or years ago!

'Are you sure you've seen Jara in here?' Pelathina repeated. She'd slipped round to Halfen's left side, to be sure he heard her question.

'He's deaf, not blind,' Nathine snapped. Aimee almost smiled to see her defending someone, but the cold shock in her chest had seeped up into her face, freezing it.

'I'm sorry,' Pelathina was quick to apologise.

'It's okay.' Halfen shook his head and threw Nathine a small smile. 'And I'm only half deaf. But yes, it's definitely Jara that visits. Tall, blonde, kinda intimidating-looking, with a blood-red dragon, that's her, right?'

Pelathina nodded.

'You said visits, plural, meaning she's been here more than once.' Aimee felt like she was dragging the words up.

Halfen nodded. 'Oh yes, probably once every other month she flies in. It might be more. I'm not always on duty here. Sometimes my sergeant lets me patrol the practically empty streets around Lufenjen Square, checking for pickpockets.'

'That's near Palkstan's bakery, though. Have you had his potato pancakes, with fried onions?' Pelathina asked.

'Oh, they're so good.' Halfen grinned.

Aimee stared at them in disbelief. How could Pelathina even think about food right now? And how could Halfen smile? She felt like everything was crumbling around her. She turned around and saw Jess had curled up on the floor, her long neck stretched out, yellow eyes staring up at Aimee.

'What do I do now, girl?' Aimee whispered to her.

Jess shuffled on the floor. She had no answers. Aimee looked around the large cave at the shadows, thick and deep, beyond the dragon's breath orbs.

'Kyelli!' she yelled.

The name echoed back from the walls, mocking her, then there was silence.

'Kyelli, we're your Riders. And I'm sorry that we can't work out your last clue, but can you come and help us anyway. Please!'

This time the echoes of her words rolled over each other as they bounced back. Aimee felt a hand slip into her own and give hers a squeeze.

'I don't think she's here,' Pelathina said softly.

'She is,' Aimee insisted. 'This is where the clues point to. We just haven't proved ourselves yet. There's one more puzzle to solve, or Rider-ish thing to work out, then she'll know we're worthy of her help.'

Aimee felt Pelathina take her other hand, and slowly pulled her around so they were facing. Aimee looked up into her face. Pelathina's darker skin seem to suck in the orange light from the flames, then glow with it from within.

'You are worthy of being a Rider,' Pelathina said, her words gentle. 'I've watched you, and not just today. I saw you sometimes when you were training, and you never gave up. It takes bravery to look out at the world from your face. I remember the way you pulled your hair over your face after you'd first made the climb, hiding yourself. But look at you now.' Pelathina let go a hand and flicked Aimee's short curls, making them bounce. She twirled her fingers in the pure white ones. 'And I've seen how quickly you've bonded with Jess, which is amazing given that Jara rushed you, and you've only had a few months together. I'm sure it took Skydance and I closer to a year to get to where you two are already. So, Aimee Wood, you are worthy of finding Kyelli.'

Aimee felt the prickle of tears in her eyes and tried to blink them back inside.

'Yeah, I've been telling her that too.'

Nathine threw in the comment in an offhanded way. And completely ruined the moment, if in fact she and Pelathina had been having a moment. Still, Aimee was grateful for her typically blunt vote of support. Reluctantly she retracted her hands from Pelathina's, and turned to Halfen.

'What does Jara do when she's here?' Aimee asked.

Halfen had been looking at the floor but now his head popped back up, cocked to favour his good ear.

'Well, she doesn't check the tomb actually, I guess maybe because it's our job to guard that. She always just checks the tree then leaves again.' Halfen pointed with his spear, off into the shadows behind them.

'The tree?' Aimee felt a prickle of excitement. She thought of the tree symbols on the map that marked the clues, and the tree embossed on the leather cover of Kyelli's diary. Perhaps the quest wasn't over yet. 'Can you show me?'

Halfen cocked his head at her and she had to repeat the question. He nodded. 'Do you have an orb? I can light a torch, that's how I get back here from the waterfall, but if you have an orb that'll save me faffing about with the kindling.'

Aimee pulled a fist-sized dragon's breath orb from her pocket, its orange light creating a glow around her.

'Great.' Halfen looked at Nathine. 'Don't suppose you could get me one of those?'

To Aimee's surprise, Nathine looked flustered, and guilty. Halfen smiled and waved away his question.

'I was only kidding. Okay, the tree is this way.'

He beckoned Aimee with her orb, then stepped into the shadows beyond the tomb. She sent a command to Jess, telling her to stay, then caught up with Halfen. She walked on his good side, and held her orb out, lighting their way along the cave floor. While they had a moment, she couldn't help asking him something.

'You haven't said anything about my face. It…it doesn't disgust you?'

'I've been deaf in one ear for four years. I know that's not something you can see, not like your face, but when people realise, they treat me different. But to me I'm still the same boy I was before it happened. I've still got goals, things I want in life, that's not changed just because I need people to speak a little louder around me.' Aimee heard the scratch as he ran a hand over his closed-cropped hair. 'I can still be handsome even if one of my ears doesn't work. So I reckon you can still be pretty with a mismatched face.'

He smiled at her as they walked, and Aimee decided she liked him.

'Does Nathine think you're handsome?' she blurted out.

His smile turned wistful. 'She used to.'

Aimee was about to ask what happened to his ear when he stopped, and pointed upwards, the tip of his spear disappearing into the thick shadows. Aimee held up her orb, orange light pushing away the blackness. They were right by the cave wall and it stretched up and up, the ceiling lost in the shadows. A vein of sparkling rose-pink quartz wiggled up through the rock, like a river on a map. At about the height of a house it split in two, snaking either side of a small wooden door.

'Well, I was not expecting that,' Pelathina said behind them.

'Ugh, it's another clue. I'm getting fed up of Kyelli and her games,' Nathine complained.

'Shh!' Aimee rounded on her, still worried Kyelli might be watching them, testing them. Nathine just shrugged.

'That's the tree,' Halfen wiggled his spear tip up at the door.

Aimee held her orb higher so they could all see the tree, in a circle, chiselled onto the wooden door. It was just like the ones Kyelli had drawn on the map.

'Well, if that's the entrance to Kyelli's house, she must have shrunk. I doubt even scrawny Aimee would get her shoulders through it,' Nathine pointed out.

She was right, it wasn't really a proper door, more like a cupboard door. But who put a cupboard in the wall of an empty cave?

'What does Jara check?' Aimee asked.

Halfen shrugged, in manner that was so like Nathine she almost smiled. 'I dunno. She doesn't let me come with her. Not that I've ever asked. She's quite intimidating, and her dragon's always watching me.'

Aimee looked back the way they'd come, beyond the tomb, where their dragons waited.

'Jess!' she yelled.

Nathine shook her head despairingly and Pelathina burst out laughing.

'What?' Halfen looked around at them all, worried he wasn't getting the joke again.

'Normally Riders whistle to get their dragon to come, or the older ones who've been bonded for a while can summon their dragons just through the connection in their mind. Aimee, though, she just yells.' Nathine was still shaking her head.

'So? It works.' Aimee pointed to Jess who was swooping over the tomb. She landed beside them, her talons clicking on the rock, and began head-butting Aimee, getting her spiralled horns caught in Aimee's hair.

'Yeah, I love you too girl,' Aimee said, as embarrassment crept up her cheeks in a red flush. She was glad it was dark. 'But we've got a job to do right now.'

'Wow, she's amazing,' Halfen breathed. Then he quickly looked at Nathine. 'Her dragon, I mean, not Aimee. Well, Aimee is amazing because she's a Rider, but then so are you and your dragon's incredible too.'

Aimee suspected a similar red flush was warming Halfen's cheeks right now, and she smiled. Nathine didn't. She still somehow looked guilty. Aimee couldn't spare that much thought however, there was a final clue to unlock. She climbed into her saddle.

'You don't give up, do you?' Pelathina asked, looking up at her, dark eyes sparkling in a way that made Aimee want to be closer so she could stare into them better.

Aimee pulled her own eyes away, with effort, and gently pushed on Jess's horns. Even though she was used to it now, her stomach did a small flipflop as they lifted off the ground. There was a rock ledge in front of the door, just large enough for a dragon to perch on. Jess landed and tucked in her wings.

'Good girl,' Aimee told her as she reached out, touching the door.

There was no handle, so she pushed. She heard a quiet click then the door swung outwards. She jumped, slid back in her saddle so far that she was nearly falling off, quickly grabbed the pommel, pulled herself forward again, and hoped the others hadn't seen.

She knew the door was too small to be the entrance to some amazing cave palace, but still her hand shook as she reached out again. Surely this had to be the last hurdle to jump and then Kyelli would appear.

She wrapped her fingers around the edge of the wood and pulled the door fully open.

'What's in there?' Nathine called up.

'Can I see too?' Halfen asked, getting caught up in their excitement.

'Is there cake?' Pelathina asked, making Aimee smile.

The little wooden box was about the size of Aimee's

outstretched hand. She carefully slid it out and felt around. There was nothing else in the shallow recess behind the door. Leaving the door open she slipped the box into her coat pocket and pulled Jess's horns. With a snap she unfurled her wings, flapped twice and pushed off from the cave wall. Aimee guided her back to Marhorn's tomb and she landed beside Malgerus. He stretched out his neck and playfully snapped at her.

The others' footsteps echoed around the cave as they ran back to Aimee. She put the little box on top of Marhorn's tomb. She didn't think he'd mind since it was his daughter's box. There was a charged silence as everyone gathered round, as if they were all holding their breath. Aimee was. Her mind was racing, running through answers to what was in the box. Kyelli's front door key and a note of her address?

There was a small metal clasp, like you might find on a jewellery box. It was tarnished with age and the hinge was stiff as Aimee lifted it with one finger. The lid fell back and banged on the rock of the tomb, making everyone jump.

'Sorry,' she whispered.

There was some sort of yellow fabric inside the box. Aimee touched it. Silk. There was something hard inside the fabric. She very carefully lifted the whole lot out. The ends of the silk trailed and fluttered as she moved it and she thought it might be a scarf. Holes marred the fabric and one end had begun to rot, but it must once have been a beautiful yellow scarf. Just the sort of thing she'd imagined Kyelli wearing.

'What are we supposed to do? Wave that scarf at the Empty Warriors and hope they disappear like a magic trick?' Nathine crossed her arms, looking skeptically at the scarf and box.

'Shh.' It was Halfen who hushed her this time.

'There's something wrapped in the scarf,' Aimee said, and began to unwind it.

Her heart was thumping against her ribs, and her fingers shook. The scarf seemed to go on forever, until finally a wide band of gold dropped into her palm. She let the silk flutter down onto the tomb. The gold band was as wide as her little finger, and its entire surface had been engraved with minuscule writing in a language Aimee couldn't read. She turned it over in her hands. There was a hinge on one side and a hook and clasp on the other.

They'd found Kyelli's bracelet.

As Aimee realised what she held she felt no elation at all, but instead a huge swell of disappointment. A line from the poem carved on the council chamber table sprang into her mind. It had said *the essence of me, always here*. Aimee had thought that meant Kyelli was here, but she'd meant this. She'd left her bracelet in the city, but she wasn't here.

She looked up at the others. Nathine was scowling at the bracelet, looking like she might ask Malgerus to eat it. The flush of excitement had gone from Pelathina's face, and now she wore her sister's frown. And Halfen looked confused, and perhaps a little scared.

Aimee had let them all down, again. They hadn't

found Kyelli. The Empty Warriors would break through the second gate and they had no way to stop them.

Aimee didn't even realise she'd slumped until her bum hit the floor. Her back was against the cold rock of Marhorn's tomb and her legs splayed out along the cave floor.

'She was supposed to come and save the city,' she said quietly, her words falling on the gold bracelet cradled in her hands.

Jess lay down beside her and wriggled her head into Aimee's lap, under her hands. For a moment Aimee wanted to climb onto her back and fly far away. But she wouldn't. She couldn't leave the city or all the people, like the baker she'd met this morning. How could he, with his floury hands, fight the Empty Warriors? How could any of them? How could Callant, with his cough? Or Nathine's little brother?

'Hey.'

The voice was soft and Aimee looked up into Pelathina's dark eyes. She wore a gentle smile and Aimee wondered, again, how she did it? How could she choose to smile right now?

'It's not okay, so don't say it,' Aimee ordered, before Pelathina could say anything. 'Kyelli was supposed to save us. I was going to find her.' She felt the tears come and did nothing to stop them. 'What if I failed because I'm not good enough?'

'Stop being an idiot!'

Nathine kicked Aimee in the shin, not hard, but not to gentle either.

'I'm not sure that's helping, Nathine,' Pelathina said, still looking very intently at Aimee.

Aimee sniffed up some tears. 'Actually, weirdly, it does kinda help.'

'Oh, well in that case get up, *bubadysh*!'

'What's a *bubadysh*?' Aimee asked.

'It's Irankish and it roughly translates as someone who's so stubborn that they won't see what's right in front of them and they are like a mole digging backwards.'

'All that insult in one word?' Nathine grinned. 'I like your language. You'll need to teach me some.'

'So you can insult me more?' Aimee asked, getting to her feet.

'Exactly.' Nathine punched her on the arm, her non-injured one. 'What's the Irankish for mushroom head?'

Aimee looked down at the bracelet in her hands. The disappointment of not finding Kyelli still made it feel like her ribs were caving in and squishing her heart, but Nathine and Pelathina were right, to give up now would be pathetic. She looked over at Halfen who'd been lingering at the edge of the conversation.

'Why did Jara come and check this bracelet?'

He shrugged. 'Sorry, no idea. It was like she'd just check it was still there and then go again. Though I'm not sure how or why she expected anyone would steal it.'

Aimee was sure any of the scholars at the university would have loved to have this bracelet, and Callant first among them. Perhaps they could have learned more about Kyelli, or their past, from studying it. So why hide it away and keep it guarded? Halfen said Kyelli had left instructions for the city guards to protect her father's tomb, but Aimee thought now that was a cover. They were really protecting the bracelet, even if they didn't know it. But why? It was just a bracelet.

Disappointment aside, Aimee did still feel a small thrill at holding it. It belonged to Kyelli. She'd worn it. She was wearing it in every statue, carving and painting across the city. So why did she take it off? Aimee turned it over and over in her hands, looking for another clue. She flicked open the clasp with one nail, opening up the bracelet, then placed it around her left wrist. Maybe it was an important relic and she shouldn't put it on, but right then she needed to feel closer to Kyelli.

She snapped the clasp closed.

Sharp pain stabbed her wrist and shot up her arm, just as someone yelled from the air above them.

'No! Don't put it on!'

CHAPTER 30

## BLADES AND SPARKS

THE PAIN STOLE Aimee's breath. It was like someone had stabbed an icicle up through the veins in her arm. It was cold, and sharp, and went from her wrist, under the bracelet, all the way up to her shoulder. Just when she thought it would pierce down into her heart, the pain vanished. Gone completely.

She blinked and looked around. The cave was a lot brighter. There were lights that hadn't been there before, hovering at chest height. Not yellow lights, like dragon's breath orbs, but white lights, tinged with green.

'No! What have you done, you idiot!'

It was the voice that had shouted a moment ago, and it was Jara. Faradair landed right in front of them, making the other dragons skitter to the side. His scales rippled like freshly spilled blood. Jara leapt from his back before he'd even tucked his wings and stormed towards Aimee.

'Jara, wait!' a voiced called and Aimee heard another

dragon land. Dimly she was aware the voice of caution was Dyrenna's.

The other Riders jumped aside from Jara's fury, just as their dragons had scattered from Faradair. The white-green lights bobbed around making Aimee feel dizzy. Jara grabbed her wrist, the one now wearing Kyelli's bracelet and horror washed over her face.

'You stupid little bitch,' Jara hissed.

Aimee heard the rasp and a second later Jara had both scimitars in her hands. Aimee screamed and threw herself to the side as Jara's blades sliced the air where she'd been. She scrabbled around Marhorn's tomb and, crouching on the other side, drew her own blades. She heard the others yelling, and behind them the roar of dragons. Then Jara vaulted up and over the tomb, landing beside Aimee.

Their blades crashed together with an ear-piercing screech of metal. Jara was taller than Aimee, her reach longer, and the weird light was still shining in her chest, half blinding Aimee. Jara danced forward, her right blade sweeping high as her left cut low. Her movements were shadows against the white-green light and Aimee only just managed to catch the slices with her own scimitars.

Jara didn't give her a moment to breathe. As Aimee twisted her right blade free and lunged at Jara's hip, Jara spun to the side, snaring up Aimee's other blade with her own. Jara stabbed forward with her left blade and Aimee felt the point of it cut through her coat and shirt, just missing her belly. She squealed and jumped back.

Despite her months of training, she knew her swordwork needed more practice. As she barely parried Jara's next series of attacks she knew she'd never outfight her.

The clang of blades echoed around the cavern making their fight sound like a battle. Aimee felt a low slice from Jara cut along the outside edge of her thigh and cried out in pain.

'Jara, stop!' someone yelled.

But she didn't stop. Aimee felt her injured arm quivering as she raised both blades just in time to stop Jara slicing her head off. Jara lowered one blade, slicing for Aimee's knees, but Aimee pushed it aside with her own. They still had two blades locked together but now Aimee was off balance. With a skilful flick of her wrist Jara unlocked their blades and at the same time sliced the edge of hers along Aimee's knuckles. The pain flashed a moment later and Aimee dropped the scimitar from that hand.

Jara's next cut would have opened her throat but, forgetting all Rider finesse, Aimee tucked her head down and barrelled into Jara's midriff. The white-green light in her chest filled Aimee's vision. Jara wasn't expecting it and she lost her footing, tumbled backwards, landing on the floor with Aimee on top of her. The cuts on Aimee's thigh and across her knuckles screamed at her, and it felt like she'd torn the scabs on her burned arm.

One blade flew from Jara's hand, clattering against the cave floor. Before Aimee could take advantage of that, Jara put both fists against Aimee's chest and shoved her with such force that she slammed up against the side of Marhorn's tomb. She wheezed, winded, and before she could slump to the floor, Jara had sprung up and pressed a blade to her throat.

'Jess!' Aimee yelled. Her dragon had always appeared to rescue her when she needed it. Where was she? 'Jess!'

A blast of dragon's breath lit the shadows above them and both Aimee and Jara looked up. Jess swooped through the air, Faradair's flames just missing her. Jess tried to retaliate but she wasn't yet fully grown, and all she managed was a puff of smoke. Faradair flew through it, right at Jess. She slipped sinuously away, twisting through the air. She flicked out her barbed tail but Faradair dived beneath the attack and came up behind Jess, snapping at her wings. His teeth caught the edge of her wing membrane and he tore it.

Aimee felt Jess's pain and fear in her mind, swelling her own till she felt like her head might explode. Jess's roar echoed around them, and drops of her blood rained from the sky. Halfen jumped aside to avoid the splatter. Jess flew up into the shadows, growling as Faradair followed her. Then she tilted her body and swooped back down towards the horrified Riders watching. She was no longer trying to attack, she was trying to escape.

'Jara! Stop this now! And make him stop!' Dyrenna yelled, pointing up at the dragons tearing around the cave above them.

'Please,' Aimee whispered. She felt tears on her cheeks and they splashed down onto Jara's blade at her throat.

'I have to Dyrenna!' Jara called over Aimee's head.

Aimee heard footsteps and guessed Dyrenna was moving slowly towards them.

'You don't.'

'I do!'

'Jara—' Dyrenna continued but Jara shouted over her.

'She put on the bracelet. She has the power to kill us all!'

Jara's words hit Aimee like a punch to the gut. 'What?' she asked, but her voice came out as a whisper no one heard.

She looked down at the gold cuff on her wrist. Why would Kyelli's bracelet make her a killer? She was squinting, because the white-green light from Jara's chest was shining right in her eyes.

Then she finally realised what it was.

She could see Jara's spark.

Jara and Dyrenna continued arguing over her head. Other voices had joined now too but their words were indistinct because Aimee was transfixed by what she could see. She was looking at Jara's life spark, her energy. It was right in the middle of her chest, and pulsed faintly in time with her heartbeat.

Jara's blade had slipped away from her throat as she argued with Dyrenna and the others. It gave Aimee space to turn her head. She looked around for Nathine and Pelathina. They each had a white light in their chests too, both of theirs slightly brighter than Jara's. Aimee was confused, then with a jolt of shock she realised she was seeing not only their sparks, but how much energy they had left in them. Nathine and Pelathina were ten or more years younger than Jara, their sparks were brighter, more full of energy. Aimee's eyes flicked to Dyrenna, almost dreading what she'd see. The older Rider's spark shone with less luminance, but Aimee was pleased to see it wasn't as dull as she'd feared. Dyrenna still had many years to live.

Then Aimee realised with a rising horror, that if she looked down she'd be able to see her own spark. Did she want to look? What if it was duller than everyone else's? What if her weird skin really had been draining it all these years and it had less shine than Dyrenna's? What if she looked down and then knew she wouldn't have a long life? She couldn't un-know that.

Before she could look the cold edge of Jara's scimitar pressed against her throat again. But the urge to know was overwhelming. She tilted her chin down and felt a hot prick of pain and a trickle of warm blood as Jara's blade nicked her neck.

And there, below the blade, in the centre of her chest, was her own spark.

Its white-green light was as bright as Nathine's. Aimee felt tears of relief spring to her eyes. All her life she'd feared there was something wrong with her, but her spark was there, as bright and shiny and full of energy as any other girl of seventeen. She had years and years of life in her chest. But not if Jara slit her throat. Then her spark would burn though all its energy trying to save her from a fatal wound.

'She can't have this power, no one can.' Jara's words were as sharp as her blade.

'*Gari chingreth*, Jara! Just let her take off the bracelet.' There was a desperate edge to Pelathina's voice.

'She can't,' Jara snapped.

With her free hand she grabbed Aimee's left wrist, slid her fingers over the wide cuff of the bracelet and yanked it upwards. Aimee screamed. The cold icicle of pain shot up her arm again. The bracelet didn't budge, even though on Aimee's skinny wrist it should have slid up to her thumb joint. Jara tried twisting it and Aimee screamed again.

'Stop, please,' she whimpered. She'd half fallen to her knees the pain was so intense. Only Jara's grip on her arm kept her upright.

Through the pain Aimee heard a growling and the rustling of wings, then felt a surge in her connection. Jess was coming to her rescue. She was flying straight for Jara, who held her ground and ducked at the last moment. Jess's talons raked the empty air where she'd been. Then in a flash of red scales Faradair followed Jess, caught her, wrapping his wings around her. They both plummeted, crashing into the cave floor. Much bigger and stronger, Faradair quickly pinned Jess to the floor. Both dragons growled and snapped at each other, the noise filling the cave with roiling echoes making it sound like a hundred dragons were fighting.

'Jess!' Aimee wheezed, forcing her wobbly legs to stand up. Jara still gripped her wrist, and her blade hovered inches from Aimee's neck.

Faradair snapped at Jess's face and she flicked her head aside. Their spiralled horns clacked together and Jess tried to twist her head free. Her wings fluttered useless against the cave floor and she clawed at Faradair with her back talons. Faradair clawed back, opening a cut along Jess's neck that oozed viscus blood. Aimee cried out as she shared Jess's pain.

Then with a snap of his huge wings, Black landed beside the fighting dragons. He roared so loudly that Aimee clamped her hands over her ears. Faradair and Jess cowered before him, their bellies to the floor, heads down. Faradair might have been leader of the dragons, because Jara was leader of the Riders, but right then it was all about size and strength, and Black had more of both than any other dragon.

As the echoes of Black's roar faded, there was an uncomfortable silence in the cave. Jara swivelled her eyes back to Aimee.

'You should have listened to me and not got involved.'

Her blade moved for Aimee's throat. On instinct Aimee reached up and grabbed Jara's wrist, trying to stop the inevitable.

The moment her skin touched Jara's she felt it. And so did Jara. They both gasped, Aimee in surprise, Jara in pain.

Energy rushed into Aimee, flowing from Jara up her arm and into her chest. Jara gasped, dropping her blade and fell to her knees, but Aimee couldn't let go. Her hand felt stuck to Jara's wrist, and every second she held on she stole more of Jara's energy. Aimee watched in horror as Jara's spark started to dim, and a second smaller spark appeared in her own chest.

She was draining Jara's spark, stealing her life.

'No, stop, please stop!' she cried, begging with whatever was doing this.

She tried to uncurl her fingers but they wouldn't obey. Jara moaned pitifully. Aimee stood over her, unable to let go. Unable to stop killing her.

She could feel the bracelet pulsing, eager to keep draining Jara's spark. Jara was still clutching the bracelet and Aimee pulled against Jara's grip, trying to get the bracelet off. The icy pain fired up her arm again and she collapsed to her knees beside Jara. The bracelet stayed where it was. Dimly she was aware of the others shouting but the rush of someone else's energy inside her was overwhelming and she couldn't focus on them.

Jara's energy felt different. She wasn't aware of her own, it was part of her, like her blood, but she could feel Jara's. It felt wrong, like something familiar that had been twisted—the page of a favourite book with the words all written backwards, or walking into her bedroom and the furniture being in different positions.

The second spark in Aimee's chest was growing brighter, and Jara's own was half as bright as it had been before Aimee touched her. Aimee felt tears stinging her eyes as she grabbed her own hand and pulled, trying to release Jara.

'Let go!' she screamed at her hand.

The world went blurry as her tears fell, and she was grateful because Jara was staring at her, and her piercing green eyes were pleading. But the bracelet wouldn't release her, it just kept sucking. It was like having an unruly dragon in her mind that she couldn't control. And it was killing Jara.

'Help me!' she yelled.

Someone must have understood what she was trying to do because other hands appeared, grabbing hers and Jara's trying to pull them apart. The wrong energy, Jara's energy, continued to flow into Aimee. Jara collapsed, pulling Aimee's arm down with her. Dyrenna skidded under Jara, trying to pull her up to sitting but she was too weak now.

The fingers kept pulling at Aimee's, and finally she felt her index finger lift from Jara's hand.

'Yes, get the others, please!'

She felt her other fingers being prised upwards, bending backwards to the point of pain. She didn't care if they broke all her fingers, as long as they could make her let go before she killed Jara.

The pulsing in the bracelet began to ease, Aimee felt the change, and it was like when she took a firmer hold of Jess through their connection. She pictured throwing a wall up between herself and Jara, and at the same time, yanked her hand back with all her force. It popped free and she fell backwards, gasping.

Jara slumped back in Dyrenna's arms. Aimee felt the others who'd been beside her all step away. Dyrenna checked Jara for a pulse.

'She's still alive,' croaked Aimee, 'I can see her spark.'

What she didn't say was that Jara's spark was wavering like a candle about to go out.

CHAPTER 31

GIVE IT BACK

Jara's eyes were closed as if she no longer had the strength to open them. How long could she live on the little energy Aimee had left her with? Faradair was curled on the floor beside her, head resting on her prone legs.

'What did you do, Aimee?' Nathine yelled at her.

'You just touched her and she collapsed.' Halfen's voice was shaky. He'd dropped his spear and hidden both hands behind his back, as if afraid Aimee would grab them. It was what people used to do when they didn't want her to touch them with her weird skin.

Aimee recoiled from them. 'I didn't mean to,' she whispered.

'What did you do, little one?' Dyrenna's voice was softer but still accusatory.

'I drained the energy from her spark,' Aimee wailed. 'I'm sorry. It was Kyelli's bracelet.' Aimee held up her left wrist, the gold gleaming in dragon's breath light. 'When I put it on, I could suddenly see all your sparks, shining in your chests. They're kinda white with a greenish tinge at the edges.'

Everyone was looking at her, and she didn't like the wariness in their eyes.

'No one can see people's sparks,' Nathine said. She'd taken a step away from Aimee.

'The Quorelle could.' Jara croaked. Her eyes were closed but she must have been following their conversation.

'But scrawny little Aimee isn't one of the Quorelle,' Nathine pointed out. 'I've seen her bleed, and her blood's no more sparkly than mine.'

'How do you know the Quorelle could see sparks?' Dyrenna asked Jara in a soft voice.

'It's written in Kyelli's diary.' Jara's voice was barely a whisper.

Aimee looked down at her hands. They were the same small hands as before, short fingers, knuckles speckled with colourless skin and a cut across one hand from Jara's blade. But now if she touched someone she could kill them. All her life people had avoided her touch, scared she'd infect them with weird skin too. People thought there was something wrong with her spark. She remembered Hayetta saying she was scared to touch her in case she too was infected by something that would drain the energy from her spark. Jara was right, this was a power no one should have.

Aimee's knees buckled and she slumped to the cave floor. She pulled her legs up, hugging her knees to her chest and letting her tears fall. She'd become the freak everyone always thought she was. Now she could never touch anyone without killing them. It wasn't fair. She'd just wanted to find Kyelli so she could save them.

'Aimee, are you—'

'Don't touch me!'

Pelathina had crouched down in front of her and Aimee scrambled back on her bum. She tucked her hands into her armpits so she wouldn't accidentally touch anyone. She could still feel Jara's energy inside her, all wrong, like boots put on the wrong feet. She glanced down and saw Jara's spark glowing in her chest beside her own. She hurriedly pulled her eyes back up. She didn't want to see the evidence of what she'd done.

She felt something pluck at her hair and almost jumped away until she realised it was Jess's horns. She rested her head on Aimee's shoulder, scales cool against her neck. Aimee stroked her feathers. At least she could still touch Jess. Dragons didn't have sparks, so Aimee couldn't kill her. She reached along Jess's neck to check the cut Faradair had given her but it was already clean— Jess had coated it with her saliva. Sensing Aimee's concern for her, Jess returned it by gently licking the cut along her knuckles. Her tongue was rasping but her saliva was cooling, taking away the pain and helping the wound heal. She did the same to the slice Jara had cut along her thigh. Aimee closed her eyes and breathed deep Jess's warming smell of woodsmoke.

When Aimee opened her eyes she saw Pelathina had stayed crouched where she was, and hadn't followed Aimee across the floor. Aimee was glad of that, but also it hurt.

Then a hand slapped down on her shoulder, grabbed her coat collar and yanked Aimee to her feet. Jess's head slipped off her other shoulder and she stayed huddled to the ground. Aimee had no fight left in her, so neither did Jess.

'Don't touch me!' Aimee repeated, shoving her hands deeper into her armpits.

Nathine's round face was flushed with her anger. Somewhere in the back of her mind Aimee noted that there was no disgust on her face.

'You have to give Jara her energy back,' Nathine ordered, one hand still clutching Aimee's coat collar. Her words were fast and panicky, and that did nothing to help Aimee's racing heart. Did it beat faster now she had twice as much life energy?

'I can't put it back, I don't know how.' Aimee's words came out as a wail. 'I just touched her and the bracelet started sucking. I couldn't get it to stop. And now I can feel Jara's energy all inside me, and it feels wrong! Oh sparks!' She would have slumped to the floor again if Nathine hadn't been holding her up. 'Her spark's fading, I can see it.'

Nathine gave her a shake. 'Then fill her spark back up.' She made a grab for Aimee's left arm but Aimee twisted away. 'Damn it! Jara's going to die!'

'I know! It's my fault! I killed her!' Aimee yelled at Nathine, then her anger was gone as fast as it had come. 'I don't know how to give this back.' She waved a hand at her chest where Jara's spark glowed, even though she knew Nathine couldn't see it.

'The bracelet works both ways.' Jara's words were so quiet Aimee almost missed them. Dyrenna had helped her up to sitting and it looked like it was taking all Jara's strength to stay there. 'The bracelet can steal a person's spark, but it can also transfer the energy into someone, or something.'

'How... how do you know that?' Aimee asked.

Jara fumbled with her coat, shoved away Dyrenna's helping hand, then pulled something from her inside pocket. It was a wad of folded papers. She held it tightly for a moment, as if not quite ready to hand it over, then she held it out. Aimee could see her whole arm was trembling with the effort. Aimee took the papers, being careful not to touch Jara's fingers. She unfolded them and a jolt ran through her. They were covered, on both sides, with Kyelli's handwriting.

'These are the missing pages from Kyellis diary. You tore them out? You knew about her diary? Why did you keep these hidden?' Aimee threw her questions at Jara.

Jara had slumped back against Dyrenna, her eyes closed.

'I don't think you'll get any answers, little one,' Dyrenna said softly.

'She's been keeping secrets that could have helped us find Kyelli!' Aimee yelled.

Despite Jara's weakened condition, all the anger Aimee built up against her leader seemed to be bursting from her. Anger at forcing them to steal their dragons too early, at rushing their training, at pushing Hayetta to fly when she wasn't ready, at trying to exclude Aimee and force her from the Riders, at threatening Jess, and at letting Aimee race across the city solving clues when she already had all the answers.

'Aimee, just read the damn pages and find out how to put Jara's energy back. Then you can annoy her with all your questions.' Nathine flicked the pages in Aimee's hand.

She was right. Answers, and anger, could wait. She had to save Jara. Everyone was huddled around Jara, though whether consciously or not, they all left a space between themselves and Aimee. She could see everyone's sparks, and beside the others, Jara's looked like a faint star seen in daytime beside the sun. Aimee couldn't tell how much energy she had left. Days? Hours?

She flicked through the pages until she saw Kyelli's now familiar spiky handwriting surrounding a sketch of the bracelet. She held up her wrist and compared the real thing to the sketch. The bracelet was tarnished from so long languishing in a box, making the writing engraved on it hard to read in places. The sketch on the page showed the bracelet from both sides, and Kyelli had added writing, neat and clear.

*The purpose of our bracelets is twofold. I believe the originals could only give sparks, but somewhere in our history another Quorelle discovered how to create ones that could also take sparks from humans. It works on Quorelle too. If he'd let me, I would have given my father some of my sparks.*

*There are two settings on the bracelet. The first* Ura *means to take, and the second* Zurl *means to give. The dial switches between the two. And in the neutral position, you can touch someone without taking their spark or giving away any of yours.*

'There's a dial?'

Aimee rushed over to stand underneath one of the dragon's breath orbs. She held her wrist up to the light. On the back of the bracelet, the part that rested against the top of her wrist, there was a small dent, like a circle set into the gold. Aimee peered closer and saw the dial, a tiny gold lever and the words *Ura* and *Zurl*. The lever was set to *Ura*. Aimee quickly flicked it to *Zurl*, give, and ran back to Jara.

Her bloodshot eyes flickered open as Aimee knelt beside her.

'I'm going to give you back your life.' Aimee made her words sound more confident that she felt. Kyelli's instructions said she could give Jara her spark back, but they didn't actually say how to do that. Aimee reached out towards Jara.

'Please work,' she whispered, really quietly so no one heard.

The moment her hand clasped Jara's, she could feel it. This time the bracelet was tugging at the energy inside her. She picked out the thread that felt different and let it flow through the bracelet and back into Jara. Relief washed over her as she looked down and saw the extra spark in her chest growing dimmer, and Jara's own spark brightening as it filled up again. This time she knew what was happening and felt more in control. When all of Jara's energy was gone the bracelet tugged at Aimee's own spark but she pictured slamming a door closed and pulled her hand back.

She'd done it. Jara's spark was glowing brightly in her chest, and so was her own. She looked up to smile at Jara but she leapt from Dyrenna's arms, barrelling into Aimee and knocking her backwards.

Aimee slammed into the cave floor, breath squeezed from her lungs so she couldn't even yell. She felt Jara's weight on top of her, then pain exploded across her cheekbone. She twisted her head back in time to see Jara's arm swinging around for another punch. Before it could land she head-butted Jara in the stomach, and the punch glanced off her shoulder.

'You nearly killed me, you idiot girl!' Jara yelled. 'Why did you have to do this? Why couldn't you just have left things alone like a normal person?'

'You lied to us!' Aimee felt her own anger rising. Jara was keeping secrets that could damn them all to a gruesome death at the burning hands of thousands of Empty Warriors. 'You've had the pages from Kyelli's diary all along. And you knew her bracelet was here. Do you know where Kyelli is too? You should have—'

'Shut up!'

Behind Jara, Faradair growled, then so did Jess. Aimee wasn't going to be bossed around by Jara any more. Jara didn't deserve her respect, or her fear. She took a deep breath, ready to argue, but the look on

Jara's face stopped her.

It was as if a stone wall had suddenly crumbled, revealing behind it a yawning pit. Jara's eyes were brimming with tears and despair. She reached out to put a steadying hand on Marhorn's tomb, but missed and fell to the floor. It was like the weight of something she'd been carrying had suddenly become too much for her. Dyrenna sank down beside her, wrapping an arm around Jara's heaving shoulders. Faradair laid his head in her lap and snorted a small puff of smoke.

'Sparks, I can't do this,' Jara sobbed.

Aimee looked at her in growing horror. She was broken. Whatever she knew that they did not, it was a secret that was crushing her. Gone was the confident leader of the Sky Riders, the angry one had vanished too, leaving behind this crying woman. Aimee had seen her once before, when she cried up in the mountaintops after the city elections, but that woman had been sad, this one was heartbroken.

'Aimee, it wasn't me who tore out the pages from Kyelli's diary.' Jara's voice was thick and snotty. 'It must have been one of the Sky Rider leaders sometime in the last hundred years. I was given them by Viana, who was the leader before me. She'd been passed them by the previous leader, and she knew they came from Kyelli's diary, but she didn't know where the diary was. I don't think anyone did until you found it today.'

'Why didn't you tell me?' Aimee asked.

Jara ran her hands through her hair, pulling it back tight from her temples, then let it fall. 'Those pages contain a secret that the Sky Rider leaders have passed down and protected.' She blinked through her tears and looked away into the shadows around them. 'It's knowledge I wish I'd never had.'

'What is it? What's the secret?' Aimee pressed her.

'I... I can't,' Jara wailed and a fresh flood of tears ran down her cheeks and dripped off onto Faradair's head.

Aimee looked down at her wrist, at the bracelet that had turned her into the freak she always feared she was. How could this evil thing that held the power to kill people belong to Kyelli? Aimee didn't want it anymore. She wished she'd never put it on. She tried to flick open the catch but it wouldn't budge. She grabbed the bracelet and twisted, trying to pull it over her hand. The icy pain shot up her arm. Aimee screamed and felt to her knees.

'Get it off me!' She held out her arm, waving it at someone, anyone. 'Please!'

No one touched her. Why would they? Her touch was death. Aimee's whole chest shuddered as she began to cry. Jess curled her long neck around Aimee's shoulders and sent a pulse of love along their connection. Aimee felt it, but it was like a single ray of sunshine in a whole day of rain.

'Hey, Aimee.'

The words were soft and came from right beside her. Aimee flicked her head up and pulled her arm back in, scared of accidentally touching Pelathina.

'Can you switch the bracelet to the neutral position

that Kyelli describes?' Pelathina asked. Aimee glanced at the sketch then at the bracelet's dial. Between the words *Ura* and *Zurl* there was a little circle, a closed loop that was neither giving nor taking. Aimee flicked the dial to that.

'Okay great, now.' Pelathina reached out to touch her and Aimee quickly pulled her arm back.

'What if it didn't work? What if I still hurt you?'

'Only one way to find out.' Pelathina smiled at her.

'No!' Aimee yelled as the other girl grabbed her hand.

Nothing happened. Aimee felt no pull on the bracelet. She looked down at her chest. Her own spark was still there, not getting any dimmer, and Pelathina's spark was bright in her own chest, not being drained.

'You shouldn't have risked yourself like that,' Aimee scolded her.

'I trust you to put my energy back if you accidentally steal it. Otherwise how can I take you for those amazing cheese rolls?'

Pelathina turned over Aimee's wrist, examining the bracelet. She gave it an experimental tug and Aimee gasped as a short burst of the icy pain stabbed her arm. Pelathina squinted right down at the bracelet's catch, her cheek practically touching the bare skin of Aimee's forearm. Aimee suddenly wished she'd move a little closer so she could feel Pelathina's skin against her own. But how could she ever touch another girl again? Even with the bracelet in neutral, Aimee didn't trust it. One little nudge and she could suck the life from someone as she held them. She swallowed around the lump of tears in her throat.

'Can you get it off?' she asked, and could hear in her own voice how desperate she sounded.

Pelathina shook her head and Aimee's heart collapsed. 'It's stuck into you, here.' Pelathina gently pushed it under Aimee's nose. 'When you closed the catch, there must have been a needle or spike, and it pierced your wrist. I can't get the catch open and I can't get the needle out without tearing open your arm. I'm sorry.'

Aimee saw it now, a thin trickle of blood had run down her arm from under the bracelet. That's why it hurt when she put it on, and that's what the shooting pain was when she tried to remove it. She was stuck with it.

CHAPTER 32

BROKEN

THE SILENCE IN the cave was heavy. It was Dyrenna who finally broke it. She gently propped Jara up against Marhorn's tomb and stepped over to Aimee. Black was a dark shadow just beyond the dragon's breath light, standing still and silent as he had this whole time.

'May I see the diary and missing pages, little one?' Dyrenna asked.

Aimee looked down at them, still clutched in one hand. She wasn't sure she wanted to know the secret they held. Carrying it had tormented Jara. She knew, though, that they had to read it. But she didn't need to be the one to actually say the words and bring the secret out into the open. Aimee passed Dyrenna the diary and pages. The older Rider flicked to the beginning of Kyelli's section on Empty Warriors.

'"Only an immortal could stop them, only we Quorelle could undo them",' Dyrenna said, reading aloud. Her eyes ran along the other lines of writing.

'Her voice is full of remorse.'

'Kyelli's?' Aimee asked.

Dyrenna nodded. 'Yes, if you've felt it enough, it's easy to recognise in others.'

She didn't elaborate, and it reminded Aimee that she didn't yet know Dyrenna's story.

'Aimee, what were the lines engraved on the Empty Warrior's breastplate?' Dyrenna asked.

Jara spoke before Aimee could answer. 'You've figured it out, haven't you?'

'You shouldn't have had to carry this secret alone,' Dyrenna said to her, voice soft.

'It was a leader's responsibility.' Jara looked up at them all and Aimee could see the strain pulling at the edges of her face.

'So what's this big secret?' Nathine asked, hands on hips.

The pieces had started to slot together in Aimee's mind and she shook her head trying to dislodge them, because the pattern they were making couldn't be right.

She spoke slowly, trying desperately to twist the theory in her head, to make it fit a different way. 'The words on the breastplate say, "We are created through sparks and fire" and "All that we are is hatred" and "We are fuelled by our purpose". The last one was "We will not cease until Kyelli's city is in ashes".'

'So, the Empty Warriors are created using sparks,' Dyrenna said.

'But they don't have sparks,' Pelathina pointed out.

'Perhaps the energy of a spark is used up in creating

them,' Dyrenna suggested.

A few more pieces slotted into place and Aimee shook her head vigorously.

'There's a whole army out there.' Pelathina gestured towards the waterfall, and the city and mountains beyond. 'You'd need thousands of sparks, all that energy, and oh!' She clamped her hands over her mouth and turned horrified eyes on Aimee, and the bracelet. '*Jalsparsh*!'

A single tear slipped down Aimee's cheek as she kept shaking her head. 'She didn't. She wouldn't.' But Dyrenna, Jara and Pelathina's faces all told Aimee she was right. Nathine was still standing with her hands on her hips. Halfen was gently holding one of her elbows but she didn't seem to notice.

'We're wrong somehow,' Aimee insisted.

Dyrenna held out one of the missing pages and Aimee read the first few lines.

> *The first Empty Warriors we created weren't soldiers, they were workers. I guess we should have known it wouldn't always stay that way. Our good intentions fuelled those first workers but it was our twisted hatred that gave purpose to the ones who came later. It felt so good, the first time I poured out my anger into the Empty Warriors I created.*

Aimee's legs felt like jelly. She took the diary from Dyrenna, closed it and ran her fingers over the tree embossed on the cover. She thought of the little trees on the city map that marked the statues and clues. And the tree carved into the cupboard door that hid Kyelli's bracelet. Then she pictured the tree engraved on the Empty Warrior's breastplate. They were all the same. Why hadn't she seen it before? Because, she thought, she hadn't wanted to.

'Kyelli created the Empty Warriors. She's the Master of Sparks.' Aimee felt like her own voice was coming from really far away.

'What?' Nathine demanded of everyone and no one. 'See, I've been right to be pissed at her and her stupid clues.'

Aimee ignored Nathine and looked at Jara. 'That's why you didn't want me to follow the map and find her. You knew she wouldn't help us because the Empty Warriors are her monsters.'

'I told you it was a secret you wouldn't want to know.' Fresh tears were making shiny tracks down Jara's cheeks. Dyrenna quickly knelt back down, wrapped an arm around her and gently helped Jara to her feet.

Jara was right, Aimee wished she could rewind time to an hour ago before she'd found the bracelet and before she knew Kyelli had used her sparks to create monsters. It wasn't fair. Kyelli was her hero. She was supposed to save the city, defend Aimee from her bullies and be an amazing woman. But she wasn't. Aimee felt a single tear run down her cheek.

'Why have the Sky Rider leaders kept this a secret?' Pelathina asked. 'Why do you still have a city full of Kyelli's image, and talk about her being your saviour, when she created the monsters that destroyed your old home?'

Jara choked as a huge sob suddenly wracked her body. 'What else was I meant to do? I swore on the life of my dragon that I'd keep this secret, because Kyelli also created the Riders. We exist because of her. Our mandate to protect the city comes from Kyelli. Our right to bond with our amazing, but deadly, dragons was given to us by Kyelli.' Jara placed a hand on Faradair and he nuzzled her neck. 'What do you think the Uneven Council would do if they knew? Our patron was responsible for the deaths of thousands of our ancestors, for the destruction of an entire island and now her handiwork threatens every life inside Kierell.'

'Your brother doesn't know?' Dyrenna asked. Aimee was amazed that she could keep her voice so calm and soft.

Jara shook her head, tears dripping from her chin. 'No one but the Sky Rider leader has ever known. And I never told Myconn. I am… was, the only person in Kierell who knew.'

'That's a weighty burden for one woman to carry.' Dyrenna brushed her wet cheeks with a gentle thumb.

Aimee tried to imagine what it must have been like to carry the secret of Kyelli's betrayal. To the whole city she was their saviour, and Jara knew she wasn't, but could never correct anyone. Each woman in the Sky Riders looked up to Kyelli in their own way. Jara must have seen that every day, but instead of destroying the source of their inspiration, she protected them from knowing the truth. Because she knew what that truth would do to her Riders. It would shatter them, just as it had broken her.

'But, even if the council did know, they wouldn't blame us Riders for something Kyelli did hundreds of years ago,' Pelathina said.

'Would you risk Skydance on that assumption?' Jara countered.

Pelathina's face crumpled into her sister's frown and she didn't reply.

'But thanks to Aimee's continued disobedience, everyone will know now.' A flush of anger reappeared on Jara's cheeks. 'You'll all tell the other Riders, and he'll tell his guard friends.' Jara pointed at Halfen.

The young guard had been staring at Nathine and pulled his eyes away with a guilty start, though he kept his hand on her elbow. Under Jara's stare and accusing finger he hunched his shoulders but didn't deny that he'd spread the secret.

'So what do we do now?' Pelathina asked.

Jara shook her head. 'I don't know. The Empty Warriors are going to break through into the city and we can't stop them. We don't have an army and I don't have enough Riders to fight them without us all getting killed. The guards will do what they can but they're used to patrolling our streets, not forming up battle lines. They'll be overwhelmed. I can't save us.'

Jara's words trailed off into a sob and she leaned against Dyrenna. The older Rider wiped away her tears but she too was fighting a losing battle. Aimee saw again the broken woman who hid behind Jara's perfect face. All the anger and resentment she'd felt at Jara melted away. Now she knew why Jara had done what she did, Aimee pitied her.

'Oh sparks, they're never going to forgive me.' Faradair had wrapped his long neck around her waist and Jara's tears dripped onto his head.

'Who?' Dyrenna asked softly.

'My Riders.' Jara looked up at them and her green eyes, normally as hard as emeralds, had softened to moss. 'I've lied to them, and they'll never trust me again. And I've put them in danger. Oh Lwena!' Her eyes flickered around the cave as if looking for the Rider who'd died only a few hours ago. Instead her eyes found Aimee. 'I'm sorry I threatened Jess, but what else could I do?'

Aimee was sure Jara would have collapsed then if Dyrenna and Faradair hadn't been holding her. Seeing the toll that keeping the secret had taken on Jara, Aimee felt angry. Not at Jara, or any of the other leaders from the past, but at Kyelli. She was the one who'd lied to them all. When Aimee had realised Kyelli had created the Empty Warriors, it felt like her heart was breaking, but now it felt like it was hardening. No one should have to cry as hard as Jara was crying.

She'd thought learning the secret would crush her but the past year had made her stronger than that. Her life had taught her to be tougher than that.

Kyelli wasn't going to save the city. That fact hit Aimee with force, but she rolled with it, letting it glance off her. She knew what she had to do, and it terrified her. She wondered if she could give the task to someone else.

She looked around. Jara's sobs had turned to little whimpers and she had her face buried in Dyrenna's shoulder. The older Rider was stroking her hair with her scarred hands. Nathine had clenched her hands into fists and looked like she was searching for someone to punch. Halfen loitered beside her and Aimee reckoned if Kyelli had suddenly walked into the cave he wouldn't even have noticed. None of them were in a fit state to take on a mission. That only left Pelathina.

Aimee turned to the other Rider. She was singing quietly to herself in a language Aimee didn't know. Her voice was low and pretty. For a moment Aimee considered giving Pelathina her plan and then flying away. She and Jess could hide somewhere till it was over.

Jess growled as if sensing Aimee's thoughts and disapproving.

'I know, girl, I won't,' she whispered.

She was the one wearing the bracelet and that was a responsibility she couldn't just shove off on someone else, no matter how much she wanted to. But she couldn't carry out her plan alone. She pulled her shoulders back, shoved her hands into her coat pockets so no one would see them shake, and stood up straight. She realised that was much easier to do without Jara's overbearing confidence filling the cave. She took a deep breath before speaking.

'Okay, so my plan to find Kyelli hasn't worked out the way I thought it would, but the city is still in danger and we're running out of time. Jara, how long do you think we have before the Empty Warriors break through the second gate?'

Jara didn't look up from Dyrenna's shoulder and showed no sign of having heard Aimee.

'Jara!' Aimee yelled, making everyone jump.

This time Jara slowly turned her tear-streaked face and took a shuddery breath. 'The inner gate's thicker and there's less space inside the tunnel to manoeuvre their battering ram, but considering they broke through the outer one in less than a day, I'd say we have till tomorrow morning if we're lucky.'

'Unless the council have already voted to collapse the tunnel,' Pelathina added.

Anguish swept across Jara's face but Aimee cut in before they lost her to her tears again. 'They might not have done that, but if they have we can't stop it.'

'All it'll do is buy us some time anyway,' Dyrenna said. She'd gently pulled her arm from around Jara and was encouraging her to stand by herself.

'Let's assume they don't collapse the tunnel because that's the shortest time we have to work with. Does that make sense?' Aimee's cheeks weren't going red and her hands had stopped shaking, but it was still hard to articulate her thoughts with everyone staring at her.

'Yes, it's our worst-case scenario.' Pelathina nodded.

'Okay, so that gives us about twelve hours,' Aimee told them.

'To do what?' Dyrenna asked.

'You've got that determined look on your face, but the mission is over,' Nathine cut in. 'We failed. Kyelli can't save us. And neither can that thing you're wearing.' She gestured to the bracelet.

'I know, so we have to find Kyelli, because she's the Master of Sparks, and...' The words stuck in Aimee's throat like a fish bone. She swallowed and forced them out. 'And assassinate her.'

A deep silence followed Aimee's words. It was Nathine who broke it, unclenching her fists and shrugging. 'I thought she was your hero?'

Trust Nathine to point out the one thing Aimee didn't want to think about. 'She was, but... if she made the Empty Warriors then I was wrong about who I thought she was. And if she's controlling the Empty Warriors then we need to try...' Aimee forced the words out, 'try killing her and see if that stops the army.'

'Another of your crazy plans?' A wry smile hovered at the edge of Nathine's lips.

'Actually this one was Jara's plan, so I'll be doing as I'm told for a change.' Aimee risked a small smile, aimed at Jara. She didn't return it, but from the corner of her eye Aimee saw Pelathina did. 'Jara sent us out to the army to assassinate the Master of Sparks, but we didn't know who we were looking for then.'

'But Aimee, Kyelli wasn't with the army,' Pelathina pointed out, her smile slipping.

'I know, so we still need to find her,' Aimee replied.

'And how are you going to kill an immortal?'

Dyrenna asked.

Aimee felt flustered as everyone questioned her plan, and the old familiar urge to hide tugged at her. She ignored it. She pulled her hand from her pocket and held it up so the cuff of her coat fell back to reveal the bracelet.

'If I can suck one spark out of a person, then maybe I can take all of a Quorelle's sparks. So no matter how many Kyelli has in her blood, perhaps I can pull them all out of her and she'll die.'

'This sounds like a typical Aimee plan, it's full of maybes and perhapses,' Nathine said, trying to look dubious, around her smile.

Aimee felt a hand take hers and looked down to see dark fingers intwined with her pale patchy ones. She almost jerked away then remembered the bracelet was in neutral. Still, she double-checked the dial before looking at Pelathina as she spoke.

'You don't know what using the bracelet like that will do to you. What if a Quorelle's sparks are different from ours and pulling them into you overwhelms your body and kills you?'

Aimee hadn't considered that. She thought of the people out in the city, of the young baker she'd met this morning, of Callant and his cosy study heaped with books. She thought of the people on Mill Street that she'd known growing up, even the ones who'd bullied her—Nyanna, Parien and the others. So many times she'd wished they were dead so they'd leave her alone, but no one, not even her bullies, deserved to be hacked to pieces or burned alive by monsters.

'We've got twelve hours,' Aimee reminded them. 'Does anyone have a better plan?'

This silence was even heavier than the last. Aimee looked to Jara.

'Will you tell me not to go this time?' she asked.

Jara seemed to be pulling herself together. She was no longer leaning on Dyrenna and her face was reconfiguring from the crying woman to the confident leader of the Riders. Though she still looked pale and shaken.

'If I had a choice, I'd assign a mission like this to an older Rider, someone experienced,' Jara began and Aimee's heart thumped uncomfortably. 'But maybe my choice would have been wrong. I pushed you, and Nathine and Hayetta. Recruits should have had at least twice as much training as I allowed you, and months more time to bond with your dragons before flying into fights.'

Aimee noticed she didn't apologise for rushing them, or for indirectly causing Hayetta's death. However, there was a look in Jara's green eyes that Aimee hadn't seen before—respect.

'So no, I won't forbid you to go. In fact, I'd order you to get on your dragon and go right now, except we still don't know where Kyelli is,' Jara pointed out.

'But Aimee's got a plan, don't you?' Pelathina said, and Aimee realised with a pleasant jolt that she was still holding her hand.

'Don't expect it to be a fully baked plan,' Nathine

threw in.

'When I was little and my ma was making cardamon biscuits, I used to always eat the dough. I liked them better before they were baked,' Pelathina told her.

Aimee ignored the talk of biscuits, even if it made her stomach growl, and looked hopefully at Jara. 'There must be something in the missing pages that says where she went.'

Jara swished her hair in disagreement. 'There's nothing. I've read those pages dozens of times. And if I knew where she was, after finding out that she created the Empty Warriors, don't you think I'd have sent someone after her already?'

There was a flush of anger in Jara's cheeks. On the one hand Aimee was pleased to see her looking more like Jara, but she didn't want to fall out again, not when she'd just won Jara's support, so she said her next words carefully. 'There might have been a clue and you didn't know it was a clue because you've not been on this quest.'

'There's nothing.' Jara's words were firm like a door closing.

Regretfully letting go of Pelathina's hand, Aimee flicked through the pages in her hands. Eight full pages, and she was a really slow reader—she hadn't had much practice, and she'd be even slower with everyone watching her, waiting.

'The only part I couldn't read were the few sentences in Glavic.' Jara's words jerked Aimee's head back up.

'Where?'

'The last page.'

Aimee scrambled to find that one, nearly dropping them all. Right at the bottom, beside a tiny drawing of little houses, were words Aimee couldn't read. She turned to Pelathina all hopeful.

'Can you read Glavic?'

She nodded and took the pages, her fingers brushing Aimee's and sending tingles through them.

'No one else speaks Glavic?' Pelathina looked around at them then shook her head. 'You all really have been locked inside your mountains for too long. It says "Please remember this is a last resort. For the safety of Kierell, I have gone. It pains me to leave my people, our survivors, but I will make a new life in the town of vines." And that's it.'

CHAPTER 33

CONFIDENCE AND HUGS

'What does that mean? The town of vines?' Aimee asked, really hoping someone knew.

'Remember earlier when I said Kyelli was really starting to piss me off with her cryptic clues and you shot me down?' Nathine was looking pointedly at her.

'Vines? Where has vines? And what sort of vines?' Pelathina was musing.

'Wine?' Dyrenna suggested.

'Thanks, but I'd rather have a coffee. Oh wait, this useless city doesn't have any coffee houses.'

The charmingly smug smile Pelathina gave Dyrenna suggested to Aimee that this was an old joke between the two. She felt a sudden pang of jealousy and wished Pelathina could tease her with old jokes and cute smiles.

'You could be right about grape vines,' Pelathina continued, her voice thoughtful. 'Grapes don't grow this far south though, it's too cold. The only wine we get comes from the city states, especially… *ool-jao*, what's that small town called?'

'Vorthens. It's about a day's flight south of Nallein,' Jara said. 'My parents used to keep their wine from there locked away. One bottle is worth about a month's wages for one of our brewers.'

'That's the one.' Pelathina nodded. 'When I lived in Taumerg the other girls working in the wash house used to fantasise about having a house in Vorthens, on the slopes among the vines, and sitting in the sun all day drinking wine.'

Aimee looked around at everyone. No one had any other suggestions about where the town of vines was, and no one disagreed with Jara and Pelathina. Perhaps it was a leap. Perhaps they were wrong. But today had shown Aimee that she could trust the people around her, and taught her that a group pulled together increased everyone's knowledge, everyone's skills. She'd never had that before.

A plan had formed in her mind, but she couldn't do it alone. She'd take Nathine with her because she'd gotten so used to her sassy presence that she couldn't imagine going on a mission without her. Besides, Nathine had been loyal enough to come this far with her, Aimee wouldn't leave her behind now. And she'd take Pelathina because she spoke Glavic and that would be useful. There was perhaps another reason Aimee wanted to have Pelathina's pretty face beside her but she told herself she was being silly. Pelathina smiled at everyone, not just her.

'Okay, so I'll fly to Vorthens with Nathine and Pelathina, and find Kyelli,' Aimee said, laying out her plan. 'I don't think there's any point in sending more Riders. I'm the only one who can assassinate Kyelli, and she doesn't know we're coming. Three should be enough to sneak in and get her. And Jara, you'll need everyone else here. I don't think we can fly to Vorthens in under twelve hours.' Aimee looked to Pelathina for confirmation.

'It would normally take two days of flying to reach that far north. You might make it in closer to a day if you really pushed it, but Jess and Malgerus aren't fully grown yet, and you've been flying them back and forth across the city all day, and they both have injuries. They're going to start tiring soon.'

'We'll go as fast as we can, but Jara, you'll need to be prepared in case the Empty Warriors break through the inner gate before we can get to Kyelli,' Aimee continued. 'I know you were at the gate sorting all that before I dragged you in here, so I'm sorry about that.' Aimee said her words direct to Jara and her voice didn't wobble and her face didn't flush. 'I know you said the guards aren't used to fighting battles, but you need to hold the Empty Warriors in the caravan compound as long as you can, till we get to Kyelli.' Aimee thought of the crowd in Quorelle Square, and the scared people probably hiding in their houses. 'Please don't let them get through into the streets.'

'When I left, Captain Tenth and his men were tearing down the buildings where the wagons are kept to build a stronger barricade,' Jara said.

'Good.' Aimee nodded at that. She could see Jara

had almost pulled herself back together, but there were still a few cracks, a tightness to her face, a shakiness in her hands. She needed to take control of something and be herself again. 'You should probably go back to the caravan compound. I'm sure Captain Tenth is great,' she threw a reassuring smile at Halfen, 'but you should be there to co-ordinate the Riders, and it'll make people feel better to see the Sky Riders' leader protecting them.'

Aimee happened to catch a glimpse of Nathine. She was wearing her smug *told you so* look. Earlier she'd pointed out that Aimee had been dishing out orders all day, to people more important than she was. She hadn't realised it at the time, but Nathine was right. Though it was weird, because it didn't feel like being in charge— that was a scary thought—she was just trying to get things done, and get others to help her. And sometimes the only way to do that was to tell them what to do.

Her aunt Naura's face popped into her mind, smiling. Aimee knew she would have been both amazed and proud if she could have seen Aimee now.

'Dyrenna.' Aimee turned to the older Rider. 'Can you go to the council chamber and let Callant know what's happened here, and where I've gone?'

Aimee needed someone to go there and she didn't want to send Jara. The councillors were probably still arguing, but inside the high gallery their emotions were like flames in a dragon's breath orb, deadly but contained. Throwing Jara in the mix would be like cracking the orb and the flames would burst out.

Dyrenna clasped her scarred hands, held them to her

lips for a moment, then spoke. 'And tell the Uneven Council your plan? Everything? Including who you're going to assassinate and why?'

Aimee's eyes flicked to Jara. Her thin lips disappeared as she pressed them closed, and she ran her fingers through her flyaway hair. She gave an almost imperceptible shake of her head. The crying version of Jara was resurfacing.

'Yes,' Aimee told Dyrenna, her eyes still on Jara, 'tell them everything. It'll hurt but it's better for people to know the truth about Kyelli.'

Dyrenna nodded. 'That's the right call.'

'Everyone will know I lied to them.' Jara's words were sharp, but tinged with sorrow.

'You didn't lie, you kept a secret that you were sworn to keep because you're our leader.'

Aimee made her words soft, even though not long ago she'd been yelling at Jara for lying to them all. When she was younger and her bullies had beaten her, leaving her face mottled with bruises, making it look worse than it already did, her uncle had never pointed out how bad she looked. He'd always told her she was pretty. It wasn't true, and she didn't believe him but it was nice to know someone was on her side. Jara looked like she needed someone on her side about now.

'We all understand why you didn't tell us before,' Aimee gestured round at the other Riders, and to her relief they all nodded, 'so others will too. And if anyone doesn't, a Rider or someone on the council, let me know and I'll get Jess to bite their head off.'

Aimee smiled to show that she wouldn't really, and to her delight Jara actually laughed. It was more of a surprised exhalation than a laugh, but Aimee would take that.

'I'm supposed to be the one who defends you,' Jara said. She was stroking Faradair's head as she spoke. 'You've just shown me how badly I've failed today.'

'I think everyone, no matter who they are, needs looking after sometimes. And you haven't failed, you've just not done as good today as other days, but that's alright. I used to have days where I never left the house. Those were failed days.'

Pelathina stepped close to Aimee, dark fingertips brushing her white ones. 'And look at you now.'

Nathine too joined in. 'Be careful though, she looks like she's about to start dishing out hugs.'

Jara left Faradair, stepped over, and wrapped her arms around Aimee. 'Actually, I could do with a hug.'

Aimee's head only came up to Jara's shoulder so her face was pressed against her chest, Jara's spark shining in her face. Aimee closed her eyes and smiled. She smiled because someone was hugging her, touching her, was not disgusted by her. She smiled because Jara's spark was in her own chest where it belonged. And she smiled because when she opened her eyes and looked down, her own spark was shining as bright as anyone's.

'Thank you,' Jara whispered so only Aimee heard.

Aimee smiled so much her cheeks hurt. 'Does this mean we can be friends?'

Jara laughed that surprised exhalation laugh again.

'Yes, Aimee, we can be friends.'

Aimee looked over to see Jess gently head-butting Faradair as if she wanted to play. Faradair was older, more sensible, but still he nudged her with enough force that she tumbled sideways. She leapt back up and onto him, no aggression, just a childlike joy. Faradair tussled with her, bigger and stronger, but he didn't hurt her. Aimee felt Jess's playfulness in her mind and it made her laugh.

The dragons mated away from Anteill, but Aimee suddenly wondered if Faradair was Jess's father. She decided she liked that thought, and would believe it even if she had no way of ever knowing.

'Alright.' Jara pulled back from their hug. Her face had rearranged itself so her old confidence shone through again. But Aimee noticed Jara's brittle edge was missing, broken off now she no longer had to carry Kyelli's terrible secret all by herself.

Jara looked around at them. 'You all know what you have to do?'

'You mean Aimee's vague plan where we fly all the way to Vorthens then "sneak in and get" Kyelli? Oh yeah, easy.' Nathine's words dripped her usual sarcasm but she was smiling.

'You don't have to come,' Aimee told her.

'I'm coming,' Nathine said firmly, pulling the knot of her ponytail higher up on the crown of her head.

'Aimee's right, we can manage without you,' Pelathina said, smiling and waving Nathine away.

'Not a chance. I've seen the sneaky glances you two

have been giving each other. You'll get halfway across the tundra, fall in love, forget what you're doing and fly off somewhere. You'll have ripped off each other's clothes before you've even landed.'

The flush to Aimee's cheeks was instantaneous.

'Well, even if you're with us, we might still do that.' Pelathina grinned and shrugged.

Nathine snorted a laugh. Aimee couldn't tell if Pelathina was being serious or just goading Nathine, but her belly tingled at the thought of finding out. Lyrria pretended to everyone that she and Aimee weren't lovers, but here was Pelathina hinting in front of everyone that maybe she and Aimee were, or could be. She quickly checked Kyelli's bracelet was in neutral, just in case Pelathina touched her. She could see herself doing that a lot, always checking.

Pelathina was first into her saddle, Skydance skittering beneath her, keen to be out of the cave and back in the sky. Nathine was about to mount up too when Halfen took her hand.

'Be careful,' he told her.

Nathine's round face twisted with emotions—guilt, confusion and something else. It was a long flight to Vorthens, and Aimee promised herself she'd ask Nathine what her story was with Halfen. Then Nathine was in her saddle and Halfen had stepped back, clutching his spear. In the yellow light from the dragon's breath orbs he looked like a scared young boy, more than a city guard. He had a bright spark in his chest, though it was perhaps a little duller than Nathine's.

Perhaps whatever had happened to damage his ear had drained some of his energy.

'What do I do now?' Halfen asked, and Aimee was surprised for a moment when he directed the question at her, not Jara.

'I don't think there's much point in you staying in here anymore,' she told him.

'My sergeant will yell my face off if I abandon my post before my shift is over,' Halfen said, his head tilted so his good ear could hear her reply.

'He won't if you're carrying a message from the leader of the Sky Riders,' Jara said. Aimee was pleased to hear her voice sounding strong with authority again.

'What message?' Halfen still looked worried.

Jara glanced at Aimee for a moment and Aimee nodded.

'I'm ordering you to tell your sergeant, and your friends in the guards, what happened in here, and tell them Kyelli's secret.' Jara looked at him sternly until he nodded.

Jara was flying to the caravan compound, she'd tell Captain Tenth the secret and the new plan, but Aimee was glad she'd given Halfen a task too. She watched as he straightened, and glanced down at where his spark was, just like she did when she felt good about herself.

'It's bright,' she told him.

'Promise?' he looked up, seeming like a boy again instead of a guard.

Aimee smiled and nodded. As Halfen gathered up a small bag he'd stashed behind Marhorn's tomb, Aimee reflected that telling him his spark was bright had been easy. But what would she do if someone with a dull spark asked her? It didn't seem right to lie to them, but then knowing their spark was dull would change a person's whole life. How had Kyelli stood to live with this knowledge, and power, every day?

'Aimee?'

Dyrenna pulled her from her thoughts just in time to be enveloped in a hug. The older Rider smelled of leather oil and it made Aimee think of her quiet workshop back in Anteill. She hoped Dyrenna would get back to her workshop once this was all over.

'You've done good today, little one,' Dyrenna said, then gave the top of her head a kiss before pulling away. 'But you still owe me a cup of tea.'

Aimee laughed. 'When I get back, I promise I'll make you a cup of tea. I just need to go and save the world first.'

Skydance was first into the air, his sapphire-blue scales glittering like the sky on a sunny day. Malgerus was next, and he and Skydance flew in circles waiting impatiently for Aimee. She could still see Pelathina and Nathine's sparks, glowing bright in their chests and weaving through the air like fireflies. Jess gave her a nudge and she could feel her dragon's desire to be back in the open sky.

'You have no idea where we're going, or the danger we might face, do you girl?' Aimee asked as she grabbed the tall pommel and cantle of her saddle and pulled herself up. The moment her bum hit leather Jess opened her wings with a snap and began flapping. 'And you don't care, you just want to fly.'

She pulled her gloves and goggles from her coat pocket and slipped them both on. The cut on her knuckles stung as her glove slid over it, but Jess's saliva was doing its job and it wasn't nearly as painful as it should have been. As they took off Aimee could feel Jess's delight at the air passing over her wings, and at the feeling of weightlessness as they left the earth behind. It was a wonderful tonic to the fear and responsibility she felt like she'd swallowed when Kyelli's bracelet clicked closed on her wrist.

For a moment Aimee imagined having to do this herself, without Jess to come to her rescue or temper her fears with her simple joy of flying. On her own, she'd fail, she had no doubt about that. Jess reached Skydance and Malgerus, and the three dragons turned their snouts towards the distant waterfall. Aimee realised that without Nathine and Pelathina, she'd fail too. This morning she'd managed to persuade Nathine to come with her on the quest to find Kyelli, and now she had Pelathina too. And although they weren't coming with her, she had the support of Dyrenna and Jara as well.

Aimee looked down just before they flew off. Jara was watching them, her face turned upwards, flyaway hair whipping about in the wind from their dragons' wings. She wasn't yelling at Aimee, or forbidding her to go, or sending Faradair after Jess. Instead she gave Aimee a single wave, and in that simple gesture she knew she'd earned Jara's respect today.

She looked down at the spark glowing greenish-white in her chest. Was it a little brighter than it had been when she first saw it? She thought it might be.

CHAPTER 34

TOGETHER

AIMEE, NATHINE AND Pelathina flew through the waterfall in a burst of glittering spray. If anyone had been watching, Aimee thought it must have looked pretty awesome to see three dragons suddenly appear from behind the falls. Jess shook her head, sending water droplets flying from her feathers into the sky.

Back in the city it was evening now, the sun sinking behind the mountains, though at this time of year it would never quite set. Aimee was glad of that. She was about to fly all the way across the tundra for the first time, and it was better to do that with some light. Flying through the darkness into the unknown would have been scary, though she'd never have admitted that to Pelathina and Nathine.

Aimee wanted to fly over Kierell, but that wasn't their route. North was behind them so they would fly up over the mountains and away without going near the city's streets. Pelathina was already turning Skydance in a wide circle, his wings tilted to catch the wind. Nathine followed her but Aimee lingered for a moment. She could feel Jess's impatience as the other two dragons pulled away from her, but Aimee kept a firm hold, her hands squeezing Jess's spiralled horns. The cuff of her coat had slipped back and Aimee looked at the bracelet stuck on her wrist.

She knew she might not come back from this mission. She might never see Kierell again. Or if she did survive but failed, she might come back to find her city destroyed, the streets littered with bodies.

A last shaft of sunlight pierced the sky between two mountain peaks and shone right on the council chamber's green dome. Aimee longed for half an hour to fly back to the high gallery and say goodbye to Callant. From there she would go to the graveyard where her aunt and uncle were buried, sit with her back to a birch tree and say goodbye to them as well. Then she and Jess could dive down into the Heart and Aimee could sit on her own bed, in her own room, just for five minutes.

But there was no time. She had twelve hours to fly a distance that normally took two days. And then assassinate an immortal.

Jess roared, snapping at the air. She'd twisted her long neck around and was watching Skydance and Malgerus spiralling up towards the peaks.

'I know, girl, you're right, we have to go.'

Aimee tugged on Jess's right horn, pushing against her ribs with her left knee and they turned towards the mountains. Jess sped up to catch the others and Aimee let her go fast. Fear about where she was heading made a nauseous swirl in her belly but Jess was a solid presence in her mind. Her dragon wasn't afraid, she was simply happy to be back in the sky. And Aimee knew that whatever happened, Jess would be there and she'd protect her. Whenever she felt afraid she'd touch her connection and steal a little bit of Jess's strength. Jess wouldn't mind.

They caught up with the others as they flew around a jagged peak, snow clinging to the north-facing crevices. They reached the outside of the mountains and flew along them, the Griydak Sea looking grey and cold beneath them.

'I'm starving,' Nathine complained.

The moment she thought about it, Aimee realised how hungry she was too. They'd hardly stopped all day and barely eaten. And now Nathine had brought it up, it was all Aimee could think about and her stomach growled so loud that for a moment she thought it was Jess.

'Why do your stupid plans never involve dinner at an inn?' Nathine continued.

'When I was out with Pelathina above the army, being shot at and risking my life, and you waited at that cafe with Callant, didn't you have a pie?' Aimee accused.

'Yeah, so?'

'Well, I didn't get a pie.'

Nathine shrugged, but Aimee could see the grin on her face. 'That was lunchtime. It's well past dinner time now, and one little pie wouldn't fill anyone for a whole day.'

'Is she going to complain like this the whole way?' Pelathina asked, neatly guiding Skydance in between Malgerus and Jess.

Aimee nodded. 'Probably.'

'You didn't have to come.' Nathine threw Pelathina's comment from earlier back at her.

Aimee was worried Pelathina might take offence. She was used to Nathine by now, her sarcasm, her insults, but Pelathina hardly knew her. Aimee opened her mouth, about to say something to try and mollify Pelathina, but the bronze-skinned Rider just laughed. She must have caught Aimee's puzzled expression because she grinned at her.

'I told you I made a choice, before I reached Kierell, and before I became a Rider, to be happy. I decided not to not let things get to me and to always chose happiness as my first reaction.' She gestured at Nathine, still grinning. 'It'll take more than one grumpy girl to ruin that for me.'

'Sounds like a challenge.' Malgerus had pulled ahead and Nathine threw the words over her shoulder. She didn't mean them, though—Aimee caught the smile on her face and noticed the way Malgerus's big wings were eating up the sky, his tongue flicking out, tasting the air. Their mission might be desperate but he and his Rider couldn't help but enjoy the freedom of the sky.

'Well, you won't want any of my picnic then?' Pelathina called to Nathine, and winked at Aimee.

'You've got food?' Nathine practically turned all the way round in her saddle to gape at Pelathina.

Pelathina laughed again. She had such a genuine laugh that seemed to burst from her, as if she was filled with laughter and couldn't keep it all in. The glowing spark in Pelathina's chest looked even brighter in the evening light. Did her happiness make it stronger?

'I've learned to always have a stash of food in my saddlebags. I don't have any pies, but I've got enough that we can have some dinner.'

Aimee remembered Lyrria telling her ages ago that Pelathina was hardly ever back at Anteill, that she always liked to be out flying, scouting on missions, as if she couldn't stand to have her feet on the ground. It seemed she was always prepared to be off somewhere.

'Great.' Nathine had managed to slow Malgerus so Jess and Skydance flew level with him now. 'Aimee, from now on all your missions need to include the three of us. You can make your daft plans, and hurry everyone along with your determined little face. I'll be here to keep everyone right and save the day. And Pelathina can bring the food.'

It was another of Nathine's silly comments, meant to rile her, in a playful way, but it touched Aimee's heart. It was just the simple assumption that there would be more missions, and that they'd do them together. Aimee had Jess, and she'd be forever grateful for that, but she also now had friends. More than one. The grin on her face was so huge it made her cheeks bunch up and press into her goggles.

'When do we get to have Pelathina's picnic, Aimee?' Nathine tossed the question across the sky.

Aimee looked ahead. The curve of the Ring Mountains stretched out beneath them, the highest peaks glowing with the last of the sun's rays. The sky was still blue above them but ahead it was painted with pink and rose gold as they flew into the sunset.

Directly ahead Aimee could see the strip of land that connected Kierell to the tundra. Many of the Empty Warriors must have poured into the tunnel once they broke through the outer gate, yet still the black army covered the isthmus. Seeing it she felt her chest tighten as fear wrapped around her. Remembering Lwena and the horrible way she and her dragon had been shot down, Aimee was terrified of going anywhere near the army.

To their right the Griydak Sea rolled beneath them. It was cold flying over the water, as if the sea gave off coldness the way a bonfire gave off heat, but it was better than going near the army.

'We'll turn here and head north, flying above the sea. We can head back in towards the tundra once we're really far past the army.'

The other girls nodded and the three dragons turned on the air, wings tilting, one wingtip pointing towards the sea, the other towards the sky. It was beautiful the way the three dragons flew together. Their scales shone in the soft light from the sunset—emerald green, blazing orange and sapphire blue.

Aimee could feel Jess's joy at being in the air but she could also sense her dragon getting tired. If Aimee forced her to, she'd keep going till she dropped from the sky. Aimee turned to look at Pelathina.

'Do prowlers hunt at dusk, is that right?'

'Mostly, though if they don't catch any prey they'll keep hunting through the night.'

They couldn't fly all night. Maybe Skydance could, but Jess and Malgerus would need to rest. The younger dragons both had injuries, and so did Aimee and Nathine. None were serious but all would need attention soon, a fresh dressing or more dragon's saliva.

'Okay, we'll wait till after dusk,' Aimee decided. 'By then we should be above the tundra and away from the army. We'll land, let our dragons rest, and feed Nathine.

The other girl stuck her tongue out at Aimee, but didn't object to the plan. They'd just have to hope they didn't meet any prowlers, or that three dragons would scare them off.

The girls flew in silence, the restless grey sea below them, and the army to their left. Aimee made herself turn and watch the Empty Warriors. They were too far away to see their identical faces or their unnerving eyes, or the tree carved on their breastplates. Kyelli's tree. The disappointment hit her again, that Kyelli could have created these monsters and sent them to destroy her city. Aimee felt betrayed by the woman she'd always idolised. And now she was flying off to assassinate her. It was horrible, but she'd do it to save the thousands of people in Kierell. That was what Sky Riders did, they protected people.

She was scared, though, by the thought of what she might face when they got to Vorthens. She could feel the bracelet on her wrist, a constant reminder of the power she now held. That and the bright lights of the other girls' sparks glowing in their chests. She looked down at her own spark. It pulsed faintly in time with her heartbeat. Jara was right, this was a power no one should have. Kyelli had abused it, but Aimee wouldn't. She'd use it to save them.

She felt the familiar tug of her own determination and knew that whatever they found in Vorthens, she wouldn't give up until their mission was complete. She looked at the girls flying on either side of her. Malgerus had pulled slightly ahead, as always, and Nathine's high ponytail streamed out behind her. Pelathina felt her gaze and turned, giving her a wink, eyes magnified by the glass of her goggles.

Aimee might be scared of what she'd have to do, but she was incredibly grateful that she wouldn't have to face it alone.

## Acknowledgements

As an indie author I don't have a team of publishers and marketeers behind me and my books. What I am lucky to have is a small group of wonderful individuals who give up their time and share their expertise, helping to make my books the best they can be.

I need to say a huge thanks to my beta readers extraordinaire—Colin and Penny. Thank you for reading those first drafts, giving me honest feedback and letting me bounce ideas off you.

Colin, you give me encouragement when I need it most and you always believe in me, even when I don't.

Penny, thank you for your assistance with the map, and for encouraging me to draw it in the first place.

My editor, Rheanna, did a brilliant job of hunting down rogue hyphens and fixing clunky sentences. Thank you.

The cover of this book was created by Stefanie Saw. Thank you for once again giving me a beautiful cover that makes me smile.

One of the most lovely things I've discovered on my self-publishing journey has been you lot—my readers. I've been absolutely blown away by the way you've embraced Aimee's story and I love that you're all rooting for her.

Thank you for all the brilliant reviews (keep them coming!) and for the shares and likes on social media. I've loved sharing the world of the Sky Riders with you. I'd give you all dragons if I could. What colour would you like?

# About the Author

Kerry Law grew up reading Tolkien and David Eddings, and has never looked back. A love of the past took her to the University of St Andrews where she did an MA in Medieval History. During her degree she learnt all about castles, but her imagination had to fill in the dragons.

*The Rider's Quest* is her second novel and is book 2 in the *Sparks* trilogy.

She enjoys exploring uniqueness in her books and takes inspiration from her own interesting skin condition—vitiligo. She's also inspired by the incredible magical-looking landscapes of her home in Scotland.

Kerry lives with her husband and cat, in a small town in the Scottish Borders where there are more trees than people.

Contact Kerry:
kerrylawbooks.com
facebook.com/kerrylawbooks
instagram.com/kerrylawbooks

# Also by Kerry Law

Sparks Trilogy
*The Sky Riders*
*The Rider's Quest*

Printed in Great Britain
by Amazon